Dark Heart: Execution

P. MAIL

MY FAMILY & FRIENDS

To all those who assisted in making this dream come
true: I thank you from the bottom of my heart for your
tireless efforts and patience with me.

PART I

PROLOGUE

"Habitamus in tenebris." (We live in darkness.)

The assembly hall is nearly pitch-black as I attempt to make my escape. I have only been running for a few moments, but darkness eliminates all concept of time. Seconds feel like minutes, minutes feel like hours, hours like days. But no matter how long I run, I am only running from one form of darkness into another.

While society fears the darkness, I once relished it. I have familiarized myself with its paralyzing effects; the shadowing of one's vision, the mind's disorientation, and the rendering of senses senseless. I have never felt the common emotions evoked by it; the fear, paranoia, depression, and isolation. My training has provided me with immunity to these weaknesses of human nature. For years, I have devoted my life to this calling; I had purpose and occupation. I have never felt remorse for any cruel atrocities I have committed throughout my numerous missions. I have willingly allowed my body and soul to be engulfed, in the name of darkness. Yet now, I am struggling with the one thing that gave me purpose and reason for living. I am running away from a life of murder and evil.

Focus. Habitamus in tenebris. You are the darkness, a demanding and familiar voice echoed in my mind.

"And now the light is what I long to fight for," I whisper back.

The hall is sealed like an impenetrable fortress, not even allowing the cool night breeze to enter through its walls. My sweat beads trickle behind me and my once calm breathing becomes a sluggish pant as I struggle to maintain a rapid pace.

Someone has found us.

I suddenly sense another presence nearby. His footsteps are precise, each movement uttered in subtle silence. To the untrained ear, it would seem the room was vacant and the mind was playing tricks in the dark. However, my training has prepared me to feel his footsteps and judge his location. For once I am the prey, and if they have arranged this execution then this hunter must have killed countless without fail. Nevertheless, they underestimate my abilities; this will be their undoing.

At age eleven, I was recruited and trained to be a merciless and relentless killer. For seven years, I religiously obeyed my orders for a cause I sincerely believed in. Aside from my beliefs, a part of me also enjoyed the musicality of manslaughter – the screams and torture I inflicted on my helpless victims. Nothing matters more to an assassin than the unique preparation in plotting their next kill and the successful execution of each mission.

This decision to betray and no longer be guided by darkness leaves my stomach in knots. For the first time, I seek a life beyond existing as a simple tool of destruction. However, even a small sliver of light is a reminder of the consequential weaknesses of human emotions, and human emotions alarm me.

There is no life in the light. We belong to darkness.

Negative thoughts start to cloud my mind. What if I don't surpass this? What if there is no place for me in the light?

I increase my speed.

This new revelation will be my saviour, I think reassuringly. I want to submit to the light, but all I understand is darkness. *Stop thinking; thinking is a burden. Run before you get yourself killed,* I remind myself.

I feel the hunter's eyes leering at me in the dark, as a praying mantis does before decapitating its victim.

Which vermin has the audacity to challenge someone of my caliber? The confident voice in my mind demands an answer.

I know as long as they did not send him, my

escape is guaranteed. He is the one man who can claim to have taught me all I know about the life of an assassin.

I despise how highly you think of that decrepit old man, the sinister voice in my head complains.

I understand why he tracks me, I respond, justifying my admiration. *I broke the coveted vows: "Give myself to the night. Allow darkness to enter my soul and cleanse my impurities. I denounce my past, in order to fulfill my duties as an avatar of justice."*

The voice immediately disagrees. *Everything you believe is false. I am above humanity. I am above our meager class. I am above a god.*

The only falsehood is the portrayal of ourselves within our profession. Assassins are considered gods amongst men, lurking in the shadows to protect the realm and bring forth swift justice. Gods… if gods do exist, they would not be looking down upon me with forgiveness. How could they, when I have maimed, stabbed, and mutilated their supposed creations in the name of justice? I have strayed far from our sacred vows and now only see us as we truly are; mere men decorated with weapons and skills used only to murder.

You are being weak. There is only you and I. You may feel human but remember who I am. I am beyond mortality and humanity, I am Dark Heart and lest you not forget that. You are nothing without me.

I no longer remember my life and name before the existence of Dark Heart. This name was bestowed upon me for my twisted ritual of collecting trophies; a ritual which involved cutting through the victim's chest, exposing and extracting the heart all in the name of darkness.

I locate the giant gate entrance that leads outside.

Almost there, my heart pounds as if it might break through my chest at the thought of escape. As I approach the doors, I hear a sudden snap and *whoosh* of the crossbow firing from a higher ground behind me. The sound is all too familiar: the *thunk* sound indicating the fully extended wire, followed by the *swish* of a bolt in flight. I instinctively shift to the left and move in time so it skims the tip of my right helix, nearly piercing my eye. Though I am unable to see the bolt, I taste the evidence of its impact from the blood trickling down my brow and onto my lips. It left an elongated fissure which trailed from the top of my left eyebrow down my cheekbone, nearly touching my mouth. Even on slight impact, the arrowhead sent a hammering pain through my skull and a voice echoed from a distance.

"Let that scar remind you of your betrayal, traitor!"

I recognize the bastard's voice. They did send him after all; the one man responsible for my conversion into a soulless killer. He was my former mentor, devoted to the cause like no other. I readied myself; unsheathing two steel daggers I named the *Silent Sisters*. They are truly beautiful and my most prized possession. Identical in their appearance, the blades are sheathed in black with gold-covered hilts. Heart shaped pendants dangle from a chain at the end of the hilts. These hearts are iconic to represent my favoured ritual. I am not a killer who demonstrates clemency for my victims, and now is no exception.

"I have seen the light," I proclaim, "I have felt its warmth and I will fight for it." As the words leave my mouth, I hear the crossbow fire again, signaling a second bolt shot in my direction. Prepared, I duck and it hits the gate with an echoing *clang*.

"Next time, I won't miss," he warns. "Stop this treachery and come back. There is no light for you, Dark Heart. If you fulfill your mission, we can overlook your betrayal. *Habitamus in tenebris.*"

I must finish him before he finishes me.

I crouch low and press my back against a bench, visualizing the layout of the assembly hall. The lower court of the chapel is lined with rows of parallel oak-crafted benches used for morning prayers. A sermon table and isle stood ahead of the benches, raised by an altar for the prophet to speak to the masses. An angel statue with a missing wing towered behind the aisle. Above the first floor lay the upper court sanctuary – a balcony which was built for high priests to monitor the masses during sermons. The balcony was lined by stone pillars which enveloped both the left and right side of the church. Windows were scarce on the first floor but covered the balcony in order to allow light into the top floor of the sanctuary. The rear end of the church contained a massive stained glass window depicting the same fallen angel blessing a figure cloaked in black. I visit this place to meditate before certain missions and envision the methodology behind my next victim's demise. But now there is no time to strategize. I look to the left and then to the right, imagining blind followers and false believers resting on the benches.

Fools, all of them are stupid fools. There is no God. If one did exist, He is the cruelest assassin of all.

My hunter waits, perched above me on a ledge at the back of the church. With a fifteen-foot vantage point, I am as good as dead. From our past experiences, I recall his fondness for the number three. He was likely carrying no more than three arrows.

The arrogant bastard will die. Tonight, he will wish he'd brought a full quiver.

I move towards him, silent and light in my footwork, barely touching the wooden planks beneath me. He too can sense my approach and reloads his crossbow with his last bolt. Rarely does he permit his victims to survive the initial two arrows. The third serves as assured execution, and a punishment to his opponents. Coated in the venom of a Death Adder, the poison instantly enters the bloodstream and within ten seconds causes paralysis. Once struck and subdued, he uses his saw blades meticulously to cut through the neck.

You know better than to attempt escape before ridding ourselves of this pestilent, aging wretch.

Although I am eight feet away from the chapel exit, my body strays from the gates and moves towards my mentor. I must get to that balcony if I intend to get close enough to use my daggers. The veteran has not made a move.

Damn him and his patience, I think to myself in frustration.

The only benefit to aging in our profession is refining one's patience, and this man has too much of it. As I slide along the benches, I picture the corrosive venom dripping from the tip of what I hope is his last arrow.

He is as ready to make his move as I am. As I make my way towards the back of the church, I hook around the final bench and step up onto the seat and its backend. I propel myself up, towards the right side of the second floor, and grab the edge of the balcony. Dust immediately scatters in the air, entering my nostrils and I taste the bitterness of dirt in my mouth. My right hand trembles in anticipation under my weight as I lift myself up with a grunt and rush towards him as he unleashes his third arrow. It connects with a *cling*, ricocheting off the metal of my left-handed Silent Sister, rather than penetrating my jugular. My adversary unsheathes his saw blades from both sides of his snake skin belt and assumes a forward stance for my incoming attack. Closing in, I can smell the repulsive odour of mixed venoms on his tongue, his personal practice to ensure his own immunity. The darkness takes over.

You live for this carnage, this mayhem.

The light fades from my memory. He was right. The clash between murderous intent, the thrill of potential death, and my attempt to transcend beyond all I have known and performed collide. All I know for certain is the darkness that occupies my mind. There is only darkness in my world.

There is no place in the light for me

CHAPTER ONE
MARCUS SUNBORN

Darkness… I feel as though I am floating in an abyss. My birth, as my mother would describe, was a miracle. Even with everything my noble family possesses, she would always say I was the light in their lives. She retells the story to me daily but something sparked the tale to appear in a dream. It is vivid, beautiful, grotesque, painful and agonizing all at once. I am not myself, but an infant version. This feels right and I escape the daily hardships of my reality. As I float aimlessly, my body feels light and my mind at peace, until I hear a familiar voice echoing.

"You are almost there Lady Sunborn. Push, breath and push".

What is happening? I wonder and suddenly something grabs me and I feel helpless. The peace I felt earlier turns to chaos as my body is pulled through a confined space which didn't exist before. I cannot fight back; it is hopeless, and I watch helplessly as this infant version of me continues to be dragged from its dwelling.

The voice continues, "I see the head, Lady Sunborn, just a little longer and it will be over."

The warmth that once surrounded me is replaced with a chilling air. My body flails to keep warm while trying to adjust to this new environment. The only thing that truly unsettles me is the screaming which persists and grows louder.

What is that excessive wailing? I wish someone would silence that shrill cry - I think, irritated. I then realize that the annoying sound is involuntarily coming from me.

My body continues to move uncontrollably as sensations come pouring in, the likes of which I have never experienced. I have a sudden awareness of vivid and grotesque odours. Something makes me believe I am partially responsible for this. Sounds become clearer, sounds I remember. They were faint in the dark but now they are easy to hear.

"Marcus. His name is Marcus. Lord Edward, my love, come see your son. He looks just like his handsome father."

My mother looks vibrant, youthful and full

of joy but my infant self cannot understand these traits as he has yet to even open his eyes. From this removed state of awareness, I admire my mother in her youth for what felt like seconds standing still in time. Then, suddenly, my outer body awareness shifts – my consciousness is thrust into the mind of this infant version of myself.

The darkness starts to retreat as my eyes open. At first, it is utter torture. Darkness has been blinding, but this differed. This was blinding in a way that was beautiful and painful at the same time. Slowly the pain dissolves and is replaced by awe from the rays of light.

Mother brings me closer to her body and even through this dream I can smell her sweet aroma. The scents of floral oils fill the air. She still has soft skin, long blonde hair and green eyes. A baby would not be able to appreciate the beauty that is my mother but this dream has graced me with this pleasure. Her hair tickles my face. Beside her stands a man, harsher looking and with rough features. This is my father, yet ten years younger and almost unrecognizable. This dream is fabricating his physical characteristics on what my mother and servants have told me he looked like when I was born. His presence is uplifting, yet terrifying; and he stands firm and protective. I feel safe, and slowly the crying ceases.

"You did well, my darling. God has finally answered our prayers," says my father.

"We love you Marcus, our beautiful son. I am your mother and this is your father. God has smiled upon us," whispers my mother.

I never want this dream to end; I think to myself as the warmth of morning sunbeams kiss my face. I open my eyes, and the flood of senses from my dream slowly leaves me. I shut my eyes again, but it's gone. I lie awake, holding onto the last moments of this reverie before it fades into a memory.

CHAPTER TWO
MARCUS SUNBORN

The Sunborn name has been associated with pride, honour, nobility and charity. In all the realm of Thalia, there is no other family, other than the Monarchy, whose prestige matches ours. My father is the Duke of Apollon, a small peaceful province named after his lineage. Due to our wealth and power, my father deemed it only fitting that we used some of our influence and privileges to help the needy.

This is where we differed from the other noble families. When I was the age of 5, my Lord Father told me tales of the valiant Sunborn clan and our origins. Edwin Sunborn was the first Sunborn that our history recalls to have changed the landscape of Thalia. Starting from lowborn roots, Edwin built an empire through hard work and intelligence. Legendary stories told of his heroic exploits; Apollon before him had been one of the worst poverty ridden lands in all of Thalia. The monarchy lost the realm to bandits and outlaws, and eventually gave up on conquering it back. Apollon's citizens lost hope and started to join the ranks of the outlaws. Good people turned corrupt and savage resulting in rape, pillaging, theft and murder as a living. In those harsh years, Edwin was the light in a world filled with darkness. He was a farmer who fed the hungry and sheltered the homeless. The bandits took notice the unity that Edwin's kindness harboured. Afraid of a rebellion within their ranks, they decided to set Edwin's operation ablaze. With torches and killer intent, the outlaws marched to Edwin's farm and burned it to the ground. This had only infuriated Edwin and strengthened his resolve. Edwin Sunborn was a born fighter who fought in many wars as a squire. He took it upon himself to train the peasants of Apollon to fight back the darkness. Slowly but surely his ranks grew as the helpless became confident and skillful with various weapons. Pitchforks, knives, lumber, hatchets, axes, swords and anything that could be used for defence or offence were utilized in his crusade. Once Edwin gathered enough followers, he set his sights on the castle that held the leader of the rebellion and set a plan in motion to topple him.

He sent the mass force of his army through the main gates as a distraction for the outlaws' main forces while a few men infiltrated the castle walls. Five brave men including Edwin took the leader captive and took back Apollon. The Royal family granted Edwin nobility, gold, and treasure and declared Edwin Sunborn the Duke of Apollon. While he struggled for years to rebuild, he received help from the people who loved him dearly and transformed Apollon from an inhabitable and desolate land into a blissful paradise. All of this was accomplished with the help of lowborn peasants. Without their expertise and valour, Apollon may have never recovered from the rebellion. That is why the Sunborn shelter and protect the lost. To honour Edwin's legacy as well as Apollon's struggle.

"There are none more noble or wealthy in the land of Thalia. The monarchy favours us above all the noble houses in the kingdom. Respect and love is not easy to attain, Marcus," he would explain with pride. "Your ancestors always found a way to take in the poor and give them light. The darkest times in any man's life is when they are lost. Thalia is filled with many lost souls. Our goal as the noble Sunborn is to light their path so they may become an integral part of society. This is why you learn from peasants. A peasant will teach you struggle, hardship and survival, while your role will be to teach them nobility, honour, manners and eventually light their path. Do you know how we light their path Marcus?" He liked to ask.

"We give them shelter, we give them food, we give them family and we give them use," I would recite.

"That is correct, Marcus. Once I feel that they have learned from us and us from them, I send them back to society with a home and some gold to begin their new lives," he would remind me. I love when father told me of our ancestry.

"Lord Marcus! It is time to break your fast." That is Liza. The Sunborn family has many servants, but only five servants who hold prestige due to their significant skill sets. Among these are two maids, a giant blacksmith, Master of Coins, and a Master of Blades and Potions. All of these roles are occupied by peasants who my father takes in on behalf of our noble name. Liza is the pregnant midwife who also serves as a dear friend to me. However, she has never hesitated to give my Lord Father and Lady Mother an earful every time I am late for a meal. Liza calls out again. "Lord Marcus. You cannot be late. Your Lord Father will scorn me if you do not have your meal on time."

"On my way Liza," I proclaim. I rush hastily down the steps of my future keep and bolt past her as I make my way to the main hall. The meal is prepared on one of my father's enormous tables. The meal consists of goat's milk, two bread loaves, cheese and eggs. I devour my food as Liza stands leaning against the wall, admiring my appetite.

She smiles and says, "A healthy Lord is a wealthy Lord." I smile at her with a mouth full of cheese and she laughs aloud.

Liza looks different from most women of our province. In fact, she is darker than almost anyone I have ever met. Her nose is wide, contrasted against small perky lips, and she possesses eyes as black as night. She has wide hips but skinny legs, small feet and lovely slender hands. Despite these contradictions, when garbed in her maid clothing which consists of a brown cotton blouse and black skirt she looks the part of the dutiful maid. But Liza is more to me than that. Liza loves me as much as a mother, so much so that she would only trust me with the secret of her pregnancy. But lately, there is something mysterious about Liza, as if she is hiding something important from me. Regardless, as little as I know of Liza's past, there is even less I know of any of the other four who serve our home.

I believe that all of my father's servants are strange in their own unique way. Gwyneth is a younger version of Liza, but less stern and more childlike. She treats me like a sibling. When mother is not around, Gwyneth is always visiting my parents keep to speak with father and keep him entertained. Sometimes I can hear father's booming laughter ring from various locations within the keep as he carries about his duties as Lord of Apollon. My mother is not at all pleased with Gwyneth shadowing Lord Edward.

My mother and I would spend some nights discussing my studies during dinner and it would be interrupted by Gwyneth's laughter while she accompanies my father. "Laughter like that is different than the way someone laughs at a joke," my mother would hiss.

Mother begs my father to rid our noble house of Gwyneth as she has always considered the woman to be a harlot. My father would always have a quick defensive response, "Who will keep up with Marcus and his studies? Besides she is like a sister to him and we cannot turn our backs on the poor and helpless." *Harlot...* whenever I asked my father the meaning of the word, he would always answer with, "A Lady who is *friendly* in more ways than one." Being ten years of age, my understanding of friendly is limited within practical pranks and funny jokes which involve bodily noises.

The two maids are responsible for dressing

me, preparing my supper and my bed chamber. They also reassure my parents that I have completed the assigned tasks from my studies. Recently, both Liza and Gwyneth have taken an interest in learning to read and write. Neither of them could, so they were naturally pleased to hear that my father would allow them to partake in my lessons. Liza is intelligent and focused, while Gwyneth is always immature in her approach. She giggles at every mistake Liza commits, but would storm out cursing when she struggling with spelling or writing simple words.

My mother believes that a strong mind always triumphs a strong hand, while my father stresses both fighting skill and mental aptitude in his noble bloodline. He has been grooming me into an heir that would protect the family name and capital through the use of both intellect and physical prowess.

Lord Father has been losing his radiant colour since the first day I was born. While my mother's hair shines golden, my father's is becoming frail and silver. When I was six, I recall asking my mother why father's hair was different than our own and she told me that he was passing down his legacy to his beloved son. My hair is bright blond and kept at shoulder length, no lower.

I have my mother's light green eyes and my father's skinny and slender nose. Everyone tells me I have father's handsome appearance but possess my mother's gentle heart.

"Those are the perfect qualities to inherit from your parents," Liza would always compliment. Sometimes Liza would proclaim there is no one more handsome in Apollon or even as far as all of Thalia. She would foretell tales of my future heroic deeds, jokingly calling me *Radiant Knight Marcus.* I was deemed to be the most courageous and dashing knight there ever lived. I never believe her, but the idea would always boost my ego. I would simply laugh at the notion but Liza seems convinced I am destined for greatness. "That is why you must endure these hardships Lord Marcus. They are to prove to your father and mother that you are worthy to be called a Sunborn," she consistently reminds me. I want to make my mother and father proud so I endure all physical obstacles my father puts in my way. Liza's support has been unwavering. Every morning, she plants a soft kiss on my forehead, the only form of affection I have been receiving as of late, and wishes me luck as I prepare to endure the hardships of blacksmithing, jewel crafting, and my combat ability - the trial I dread most.

My physical training is scattered north of our keep. East of my home lies the merchant town of Sallandar. Although the town is less than a three day ride, it looks much different than Apollon. Apollon is filled with healthy grasslands, blue rivers, robust colourful trees, flowers, farmers and fisherman, and homes made of solid stone. In comparison, Sallandar looks much like a wasteland. There is nothing but miles of sand in every direction. The homes are made of straw and hay. Scents of manure, fish and body odour linger in every direction. Yet travellers from all over Thalia flock to Sallandar with various merchandise. Even with all the inferiorities of the Merchant town, the people who live there have freedom. One of my greatest wishes is to freely travel to Sallandar and explore the world.

Apollon is surrounded by many other wonders and different provinces. On the west side of Apollon lies Pesoleen Harbour, the fishing village, also known to possess the swiftest ships in Thalia. Nasgrath is southwest of Apollon; and though it is known to invite the richest and most dignified families to its famous Noble District, it is also notorious for its bustling market place and impoverished slums. There is twice the amount of poor folk in Nasgrath living in the slums as there are rich in its Noble District. Grey Axe stands erect northwest of Apollon and is said to be inhabited by men who are descendants of the extinct giants. They were said to wield two handed axes the size of grown adults in each hand, and are the fiercest of warriors in all the land. However, what they held in size they lacked in number. Destonia and Castle Fate is found northeast of Apollon and had the second largest army, even rivaling the Royal families. They are a peaceful province, one ruled under God; but when time comes for battle, none other stands mightier in number. The last and most famous location is directly north of Apollon, and is the royal city and capital of Thalia, Alexandria. The royal family and powerful Royal Guard reside here and rule all of Thalia. It is rare to see the royal family, due to their duties to serve all the people of Thalia. They rarely make leave of Alexandria unless completely necessary. I have only once had the privilege to sit in their company in my ten years, even with my renowned name. Father informs me that seeing the royal family even once in a life time is a sacred privilege; only the important and influential families are ever graced with their presence. When my father is not home occupied with signing treaties and reading parchments from citizens and other noble families, he and his guards visit other nobles by horseback to conduct business for the monarchy. I know little of the political world but even less of the men behind it. "Your time will come Marcus. When I deem you worthy to meet the other noble homes of our land, we will voyage all of Thalia and introduce you to the fair maidens and their lordly fathers. First you must train to be worthy of that opportunity. Practice, Marcus. Practice and they will respect you as they respect me," my father would tell me encouragingly.

With this in mind, my attention draws back north. I travel by foot from dusk till dawn. Each day, I take time to reflect and appreciate the beauty of Apollon. I feel the lush green grass underneath my feet as I walk to my first lesson of the day. Large full trees stand on each side of my path and they brim with magnificent, colourful leaves and pines. The scent of blooming flowers is carried in the wind. Each lesson represents values in which father believed vital to my growth in becoming a worthy successor. As I approach my destination, the scent of flowers is replaced by the stench of smoke, steel, fire and sweat. In front of my eyes lies the weapon shop and the first of three daily trials.

My first lesson is for muscle growth and craftsmanship, which blacksmithing as an art form offers. The blacksmith is a towering beast of a man, whom I call Timber. Age seems to have no effect on the giant since the day I first laid eyes on him, though his face shows signs of a harsh life. Behind dents and permanent streaks of char are subtle hints of creases around his eyes and mouth. His arms are as big as tree trunks and hands larger than my head. His fingers are so plump that it makes me think of giant sausages. Timber's legs are monstrous as well. His feet are at least three of mine and no shoes could fit him. He walks around bare foot without a twitch or show of pain. *The man's skin is as hard as the steel he creates*, I imagine. He has long curly brown hair that lies on his massive shoulders. His crooked teeth are rarely on display, since Timber never speaks. A deep and grotesque scar runs vertical across his upper and lower lip. It may be the reason why he never speaks and the cause of him to be a mute. Consequently the permanent silence only heightens his nature to intimidate. The man has a stare that without fail will send chills down my spine.

When first meeting, my father questioned Timber's inability to speak. Liza had informed him that Timber protected their group from bandits and lost his tongue during the battle. My father did not further inquire about the story, but I could tell from his expressions that he had his doubts.

Learning from Timber would have been impossible if blacksmithing was anything other than physical. Timber would grasp his giant hammer and bring it down on the hot metal. He would continuously pummel it until the metal slab took recognizable shape. His creations were majestic. He could craft swords, daggers and axes within hours. Although my father considers blacksmithing to be a peasant trade, he appreciates the value of good weaponry and significance of weapon crafting. Father feels all Sunborn men should at least have some basic skill in it.

I watch Timber for hours in awe. Every strike makes numerous sparks that mimic fire dancing on the rough surface of metal. The red hot steel looks like the sun crafted into every *clang* of the hammer. He cuts the long slab of metal with his chisel and makes two short pieces. Once the metal takes shape, Timber heat-treats the steel next. This takes the deformed parts of the dull steel and gives it a sharp edge. Timber points at the large bucket near the anvil and begins to push me towards it. He wants me to carry the bucket over to his workstation. I lift the bucket of water and wobble towards him. As soon as I drop the bucket, Timber grabs both pieces of steel and seeps them into the water. Hot steam comes rushing with a hiss as the hot metal starts to cool. The entire workshop is now covered in the fog. He then removes the blades from the bucket and roasts them in the fire. I gaze at the wondrous change in colour. The steel turns various shades of brown, purple, blue and yellow. When the metal becomes bright yellow, Timber removes it once again and cools it down in the bucket. He then instructs me to remove the bucket and sit by the grinding stone.

I sit idle while waiting for the steel to be ready. Once the steel is hard enough, I sit at the grinding stone and sharpen the blades. Sparks fly in all directions as I rapidly move the blades in a vertical motion. By the time I complete sharpening the blades, my hands grow callous and the skin on my fingers is left raw and peeling. When the steel is cold enough, I use leather strips to cover the hilts and take the weapons over to my next lesson. Today we created two daggers, and off I go to complete them.

My next lesson is crafting jewels, setting them into weapons and naming various coins and their origins. Admittedly this is the easiest of the three trials, and I enjoy Pyke's demeanour the most. If Timber is to be compared to a tree, then Pyke would be a mushroom. He is an obese man appearing to be made of dough. Pyke likes to wear tight doublets and slacks which allow his numerous rolls to bulge out freely. He constantly sniffs and wipes his nose with his hands.

Sometimes it looks like he is drooling from the corner of his mouth. His teeth are covered in gold, and some are just plain yellow. Jewels are his obsession. He treats jewellery as if they were his own children. At times, I would see him kissing his rings and speaking to them. He wears nine rings on his fingers and has a name for each one. I once inquired about his rings and how he acquired them.

He answered, "I won them from the hearts of beautiful women whose husbands could not satisfy them, lad."

My next question would always be answered with the same response. So I decided to ask again, to see if the answer would differ.

"Why are you missing a ring on your commitment finger?" I asked.

As usual he remarked, "I told you a thousand times lad, my commitment is to gold and I will marry her once I find something *suitable*."

Occasionally, Pyke would just look at his rings and a trail of drool would start oozing its way out of his mouth. *He is probably thinking about those beautiful women,* I would tell myself.

Although Pyke was awkward, he knew how to make me laugh. We would constantly play pranks on Timber knowing that Timber would not be able to speak against us. When it came to history and understanding of jewellery, there was no one more suited and knowledgeable in Apollon. It baffles me that my father would allow a stranger such open access to our keeps' treasures and coin. Yet the principle behind the Sunborn's philosophy is to be the guiding light to those in the dark. Pyke has all the jewels and coins he needs to become a successful Master of Coin. Pyke claims that becoming a Master of Coin for a noble home has been his dream, and now he lives it happily.

"Have you brought today's weapons to decorate?" He asks. Placing the daggers on the wooden table, I watch as Pyke examines them carefully. "Yes… fine piece of art, as expected from Timber. I am sure you played your part as well, Lord Marcus."

When we were in good spirits, Pyke called me *lad* as if I was his friend. However, during lessons he called me *Lord Marcus,* almost mockingly. He picks up the daggers and admires the craftsmanship. Pyke stares at them for over a minute before I interrupt him.

"Pyke, what's the matter? You have been

staring at those daggers forever! Can we get on with our lesson?" I ask.

"Oh yes... yes, sorry my *Lord*. Let us continue."

Pyke requests that I remove the leather strips off the hilts. He wants to introduce me to gold infusion. I am exhilarated to learn something new. Lately, all we had done is count coins and memorize where they originate. There are over three hundred provinces that occupy Thalia, and most of the coins look the same. Each coin is embedded with the King's royal emblem on one side and the province's richest family on the other. Apollonian gold has the Sunborn emblem embedded on it but not all provinces possess gold coins. Depending on where the coin originated, they are molded with gold, silver, copper, or bronze. We walk over to the table full of gold and Pyke grabs two bars. He then stumbles over to the smelting pot and proceeds to melt those bars on top of the dagger hilts. The gold is not going to cool off until the evening so I am instructed to go have supper and return in a few hours.

After a few hours, I return to Pyke and cannot believe how different the daggers look. The golden hilts glimmer in the light; they seem infused with the very essence of it. A heart was crafted at the end of each hilt and the letter "S" was inscribed into the golden handles. The S is shaped into two head dragons with each head beginning at the top of the letter and ending at the bottom. The steel itself is a matted black with three sharp edges jutting out of the top while the bottom of the blade looks sharper than any blade I have ever seen.

I ask Pyke how he managed to turn silver so dark, and he replies,

"A secret art I learned from my old master which uses magic to seal darkness into steel." It sounds far-fetched, but I am excited at the idea of magic. Later, Pyke admits he smelted onyx into the steel but he chuckles at the fact that I believed in the absurd notion of magic existing. He carves two diamond shapes into each dragon head on both the blades. Moving along quickly for a man his size, he arrives at the table where the collection of rubies lies. Pyke begins to socket a ruby into each empty diamond shape slots.

Once complete, the daggers look surreal. The blades are as dark as night. Staring at them makes the sun look as if it was eclipsed. There is something malicious and deadly about them, but I cannot pull away my gaze. With the golden hilts, it is a perfect combination of light and dark. Pyke clears his throat to catch my attention.

"Run along, *Lord Marcus*," he says in his sarcastic tone. "Take the daggers to your next lesson. You don't want to make Payne wait longer than he has too."

All of a sudden, the beauty of the blades no longer intrigues me and the numbing feeling of fear creeps its way into my body. *Payne.* The name is not literal, but my Lord Father's next servant is the one who intimidates me the most.

He has been titled the Master of Blades and Potions, and rightfully so. He has only ever lost a single duel, to my father, and I believe it was purposely. The man beats me during our combat trials relentlessly since he believes that a real man should be able to stand up to any foe at any age. He calls me *Light Heart* and scowls at me to learn to accept darkness or else I will never become a warrior like my father wishes. My mother detests Payne.

"He should be less physical with a ten year old," she would tell my father. But he would always reply, "if it does not kill him, it will teach him."

As I look up at the unusually crimson sky, the sun slowly started to descend into darkness, taking with it my confidence.

CHAPTER THREE
PAYNE BLADESTORM

As the sun sets behind the mountains, I sense Marcus Sunborn sullenly marching up the hills. I was hoping the boy would have given up by now, as I could have done with an undisturbed night's rest. However, Lord Edward is keen on Marcus becoming a stout and noble warrior. The boy does wish to learn, but he does not have the mindset or principles to defeat any competent opponent. Apollonian nobles are born and raised with a silver spoon in their mouths and a ray of sunshine beaming up their arses, and nobody in all of Thalia is more charitable than Edward Sunborn. They are fanatical in their belief of helping others, and Edward claims it is proof of their strength; he does not realize it is also their greatest weakness. He would put a roof over a garrison of rapists and murderers if they were seeking shelter. The only thing he would learn from those low life delinquents is how cruel the world really is.

The Sunborns have survived all these centuries due to their wealth and numerous allegiances. Once a powerful military province, it has now become weak and meager due to its founding principles. Apollon's militia have dwindled and their skills weakened after the Second Great Holy War, and Edward realizes his time will soon pass. Before his inevitable departure to the afterlife, Edward wants to equip Marcus with a fighting chance to defend his land. The little *Lord* may have the spirit to train, but he battles for the wrong reasons. Marcus fights to impress his father, and this foolish notion is going to cause the boy his life one day. The only true reason why anyone should step into battle is for survival. I would have ended his misery by now if it were not for his whore of a mother watching my every move. Those judgmental bright green eyes have stared at me with contempt and caution for so long that I keep a purposeful distance from the main keep. One day, when the time is right, I will pluck them out of her smug, pretty little face.

The year before Marcus was born, Timber, Pyke, Liza, Gwyneth and I had approached the home of Edward Sunborn seeking shelter. Lord Edward was a pale, skinny man who looked as though any day would be his last. Mortality did not favour poor Edward. His aging was rapid and he looked nothing of how the tales describe him. The legends spoke of *Edward the Light* to be a gallant man with hair that shone as bright as gold and the fighting prowess to best any warrior in Apollon. The man who had stood in front of me looked as if a mere child would be able to topple him. The Sunborns' simple principle ensured that we "peasants" would be accepted into their servitude as long as we could be of use to them. Edward pompously called their home *The Guiding Light*.

The decision to take Timber, the lumbering giant was simple, since Edward found more than enough uses for him. Pyke immediately claimed to be all knowing of coins and jewels; coincidentally, Edward needed someone to look over his finances while he was away on royal visits. For five years, Pyke gained the trust of Lord Edward by guarding coin and treasure, so Lord Edward entrusted him with the house wealth and bestowed upon him the title of Master of Coin. Gwyneth, who was fourteen years of age, was quickly brought into servitude due largely to her maturing, attractive looks. She was immediately taken in under Lord Edward's wing. On the other hand, Lady Jaina was presently with child and required her own young maid with energy that could keep up with the soon to be new born. At the time, Lady Jaina did not have any mature female companions living with her, and Liza was a friendly and compassionate soul. Her personality gave Lady Jaina comfort and Liza's experience as a midwife would prove useful on the day Lady Jaina's new born entered the world.

My acceptance seemed to be the most difficult. Lady Jaina did not trust me because she claimed I was *born of darkness* and could not be guided. Everyone but Timber testified that without my ability in battle, they would have been taken into slavery or killed. Edward, having always prized a man's value in the field of battle was intrigued by my fighting potential. Edward would place me in his service as a guard if I was worthy, but I never forgot that it was Jaina's accusations which led to my trial of combat. My test was to best their champion, the reigning "Master of Blades and Potions", in a one on one duel.

The man chosen was not only bigger than Timber but he unfortunately also had his tongue intact. He would not cease barking insults my way. His armour consisted of plated steel coated in gold with a sun emblem embedded on the chest. Holding a towering shield in his left hand and a six foot lance in the right, the man looked like the Sun incarnated into a human. I was given a rusty rapier, which looked as a twig ready to snap under its weight if held up for too long; in my other hand, a simple wooden shield for protection. Coming from a weary travel, the only armour that I bore was my linen doublet, stained with dirt and mud, and my short slacks which had rips at the seams on either side. Some of the other guards laughed and took bets, convinced that I would lose within the first three strikes.

With my poor weapon disadvantage, I analyzed the situation rationally to gain an upper hand. *The giant man's armour will tire him out, I thought. His lance is a weapon meant for jousting, but will leave him open to many quick strikes in a one-on-one battle.* Eyeing his armour, I noticed there were very minimal weak spots. I remembered the enormous warrior lifting the spear with his arm fully extended as a show of strength. It was at that moment that I recognized the steel plate armour did not exist under his right armpit. Leather replaced steel in order to grant superior mobility for the large spear in his attack arm. *I could pierce him under there to slow his movement,* I told myself. The only other opening was his helmet; as beautiful and elegant as it was crafted, it had many functional weaknesses. On top of his neck left partially bare, his eyes were left exposed under a narrow opening. This placement would block me from his vision every time I sidestepped his blows. As I examined him, the lance came at my chest with blinding speed. I parried to the left but not before he tore my shirt in half. It would have impaled me if I lost focus for a split second longer.

The behemoth was much faster than he looked. I kept my distance and allowed the lance to come at me. "Stop running coward! You fight like a whimpering dog! Did your father mate with a bitch? I will tear you to pieces and have your head on a stick. Bloody hell, hold still!" he growled.

Any attempt to manoeuvre my way in was being thwarted by his shield. After a few minutes of dancing around his blows, I noticed the man was beginning to slow down under the weight of his fancy armour. Sidestepping left and right had kept him guessing my pattern of movement. It was a matter of time before I crippled his attack arm. His lance came at me sluggishly, and I saw my opportunity. As soon as he threw out his arm, I attacked.

Dodging the lance, I slide to his side and stick the rapier right through the leather opening and into his arm pit. The giant roared with pain and tried to free himself with his lance but the weapon was strapped onto his forearm. Instead of removing the rapier, I twisted it, feeling it rip his tendons and muscles. A river of blood came gushing through his armour. The fear in his eyes was exhilarating. There is no other euphoria like the one you feel when a life is in your hands. He continued to try and pry me off, but I clung on securely. As he fell down to one knee, I snapped the steel inside and swiftly spun behind him. I was inches away from having my rusty and broken sword from slitting his neck. Lord Edward put his blade to my back and asked me to step away. He had seen enough. From that day forward, I was known as the Master of Blades and Potions.

Edward deemed me worthy and fit to educate his future heir in the art of battle. Lady Jaina was not all too pleased by this turn of events, but I did not care what the whore thought. Once in a while, Edward's manhood wanted to test itself and he would challenge me to a duel to prove himself still a capable fighter. I could have killed them all without hesitation but I always allowed Lord Edward to defeat me so his precious slut of a wife would feel safe in her high walls. It infuriated me looking into her judgmental eyes. That is why I always punish and show no mercy to Marcus during our training. The rage I feel for Jaina is equal to the love she feels for Marcus.

Speak of the devil, here he comes. Young Light Heart, in all his glory. I snickered to myself as my mind returns to the present and my task at hand. *As usual his head is down and his confidence low. He has his mother's loathsome eyes. At the very least, I can take my rage out on him. Another night of pain for our dear little Lord.*

CHAPTER FOUR
MARCUS SUNBORN

Payne Bladestorm is not someone whom I prefer to cross. The man has a slim yet toned physique and his body is covered in numerous scars.

"My scars are self-inflicted to remind me of the men I have killed", he would say whenever I was mistakenly caught gawking at them.

Long, sleek black hair hangs down to his lower back like a velvet cape. He has a pointed, slender nose, thin eyebrows and always has dark bags under his discoloured, mysterious eyes. His gaze is cryptic and his stare never fails to give me chills. The eye on his left is dark brown, while his right eye is an unnatural crimson red. A scar stretches from his brow to his jaw on the right side of his face where his red eye looms. This strange man only ever left his tower after the sun set into the mountains. Avoiding the sun at all costs only resulted in ghostly skin as white as a spectre. At times, I wonder if he would combust into flames if he was to step in the sunlight. Beside his love for battle, he has a passion for alchemy and is a master of mixing concoctions for every situation. His quarter has numerous ingredients which he gathers from the nearby forest and far beyond. Mortar and pestle lie in every crevice of his tower. The numerous smells of mixed ingredients overwhelm all other senses. Sometimes the air smells of rotten eggs and other times of rich, mysterious scents yet Payne himself remains the same. There is no scent to Payne, almost as if he is covered in an invisible barrier that rejects all smells from his body.

My father has been asking Payne to create potions for him since before I was born. "May I try your drink Father?" I would ask. Curiosity always got the best of me. I loved snooping and spying on everyone. It is unfair that secrets are kept from me because I am ten years of age.

My Lord Father would patiently respond, "If you drink that potion, you may never grow to be an adult and will stay a boy forever." The potion was a creation to keep my father young, although there was nothing young about my father. He has grown tired and looks twice his age. The only noticeable result from the potion is my mother's fury and frustration with his addiction. She refers to the potion as the *devil's drink* and mother is convinced it is changing father. A few nights prior, after my training with Payne, my father had entered his keep and spoke in whispers. This night my curiosity took no heed of previous warnings and clouded reasoning. I hid behind a bush only a few feet away and witnessed my father desperately plead for the first time. He seemed to have been begging Payne to compose an elixir that would calm my mother's nerves. She seems to have been angry as of late as a result of all the attention my father has been paying to Gwyneth. Payne agreed under the conditions that my father provided Timber with a rare steel and Pyke some golden bars and rubies. That did not seem to perturb my father, as wealth was not something he lacked; what he lacked as of late was his wife's love and attention. I stood wishing he would have just banished Payne. Instead, I was left having to spend another night with the Master of Blades and Potions.

His keep was lit by torches and the tower itself reminds me of a manifestation of

Payne. It is lean and long, made from cold, grey stone. It stands on an open field with practice targets for training. There are few straw men for sword practice, round wooden boards for archery and instructional human skeletons for studying human anatomy. Payne believes that all living creatures have individual weak points in the body. He told me, "If you remember these points and practice striking them precisely, you can annihilate any opponent."

Father once instructed one of his personal guards to participate in one of our sessions of human anatomy. The guard, Samuel Richter, was one of our veteran soldiers. He had fought in two Great Holy Wars, and was esteemed and praised for his savvy and stalwart defence. The stories referred to him as the "Meat Shield"; during the Second Great Holy War, Samuel's lone efforts to save his wounded comrades against five other opponents made him a legend. He had been surrounded by the opposition and withstood every attack that the soldiers sent his way while answering back with relentless blows. By the end of the battle he was still standing, even with several deadly deep cuts and wounds. That courageous act of heroism had the bards singing of his action. I hoped at least he would have made a mockery of Payne. Instead, Payne only toyed with him.

It infuriated Samuel knowing that Payne was planning to fight barehanded. At first, the guard refused to sheathe his sword against Payne because it was dishonourable to fight a man without a weapon. "What kind of 'Master of Blades' fights without a blade?" Samuel barked. Payne did not respond, and Samuel turned impatiently towards my father. "Lord Edward, does it please you for me to fight this man while he stands before me without a proper combat weapon?"

My father nodded and said, "Sir Samuel, please proceed. Payne is merely showing Marcus the value of attacking specific junctures. You were chosen because of your experience and legendary defensive tactics."

It did not take long for Samuel to realize that Payne was as deadly, if not deadlier, with his bare hands. Payne slithered around like a snake, avoiding each swing and dodging every hack. He would pinpoint each jab by using only his index and middle finger at rapid speeds. The first hit landed on the guard's temple, sending him reeling back and dazed. "If you do not fight back seriously, I cannot guarantee you will survive our training session. It would be a shame to have a coveted warrior like yourself crippled due to his arrogance," Payne declared. The guards face turned bright red, reminding me of an overgrown tomato. He then began to swing wildly at Payne, but he could not compare to the speed of the Master of Blades and Potions who made it seem as if everything around him moved sluggishly while he danced circles around his opponent.

He quickly hit the guard's inner bicep, stopping his swings as fast as a heartbeat. Then he switched to three blindingly quick stabs to the abdomen, bringing the opponent to his knees and allowing Payne to finish quickly with a closed fist thrust to the back of the neck. The "Meat Shield" was unconscious for weeks and still cannot manage to keep down his food every day. His abdomen has never recovered, and likely never will.

This is the man who I am training with. If Payne ever feels fear, his eyes never showed any sign of it. These are the same deadly eyes that are staring at me as I approach the top of the hill.

"*Young Light Heart,* good of you to make it today. I see you still walk with no confidence. Pick yourself up when you are in my presence. I despise those who do not believe in their abilities," Payne said. I straighten myself out quickly so as not to anger him. There will be plenty of anger to endure during the actual training. Payne acknowledges the daggers almost instantly.

"Oh, what are those hanging from your belt? Ah, so Timber and Pyke have finally completed what I have requested of your Father. Excellent," he says with a smile. I realize this is my first time seeing Payne smile. It is disturbing, twisted, and unnatural. He has perfect teeth and thin lips, but the way in which he smiles makes him look inhuman.

"My father has not mentioned giving these to you. How am I to know these are not my gifts for being a good student," I proclaim.

"If you were a good student, then I would not have caught you spying on your Lord Father and I speaking about a certain elixir he requested. You remember over-hearing my request don't you? I asked for specific steel and golden bars with some jewels. What you hold there is my reward for completing your father's wishes. And if you do not take me seriously and I catch you sneaking around again, I will punish you in the same manner as Samuel."

Utter shock and terror took over my mind. *How did he know about me hiding that night,* I thought perplexed. He really is inhuman.

"Pick up your training sword, Marcus, and go work on your swing. In one hours' time I will return from my keep and I expect you to be ready for your lessons today. Tonight is a special occasion. It will be the first time I will allow you to use a real sword and we will test these daggers," he announces. "Remember that to defeat an opponent such as myself, you will need to let go of your light and embrace darkness. I will return in an hour." As he walks away, I pick up my sword and feel uneasy. *What will happen in an hour,* I wonder warily.

There is definitely something different about him today. Payne usually likes to end lessons quickly and quietly. I cannot shake the uneasy feeling that washes over me. *First that smile and now an hour of training on my own,* I ponder. I best be careful not to anger him anymore today. I may not live to see another sun rise.

An hour passes and I am already fatigued from swinging at the straw practice figures. Payne must have already been behind me, watching my technique. I do not even feel his presence until I drop my training sword and I hear, "done already?" Startled, I quickly pick up my wooden sword and move into a defensive stance. I do not know what to expect of him today. He throws a steel short sword by my foot and gestures for me to pick it up. As I kneel down to pick up the blade, I suddenly realize it is my father's. The blade is engraved with his name, and I see it is the gift he was given by the King and Queen for his service as Duke. "You recognize it, don't you," Payne stares at me.

"Yes, that belongs to Lord Edward, your Father. Do not worry, *Young Light Heart,* it is simply being borrowed and will be returned without him noticing. After all, you have become accustomed to sneaking around. I am sure you will put it back before anyone notices."

He plans to make this look like it was my doing? Surely, my father would believe my word over his.

"Do not even think about telling your father that I took the sword either. If you do, that will be the last time you ever draw breath," he threatens as he walks towards me.

My legs are shaking. *I am a Sunborn and not some peasant,* I remind myself, but that was the point in all this. Payne was trying to make me feel as if I was lower than him; As if I have to struggle by any means and do whatever I have to in order to survive. Picking up the sword, I quickly swing it at his chest. Almost startled, Payne jumps back and laughs.

"That is more like it boy. Are you scared? Fear is a weak emotion. Fear is what the prey feels when he sees a predator approaching. Do you feel like prey? If so, then come at me like you mean to kill me!" he yells.

I come at him with all my strength. Running with my blade out, I want nothing more than to pierce Payne through his abdomen and watch his guts spill on the floor. This is the first time I have truly felt hatred in my heart. My feet pick up speed as my mind blanks from rage. My mouth opens and lets out a long roar as I charge with my father's blade in hand. The blade is about a hand away from his stomach, but it is as close as I would ever get.

With one ferocious swing, his dagger sends my sword hurling in the air and he is instantly behind me, the other dagger cupping my throat. "Your technique is embarrassing but your heart is in the right place. Perhaps I shall begin calling you Dark Heart," he whispers with a devious smirk.

As he removes the dagger from my throat, I feel the life spill out of me. The tears begin to stream from my eyes, like ferocious waters. This is the closest I have ever been to experiencing death. "Stop your blasted crying Sunborn," Payne replies without an inkling of emotion. "Today is a step forward in your training. You came at me with the hate required to defeat an opponent. Rejoice, young Marcus."

There was nothing to be proud of. A boy my age should never feel the urge to kill or hurt anything. My parents raised me to love all life and resort to violence only when necessary.

"You know I killed a man at the age of six," Payne mused. "It was my father. Nothing the likes of Lord Edward, but he was my father nonetheless. He was a sadistic womanizer who spilt his sorrows in his tankard. We were a poor family that lived on a daily income that was spent keeping my pathetic excuse for a father drunk. Wine and mead were his pleasures. And every night the alcoholic fuck used to come home with random women and sleep with them, all the while making me watch. My mother was simply useless. She hid from my father as he committed adultery with the pigs he picked up from the streets. He believed that a boy my age should see how women should be treated. "This is a woman's worth, boy," he would say as he shoved himself in the filth. His hairy gut hung on the back of the whore as sweat formed on his forehead and chest. Grease would drip from the back of his slick hair all over the bed as he moved back and forth. The lard could barely breathe as he fought gasping for air. The women were always battered and bruised when he was done with them. I could see the fear in their eyes. Their pleading disgusted me. They expected a child to free them of their misery. All I did was look away but he would jump off the bitch as if he were riding a horse and beat me until I was unconscious.

Well, one night I snuck into his room while he slept. My   father was as naked as the day he was born. I brought a butcher knife with me for protection, but that time he was the one who needed to be protected and not me. The first thing I did was cut off his little prick. The moment he awoke screaming, I jammed my knife into his heart. I felt no pity or remorse because I lost a father. What I felt was justice. That was how I helped those sluts. I took the life of my father so he would not be able to harm me or anyone else. Of course, my cowardly mother disowned me because she still loved the drunken fool. I was left as a child without parents, money or food. But I survived because of my hate and so will you, Marcus, if you learn to control it." I stood speechless, as I could not imagine what kind of man would kill his father and tell the story proudly. The thought of being without my mother and father was terrifying. They are my foundation and my inspiration. They are MY guiding light.

Not knowing what else to do, I wipe the tears from eyes and rise. Payne begins to walk towards a table where some of his potions stand. He grabs a small and round shaped, purple elixir and hands it to me. "*This* is your Father's request. Give him this potion and tell him to follow my instructions exactly. Empty the flask completely into a cup of mead and give it a few minutes to settle. Your mother must drink every last drop. If she does not, then it will not work." As I turn around to take my leave, Payne says one last thing. "*Young Dark Heart*, it is very important that your mother drinks this elixir at night. It is the most potent then." I nod solemnly and begin my dark journey back home.

CHAPTER FIVE
LIZA SKYLAR

The plan was simple. Live together, survive together, and assist Payne in completing his mission. These are our sole objectives; the values in which Payne has instilled upon us. It all began with Payne, Pyke and I. We stole from rich nobles and made our living off the misery of others. Although Payne and I met through sheer coincidence, I would like to believe it was bittersweet fate.

I was born into slavery and could not recall who my parents were or where they were from. I knew I was foreign in the land which I resided, but it had been the only place I recognized as home. All my life I knew I would be different. I would always live a life of duty, obeying every command of those who opened their houses to me, while others lived their lives unquestionably in exorbitant luxury. I recall vividly daydreaming of a white knight from silly fables to rescue me from this plight. We would be married and have children, and I would have my own servants whom I would judge as equals rather than slaves. Part of me knew my dream was likely never to happen, so I would have to remind myself that my life could be much worse. At the very least, I live in the noble sector with a roof over my head and a warm meal for my belly. Every day, I travelled to the nearby forest of Nasgrath to pick fruit for my Masters, and it was one very normal day that my life had changed forever.

I gawked from a distance, mesmerized by a figure that stood in my view. Unsatisfied, I decided to have a closer view of the fascinating specimen. Hiding behind a tree, I stared as he bandaged himself. He was a tall and muscular man, with skin that shimmered like silver. His hair was long, sleek and black. The attire he wore was dark and skin tight. His hooded tunic lay on his lap, resting on his leather pants. What seemed to have been black hide boots were now muddy and brown from the murky land which surrounded the river. When the stranger completely covered his wounds, he turned his attention to washing the dirt off his body. Water trickled from his hair, to his brow and onto the rest of his toned body. *Who is he?* I wondered, *He is beautiful.* The only residents who ventured into the forest were the slum infected lowborne and nobles' slaves. He looked to be neither.

I wanted nothing more than to have a better

view of his face. Fog covered most of the perimeter where the forest met the river. I was fifteen years at the time and my womanly desires were fierce. Coming into womanhood at an early age, I started feeling a desire to be around the opposite sex. As I matured with age, that yearning only intensified. I have never felt the touch of a man, but craved the idea and was aroused by it. The idea of touching him and having him take me in the forest was exciting. Lost in a lustful fervor, I took a few cautious steps forward, watching my feet move instinctively through the cold forest ground. The last thing I wanted was to step on a fallen branch and make a noise. After taking no more than a few steps, I gathered myself and looked up. The stranger had vanished without a trace. *Was he an illusion or is my mind playing tricks on me?* I looked around and was surrounded by an empty forest.

Disappointed, I picked up my skirt, careful not to get it dirty, and turned around to take my leave. Suddenly, there was a bare and muscular chest in my path. My mind filled with doubt, and the lust I felt earlier quickly turned to terror. He was breathing heavily, and I focused my attention on his chest moving in and out in a rhythmic fashion. I slowly and nervously raised my chin to look at the figure in the face. He was nothing like I had imagined. The aura he exuded was cold and emotionless. He possessed soulless eyes with a look that seemed almost bloodthirsty. His lips were thin and nose pointed. This man was not handsome, nor was he ugly, but there was something definitely dangerous about him. We stared at each other in silence for a few moments until I found the courage to speak.

"Are you hurt?" I asked. "If you need antidotes or medicine, I can request my Master for his aid. I am sure you would like to clean those cuts and gashes." He continued to glare at me. "Do you understand?" I asked. No answer again. Instead he reached into his black tunic and swiftly grabbed a dagger. The sight of the weapon instantly left my throat parched. I tried swallowing to regain some moisture in my throat but all I felt was a scratching sensation. I could feel, instead, that moisture that once inhabited my throat move to my eyes as they glistened with tears. I wanted to scream for help but my voice was lost. My heart stopped and I could feel sweat uncomfortably coat every inch of my body. *I am going to die at the age of fifteen*, I cried silently. *I will never feel a man inside me, never bear a child, and never find someone who I can call a husband.* Regret began to fill my mind as I closed my eyes and braced myself.

My body stood motionless and cold while

my mind spun in circles. *Is this how death feels?* I asked myself. Bumps began to rise on my arms and legs from the chill. My eyes began to open cautiously. I could not help but wonder how the stranger chose to end my life, so I attempted to pry my eyes open to see if I was in fact in the afterlife. As I looked down, I realized my maid dress was sliced through the middle and lay beneath my feet. I was naked except for the under garment that protected the private area between my legs. Without warning, the man suddenly cupped my breast with one hand and began groping violently. *This felt wrong,* I thought. It was not how I imagined my first sexual experience with a man. I wanted romance, excitement, beauty and someone I loved touching me. Instead, I had a silent stranger who was neither passionate nor loving; he was rough and angry. I wanted to yell for help, but realized it would be useless since no one could hear me. Besides that, who would bother to help a lowly peasant in the forest when there were countless women being raped in broad daylight on the streets?

My nipples involuntarily hardened in his mouth as he suckled them. He grabbed my other breast and this time fondled it gently before squeezing them forcefully. My mind told me to not give in, but my body was defying sound reason.

His mouth moved up and found my neck. To my surprise, he gently kissed me in a way which left no marks, but then jerked my hair back and shoved his tongue in my mouth. To this day I vividly remember his taste. His mouth had no odour, but his tongue left a flavour of blood and saliva. My tongue naturally responded and found its way to his. We kissed passionately. My mind eased at that point and my slit was damp, my white undergarments becoming completely wet. I could feel him against me, stiffening up and becoming elongated. I impulsively reached out in curiosity to touch his manhood. He responded startled and jumped back. This led me to believe it must have been his first time as well.

As he stood there erect, I saw him differently under the moonlight. The fear which previously occupied my body transformed completely to desire. I wanted nothing more than to have him there and then, and boldly realized there was nothing left to stop it from happening. Unable to control my urges, I pulled my undergarments down to my knees, bravely and invitingly sticking a finger inside. I heard the mature slaves discuss topics on self-pleasure and this was one that they raved about. The magic of two fingers entering their moist hole and the sensation that followed would send them into a frenzy. It was a way to please them because noble slaves were under strict rules to never sleep with men. The rule was manifested to avoid scrutiny to the noble family that owned the slave. I slowly went down on my back and lay waiting for his manhood to enter inside me. The man was a swift learner.

He was inside me for some time, thrusting at various speeds but never said a word; he simply grunted and made noises of passion. I, in turn, was loud enough for the both of us, rivaling even the howling of wolves. I can remember savagely reciprocating every time he thrust with my own hips. He seemed to enjoy the challenge. I felt liberated. Our bodies were sweating and our distinctive odours were in the air. His face was against mine, cheek to cheek as he panted with lust. His moans grew louder as the inside of my thighs moistened with every plunge. I do not know whether it was the effect of being in the forest or being with a complete stranger, but I relished every moment. "Leave it inside," I told him. He was not even listening and continued to move in me until his seed was pouring down the side of my leg. This was the most memorable night of my life.

He had not said a word afterwards. I lay on the cold, soggy ground while he put his black attire on. I did not know what to say at the time. Once he was dressed, he quickly kissed me again on my lips and disappeared. I slowly gathered myself and tried to regain control of my shaky legs. A trickle of blood ran down my leg which I quickly wiped away with what cloth remained. The outfit I wore was torn down the middle and was not salvageable, but I had to make due. I resourcefully wrapped the cloth around my breasts and stomach, making me look like I was one of the working ladies who sold their bodies for copper. *This will be suitable for now,* I decided. My fruit basket stood beside me full of lush and ripe fruits and reality crept back. I needed to get back to my Masters before I was punished for being too late.

I thought of him the entire way back. I felt empowered, fearless, as if nothing could stop me. Deciding to pursue my new found identity, I took a shortcut home which my Master had prohibited. This shortcut led through a deserted alleyway into the back of my Master's home. I had never ventured through this path at his behest, let alone at night, but I was a *different* woman today. Sadly, the feeling of confidence dispersed as quickly as it arrived. It was at this time that my world was turned upside down. While the event in the forest was frightening at first, it became magical. What was about to happen was far from my previous experience. What happened next was every woman's nightmare. That was the day my innocence and trust of most men vanished.

A man took me by surprise, and clutched my waist with such force that it left me winded at first. His meaty and hairy arm pulled me towards him as his free hand found its way to my mouth, holding it shut as dirt and sweat covered my lips. I began kicking and biting to break free but it was hopeless. The man was three times my size and weighed as much as a horse. His breathe smelled of alcohol, and he was slurring profanities at me. Spit and saliva covered his hands while I tried hardest to bite and scream; this only made him angry. He twisted his body left and right which forced me to follow his motion. My head was spinning and I felt nauseous from the rapid movement. Once he was tired of flailing my body like a child's play toy, he threw me on the floor and dropped himself atop. He looked crazed and seemed to enjoy what was transpiring. My arms were pinned to the ground as he held them, and my legs were spread open by his. The slacks that barely fit him were already to his knees and his cock was ready to enter. *I have to do something,* I panicked. As his mouth came down, I spat on his face and bit his ear, ripping off a piece of his ear lobe along the way. Blood ran from my mouth as his fleshy ear wiggled. I spat it to the side and watched his hand cover his bloody head with pain. "You stupid bitch!" he screamed. His closed fist came crashing down on my nose. That was when I stopped fighting; I felt like a child again. All the courage in the world would not stop him from ravaging me. All the innocence and light in my soul was replaced by darkness. Hatred I had never felt before became my new way of life. I was left broken and battered in the alley that night.

The next morning, I managed to make it to my Master's home bruised, beaten and battered. I wish I had died that night following the raping but something in me wanted me to survive. There was no pity or remorse in my Master's tone. Instead of compassion he was furious that I was out all night "whoring myself" to strangers and no matter how much I pleaded, cried and tried to explain, it fell on deaf ears. The worst type of punishment next to death was given to me by a noble. He disowned me and took away my rights to live in the Noble District. Nobles kept slaves such as I so long as we served diligently and committed no crimes. My Master contrived the assumption that I worked as a prostitute when I was away running his errands. "I will not have prostitutes in my home," he spat with disgust before he shut the door in my face.

For the first time in my life, I had no

direction for my future nor a Master to guide my actions. My new home was less than flattering. Anyone who does not live in the Noble District or make a living in the market place is forced to live in the vilest location in Nasgrath: the slums. Everything and everyone that lived in the slums shared a few things in common; the last name *lowborne,* hunger, poverty, death and a desperate need to survive. I found myself in the slums plotting revenge on the man who raped me to the point of obsession. Vengeance took precedence over everything. Killing the man who robbed me of my dignity was what fuelled me to live on. I always thought the life of a slave was unfair; but at least with slavery, food and shelter had been provided. I was now homeless and below slave status. I was nothing.

Survival became second nature. Soon I was stealing food from merchants and scrounging for any clean water I could find. When it poured rain, I would fill buckets in order to preserve my water supply. I endured through all of this just so one day I would have the chance to exact my revenge.

Few months passed and there was word that a man, described as having similar physical characteristics as the one who raped me, had been murdered. This news spread throughout the town of Nasgrath, from the Noble District to the slums. Unfortunately, there were many men whom shared the characteristics of the rapist. He was obese, reeked of alcohol, hair was receding, and his nose was flat. It was entirely possible that the murdered noble was someone different, but the last description gave him away. The one characteristic that I left him as a parting gift after my rape was his torn ear lobe. There was a large crowd gathered in the market place so I decided to follow the trail of town folk who lined up to see the murder. His intestines were ripped out with a note on his crotch. I heard the crowd whisper to one another that the note said, "I Am Sorry." I was stricken with grief because I was the one who wanted to kill the pig. Instead, someone else murdered him before me.

My life lost all meaning after that. I belonged in the slums with all of the other disease stricken and poor lowborne. Feeling sorry for myself and wanting for someone to end my miserable life because I was too cowardly to do it myself, I dragged my dirt covered feet from one location of the slums to the next. I was damaged and nobody wanted to have me. Homes in the slums were built from what people could salvage from the forest. Constructing one took time and dedication, and I possessed neither. Instead, I slept on the hard ground and let the dirt and cold air cover my body. Desperation of a different future took its toll on me and I was slowly building the courage to take my own life. It would have become reality if not for that one faithful night when I was fast asleep and received an anonymous written message tucked beneath my dress. When I awoke and rose to my feet, I noticed the letter neatly folded on the dirt filled ground. I unfolded the letter but could not read it as I have never learned the art. Bewildered and confused, I began to wonder if it was mistakenly given to me. There was something familiar in the penmanship. The careful curvature in the writing and the way the capital letters were written larger and fancier than the rest of the letters. It reminded me of the writing that was branded on the dead body of the rapist. Then it dawned on me. It *WAS* the same writing as the letter that was discovered on the fat rapist.

I searched frantically for someone able to make out the message in the letter. The only part of Nasgrath which was accepting of both nobles and lowborne was the market district. Cursing my inability to read, I rushed over to random shop owners begging someone to read the letter to me. A kind, frail man saw my desperation and yelled out to me and beckoned me forward. Opening the letter in his hand, the man rubbed his scruffy chin as he read it quietly to himself. He pronounced each word slowly and looked up to me. "This letter must be personal, miss. It reads, *Meet Me Where It All Began.*"

I was sure it was *him,* and I believed *where it all began* meant the forest; the night we spent together, the night I transformed into a powerful woman and the same night I reverted back to a helpless child. I rushed to the forest to meet him. My heart was pounding and adrenaline rushed through my veins. I wanted to believe that he would make the horrors I faced in the last few months go away but he never appeared.

After waiting a few hours I decided to head back to the slums. The sun was setting and darkness was swallowing the world whole. Making my way down the street, I noticed an awkwardly dressed man following me. He was fat and wore clothes too tight for his body; he reminded me of the rapist. My heart jumped into my throat and I felt my body stiffen, but I had to be strong and confront my fears. *I was not going to be put through that torture again,* I told myself. I quickened my pace hoping he would continue on but he sped up as well. Distracted by the thought of escaping, I entered an alleyway. *Where it all began,* I finally understood the letter. The letter was not referring to our night in the forest; it meant the night I was raped. I looked around anxiously, trying to find an item in order to defend myself. Eyeing a lose rock on the ground, I picked it up and readied an attack. As the fat man turned the corner, I closed my eyes and swung with so much velocity that I imagined his head would come clean off. The fat man moved faster than I expected and the only thing I hit was the air. It made a loud *whoosh* sound.

"Whoa!" He screamed, startled and disoriented. "What in the world are you doing, you crazy bitch? I am not here to hurt you!" He proclaimed as he quickly backed away with hands in the air. As he lifted his hands, the tight shirt he was wearing moved up with them and uncovered his hairy and sweaty belly. It jiggled and moved when he moved and his breathing was heavy from following me. He truly looked like a swine had a child with a overweight human. "I came on *his* behalf. Put the stone down my Lady, there is no need for violence."

This is a trap. It has to be, I tried convincing myself. The last time a fat man raped me in a dark alley. "Prove it," I demanded. "Describe him to me. Mark my words, fat man, if you get anything wrong I will not miss with my next swing!"

He laughed as drool rolled down the

corner of his mouth. "If my *Lady* wishes, but first you may call me Pyke. I do not like being called fat. I have feelings, you know."

It was difficult to trust anyone anymore, especially people that reminded me of the rapist. Pyke described the man in the forest with accuracy, even down to the bandaged scars and his spectre like appearance. I did not want to follow him of fear that I might be raped again, but I was overtaken by my desire to see *him*.

"Alright, lead on...but put one hand on me and I swear I will make sure your face is uglier than it already is," I threatened. He flashed a big smile, exposing his yellow teeth and slobber filled mouth. We walked together through the alley into the Noble District of town. I had so many questions and it seemed that Pyke had the answers.

"Why is he living in this side of town," I asked. "Is he a noble? What is his name?"

Pyke laughed again. "My *Lady* is curious, and rightfully so. The man is here because he chooses to be. He is as noble as any man I have ever met but I assure you not in stature. Also, each individual has his or her own definition of *nobility*. You may call him Payne. If it is his true name, I cannot say but I find it quite suitable for his profession. Though I dare not speak of him any further; he is much more eloquent and convincing with words than I. Any other questions you may have, please save for him to answer," Pyke requested.

His profession, I wondered what Pyke meant. Pyke would not answer any more of my questions so I kept them to myself as we walked in silence down numerous alleyways. No later than an hour passed when we arrived in the Noble District. I had forgotten how glorious and prestigious it looked. Compared to the slums, the Noble District looked like Heaven on Earth. It felt as if a lifetime had passed since I stepped foot on such rich soil. *I thought Pyke said Payne was not a noble*, I wondered.

We arrived in front of a dark home full of lit torches. The home seemed luxurious enough, but was overshadowed by the darkness surrounding it. Pyke stared at me as if I was missing something.

"You must have not wanted to kill your rapist as much as Payne thought," Pyke said with a mocking tone. I stared at him bewildered and insulted, crossing my arms so he knew how I felt after that remark.

"How dare you claim to understand what that incident did to me? Clarify your accusation,

Pyke, or God help me I will leave your sight this very instant," I demanded.

"My Lady," he whispered and paused, "this is the very home of that deviant who raped you."

I stood momentarily speechless; *how was this possible? The man who raped me was a noble? Nobody cared that a noble's home was now occupied by a stranger?* Everything about this situation seemed bizarre. I decided to confront Pyke about these curiosities. "Payne is inside? How is it that—" but before I could finish, Pyke knowingly interrupted.

"If you are wondering why no one has mentioned anything to the royal guards about our occupancy of this home, it is because Payne has a way of plotting situations out in his favour. The law decrees that any noble who commits adultery will be robbed of his inheritance, lands, gold and even at times executed at the discretion of their partner's mercy. It is the only time a woman has power over a man in our culture. In this case, the nobles wife was so furious about learning of the sex crime he committed that she killed him and left a note on his body saying *I Am Sorry...* but you already knew that," Pyke snickered as he told me the story. "The wife killed herself afterwards and the man did not leave an heir to inherit his gold or his property. That is why Payne resides here without quarrel. We will be undisturbed until the Royal Family takes the land back under their possession and sells to a new buyer. Therefore, we stay as long as we can and we leave unnoticed when the royal guards come to take back the home. Now please, come in. We do not want to keep him waiting."

The fires from the torches flickered and covered the home in shadow. It was menacing. The dark terrified me ever since the incident in the alley, and I moved carefully to avoid tripping. My eyes took their time to adjust. At first blackness veiled my vision, but as time lapsed I began to see clearer in the darkness. Pyke continued to lead on as we entered a large, vacant room and noticed a tall figure seated upon a chair, one leg crossed, leaning back and holding a cupped fist to his chin. He was staring in our direction intently.

"Welcome, Liza," he said with a smooth deep voice. "Pyke was good to you, I presume?" I nodded but did not speak. He continued on, "You must have asked him enough questions to know who I am by name, but we know each other more intimately than that." I could not help but blush. Thankfully the darkness in the room covered any trace of it. "I hope you liked my gift?" he asked.

"What gift?" I inquired curiously.

"Why, the gift of death. The rapist brought to justice. His death in exchange for the innocence he took from you. I know you wanted to kill the man yourself, but there are plenty of low-life scum in this world. I can promise if you come with us, no one will ever hurt you again. You would live a life of adventure, riches and security. I would be yours and you would be mine."

The night in the forest felt so vivid and real that my nipples hardened thinking of him inside me. I wanted nothing more than to be with him, but I knew this was no ordinary man. I wanted to know more about his *true* intentions but my thoughts kept going back to the night in the forest and I pulsated between my legs for him. I steadily controlled my urges and asked the most obvious question I had been pondering, "Why? What could I possibly offer you, especially after I have been broken and beaten? I lack any special talents and I would only slow you down," I whispered dejectedly. The light flickered on him and his eyes were still staring into mine.

"You underestimate yourself. Do you remember the hatred you felt when you were being raped?" he asked, "What I want is for you to take that same feeling and learn to control it. Anyone can act innocent and proper, but feeling true hatred and manifesting dark thoughts into reality requires practice." Flashbacks of the rapist gushed through my psyche and invaded my mind. I gritted my teeth and tried to calm my raging nerves. The violent images of meat like fists crushing down on my face made me stumble back slightly. Luckily, my feet were able to regain stability and I caught myself from falling.

Payne stood up and began to walk towards me. I did not know what to expect. *He wanted me to control hate? Why?* He answered as if I said my thoughts out loud. "Pyke has told you the rule of the nobles. I want you to use your womanly charms to help me in my mission. You are a beautiful woman Liza, and that is your weapon. I want you to seduce the men of the noble homes we serve so that their wives would suspect them of adultery. You would never have to touch or be touched but you will need to show interest. I need you to harness the darkness inside you, because light is weak. It allows you to feel emotions such as pity and doubt. My mission is one of justice. Can I count on you, Liza my sweet?" he asked.

The very idea sounded evil. I would be ruining countless lives, but Payne assured me that only corrupt nobles would be targeted. I took the opportunity to ask about his mission, but that was one piece of information he would not disclose to me. That was the *only* secret he would ever keep from me. I weighed my options with a heavy heart. I did not have anything left to live for; no one would have me and I could not fend for myself any longer. The only reason for my living was to seek vengeance on the one who took everything from me, but he was killed by the very man giving me a second chance and a new beginning. I had the opportunity for a life filled with freedom, belonging and camaraderie with nothing to lose and everything to gain.

My decision was made; I agreed to join. Payne had a route he planned out on a map for us. There were specific targets he had in mind. From that point, we scoured the realm for nobles whom we could steal from. Payne would only visit my bed some nights. When he did, our bodies intertwined, full of ecstasy and lust. He would never tell me where he was coming from or why he kept the missions a secret. That information was his and his alone and it would remain that way.

Pyke and I became friends quickly and shared our goals and dreams. Pyke wanted gold and women, an unlimited amount of both. I wanted to be a mother more than anything, settling down and having a family with two children. It seemed as though one part of my dream was coming true, as I had not bled for many weeks. I wanted to share the news with Payne, but I cautiously remained patient until the right moment.

Payne arrived a few days later and climbed into my bed. As always, we enjoyed a night of wild love making. After we had our fill of pleasure, I could not hold my excitement in any longer. When I told him of the news, his face showed no sign of emotion or joy. Instead, he went away that night and did not return for weeks. The day Payne returned, he was *different* and not alone. Payne had a scar running down the right side of his face and his right eye was blood red. He looked as if he battled an army and came out barely alive. His skin was dirty and the aura of confidence that surrounded him was gone. It seemed as though this was a completely different person compared to the man whose child I carried.

Payne, caught all of us staring at his scar and scowled, "If any of you stare or ask about this scar again, I will rip your eyes out myself." That quickly ended all of the gawking and stopped anyone from asking questions. From that day forth, he rarely came to see me unless it was to give an order.

He also brought back a young female by the name of Gwyneth and a giant of a man who was a mute. Payne just referred to him as the silent blacksmith. The girl was a slave that Payne bought with gold. She was beautiful, young, and not beaten or broken down. I was beginning to wonder if Payne meant to replace me. My belly had grown and I was showing. With a protruding belly, our mission was proving difficult as of late since Nobles did not want the responsibility of hiring a maid with child. Payne had reassured me that Gwyneth was there to look after me and our baby. I believed that to be true until one night I bled profusely and lost my child in the process.

I believed Payne mixed a potion that killed our child before it was born. Over the coming weeks, he asked Gwyneth to fill my water with an odourless and colourless elixir. At first, I had cramps that lasted longer than what I was accustomed to but I paid no heed to it. I expected them to become worse as my child grew in me. Eventually I started to cough up blood. My insides burned and my throat ached. I slept and rested for three days until it happened. I woke up one night and my legs were completely drenched. At first, I thought it was my night sweats but this felt thicker. I lifted the blanket and saw blood everywhere. I was bleeding between my legs and could feel my child dying. Gwyneth knew the effects of the brew she was feeding me. For such a young girl, she showed no sign of pity or compassion. Instead, she seemed to enjoy causing pain.

For a long period of time I felt numb, as my emotions dwindled with the death of my child. Only the physical pain and fatigue remained from the blood loss. My darkness and hate clouded my mind again, and I no longer knew how to react to the death of my child. I should have grieved but I did not; instead, I went on with my life as if nothing ever happened. Payne came to me one night promising that I was everything he wanted and when he was ready, we would consummate a child together… but until he completed his mission, it was not going to be possible. That sounded like the Payne I knew and fell in love with, but ever since he took our child from me and returned home with that scar my gut feeling was not to trust him.

We lived in the same noble house for months and we were running out of gold and food. Payne had decided to finally target the wealthiest family in the land, the noble Sunborn. They had a reputation of admitting anyone in their service who they deemed to be a lost soul but still useful. Pyke believed that Lord Edward Sunborn had so much gold that could feed multiple families for centuries. If we could overtake this noble family, it would give enough resources and gold for Payne to finally achieve his mission.

We began ten years ago and this family has proven difficult. We have all grown fond of Lady Jaina and Lord Edward. Payne seems to have changed as well, including his attention towards me. He promised me that we will leave this family alone and not rob them of their lives because they are not corrupt; if the Sunborns represent anything, it is the true meaning of nobility. Marcus tells me that Payne is kind and gentle and I believe he is trying to be fatherly. *Maybe there is hope for us.* He may become the father that our future child deserves. *Yet, why have I not told him about my latest pregnancy?* I ask myself. *If he has changed, perhaps he should be told.* Then I begin to recall the blood seeping out of me from my previous child having died without seeing the light of day. I am determined to have this child without interruption. Payne has his secrets, and I will have mine. No one but Marcus knows of my pregnancy, and he has promised to keep it a secret. I have not bled for three months.

I have always wanted a son and a daughter of my own. Marcus is the closest thing to a son that I may ever have, and I promise to protect him from the darkness as long as I live.

CHAPTER SIX
MARCUS SUNBORN

The trek back home from training was gruelling and tiresome. When I began my lessons two years ago, the travel to each session took over half a day. By the time I reached my first location, Timber would be asleep and most of the steel would be already be tempered. I was thankful the first few times since the walk would sap all of my energy and willingness to learn. Following his lead, I would bundle up near the fire and sleep for hours. When I woke, light burst through the weaponry and Timber would be back to work as if I did not exist. It took several days for me to reach even the third lesson. At first, my father would order his guards to recover me, but he eventually ceased once he knew that I was safe and with my mentors. He would then allow me to take my time travelling and completing each training session without concern.

On the other hand, my mother was not as pleased with my father's leniency. One day, I hid behind their walls to listen closely to my mother and father speaking to each other in privacy. My mother was begging father to let me ride the horses to each lesson but to no avail.

"Jaina, I would not put Marcus through such an ordeal if it did not benefit him. He has worked tirelessly, day and night, and has grown tremendously over such a short period of time. If I make it easier for him, it will only deter his willpower and training," my father explained.

"He is only a child, Edward. You are taking away his childhood innocence from him. I understand the importance of a capable heir who can carry on your legacy, but these lessons are-," but before she could finish, my father interrupted her.

"These lessons are helping him become a man worthy of the Sunborn name!" he exclaimed. "What will I do next, Jaina? Let the guards fight his battles? I will not live forever, my love, and neither will you. Marcus must learn to fend for himself. We are only here to provide him with the essential tools to become a proud and noble man."

At this point, I had heard enough. My father's wish was for a son who could represent his name with pride and honour while my mother's wish was to have a son who would live a normal childhood. I decided to continue doing everything my father asked, but I would take the time to show my mother that I was behaving and acting as a child should. I played pranks on the servants with Pyke, acted childish with Gwyneth, and went out of my way to put a smile on Liza's lips. My father was correct about my willpower and training: It had paid off over time. Now my departure to and from my lessons only lasted a day, and stamina was no longer something I lacked. My parents have given me everything, and all I wanted to do in return was make them happy. Despite this, my parents are not happy. If anything, they have been miserable and distant towards each other. Sometimes they do not even share the same bed. *Am I doing enough*, I wonder to myself. I look down at the elixir and hope this potion will make them happy again.

When I arrive at the front gates, I stop and begin to appreciate the beauty of our keep; it rivals most castles and towers over many other strongholds. Each stone is plastered in gold leaf lining to represent our symbol of light. The architecture comprises of two enormous towers and a main hall for feasts. Banners hang from the balconies with our household emblem. The flags are bright yellow, each one possessing a sun insignia in the centre. Within the sun lay two crossed swords and coins scattered underneath them. The sun represents our name, while the swords represent our commitment to uphold justice and the coins symbolize our wealth. The left tower belongs to my mother and father, while the right one hosts Liza, Gwyneth and I. The main entrance contains two gates stationed by my father's guards. Within the gate, lies a stable which is attached to the side of the main hall. The hall is the main attraction as it is large enough to hold a small army; it contains twenty large ash tables, each draped in golden silk runners. In addition, every table is brandished with jewels and rubies. Even when dinners are not being hosted, my father would ensure that the tables are decorated with the finest cutlery, plate sets, and tankards in case of unexpected visitors. The King and Queen would occasionally make their stay in our home and feast in our hall; and while father may not be royalty by blood, they would respect him as one of their own when they dine with him. One day, I will inherit this fortune and be as famous as father. *I will make him proud*, I think purposefully. The two guards notice me approaching the gates and begin to open them.

"Lord Marcus," they say in unison. I thank them and walk inside, noticing Liza awaiting my return in the hall. She is smiling at me as I sluggishly approach her.

"Lord Marcus, you look like you battled your way through an army," she says. I cannot help but smile. Lately, Liza has been more a parent to me that my mother and father. Mother is too busy brooding over father's attitude and decisions to pay me any heed, and father has been busy trying to defend his every action. Liza has been supportive and attempts to cheer me up by stating that these issues are not my doing. "Just keep being yourself and doing as your mother and father ask, Lord Marcus. The rest will work itself out," she would assure me. She guides me over to one of the lavish tables and places her hand gently on my shoulder. Her light hand weighs me down and I am forced to sit. Liza snickers to herself and removes her hand from its resting place. She prepares dinner for me consisting of; warm milk, bread, cheese, and boar meat. My stomach rumbles at the sight. Liza laughs, sits beside me and asks, "How were your lessons today?"

I look at her and answer with confidence, "It went as well as I could have hoped."

"I assume they were not too rough with you? How is your training with Payne? Are you two still getting along as friends?" I let Liza believe that Payne and I have been friends from the moment we met. She has a special connection with him, and although I do not know their story I can feel how much Liza cares for Payne. However, I do not know if the feeling is mutual. I do not want to hurt her feelings by telling her Payne is a bloodthirsty brute. I cannot bear to have Liza depressed like my dear mother.

"Payne is being as friendly as ever. He tells me that my training is progressing splendidly," I respond.

She is with child, and only I know, but she will not tell me whom it belongs to. When I bring the topic to light, she always responds with, "Someone who is very dear to me, but it is our little secret." Once she finishes asking her questions, she rises from the seat and insists, "Eat and regain your strength, Marcus; you will need it for your lessons tomorrow. I will go and ready your bath so that you can wash the dirt off and retire to your bed." I nod and she takes her leave.

I have no appetite today. Any mention of Payne only reminds me of his demonic smile and the hatred I felt for him today. The name *Light Heart* is insulting, but being called Dark Heart was simply disturbing. When I rushed towards him with my father's sword, I wanted nothing more than to permanently extinguish the light from his eyes. At that moment, all fear was absent and I felt empty, as if I had lost myself to the darkness. I never want to feel that hatred again. Putting aside my own feelings, I turn my focus on more a pressing matter - my parents' relationship. I pulled the elixir from my pouch and wondered what kind of effect it would have on my mother and how it would *calm her nerves*. My instinct told me not to trust the content that was in the flask, but I cannot defy my father's judgment. If he trusts Payne then I should trust him as well. But every time I think of Payne, all I can see is that wicked smile. Lost in my thoughts, I barely notice that someone is behind me. I begin to turn when a pair of cold hands clutch my face and cover my eyes. The voice is gruff, but undeniably feminine. I hear the mischievous voice utter, "Guess who?"

I sigh in response. "Gwyneth, no matter how manly you try to disguise your voice, you will always sound like a Lady."

She giggles and removes her hands. "Lord Marcus, you are so sweet. I am here on your father's behest. Your father is curious to see if you brought a 'special parcel' with you from Payne's keep. He has summoned me to retrieve it and return it to his Lordship."

How does she know about the potion? I wonder. I try to play the situation off with ignorance.

"What parcel?" I ask.

"Oh, Lord Marcus," she coos, as she pokes my nose. "You are as bad a liar as you are a sneak. The potion Payne created for your mother's woes. Your father is eager to test its abilities. He misses your mother dearly and would want nothing more than to bed her again," she put her hand to her mouth coyly and laughs.

Gwyneth is beautiful; she also has curves in all the right places and her voice was sultry and soothing. I could see why my father enjoys her company. If her stature was one of nobility, my father would have us betrothed once I was of proper age. It is common practice for young nobles to marry older women, and Gwyneth is much older than I despite acting far less mature. However, to me, her childishness is her most redeeming quality. When I was younger, I detested her and any woman who was not my mother or Liza, but now I found myself fantasizing about her often. I may be ten years of age but I have been raised as if I was a decade older.

She takes my hand and leads me outside the hall. "Liza has prepared your bath. The water will soon be cold, so you best go on," she says with a sweet smile. I am about to take my leave, hoping she has forgotten about the elixir, but as I turn away Gwyneth reminds me, "Lord Marcus, you are forgetting something." She walks towards me and bends down. Her eyes catch mine and I feel lost in them. It is rare for us to be alone since Liza and mother always keep an eye on Gwyneth and her whereabouts. She leans forward and her fragrance overcomes me. She smells of fresh wild flowers. The closer she leans, the faster my heart beats. *Is she going to kiss me,* I think eagerly. I close my eyes, ready to embrace her. I imagine our lips pursed together as I have seen my mother and father perform during their better times. Time stands still as I wait. What is only seconds feels like hours. I await anxiously but nothing happens. Instead, Gwyneth lifts herself up and puts a finger on my chin so to have me look at her.

"Thank you, Lord Marcus. I will make sure to deliver the vial to Lord Edward safely. And next time, if you wish to kiss a Lady, do not wait for her to make the move," she says as she blushes. I turn bright red.

"Was there any instruction from Payne that I should relay to Lord Edward?" she asks, perfectly normal.

"Ah…-Aye," I stutter. My heart is still fluttering and awkward sensation in my loins stirs. "Payne instructs it is vital that the elixir is taken in full and at night. It is the most potent at that time. Every last drop must be absorbed." She bends down again and places a kiss gently on my cheek.

"You are sweet and strong, Lord Marcus. If I was of noble blood I would have been honoured to be your Lady." I felt the red illuminate even brighter from my cheeks. I bow, oblivious that I still have my father's sword on my hip. Payne warned me about being caught with it. I decide to ask Gwyneth to place it back in its proper holster in my father's weaponry.

"Gwyneth," I say, "may you return this sword to my father's keep? I used it during our training session with Payne and forgot to mention to my father that I had taken it." I hand her the sword and she curtsies and giggles.

"I will see you in the morrow, young Lord," she calls, as she makes her way towards my parents' keep.

As I ascend up the stairs to my room, my mind begins to reminisce of the days my father, mother and I were happy together. No fights, no quarrels, and no disagreements. However, if

Payne's alchemy works, then I will pay no heed to all the past torment and bullying I suffered by his spectre-like hands. I will acknowledge him a friend, as Liza would have me do; I will not need to lie to her any longer. I climb the winding stairs, looking forward to finally taking a warm bath. My room is at the top level and as I approach it, I feel the steam from my bath fill the air. Only then do I realize how sore and stiff my body is.

Liza sees me enter and asks, "What held you, Lord Marcus?" When I do not answer, she looks at me sternly. "Fine…Here you are then." She hands me a change of clothes and leaves to prepare my bed. I climb into the tub of scolding hot water. I realize Liza must have refilled the tub and feel a need to apologize. Sitting in the tub, my eyes start becoming heavy and my mind begins to wander. I start to dream of Gwyneth and how it would feel to kiss her. Our lips pressed against one another as I hold her in my arms, feeling her curves against my body. The tingle re-emerges between my legs and I wake up startled and embarrassed. I sit in the tub for a while longer, letting the warm water wash away my troubles and worries. After some time, when my skin begins to resemble dried grapes, I yearn for my bed. Rising out, I dry myself and dress for bed. Walking to my bedroom I look forward to fantasizing more about Gwyneth. I lift my blankets and tuck myself into my bed. The candle by my bedside flickers and creates dancing shadows in the dark. I close my eyes, hoping to continue my dream of Gwyneth but the only images that appear are those of nightmares. The darkness reminds me of Payne and what transpired today during our training. I cannot rid myself of the image of Payne. He means to haunt me even in my sleep.

CHAPTER SEVEN
PAYNE BLADESTORM

It is time to strike. Everything I planned can now finally be set in motion. It has taken ten long and gruelling years, but all the pieces have finally come together. I will have my revenge against *them.* With the wealth and resources the Sunborn possess, I will be able to build the army I require to vanquish my foes. All of my pawns have played their parts well: Gwyneth has seduced Edward and caused a rift in his marriage, Pyke has earned the trust and access of the Sunborn's vast wealth and treasures, Timber has gathered all of the materials required to re-create my old daggers. The only one who has lost sight of our mission is Liza.

Ever since Marcus was born, she has been irrevocably drawn to him. Perhaps she feels the need to bond with him in order to fill the void she has been carrying all of these years from the loss of our first unborn. It had been easy to manipulate her in the beginning, but now she has found new meaning in life through her love for Marcus. All the hatred and resentment she once felt appears to have disintegrated. She even had the audacity to ask me not to harm these noble bastards. That was the moment I began lying to her. I had to continue telling Liza that no harm would come to the Sunborns and that we would stay in their service for as long as Edward would have us. We would continue living this mundane life as a "normal" family. *She has become naïve,* I tell myself. All these lies are mandatory in order to keep her from opening her mouth and telling the truth about who we really were and what we mean to do with the nobles of Thalia.

Liza was someone I cared for in the past. I have never been close and intimate with anyone besides her. The night at the forest still lingers in my mind as if it were yesterday. She was a lost girl whose curiosity got the better of her. I had just completed a mission, and was marking my body with cuts to remind myself of my glorious kills. She assumed that I was oblivious to her presence, but I had been fully aware that she was eyeing me from behind the trees. The moment she began to edge closer, I made my move. I planned to severe her head from her body before she had the opportunity to see my face. I climbed a tree and catapulted myself above her, dropping down nimbly. Adrenaline was rushing through my veins and I wanted nothing more than to spill her blood on the muddy ground, but something stopped me. As she was turning, my hands steadied and I did not reach for my daggers. I refrained myself from acting on my murderous intent because something about her intrigued me. I remember her brown skin and plump lips, the way her dress hugged every curve. She had beautiful, caring and innocent eyes. Liza had an aura of kindness about her. Rather than sticking my dagger into her chest, I instinctively groped her with my hands. I remember feeling her perfect teats in my grasp and hard nipples in my mouth. That was my first sexual encounter with a woman and I had no idea what I was doing. I realized she was as lost in the act as I was and it was likely her first time with the opposite sex. We both impulsively explored each other and experienced physical intimacy for the first time. She was timid at first, but as I entered her she began to push back wildly. I wanted to live in that moment forever.

Most women were fearful and intimidated by my physical appearance, but she had found me attractive. The act of intimacy was a stranger to me, for I found murder was the only form of physical and emotional intimacy I desired. After my mother disowned me, I felt hatred towards women and especially enjoyed missions where women were the targets. The screams of agony and despair as I ripped their hearts out gave me enough pleasure to rouse an erection. Blood was my lust. Never have I felt compassion or guilt when taking the lives of those jezebels, but Liza was different. When I released my passion inside of her, the world illuminated in an unfamiliar light. The union of passion and pleasure instantaneously opened my heart to something I have long forgotten. I felt human emotion, the one thing I despised and vowed to never succumb to again. I was trained to kill without emotion, yet this human act of intimacy lit the darkness in my heart. Seeing her sprawled naked on the dirty ground, gazing at me with lustful eyes made me want her more. I was only used to seeing women lying on the floor in a puddle of their own blood. In the darkness of the forest, she was the light. I left her that night hoping to see her again but *they* followed me and it was Liza who paid the price.

When I returned to my Masters in order to debrief them on my mission, an unexpected interrogation occurred. I was being questioned on the activities that transpired after the assassination. *Was I being followed,* I pondered. Hoping that my silver tongue would keep Liza safe, I decided to lie and tell them that nothing else happened. Regardless, they already knew of everything that happened between Liza and I in the forest and were testing my loyalty. Had I realized sooner, I may have been able to stop them from ruining her. They employed a sleazy noble to do their bidding; this *filth* had a gambling problem as of late and was in desperate need of gold to continue feeding his addiction. I overheard their plans for Liza accidently during a meeting between my mentor and my Masters. I rushed back to stop what was about to occur. I was too late and was forced to watch her helplessly fight and scream for help. I unwillingly hid in the darkness, knowing I could not defy the orders of my guild. This catalyst was the trigger of a flood of memories that had been hidden away from my past. I could no longer see Liza, but instead memories of my mother's abuse at the hands of lowlife father surfaced my vision. Being in the same type of situation, standing idly and watching helpless, I felt like the child from my past. I started to hear the ever so familiar voice whisper sinisterly in my ear, *Kill them all.* I shut my eyes and struggle to forget the memories of the past; after a few moments, I am back in the present, witnessing a broken and beaten Liza.

My mentor warned me to forget her and that she was going to cause problems for me. He was right. For once I cared for something and my punishment was to watch helplessly as she lost her light and innocence because of my actions.

For months, every mission I carried out was out of spite and anger towards *them*. Whenever I killed a noble, I imagined it was the fat swine who raped Liza. Finally, I could no longer bare it and I made the decision to kill him. That was the start of my double life. I used the rape incident *they* plotted against Liza to cover my murder by portraying the kill as a marital quarrel. I had a personal vendetta against my former Masters, but I still required their trust so I could conjure enough information about them to exact my revenge for Liza. Recruitment was imminent and I knew the perfect lackey.

Pyke was a personal informant and a prostitute pusher. His prostitutes were few, but they had the newest gossip and information of noble activities and daily routines. Pyke was vile and would do anything for coin, so I promised him all the gold and jewellery in the land if he served me. To show my good faith I tossed him a bag of enough gold coins to last him a year as proof of that promise. Liza's role proved more complicated. I wanted her by my side, but I also needed to use her to further my own cause. I was more than willing to give her what she wanted, including myself, but only if she would be willing to participate in my crusade.

"No harm will come to you again," I told her, fully knowing that promise could not be kept if she stood in my way. Steadily, we began targeting nobles for gold and resources. I was determined to locate *their* identities. After the incident with the rapist, I tested to see how far the organization's corruption had spread.

After a few missions, it was evident that many of the nobles I tracked were indeed working for my old Masters. I was gaining information from each successful interrogation without their knowledge; some information proved useful, while others were trivial lies to get me off track. One way or another, it ended with their demise. The knowledge I gained led me to believe that a rich and powerful family was pulling the strings behind the shadows. However, I had no proof and only theories. My torturous examinations had brought me closer to what I sought after. Everything was going as planned, until Liza told me unexpected and miraculous news. She was with child - *my* child. The suppressed memories of my childhood came flowing back again, like a powerful wave, drowning me with contempt. I knew there was no place for a child in my world, but it meant a second chance at life with Liza. This was the first time I created life rather than taking it. It was then that I decided I was going to stop living a life of darkness and turn to the light. *They may have soiled Liza for me but they would not ruin my child*, I determined. What a fool I was. I informed the Masters of my decision to leave a life of assassination to try existing in a normal society, but was starkly informed that it was not an option. They claim to own the mind, body and soul of their subordinates. I was no exception, despite being considered the highest rank of assassin. The only way out of their services was by death. I knew too much about the organization and their members. Even though there were many secrets kept from me, such as my Master's identity and the location of various headquarters, I still had enough knowledge to threaten their existence. I made my choice, and I chose Liza and my new born.

The man they sent to carry out my assassination was the one who mentored me in the art of killing. I fought him for my new found light and he left a reminder of how miserably I failed. The scar on my face will always remind me of the darkness in my heart. I was, and still am, consumed by my hatred. The realization that a child could not exist in my world struck me harder than ever after that battle. Darkness fuelled me, and I was ready to do anything and use anyone to destroy *them*. My escape from death led me to a slave trader's ship where I coincidently located my next recruit.

Gwyneth was a slender, yet physically well-endowed, brat. Her slave Masters were looking for anyone to buy her for a reasonable price. It seemed as though Gwyneth was a violent little bitch who wanted nothing more than to puncture people with pointy things. I inquired the seller as to why they could not control her and they responded, "The little bitch fights like a savage, sir. We believe she is a curse from God. We must have offended him in some way." *By selling people, you miserable ingrate*, I thought. The seller went on to tell me how she killed another slave because they were chewing loudly and it annoyed her.

"How much are you asking for the slave?" I inquired.

"For you, noble sir, we will give you the witch for 10 gold coins. She has not been de-flowered and has energy to outlast even the mightiest man."

Gwyneth's appearance reminded me of a younger Liza, with lighter skin and more sadistic in nature. Since Liza was pregnant and now showing, someone younger and less "used" needed to replace her. Gwyneth was perfect.

I responded to the man, "I will give you 2 gold coins. I am doing you a favour by taking her with me. Less of your slaves will perish without her presence."

The slave monger pondered over the offer and smiled, "You make a good point, wise sir. Two gold, so be it! Now, please take this witch away from my caravan before she curses the rest of my people."

Gwyneth was attractive but also proved to be dangerously charming; almost as if she were a succubus, ready to steal the soul of any unlucky man to fall for her. Liza was not aware, but she was not the only woman I bedded at night. I fucked Gwyneth and spilled my seed on her belly so as not to make the same mistake as I had with Liza. While Liza is passionate in the bedroom, Gwyneth is relentless and ruthless. She loves to be spanked, choked and treated like a whore. She is the ultimate tool of destruction and sexuality. Poor Edward does not know how much he has sacrificed for the young slut. Gwyneth has been more useful than I could have possibly imagined. All she needs to do is have Edward commit adultery and the rest will be simple. And this will be inevitable; as honourable as Edward may be, he is still a man. Every man has needs, and lately Lady Jaina has not been there to oblige. A sadistic and satisfied smile crosses my face as I see torches ahead. *Time to forget the past and start anew,* I think.

I see Pyke's golden-tinged smile from a distance. The tunnels we dug have been allowing us to secretly meet and plot without suspicion. It took longer to complete than expected, but without these passages my plan would have never been possible. Marcus' lessons required all three of us to stop and interact with him every day. Timber did most of the digging, since the man was built for physical labour. His giant hands could scoop more dirt in a minute than Pyke and I could in five. I placed him closest to the Sunborn's home so that once Marcus finished his lessons; Timber could continue digging the tunnels. It spawned from our separate locations and split into the main hall as well as both keeps. In the main hall, the tunnel entrance is underneath the corner of the kitchen. The keep that belonged to Edward had the secret entrance in the dungeon which was always vacant. The trap door located in Marcus' keep was underneath Gwyneth's chambers. These tunnels were essential to completing our goals.

Only Pyke, Timber, Gwyneth and I knew about these tunnels. As I walk through the shadowy halls of dirt, I begin to imagine how glorious it will be when I rid myself of the Sunborn pests. I have asked Gwyneth to come down to the tunnel and inform me when she has given the elixir to Lord Edward. It happens to be the night of their marriage anniversary, thus seeing each other will be customary. Once the drinks have been served, Edward will carry out the rest of the plan. He will serve Jaina the elixir, they will both travel to their bed chamber after their meal, and the potion will take its effects. Once I have completed soiling his name, Edward *the Gallant* will be known as Edward, *the man whore. He will wish he never took us into his home when I am finished with my plans.* The picture plays over and over in my head - two hearts ripped out, and placed neatly beside each body.

CHAPTER EIGHT
LIZA SKYLAR

Payne has not visited me for weeks, and lately I have been crying until my eyes swell and I fall asleep. This feeling of utter loneliness never affected me the first time I was with child because I was focused on our mission. Now, as the sun sinks into the mountains, my heart follows close behind. I pray every night that God grants me a safe delivery so that I may have a family of my own. The idea of losing Payne is far less heartbreaking than the loss of a second unborn child. Serving Lady Jaina has opened my eyes to the wonders of motherhood, and Lord Marcus has broken the seal that once enclosed my emotions towards being a parent. They have both given me hope that in this cruel world, there still exists happiness and room for salvation.

My road to redemption began the moment I held Marcus in my arms. Before his birth, I only knew death. Death surrounded me, engulfing my innocence, my womanhood, and the life inside me, killing it before it was even born. Payne was the cause of my child's death. I want to hate him for his betrayal but I could not; I love him, and want to believe that he has become less vengeful and more human. I cannot hate him even after he spoiled my dreams of motherhood. How could I after he protected me in the past and helped me become the strong woman I am today? Without him, my world would have been an empty shell. He once guided me with his unwavering will and determination, and I followed like an obedient dog who loved her Master. However, things are different now that I have Marcus and another child on the way. Lately, I have been seeking advice from a higher power than Payne. I pray to God for forgiveness of my past sins and the sins of Payne.

Holding my hands together and placing my forehead on them, I begin to whisper.

"God, please look after Marcus, my friends, and my new found family. Protect my unborn child and look down at your unworthy daughter with forgiveness and compassionate eyes so I may redeem myself. I have found my light and want nothing more than to protect it."

I raise my head and look at the ceiling with a smile. I do not require a sign from God. He has already provided me my second chance at what I want most.

After my prayer, I remove my servant attire and dress in my night gown. It once belonged to Lady Jaina, but she presented it to me as a gift for my years of service. Through the years, Lady Jaina and I have become dear friends. She confides in me with her worries and troubles. As of late, Lady Jaina has noticeably not been her cheerful and loving self. Her face is drastically thin and pale. Her hair is tangled and dangly, and she is neglected to care for her appearance. Her melancholy is especially apparent in her mannerisms: she no longer walks with her head held high and her usually confident demeanor. Lord Edward's obsession with Marcus' training has put a strain on their relationship. Only a mother can understand what Lady Jaina is going through. After all, Marcus is her baby and still only ten years of age. She is watching helplessly as Marcus' innocence and childhood are taken from him.

I recall early one morning, as I was cleaning Lord Edwards loft, I was summoned to Lady Jaina's bed chamber. She had a tormented look to her as if she was waging a war within. I could tell she was doing all she could to hold the tears from flowing. Silence clouded the room but without words I understood the pain Jaina felt. I sat by her side and placed my hand on hers. She looked up with empty eyes and began to speak.

"I feel as though the only time I have truly been a mother to Marcus was the day I held him in my arms as a new born. Edward has taken my child from me in order to mold a soldier. I do not want a soldier, Liza; I want my baby," she said as she quietly began to weep.

I held her in my arms but I could not share her sympathy. I have discovered my inability to produce tears have since the day of the rape. I could not even cry for my own child when it was taken prematurely.

"I am sorry, Liza," Jaina said, this should not be something I share with everyone. I must be stronger for my child and for my husband. Please take the night off and leave me be. I have much to ponder and reflect upon."

Rising from her bed side, I bowed and left Jaina helplessly to her sorrows.

Walking through the courtyard I could not help but hear Lord Edward boastfully laughing from the main hall. He was with a female companion whose flirtatious and cheerful giggle was easily recognizable. Instead of heading to my chamber, I decided to disrupt the insensitive prattle coming from within. *How could Lord Edward do this to Lady Jaina? She suffers inside while he keeps himself happy with another woman's company,* I thought bitterly. All men, even the most noble of them, are pigs. The only one who differed from the rest was Payne, who has always been loyal and faithful to his word. I was his and he was mine, and we have shared no one else. I stormed into the feast hall, ensuring that my pronounced footsteps were heard.

Gwyneth was pouring Lord Edward wine while he drank and told stories of his courageous victories in the Great Holy Wars. I could sense the little vixen was up to something and made note to inform Payne of her agenda. As I came into view, Lord Edward's laughter faded.

He stood from his chair and hollered, "Liza! Where is my beautiful wife? Has she stopped brooding in our bed chamber yet?" Before I could answer he continued. "Never mind. Gwyneth has been a gracious Lady and reminds me of my wife when she was younger and merrier."

He picked up his tankard and chugs down his wine. *He is drunk and Gwyneth continues to pour his glass.* I fight the urge to tell her to go back into whatever snake hole that Payne found her in; I had to be delicate about this situation. Lord Edward is the Duke of Apollon and would definitely side with the bitch pouring his wine over a voice of reason. Keeping my composure, I calmly say, "Lord Edward, my Lady bids you goodnight and would ask that you join her." It was a lie, but I needed to pry him out of that harpies claws. Gwyneth gave me a wicked look as if to ask, *what do you think you are doing?*

"Would you like me to escort you back to your keep, sire?" I asked.

"No, no. You ladies best be off to bed yourselves," he replied, as he hiccupped.

I have never seen Lord Edward this way. Drinking was something he did rarely as a pastime. This was not a condition I was accustomed to witnessing from his Lordship.

"Thank you my Lord," I replied, "Gwyneth and I will take our leave." Gwyneth giggled and put her arm around mine.

As Lord Edward fumbled away towards his keep, I turned to Gwyneth sternly and hissed, "What in the world are you thinking?! Lady Jaina is in her bed chamber crying while you sit here and make Lord Edward forget about his troubled marriage? Payne specifically said that this family would not be harmed!" Gwyneth's immaturity annoyed me more than anything else about her.

She simply smiled and slid her arm from mine and responded, "I am doing the duty of a loyal house maid. If Lady Jaina cannot keep her husband happy then someone must. Now, if you will excuse me, I will escort myself to my own bed chamber Liza. Goodnight, my sweet!" Her response reminded me that I too must spend yet another lonely night in my bedchamber.

By the time Marcus turned ten years of age, Payne and I barely laid eyes upon each other. There was only one night when he appeared in my room quietly to surprise me. What a surprise it was. We fondled each other and made love that night for hours. Payne wanted to spill his seed anywhere but inside, but I forced him to stay in. Lost in ecstasy, he could not stop himself from finishing his manly deed inside me. That was the night I was most fertile, thus because of his one visit I now have my second chance at being a mother. Payne will not notice until I start to show, and by then I hope to have Lord Edward and Lady Jaina's blessing to raise my child in their home. I pray that Payne will be prepared as well. I will not allow this child to suffer the same fate as my first.

Our child would thrive in this atmosphere and would learn to become a powerful warrior like his father, or a beautiful lady like her mother. Just the idea of holding my own child made me exultant. If Payne and I can live happily as parents, I will have fulfilled my lifelong dream to be a mother with someone I actually love to call my husband. The thought of it made me happy until I realized I was in bed with child, alone, and no one knew of it but a ten year old boy.

I had to stay strong for Marcus and Lady Jaina. Tomorrow marks our Masters' fifteen year marriage anniversary. This would be the perfect opportunity for Lord Edward and Lady Jaina to make amends. Marcus, being the only adult in this strange situation, has been planning a special surprise for them with my help. The poor boy tries his outmost to please both his father and mother, but completely neglects himself. Hopefully tomorrow's gifts show both parents how much Marcus really loves them and wishes for their marriage to prosper as it once did.

The sun rose early, as did Marcus and I. We planned a trip to the market town of Sallandar today. Secrecy is required since Marcus and I will be absent for most of the day. My absence will be noticed but I am willing to endure what punishment comes my way if it helps Lord Edward and Lady Jaina rekindle their marriage. We decide to travel to the closest stable outside of the *Guiding Light* in order to acquire horses. Everyone in Apollon recognized Lord Marcus as the rightful heir to the title of future Duke and wanted nothing more than to assist the little Master. Farmers praised Marcus and the Sunborn for their kindness and years of dedication to the land, and many offered free mares for our trip. But in true Sunborn fashion, Marcus chose two horses and paid the farmers handsomely. Once we arrived to Sallandar, we noticed the robust and booming market was in full swing and crawling with merchants. We both know that Lady Jaina and Lord Edward are too stubborn to purchase anything for one another so we decide to surprise them with presents. Marcus and I saved all of our gold coins and began our hunt for the perfect gifts.

Lady Jaina was planning to wear a yellow dress with red trim along the sides; it was made of silk and glistened with jewels, mostly composed of rubies and topaz. Marcus wants to acquire a necklace and earrings to complete his mother's attire. He has asked Pyke for assistance but was rejected since Pyke was pre-occupied with a request from Lord Edward. The shops were filled with jewels, some fake and others too expensive. After visiting countless merchants and stores, we finally found what we were looking for.

A traveller from the Eastern shores possessed a magnificent collection of rare jewellery from the other side of the sea. The man nicknamed himself Jewel Tzar, which translates to "Jewel King", a name I was sure that if heard by Pyke would definitely be challenged and mocked. He asked for a hefty price at first, claiming that the jewels were all won from slaying legendary monsters.

"The topaz was from a scorpion the size of large castles," he claims, "the scorpion's eyes were made of topaz. It was just me and my trusty sword against the enormous monstrosity with six legs and its venom tail. The scorpion initiated its assault by attempting to poison me, and listen to me, boy, because the poison from a scorpion is fatal. I dodged to avoid the tail as the monster tried to impale me with its sharp tip. It began to show frustration by skittering its massive feet on the sand, trying its best to step on me. I continued to avoid all of its blows and waited patiently for an opening. With one powerful downward thrust, the scorpion's tail landed and was caught in the deep sand. Can you guess what I did next young man?"

the traveller asks.

Marcus shakes his head in awe.

"I sliced each leg off and green venom spewed from its limbs, and the scorpion came crashing down!" The merchant was waving his arms left and right, mimicking his sword as Marcus' head followed every motion with amazement. He continues to tell his story, "Finally I drove my sharp blade into its thick skull. Once the scorpion was dispatched, I thrust my sword into its eyes and acquired the jewels."

The travelling adventurer, as I have deemed him, continued with his fabled tales but this time about the giant ruby gem which lay sparkling in the sun on the counter.

"The ruby was held by an ancient Cyclops. It was the last of its kind and adventurers throughout the land tried desperately to acquire his ruby eye. Legends said that the Cyclops would shoot beams of red sun at any foe who would dare steal from its cave of treasures. I had hired many mercenaries and recruited dozens of hopeless adventurers to confront the Cyclops. I promised them all the treasures in the cave knowing full well the real trophy was its *eye*," he says with emphasis.

I watch Marcus and smile as he is entrapped with marvel at each word the traveller sputters. *What utter nonsense,* I say to myself. I almost forgot that Marcus is only ten and his innocence is still intact. The traveller continues with his legend.

"We lost many good men searching for the cave. Travel itself was treacherous because the cave was well hidden. Our ships faced dangerous storms, which threw men over board. We battled the desert sun without any water and many perished to thirst and hunger. When we finally arrived at the Cave of Treasures, the Cyclops was nowhere to be seen. I lit a torch and went inside alone," he whispers mysteriously.

"Then what happened?" asks Marcus with a look of excitement.

"As I traversed the cave, I could smell death and blood. Bones scattered everywhere. The skulls of animals, men and babies were thrown aside. I walked a few hours and stopped suddenly. You want to know what I saw next?" The merchant bends over and whispers in Marcus' ear.

Marcus shakes his head while his mouth remains open and his eyes widen.

"A red eye glared at me through the abyss of the dark cave. I knew it was the Cyclops! I put my torch to the ground as to eliminate any light. I was able to see the red eye but it was not able to see me. I crawled carefully towards the Cyclops as it shot beams of sun in all directions. The beam turned many of the treasure hunters into ash but it lit the narrow hallways of the cave. I snuck underneath him while he was distracted, shooting at the men behind me. When I was close enough I removed my mighty scimitar and struck its legs, forcing the giant to fall to its knees. Once we stood on common ground, I punctured my sword into the Cyclops' eye. The monster roared and swung wildly, like this!" The travelling merchant swings his arms, this time imitating the monster. Marcus had to jump back so he would not be struck by the wild flailing.

"I removed the eye and shot the beam of sun back at the Cyclops and it turned to a pile of ash. See, boy, this was the very sword that killed those monsters."

The man pulls out his curved scimitar from his cloth belt so Marcus could admire it.

"WOW! Liza, can you believe it!?" Marcus asks.

Of course not, I think. "Yes, Lord Marcus. This man is a legendary story teller indeed." I was hoping that the merchant got the intentional insult within my statement and that I did not believe a word that came from his fictions but the reaction and joy it brought to Lord Marcus is adorable. Watching Marcus' imagination soar as the traveller told his stories of monsters and adventure is something that no one has the chance to witness. He is so caught up in his daily training that he does not have the opportunity to be a child his age. I did not want to ruin this moment for him so I ask Marcus to wait by the merchandise as I pull the traveller aside.

"This boy is the son of the powerful and wealthy Lord Edward Sunborn," I proclaim. "We are here on his behalf to purchase a gift worthy of his Lady. It would be worn by her in the presence of other powerful and rich nobles. I am confident your name would become *even* more famous if the Sunborns were to promote it."

The traveller seems intrigued. I continue on.

"All we ask is that you make this first purchase, one of many, 'reasonable' for the little Lord, and I will see your pockets filled with future earnings," I bribe the merchant. The Sunborn's name is powerful and the merchant knows if he falls into their good graces, that his own merchandise will be sought after by many other rich nobles in the land.

"Seeing if I sell to you for half the price, will you tell Lord Edward of my glorious adventures so that he may one day accept me as his Master of Coins? Tell him I am gifted in the art of battle as well, but I prefer gold. If you do this, my Lady, then I shall grant you half the price on these rare and magnificent items."

I agree knowing full well that this man would never reach the status Pyke worked so hard to attain, as no one fought for the love of gold more than that man. We both consent to the terms and I head back towards Marcus. He is busy trying to figure out what other monsters were slain for the sapphires and diamonds within the man's tiny shop.

"Ah, little Master," the merchant says, "You tell your father of how good the Jewel Tzar has been to you and I might tell you the story of the stone colossus I defeated to in order to mine this diamond heart from its chest."

Marcus claps excitedly. Lady Jaina would have loved to see him like this. This was the motherly experience she wished to have. Instead, I am in her place, watching him act his appropriate age.

Once the purchase is completed, Marcus and I look for Lord Edward's gift. Lord Edward does not lack material objects. As a matter of fact, the man has everything gold could possibly provide. What his Lordship wants most is his youth. Payne's potions have not been working as intended, but all of Lord Edward's acquaintances have been telling him how young he looked as of late. *Blind, foolish 'yes' men*, I think to myself.

Marcus considers his father fit to be a king. Even when the Royal Family visited his estate, Lord Edward was the talk of the feast. He out drank the Prince, out dressed the King, and out danced the Queen. Not intentionally, but this was how Lord Edward was - a man of many talents and few flaws. Marcus requests to have a golden crown created just for him. It is to have a sun emblem enshrined in the middle, two swords pointing at each other from each direction and diamonds enlaced around the crown so rays of light will sparkle off it. This is the banner of House Sunborn.

When I asked Marcus why he wanted to get his father a crown, he sadly replied, "Mother told me Father has been losing his sun because he was passing down his legacy to me. I want my father to remember that *he* is still the ruler of his house. My time will come. This crown of gold and diamonds will take away from the white and dark hairs on his head."

I cannot help but smile. God has blessed Lady Jaina and Lord Edward with such a marvellous son.

"He will be honoured and pleased to receive such a gift, and be proud to have such a kind hearted son," I tell him with approval.

When we arrive at the blacksmith's shop, Marcus looks at me and worriedly says, "Liza, don't tell Timber I did not go see him for this. I did not wish to bother him with this task and this blacksmith is renowned for his ability to make helmets and headgear."

I look across the shop, eyeing the golden crown. "But of course Lord Marcus. You keep my secrets and I keep yours, right?" I reply as I pinch his nose.

He laughs and gives me a hug. This is how I want to live my life. A child of my own who loves me and that I can love in return.

The blacksmith is an older man, with large

arms and an even larger belly. He is pounding away on some metal until he sees Marcus.

"Lord Marcus! How good of you to come! Lord Edward's gift is ready," he yells.

All these years of hammering has made the man go nearly deaf, so Marcus replies yelling in return.

"Thank you, Bonsworth! Here is the rare metal you asked for!" Marcus hands him steel that looks familiar.

It has a hint of silver and gold mixed together. Then it occurs to me. *Mithril,* I remember. Only nobles have access to the precious metal. I remember Lord Edward acquired some recently for a purpose he was not willing to share. Marcus must have taken some.

"OH!" yells the blacksmith. "You are a man of honour, like your Lord Father! This will do indeed! There you are, Lord Marcus! Remember to give my thanks to Lord Edward!"

We take the crown and prepare to make our journey back to the estate. As we take our leave, I begin to feel sorry for Marcus. Marcus the child must disappear once again to become Marcus the adult once we arrive back to the keep.

CHAPTER NINE
MARCUS SUNBORN

As Liza and I begin to make our way home, I cannot contain my excitement for adventure. The travelling merchant's tales left me aching to explore the various lands found in Thalia, its inhabitants and mysteries like the mythological monsters described by the Jewel Tzar. I wonder what it would feel like to be free of the everyday burden I face as a noble. Nobility has its perks: respect, servants, a loving mother, a heroic father, riches, and acres of land. However, what I desire most is freedom. For once, I want to be free like the wind. Free like the dreams that come and go when I sleep. Free like the darkness that covers the world like a blanket and the sun that illuminates all of it yet this is not my reality. I know when we return, I will have to perform the same mundane routines that have been a part of my life since the age of five. Sadness starts to fill my heart, so I remind myself of the fun-filled day Liza and I experienced today at the market; my worries temporarily escape me.

I look up at Liza and say, "Thank you again for everything. This day would not have been as remarkable without your company. You have been every bit the mother a child could want. I know yours will feel blessed to have you."

Liza looks down at me, and her eyes fill with tears. We stop and she bends down and gives me a tight embrace. It feels comforting and fills me with happiness, yet somehow I cannot help but feel sorrow. I recall when my mother used to do this. I hope these gifts will be enough to help their marriage.

The hike home is tedious and long, but we make the best of it. Every few hours, I remind myself of Liza's pregnancy and act as if I am fatigued in order to let her rest a while. Liza is a strong and stubborn woman. I could go on for hours without stopping and she would do the same just to prove she is not a burden. Every time we halt to catch our breath, admiration fills our hearts from our surroundings. Thalia is filled with beauty and humility. We watch farmers digging holes and preparing for the fall harvest. As the men dig, their wives and daughters milk cows and goats. Gardeners plant diverse seeds of flowers and trees. Fishermen lounge peacefully in their boats while some relax on shore, waiting patiently for their daily catch. Children play in the grassy plains, carefree; some are my age and others are even older. I imagine myself playing with them... laughing, wrestling, and pretending to be famous knights. While they pretend to be adults, actually acting like children their age, I am being groomed to become a grown man. I want nothing more than to be a child.

A mixture of smells also covers the land. As we pass by farms, the scent of manure and dung seeps through the air. As we cross paths with gardeners, the wind rushes the smell of newly grown grass and lush flowers our way. Stopping to take in the fresh air, we both realize how important it is to treasure the smaller things in life. This is something I hope that my parents will remember after their anniversary. All I want them to do is love each other as they did before. I miss them so much.

After five long hours of walking, my family grounds finally come into view. The Sunborn banner greets us, waving vigorously in the wind. The sun is no longer visible behind grey clouds, and we hear a low rumble of thunder. Liza snatches my hand and pulls me along quicker.

"This storm looks evil, Marcus," she hollers

over the wind as she holds on to me.

The rain is sudden and pours down on us like arrows falling from the sky. While it was refreshing after our long walk, an ominous treble shakes the ground and flashes of lighting blind our path. The guards waiting at the gates stand still like statues until they take notice of our approach.

"Lord Marcus," they verbally acknowledge in unison as the enormous gates open.

We sprint towards the right access where our bed chambers lay. By the time we entered our keep, our clothes are heavy and drenched as if we were standing under a waterfall for hours. We look at each other and the silence in the hall is filled with our laughter.

"Thank you, Lord Marcus. Today has been the most joyous of days I have experienced in a long while."

I look at her with a smirk. This has been much more enjoyable than my typical day of lessons.

"Now, please, let us go to your bedchamber and remove your clothes. Your parents will have my head if you catch a cold and miss more training," she says in a worried tone.

We ascend the stairs while rain drips from our clothes and onto the stone steps. Holding each other became necessary, as the stairs become slippery and hazardous from our spills. When we finally make it to my room, Liza excuses herself so she may undress in her own chambers. I bid her farewell and do the same in mine.

I throw my soaked attire by the burning fireplace and promptly hide my parents' gifts underneath my bed. I hear Liza humming a soft melody in the chamber next to me as she readies herself for sleep. I look outside as the storm continues to pour mercilessly. Lightning bolts seem to increase in size and occur more frequently. I am afraid one will eventually reach me. As I stare into the rain, I start to think about Gwyneth and the idea of being caught in the rain with her.

My mind wanders, fantasizing about how she would look as water runs down her body, soaking through her dress. Her hair is wet but purposely covering only the parts of her curves that would be deemed immoral for a boy my age to see. I would hold her drenched body and make her feel warm and safe. In this fantasy, I am much older, stronger, handsome, noble, and gentle; the man my father dreams of me becoming. Once I save her from the storm, we proceed to my room where I would take my time undressing her, admiring every inch of her body. We would make love to each other all night until the sun rose from the mountains. I begin to stiffen. *What I would do to have her in my bed,* I think aroused. The idea dissipates as soon as I hear Liza calling my name.

"Lord Marcus," she yells from her room, "I will prepare your bath. Please ready yourself."

The water was scolding but Liza ensures me that it would prevent any illness that could result from being in the rain for such an extended period of time. My mind is still flirting with the idea of being with Gwyneth. Meanwhile it seems as though Liza is lost in her own thoughts. We are silent for a few moments until I decide to blurt out an unexpected question that lingers in my mind.

"Liza, do you think my father would allow me to marry Gwyneth?"

At first Liza paid me no heed but after she digests the question, she turns to me with a look of disbelief. "Lord Marcus, I do not think you know what you are asking. Gwyneth is..." she pauses to think about the proper way of explaining, "She is not a woman suitable of your stature. The girl acts younger than you but is twice your age. She is not worthy to be called your Lady my young Lord." She finishes uttering bitterly.

I do not want to pursue the conversation after this response. My question seems to have upset Liza, so I decide to change the topic and talk about her. My father always claims that women love to talk about nothing more than themselves. "They love the sound of their own voice, and think their problems surpass all else," he would say.

"How are you feeling, Liza?" I ask.

"I am fine, Lord Marcus, thank you." She replies monotonously. Liza does not seem to be in the conversational mood, but I do not allow that to stop me from expressing my gratitude for her company today.

"We had a long day and I want you to know I appreciate everything you did for me. I will definitely repay you after my parents' anniversary is over," I tell her, smiling genuinely. She does not answer. Did I upset her?

"Lord Marcus, I want you to be honest with me. Do you truly believe that your parents will allow my friends and I sanctuary for as long as we desire? Have we not overstayed our welcome? It has, after all, already been ten years."

I do not know the answer; but if my parents do want them to leave, their departure would have already transpired.

"My mother and father value you all individually, in one way or another," I answer confidently. "You have all become family and I cannot imagine our lives without each and every one of you." *I could do without Payne,* I think, but I would never say it aloud to Liza.

"I am glad to hear that," she says thankfully as her hand cups her belly.

She is worried for her child. I know my father would not abandon Liza after her birth. She will live here happily with her companions, and I will ensure my family name continues our legacy of helping those in need.

Liza takes her leave after she scrubs my back, and I finish washing the rest of my body myself. Wishing Liza a good night, I thank her again for everything today.

"It was my pleasure Marcus. Tomorrow will be a long day for the both of us. Get your rest and have sweet dreams," she says as she closes the door behind her.

My towel is hanging from the side of the tub and I reach for it to dry myself off. My thoughts drift back to what Gwyneth is doing. My clothes are already neatly folded, lying on the bed. I reach for my garment and dress in the warm cotton comfort of my nightly sleep attire. Before going to bed, I decide to take a gander through the window to see if the storm has calmed. The grey clouds subside to reveal the stars and much needed light. I crave to see Gwyneth before I close my eyes and fall into a deep sleep. I desire nothing more than to have a dream about her; but lately, all of them turn to nightmares with Payne as the culprit. Sometimes he would beat me in my dreams until I wake up, feeling sweaty, bruised and sore. Other times, his smile would linger in my mind, mocking and evil. Even then, this image does not compare to one nightmare which haunts me most nights.

This nightmare is vivid and disturbing. It always begins with Payne and I, standing in the training field. Both of us are preparing to do battle. He urges me to attack him and I comply by rushing at his heart with my father's short sword. Unlike our previous training session, my weapon does not miss the mark and I always pierce his chest. Then something turns horribly awry.

The weapon is not my father's sword; they

are Payne's daggers, with steel dark as night and hilts golden as light with hearts at the end of the handles. Both of the inscribed dragon heads come to life and sink their teeth in their victims' bodies, as blood trickles profusely. The weapon is not the only change. The person I stab is not Payne, but instead my father and mother. My father tries to speak, but his tongue is missing. My mother's throat is pierced by one of the dragon heads fangs. Their chests have holes where their hearts should be, and their hearts are also evidently missing. It seems as though a sharp knife cut right through them. I would be crying in my room with tears soaking my pillow, yet I would not wake. I realize something red and pulsating is being held in my parents' hands. The deafening *thud* grows louder in my head and I feel my own head pulsing. The cruel realization that their hearts are not missing but instead lie beating in the palm of their hands, beating and bloody red. Payne appears behind me with the same daggers I murdered my own parents with. His cheek is against mine as his weapon cups my throat.

"You did well, Marcus," he whispers in my ear. "This is the way to become a warrior. Killing requires darkness. You have potential young, Dark Heart. Look at them."

The hearts that rest atop my mother and father's hands start losing their crimson colour and slowly began turning a saturated black. Payne suddenly appears behind them, smiling.

"Kill, or be killed, Marcus. That is the way of life. Hate is your path. You are a disappointment to them. It is because of you that they fight and hate each other. They secretly want to kill you Marcus. That is the only way for them to be happy. You did the right thing by killing them first."

Payne breaks out into laughter, first softly and then progressing to such a high pitch that the last time I dreamt this I woke up screaming. *It is only a nightmare and nothing more,* I would keep telling myself. I desperately want a distraction and the only one that could give me this luxury is Gwyneth, who is usually still up at this hour. Hopefully seeing Gwyneth will give me something else to dream of; I am praying the nightmares will end. I open my bedchamber door and begin heading towards the bottom of the stairs, eagerly wanting Gwyneth to still be awake.

The damp and musky scent of fresh rain drying on stone lingers throughout the corridors. Breathing is becoming a chore as I descend with each step. The lantern I carry flickers in the dark, lighting my path as I tread carefully down each step. The chamber in which Gwyneth resides is located on the main level and faces the back of the stronghold. She enjoys the privacy of the room and never complains, even though it is considerably smaller in size compared to Liza's. Her view is less than desirable, as well; her window offers minor glimpses of few trees and is obstructed by a giant stone wall. Liza was willing to share her room at the top level but Gwyneth refused.

"This will do. A Lady needs her privacy, and my youth will permit me to travel up these stairs much quicker than Liza," she remarked playfully with a laugh.

As I creep closer to her bedroom, my ears catch a conversation between a man and a woman coming from Gwyneth's bedroom. I lean in and listen carefully to the dialogue. The man has a smooth, low pitch to his voice. It is familiar, yet hard to make out from this distance. I only manage to catch part of his question.

"...Ready for tomorrow?"

My feet move quickly and silently, and I take a step back so as not to arouse suspicion. I press my ear against the cold stone wall. Her door is open slightly, so I could understand some of what is being said. I leave my lantern on the cold floor a few steps above as to not invite attention with the light. A candle in Gwyneth's room sheds some light through the opening of the door and I am able to see Gwyneth's hair. The man is still not visible. He stands on the other side and speaks with a hushed voice.

Gwyneth replies to his question, "Everything is going according to plan. The Sunborns will be celebrating tomorrow after sunset in the main hall. Lord Edward has the elixir and the instructions."

What is going on and who is she speaking with? I wonder frightfully.

"Excellent," the man says softly. "All these years and we will finally be ready to take 'them' on. With the power and wealth of the Sunborn, I can finally exact my revenge."

Gwyneth turns, facing away from the mysterious figure. "Unlace this dress please and fuck me. I have waited all day for you."

I wish to leave, but part of me feels compelled to stay a while longer. I did not know whether to be scared for Gwyneth or aroused. My body does not budge, even though my mind urges me to flee. The man puts his dirty hands on her neck roughly. A gasp of pain and pleasure escapes out of Gwyneth. His other hand finds her breast and fondles them roughly. I close my eyes at first but my manhood takes control now. I re-open one eye and then the second. Her teats are hanging out of her nightgown, exposed and nipples hard. I cannot see any features on the man except his hands. They are silvery white and covered in dirt. It looks as if he is hurting Gwyneth, but she seems to enjoy the more he violates her.

"That's it," she exclaims. Her hand reaches behind her and begins stroking. Then she turns towards the figure and pleads, "Hurry up and put it in. I NEED it inside."

The man did something next that sent Gwyneth into a frenzy. Her body arches backwards; her hand holding his head and her back is contorted as she rocked back and forth like a woman possessed. The hands are now choking her and occasionally slaps her across the face, but not hard enough to leave marks.

"Yes! Just like that! Fuck me like a whore," she screams with lust.

This is not the woman I am accustomed to seeing. I thought Gwyneth to be innocent and pure. The person who I was staring at was neither of those things.

They were changing positions and Gwyneth turned around like a dog taking him from the rear. My eyes cannot peel themselves off the sexual event that is transpiring. It is all wrong yet I carry on watching until I hear a faint *clunk* coming from above. The noise becomes louder and louder by the second. As the noise intensifies, an item becomes visible. It is apparent that the wind had pushed my lantern down. The racket alarms Gwyneth and the mysterious man, quickly putting a stop to their lustful, inappropriate activity.

As the lantern tumbles down the stairs, I ready myself to sprint back to my room, praying that neither of them see me.

"We are not alone," the man's voice says with concern.

I run as fast as I can, leaving my lantern at the bottom of the stairs. I peer back to see if I am being followed but no one appears to have taken chase. As soon as I enter my bed chamber, I shut the doors behind me and jump into my bed and under my covers. *This is not how it is supposed to be*, I tell myself as I try to catch my breath. Gwyneth was my fantasy, but now she has become a nightmare as well. While no one comes to my door, the damage is done. Sleep does not visit me that night.

Whenever I close my eyes, all I can see is Gwyneth's body rocking back and forth with nothing supporting her. She seems as if she is floating. In my dream, I storm through the door to save her but I am too late. Her heart is cut out and placed between her breasts. The blood is dripping down her belly and between her legs. Again, I am holding two daggers in my hands. The same two daggers that kill my parents in my other dream now appear in this dream; Gwyneth has suffered the same fate. In this version, my mother is standing over Gwyneth's body and she is holding two hearts instead of one.

Her chest still has the hole where her heart is meant to be. My mother turns to me, and with a shrill voice says, "You did this to us, Marcus. You could have stopped it *all!*"

I wake up screaming and crying. Liza runs in startled, asking frantically, "Lord Marcus! What is the matter? Are you hurt?" I stare blankly into space, silent for some time.

I cannot tell anyone of these dreams. They will think I am crazy.

"I am sorry, Liza. It was a bad dream. Would you mind sleeping by my side tonight? Your company would be most welcome," I ask, almost a pathetic plea.

Liza realizes how scared I am and decides not to pry further. She climbs into bed and places my head against her shoulder. With her by my side, for the first time in a long time, I fall asleep without any nightmares.

CHAPTER TEN
PAYNE BLADESTORM

So the boy saw and heard, but how much? I wonder suspiciously.

"Are you not going after him?!" Gwyneth cries in concern.

Her excessive chatter and frantic worrying is beginning to irritate me. "No I am not going after him," I reply calmly. "We do not know what he saw, if anything or what was heard. Even if he did see the two of us together, he fears me and knows better than to say anything."

Gwyneth is quickly gathering her garments and dressing herself while simultaneously staring at me in utter disbelief. "Our plan might be ruined though! What if he says something? What if-." Before she could continue her prattle, her mouth is met with the back of my hand. She backs away and holds her mouth as her eyes tear up from the impact.

"Quiet!" I demand angrily. "The only

person that will give us away is you if you maintain that tone. There is nothing that can be done about tomorrow. The plan will not change because of some ten year old nosey brat. You know what to do, right? Repeat it again to me."

Gwyneth removes her hand from her face where marks of my hand were visible from the forceful slap. She responds in a soft and evil tone, "You, Pyke and Timber will come through the tunnels after Lord Marcus 'finishes' his lesson with Timber. While Lady Jaina and Lord Edward dine in the main hall, the three of you will enter their keep and hide in the shadows." As Gwyneth recites the plan, her soft tone becomes malicious.

She continues, "I will serve Lady Jaina the elixir right before they complete their meal. They will then retire to their bed together, happily, as if all of their troubles are resolved but before they reach the top, the potion will take effect and paralyze Lady Jaina. I will then help Lord Edward bring her to their bed as you snatch him and do whatever dastardly deed you plan on doing," she remarks with an excited giggle.

"That is correct," I stroke her hair with a smirk and then grab a handful and pull back. I place my mouth close to her ear and whisper.

"I will then fetch Liza, tell her that Lord Edward has summoned her to their chamber and then we will kill her as well. Once all three are disposed of, the final touch will be placing the dagger in the hands of Lady Jaina, making it seem as though she killed Liza and Lord Edward for having an affair. Then we will stage it as if she kills herself for the grief of her failed marriage and murder of her husband."

I release my tight grip from Gwyneth's hair, which makes her frown; I nod at her for reassurance and am pleased with her enthusiasm and recollection of the plan.

"Lastly, we will then all escape through the secret tunnels and head back to our appropriate posts as if we knew nothing."

She laughs and replies, "I cannot wait for you to finally kill that old bitch Liza."

Grabbing the back of her head, I bring her mouth to mine and plunge my tongue down her throat with passion. I could feel her tongue against mine, exchanging saliva. After a few seconds of sharing fluids, I remove my mouth from hers and give her one final message before I depart.

"I will see you tomorrow, Gwyneth. Sleep

well and do not act differently around Marcus. Do *not* raise suspicion. He is only a ten year old boy who fancies you. Take advantage of it."

Upon my departure, I begin to feel the entity inside me whisper, *poor gullible Gwyneth.* Ignoring the voice, I return to my thoughts of admiration for the fail proof plot. Marcus will have an "accident" at Timber's smith shop as I have provided Timber with instructions as to how I want Marcus disposed.

Young men always face danger, sometimes fatal, when training to be an apprentice blacksmith. Timber was the perfect candidate to commit the crime. Having a mute under my service has its advantages. If the finger of blame for Marcus' demise ever makes its way back to us, Timber would be an expert at keeping silent if being put through torture. His massive size and rough skin works as additional armour. Blows bounce off his exterior like metal sparks off a blacksmiths anvil. Once Marcus is out of the way, we will then finish off the other two pesky Sunborns.

Lady Jaina and Lord Edward are not to be disturbed tomorrow. Only their servants are permitted in their presence for the "special day". *Oh, this will be a special day indeed,* I smile to myself. The elixir I concocted in order to calm Lady Jaina's nerves is made of a deadly combination of spider and scorpion venom. It will indeed calm her, to the point of paralysis. Once the potion runs its course, the bitch will not be able to scream or beg for mercy while I take my time torturing her. With that final satisfying image, I open the trap door and take my leave from Gwyneth's room.

As I walk down the dark tunnel, Pyke and Timber await my return. I had instructed them to wait for me as I completed my *business* with Gwyneth. Pyke is leaning against the dirty wall while Timber sits quietly on the ground; the man is too big for his own good. The tunnel we constructed is too small in height, thus Timber is forced to bend his neck sideways when he stands.

Pyke discovers my presence and waves his meaty hands in the air, bidding me welcome. "Ah, Payne. How was she today? Did you slap her a few times for me? She must be a prime cunt for you to risk our plan the night before its execution."

Pyke had a habit of drooling when something excited him. I could see it forming from the side of his mouth. I answer coldly, "She knows her part of the plan well and is still oblivious about the final part she will play."

I turn to Timber, "Are you prepared to

snuff the life out of Marcus tomorrow?" Timber simply nods while continuing to stare at the wall.

"And Pyke I assume that you have forged another will that states if Lord Marcus were to die, the estate and all the treasures go to me, as Master of Blades and Potions, to protect and serve the house?"

Pyke smiles a large grin, exposing his fluorescent yellow teeth. Even in a tunnel without light, his teeth are visibly stained. He replies, "Of course I have. You keep your part of the bargain and I will keep mine." He lifts his hand with four rings and wiggles his fingers. He has had his greedy sights set on one particular jewel for quite some time. His engagement finger still lacks a ring and there is only one which he deems worthy of being placed on that pudgy finger.

I sigh. "Yes, Pyke. The ring is all yours once we have completed our objective," I re-assure him. "You two return to your posts and wait for sundown. Tomorrow marks a new era for Apollon and Thalia. We will create our army and my true mission will finally commence and I will have justice against *them*."

Pyke interrupts my speech hesitantly. "When are you planning to tell us who *they* are?

This is the one thing you refuse to share with anyone."

I touch the scar near my brow and eye on the right side of my face. I recall how I was forced to kill my own child and watch hopelessly as the blood ran between Liza's legs.

I look up at my two minions and respond, "In due time. These walls have ears, even in the secret tunnels. When we complete our goal tomorrow I will tell you everything I know."

Timber and Pyke both agree and take their leave down the tunnels and back to their stations. I linger behind and decide to spend the night in the damp, dirty and pitch tunnel. Dreams come to me tonight; glorious images of how I will exact my long-awaited revenge against my old Masters.

In my dream, I am standing in darkness; my *Silent Sisters* in each hand, covered in blood from the dark steel up to the golden hilts. A new amassed army of destruction, *My* army, stands behind me, quiet, massive, obedient and ready to kill on my command. Around my feet lie the countless dead bodies of my old benefactors. Some people I used to consider acquaintances and comrades, while others were bodies with empty faces - faces of people whom I have not yet to identify, but recognize as the *puppeteers* moving the strings in the shadows. A heart is removed from each body and placed gentle to the side of the corpses, beating, bloody and dark red. Suddenly, the ever familiar voice whispers, *Kill them all.*

Dark Heart; I can feel him again, trying to weasel his way into my psyche. I have not communicated or given Dark Heart permission to re-surface in some time but I know he is lurking within me with murderous and blood thirsty intent to destroy everything. *Tomorrow cannot come soon enough.* I close my eyes again, hoping for the final time tonight.

I awake, with Gwyneth standing in front of me with a devious smile on her face. The red mark on her cheek has transformed into a purple bruise. I rise to my feet and remove the dirt from my body. Gwyneth struts behind me and places her hands on my back and rubs the mud off. She kisses my shoulder as she cleans me. She is trying to arouse me, but I am already erect from the excitement I feel from the events that are going to transpire today. My dreams repeated themselves last night. They were filled with death, blood, decay and an unstoppable army under my banner.

I shrug Gwyneth off, uninterested, and put my shirt on. Gwyneth latches herself back on me with desperation. *Bloody leech does not give up when she wants something,* I utter to myself. Again, I pull her hands off of me and swing around to face her.

"Gwyneth, we spoke about raising suspicion. You are to look after your duties as if this day is no different than any other," I remind her. Marcus may have seen enough yesterday to cause me some concern. Not that it truly matters in the end, but I did not want to complicate matters. Gwyneth stares at me with weepy eyes as if I slapped her again and she persists lustfully.

"I dreamt of us making love on the dead bodies of today's victims. Blood covered us from head to toe, and made us more excited to be together. I woke up wet and wanting nothing more than to have you inside me this morning. I want you inside me, Payne, deep and hard. I want you to take me in this dirty mud hole," she moans while she touches her breasts.

Any sane man with function in his genitalia would be foolish to refuse her. Gwyneth has a body that only a goddess should possess, but she was far from a holy deity. Gwyneth is more demonic than angelic, though that is why I lavish shoving my member inside her body. She relishes the pain and the pleasure. Next to abusing Marcus, this was the most enjoyable form of physical activity.

Unfortunately for her, today I will not be Payne when it comes time for the execution. Today, I will give in to Dark Heart.

I have desires, needs, and even emotions. It has never been easy during my days as an assassin to kill innocents and dastardly alike. I did it for the thrill and the sport but never for the pleasure. On the other hand, Dark Heart enjoys every second of it and wants nothing to do with human emotions. Its only desire is to destroy everything and complete his disturbing ritual. The only person I will leave unharmed is Liza.

Ever since the night my seed entered inside of Liza, I struggled returning to see her. I desired her, but it was too risky. Once I complete today's plans, I will make an effort to be more open with her. Unlike this crazy bitch, Liza still has meaning to me. *The light that temporarily vanquished my darkness,* I recall. Although I lost the battle to find peace and escape the past, I will win the war and one day, regain my light. Until then, I will spread carnage and destruction on my enemies and they will lay dead beneath my feet.

I repeat myself, this time with rugged sternness in my voice. "Gwyneth, I will NOT tell you again. Be gone from my sight and do not ruin this pivotal day. If anything goes awry due to your obsessive behaviour, I will make sure you suffer dearly."

She fumes and rages. The bruise on her face now matches the rest of her skin. I am sure if she possessed a sharp object in her hand, she would attempt to kill me right now. Immaturity and Gwyneth went hand in hand. If she does not get her way, she acts like a tempered child.

"Fine," she yells. "The next time you come to bed me it will be I who refuses YOU!"

I cannot help but laugh, which only irritates her more. *You would shove my daggers inside of you for pleasure,* I think in amusement. She bangs her bare feet against the dirt ground and stomps her way towards the ladder, still vexed. As she climbs the stairs back to her room, I could not help but look upon her one last time with some admiration. *She may be a childish slut but there is nothing childish about her body. Unfortunately, once a slave, always a slave and you played your role well.* I sit back on the soiled ground and meditate as I have in the past. My mind begins to vividly imagine how the rest of the day would progress. *This will be the last sunset for the Sunborn,* I assure myself convincingly.

My meditation lasts for hours. I plan every move methodically and remove all emotion from my mind and body. I visualize the plan out in my head as if it were happening in front of me. Edward will walk in with a helplessly paralyzed Jaina in his arms. Gwyneth will assist him and open their luxurious chamber doors. Once he enters I will be waiting in the dark. I will grasp his mouth so he does not scream with one hand and my dagger in another, pressing it against his chest so he submits any will to fight back. I will not kill him right away. I am going to take my time and enjoy making him suffer excruciating pain. That prideful fool will die slowly, and I want his bitch of a wife to watch every moment, motionless but completely aware of what is happening. When I have her undivided attention, I will carefully rip into his skin, and dig into his bones until I breach the barrier protecting his heart. At this point Dark Heart should be in full control and it hears my every thought and knows my every move so it is aware of the outcome I expect from this plan. The heart needs to be placed in the hands of Jaina once it has been ripped out.

The noble and virtuous heart of Edward will be the perfect trophy for the triumphant return of Dark Heart. Then it will kill the next unsuspecting victim - my play toy, my poor, gullible Gwyneth. Her heart will join Edwards. Finally, it will take care of Lady Jaina. I know better than to get between Dark Heart and its prey but I do wish the pleasure were mine in this task. At the very least I will see everything through its eyes. My dagger will take its time silently and gradually making her throat *smile*. She will feel every bit of the anger and bitterness I have felt towards her for the last ten years. Her eyes will speak volumes for her lack of noise. As I feel myself becoming overexcited, I hear Dark Heart whisper, *Kill them all.*

Precision and swiftness is how I approached each kill. As trained, I hide in the shadows, eluding my foes while they searched for me blindly. I enjoy the power I have over my prey in the dark. The game of cat and mouse is intriguing as they run frantically, knowing that something is coming for them. Before they can expect it, I am already daggers deep into their bodies. But Dark Heart is different.

My Dark Heart persona is a murderous and unrelenting killing machine who only cares for the hunt and fear in peoples' hearts. It loves the idea of battle head on, without the art of stealth, and usually toys with its victims. Once it finishes playing with the target, it pierces their hearts and cuts them out as a ritual.

I had to learn to control this entity so I could use it against my enemies. *Their creation will also be their destruction*, I whisper back to Dark Heart, hoping that it hears me.

I remember my dream from the night before. I vividly recall all of the bodies on the floor beneath me, only this time the bodies of the Sunborn join them. Marcus is the first body I notice. His whole body is burnt from head to toe and only his mouth is wide open, as if he died screaming for help. His hair is turning to ash and his scalp is melting, skin dripping on the other bodies underneath him. Parts of his body have protruding bones, while the rest of him is mostly covered in putrid burn marks. *Marcus should be dead by now.*

I realize how long I have been waiting for Pyke and Timber and begin to wonder their whereabouts. No later than a few minutes, I hear rapid footsteps approach and see flickers of a torch in the distance. I rise to greet my comrades, but their faces look as though they have seen a ghost.

Pyke hurries along, his fat jiggling from his tight doublet. He is heaving and huffing from the jog and his face is completely pale.

"Payne!" he yells squeamishly, as he inhales loudly to catch his breath. Timber is lugging right behind him, bending low to avoid his head from ramming into the ceiling of the tunnel. "Marcus never arrived for his lessons today. We do not understand the reasoning behind it, but the little bastard is still alive. What are we going to do?"

The boy saw…. Focus at the task at hand, I remind myself. "It does not change anything. We will continue with the attack today. If he interferes, then we will kill him as well," I reassure them.

Pyke does not seem convinced by my confidence. "You do realize that this forged will only works if the boy has an accident. If we kill him, no one will follow you as their new Duke. We will have the entire Monarchy upon us. I remind you, Payne, the delicacy of how this scene needs to be handled. One unexpected mishap and we are done for," he squeals like a pig.

"Know your place, Pyke!" I holler furiously. Pyke immediately slouches and falls silent, as when a Master commands his slave. I take a few moments to relax my nerves. Calming down, I speak again with a relaxed and poised tone.

"Marcus will perish whether we kill him and rid his body, or if he dies from some unknown reason. Our hands will be clean of all this, I can assure you."

Through this entire conversation, Timber does not move, flinch, blink or show any sign of emotion. He stands, head to the side, quietly and statuesque. Sometimes I wish that the fat fool was the mute. Pyke seems to have regained his own composure after my demand. Both stand, awaiting my next set of commands. There is nothing else to say, so I turn to the tunnel on the left and begin to venture towards Edward and Jaina's keep. Every footstep leads closer to the finality of this ten-year farce. I can smell the blood in the air. It suffocates my lungs, and I take a deep breath so it all rushes in at once. Timber and Pyke are not far behind. Timber has brought his tools with him; ones he was meant to use to kill Marcus. Now it seems as though poor Edward will take Marcus' place. I guess his torture will not be quite as quick as I predicted; wondering what the giant has in store.

We climb the ladder to the lower dungeons of the keep. As usual they were abandoned and empty, not even a guard stood watch. The dungeon smells of piss and vomit, no torches are lit, and all the jail cells are wide open. When this keep belongs to me, the first thing I plan to do is make use of this waste of space and appoint an appropriate jailor. We press forward until we locate the stairs leading to the keep. Their bed chamber is situated on the fifth level and there are four floors to explore before reaching our destination.

The first floor works as an entrance and exit, and is a direct link to the stables. I hear the horses stomp and bray for attention, though their cries fall on deaf ears tonight. The stable boy is likely busy drinking himself into a coma. This day, not a single soul in *The Guiding Light* keep will be sober. According to what I have seen in the past, Edward and Jaina love to celebrate their consummation every few years. Whenever an event of this magnitude is celebrated, it affects all of Apollon thus is the perfect opportunity to avoid confrontation or suspicion.

The second floor is the garrison, where the soldiers store their weapons and armour. As we pass the room I peer in and am pleased with the view. Tanned leather armour is neatly hanging from various hooks around the room. I recognize the material from Apollonian wildlife within the forests. Some are made of bear, wolf and pig skin. A few full plates of armour are placed on wooden figures shaped as humans. Each piece of armour is ornamented with the Sunborn emblem on the chest while the jewels of Apollon, topaz and rubies, are embedded on the steel gauntlets. This is the armour worn by the champions of Apollon and the "elite" few whom represent Edward the Gallant. The detail in the craftsmanship is incredible. From the armet helmets, which shine with gold and possess a sun ornament on the top of headpiece, to the matching cuirass – I can see the work of a fine chisel engraving. Rays of light coming from the sun, the sharp ends of the swords crossing and the coins perfectly circular scattered underneath them.

I turn to Timber and wonder if he is admiring his own work as I am, but the colossus is silent and unfazed as always. On the other hand, Pyke has a giant grin on his face and points to the gauntlets and whispers, "look how glorious those gauntlets look with my workmanship added to the gem slots. They would be dull and hapless without the jewels." I shake my head in disbelief at how I have two complete opposites working for me; one talks too often while the other cannot speak, one is tall while the other short, one could very well match a giant in muscle and size and the other is so round that he could be hit with an arrow by a blind man. Nonetheless, each of them have their use and I have to credit both for their part in this plan.

Once we arrive on the third floor, Timber notices he has a much larger space to hide, so he enters the room and takes refuge within. The area is filled with salts, sugars and breads; it is primarily used as a storeroom for food. Pyke and I move on to the fourth floor. This floor possesses rooms built and kept for the Royal Family and noble guests. The rooms are beautifully decorated with yellow silk sheets, golden curtains, and fur rugs. Books are neatly organized and placed on shelves for entertainment and the beds are large enough to fit four large men. Despite this, there are rarely any visitors. Most nobles find the company the Sunborns keep in their service reprehensible and dangerous. For once, I agree with the rich maggots. Lately, the only occupation these rooms bare is that of a lonely Lady Jaina. Pyke dreams of living in a room such as this, so he points to the bed with his fat index finger and motions to it. I nod in approval and he moves towards the side of the room where the bed is placed and hides underneath it. Both men are aware that Gwyneth will be accompanying Edward and Jaina up the keep and she is instructed to make enough noise on each floor so we know when they are close to their bed chambers. Then, we can begin the festivities.

I finally reach the fifth and final floor in the keep and open the double steel doors which lead to the bed chamber belonging to Edward and Jaina. As I approach the doors, my adrenaline starts to rise and I feel the thirst for blood boil within. It is only a few hours away before all of my scheming and hard work will finally come to fruition. I hear the deadly voice inside ask, *is it time to switch places?*

There is no turning back from the takeover. Dark Heart knows the answer and patronizes me. I open the doors careful and meld in the shadows until the right moment to strike. It is only a matter of time before the fun begins and I can feel my other persona becoming impatient.

The moon is fully exposed and no cloud from the earlier storm is in the sky. Dinner has ended and if Gwyneth has not foiled anything, they should be heading to the bed chamber shortly. No sooner than the thought leaves my mind do I hear Edwards voice.

"Jaina, Jaina," he huffs in a panic. "Gwyneth, help me with the doors so I may lay her on the bed and fetch the healer. Hurry lass, go!"

The fortified doors slowly squeak open and like the wind, I instantaneously position myself behind them. First Gwyneth enters and walks right to the bed as I instructed. Next, Edward stumbles in struggling and limping like a cripple, carrying his motionless wife in his arms. As soon as both his feet pass the door, I slam the door shut and plant my foot on the back of his knee bringing him to the floor. The force of my kick sends Jaina tumbling to the ground, her eyes are wide open but body paralyzed.

As soon as he falls to one knee, I cup his mouth with one hand so he cannot scream. I place my dagger near his heart with the other hand, just as I planned in meditation. I turn to look at Jaina and flash a smile in her direction as she watches helplessly.

"You were right all along. I am born of darkness," whispers Dark Heart.

The door behind me opens as Timber and Pyke enter the room. Edward struggles to break free of my hold, but I clasp my hand around him tighter until my dagger digs through his skin, exposing blood. He quickly stops fighting once he realizes how close he is to impaling himself with my *Silent Sister*. Timber walks over and signals for me to move my hands from Edward's face. As I release my grip, Edward makes a grave mistake and lets out a scream for help.

Timber took the bark as a threat and forcefully shoves his enormous left hand inside Edward's mouth. Edward is squirming, biting and chewing but to no avail. Timber's rough skin does not feel pain and barely acknowledges the effort. With his free right hand, Timber points to his wooden tool box full of tools. I walk over and pick the heavy box off the floor and hand the lumbering giant his tools of trade. Timber reaches for his pliers and removes his left hand from Edward's mouth and pushes through the pliers. Edward is muttering profanities and curses while the metal tool searches for something. Unexpectedly, what happens next even makes Dark Heart cringe yet excited him. I feel Dark Heart slip closer with every bloody event.

Gushing red fluid comes pouring out of Edward's mouth as Timber yanks his tongue forward, exposing it with his blacksmithing pliers. Edward's body juts forward from Timber's fierce strength. The colossus proceeds to use his overgrown foot and jab it into the knees of Edward causing him to fall on the floor face first. Holding on to his tongue, Timber reaches for his blacksmithing hammer and lifts it high in the air and proceeds to pummel Edward's tongue into the floor. Blood splurges everywhere as tears run from Edwards and Jaina's eyes. Jaina wants to scream but only saliva trickles out. The paralysis seizes all of her motor functions from working.

Edward's tongue sags from his mouth, full of blood, looking like a flabby piece of meat. Timber then finishes what he set out to do; he fetches his tongs, used to flip hot tempered metal on his anvil, and places it on Edward's flat and beaten tongue before viciously yanking it out of his mouth. I strut over to Edward and bend low to face him.

"No hard feelings Edward. I am going after something grander and more powerful than both of us. If it is any consolation, your wealth and power will be used as my base to stop the biggest evil that plagues Thalia."

He tries to reply but his mouth coughs up crimson drool. Next, I stroll towards Jaina as she lays in complete stillness. Only her eyes move, looking upon me with contempt and hatred as she always has. Even in a hopeless situation Jaina looks at me with inferiority. I feel my body temperature rise and my blood boil. For a split second I lose control but that was all it took for my other half to break through. My eyes fall to the back of my head and I lose consciousness suddenly, only to reawaken through the eyes of Dark Heart.

When Dark Heart takes over, it feels as though I am a stranger watching my own body perform unimaginable and unspeakable things. I am now a prisoner and all I can do is witness the destruction and mayhem he causes around him, but not before he is done toying with his victims. I only hope he sticks to our plan.

"Leave the rest to me, Payne," he says aloud. "I will show you why everyone will bow to me and not you."

Pyke whispers in confusion at the proclamation, "Payne, what has come over you?"

I ignore him and realize that no one knows me for who I am. They think only Payne harbours this body. They will learn quickly who the one true ruler is of this pathetic excuse for a body.

Returning back to my one sided conversation with Jaina, I mockingly say, "Ah, Lady Jaina, you have never looked more lovely than you do today. If only Edward listened to you ten years ago. You were absolutely right about me. I am darkness reincarnate and now you will see me engulf your world entirely."

"Where is Liza?" Gwyneth asks, sitting on the bed with her legs crossed and picking at her nails. "I want to kill that bitch myself," she growls.

I turn to face Gwyneth with rage and demandingly say, "Undress Gwyneth, I want you to fuck me in front of everyone including Liza. She will be on her way and we can finally show her that you are the only one for me."

Gwyneth is ecstatic with the idea. She begins to quickly undress herself. First her gown comes off and then her panties. I see Edward looking at her with a mixture of pain and shame.

"This is what you wanted, isn't it, Edward?" I laugh. "You ruined your marriage for this filthy little whore?"

I grab Gwyneth by the arm and spin her back to my chest. I can tell that she has become wet between her legs. The thrill of killing others excited her to no bound, almost equaling mine and perhaps surpassing Payne's. Payne killed for his twisted version of what he believed to be justice or sport but this bitch and I have something more in common - we love to kill for the sake of seeing others suffer.

I place my hand on her breast, squeezing it roughly and firmly. I can see the lard of fat across the room smiling and clapping lightly. I lick her neck and she trembles from the sensation. *If this whore enjoys having things inside her, let us see how much she enjoys this,* Dark Heart mutters to me. I watch through my own eyes as he punctures her chest with one of the *Silent Sisters* and it buries it deep into her heart.

For the first time, pleasure and pain does not excite her. Gwyneth looks down at my dagger as I rotate it around her breast where her heart is stored. *Dark Heart reborn,* the voice exclaims. Red liquid stains the floor as Gwyneth tries to free herself but it is too late. The dagger curves around her breast and finds its way down underneath her rib cage, ripping flesh and exposing a cave to her heart. My hand reaches in, and feels around as she attempts to gasp for air. She is like a puppet and I the puppeteer. Once I feel my trophy, I rip my prize from its socket and hold it in my hand. Edward's expression turns to utter terror and his look gives me satisfaction as blood continues to persistently drip from his mouth.

I drop Gwyneth in her own pool of blood and order Timber to pick up Edward and place him on the bed. Edward thrashes, kicks, and punches to no avail. One second, Edward is on the floor the next he is thrown like a child's toy atop his massive bed. Both Timber and Pyke inch towards him. Timber is holding Edward's hands down and Pyke his feet. I climb to the other side of the bed and put my dagger to his chest.

"Now where to start cutting?" I threaten, "I wonder if your heart is as golden in the inside as it is on the outside. Shall we find out?"

The dagger cut through his skin as if I was slicing a thin piece of cheese. As I did with Gwyneth, I move my blade in a circular motion on Edward's skin. Starting from the left and going around slowly, I enjoy every moment of pain I inflict. I can feel Payne's presence becoming uncomfortable and disturbed. *This is why you are weak Payne,* I remind him. Edward elevates his chest in pain and the dagger enters right below his rib cage as it had with its last victim. He groans in pain and I lift the dagger up and out of him and calmly say, "I guess we have an opening to work with."

It only takes fifteen seconds to complete the incision, but those fifteen seconds feel like an eternity of pain for my victim. I watch his eyes overflow with rivers of tears as they come flooding out and his breathing turns erratic. The hole in his chest is exposed and his skin bright red. His heart is barely beating and he is already passed out from the torture and shock.

"I guess his heart is as red as the rest of ours," I say amused. "Timber, grab Lady Jaina and bring her to me."

Timber removes his grip from Edward's dead arms and marches towards Jaina's lifeless body. Lifting her with ease, he brings her over to me and I examine her. Her eyes speak a thousand words that her mouth cannot express. I motion Timber to drop her on Edward's fresh corpse. Jumping back on the bed and sitting on her back, I pull her hair back and whisper softly in her ear, "Marcus was killed as well. We put him inside the cauldron and burned his little body to ashes."

There is no truth to this claim but I do enjoy feeling her heart beat increase. She tries to fight the poison in her system but the potion can paralyze even the mightiest of beast for days. With her golden hair clutched in my hand and her neck arched back, my *Silent Sister* finds its way to her throat.

"Goodbye Jaina. I hope you a better afterlife with your miserable husband and child," I say as I cut her throat open.

The deed is done. I place the two trophies and Edward's sword beside Jaina. Gwyneth is still on the floor below them, chest exposed and heart missing. Pyke, who has vomited all over himself, holds one hand to his mouth and clenches his eyes shut. He extends his hand with the forged Will. I snatch it in disgust from his filthy hands and neatly put it on the table away from his other documents so that it be noticeable.

As we begin to clean any evidence of our involvement, I detect the undeniable sound of panting and footsteps running down the stairs. I knew Marcus and Liza were both watching. They had arrived as I was killing Gwyneth yet I allowed them to seem undetectable. I wanted Marcus to see what I was capable of. I wanted him to witness his family's death.

No need to worry, he is as good as dead, I assure Payne who is now trying to retake control of this body. *Today marks a new day in our chapter. It is time to rally a new banner and new cause. The Sunborns are dead. Long live Dark Heart.*

PART II

CHAPTER ELEVEN
MARCUS SUNBORN

This is a nightmare, I assure myself. *I will wake up any moment, in my bed, nestled in my warm blanket.* My eyes shut tightly; I feel my nose crinkle and my brow clench, as my face trembles under the pressure. *Please, be a nightmare, please!* I cannot wrap my mind around what is happening. Lately, all of my dreams have been violent and gruesome yet this feels real - too real. Suddenly, I hear a faint voice urgently whispering in my ear.

"Marcus, we must go. Marcus...Marcus! Look at me!" Liza's voice is calling out to me from a close distance. I turn to my right and face her. Watery eyes with bright red veins are staring at me with disbelief and pain. I feel an urge to comfort her, but I am lost in my own dismay and confusion. A sudden rattling noise inside the bedchamber allows me to refocus and turn my gaze back to the event that is transpiring ahead of me. *It will end soon,* I remind myself but the nightmare quickly transforms into a graphic and violent reality. Timber clutches his hammer and pounds the floor where my father's body is lying. Darkness masks the room in a black veil so I am unable to see what exactly is occurring but I knew my father was suffering. Ground shattering and thunderous booms resonate from the hard stone floors. A dark red slithering fluid appears, escapes from the carpet through the crack in the door and down the stone steps past Liza and I. Each time Timber lifts his massive blacksmithing hammer, a trail of blood follows behind, trickling through the many cracks of the floor in my parents' chamber.

I want to scream for my father but my voice catches in my throat. The only sound I manage to form is a dry and hurtful *gulp*. My mother is sprawled on the floor either unconscious or dead. I want to run to her and let her know that everything will be fine, and we will all be together again. But my body is frozen with fear.

In my dreams, I am fearless and armed with daggers; but at this moment, I am unarmed with the exception of the sack containing the gifts for my parents, and I have succumb to a fear I did not know could exist. *I must intervene,* I try protesting with my body. Finally, I feel my feet gradually moving forward. As I am about to take a step towards the dark chamber, a cold hand grabs my arm and forces me back down. Liza is clutching on to me with such a surprising amount of strength, she could crush my arm if she held on any longer. When she notices the pained expression on my face, Liza releases her grasp slightly, leaving behind a burning sensation on my forearm. "Marcus, if you enter the bed chamber you will be killed. We must run, now," she pleads quietly.

I manage to muster up a weak response and say, "It is alright, Liza. This is only a dream, one that I have dreamt often. It will end soon and everything will be as it was."

"This is not a dream Marcus," Liza hisses scornfully, but I pay her no heed. A lustful moan turns my attention back to the room, as Gwyneth is now naked in the arms of Payne. Her breasts are exposed, as Payne fondles her; she seems to enjoy his aggressiveness. My heart sinks into my stomach, as my perception of Gwyneth shatters with every passing moment I see her in Payne's arms. Liza warned me about Gwyneth and I refused to listen because of my own foolish thoughts about her. I was infatuated with her beauty, and at the same time, blinded by it. Her seduction over the last few months had me confident in my charm and believing that there were feelings between us.

Relinquishing my grief momentarily, I

return my gaze to the dark room. Payne laughs in my father's direction and mutters something that is unclear to me. He points his luminescent golden dagger at my father and then swiftly rotates the weapon in his hand directing it towards Gwyneth. Suddenly and unexpectedly, Payne inserts his dagger deep into Gwyneth. Unwilling and unable to comprehend what has just occurred in front of me, I turn to Liza and realize she must have just witnessed what I did. Liza's expression is one of terror. Her eyes close and tears stream down her cheeks. Placing a hand on her mouth, she attempts to silence her screams and shakes her head vigorously in disbelief while her other hand still holds onto my arm. I have seen this before; it was another version of the event, but I have had this dream in the past. *Now I am sure that this was just the re-occurring nightmare that haunted me every night,* I convince myself. My attention returns back to the bed chamber. Gwyneth lies bloody on the carpet with a hole in her chest that exposes her missing heart. Just like in my dreams.

Liza places her arms around my head and presses my face to her chest. "No more, Marcus," she whispers as she sobs quietly. "We MUST leave. If we stay here any longer they will capture us and we will suffer the same fate as your parents!" I want nothing more than to leave but I am tired of running. Every night this dream unearths its way into my mind, and every time I wake up screaming and scared. Today, I want to face my fear and conquer it. Still pressed against Liza's bosom I continue to watch the incident unfold. Payne is now on the bed above my father and he is speaking softly in his ear while holding his arm steady above father's chest, dagger firmly in hand. Father is attempting to fight back to no avail. His struggle merely assists the very weapon he is trying to fend off into entering his body. As my father moans in agony, I begin to cry but my eyes remain open. I can taste the salty tears as they find their way onto my lips. Liza cries, shaking uncontrollably as she tightens her grip around me. Payne proceeds to perform the same procedure on my father as he did Gwyneth and cuts open a hole in my father's chest before removing his heart as well. *Just like in my dream.* I know it is almost over.

I never weep in my dreams, nor is Liza there to shield me from the horrors. Perhaps, I am dreaming of her because she had comforted me the night before. *I must endure this test. I have to stand up to this nightmare,* I remind myself again. Timber lifts my mother like a plush doll and lays her atop of my father's corpse. Liza repeatedly pleas in a whisper, "Please, my Lord Marcus, it is enough. We must flee from this scene. I cannot endure this any longer. Your family legacy must live on through you." I am convicted to see this through to the gory end, so I do not budge.

"This is only a dream Liza. Please, do not interrupt. If I run now, I will never escape it," I tell her. She strikes me with such force with her open palm that I almost fall backwards if not for her other arm holding onto me. *Never has it felt this real.* A stinging sensation develops along my cheek. I rub my face trying to alleviate the lingering pain. Liza snatches my hand and pulls away from the bed chamber. I want to scream for her to stop but it is too late. We hurriedly spin down the winding stairs and I try hard to wake up. *Wake up, Marcus. It is over.* But I do not wake. I continue crying and the sting of Liza's slap still lingers on my cheek as we continue breathlessly running down the stone steps. *Wake up, Marcus! Wake up,* I plead with myself. I never awaken. I just continue running in circles down the stairs.

I recall earlier this morning waking up with the sun peering through the window and illuminating my bed sheets. Liza was in my bedroom as well, folding my attire. "Good morning, young Lord," Liza said, noticing I was awake and alert. "Do you realize the time?" she playfully asked me.

"No," I admitted. It felt as though I had not slept for days. The last thing I remember was having re-occurring nightmares of my parents dying by my hands and then waking up in my bed, sweating, panicked and yelling. Liza had rushed to my aid and comforted me. Without her presence, I would not have been able to go back to bed. She comforted me by stroking my hair and placing kisses on my forehead, as I shivered, dripping sweat on my bed sheets. Fatigue finally took over and still Liza did not waiver. I fell asleep in her arms and the next morning I woke up with her in my room still looking over me.

"Well, noon has come and gone yet you, young Lord, should be well underway to your first lesson," she smiled slyly. "But today marks the consummation of your parents' marriage. I will keep your absence between you and I, but you must hide somewhere until the proper time. If you are seen, both of us will endure the wrath of your father."

"Thank you, Liza. I shall prepare to break my fast," I said cheerfully. Liza left my attire neatly folded at the end of my bed. It consisted of a golden doublet, scaled with white borders, the symbol of my Noble blood-stitched in the middle. My bottoms matched my tunic. I stared at the symbol embedded on the chest of my shirt. *How could I hurt my own parents*? I wondered. Before I could think any further, Liza had interrupted me with a question.

"Would you like to discuss what occurred last night? What could possibly have scared my brave Lord Marcus?" she asked curiously. I wanted to tell her of what transpired in my dreams, but today was not the day to do so. There was enough pressure on both of us without me burdening Liza with ridiculous nightmares. I did not want to delve into details so I recalled the information as vaguely as possible.

"It was a bad nightmare, Liza, nothing more. I would appreciate it if we kept this between us," I pleaded. She looked at me as she dusted my wooden armoire and chests.

"Of course, but there is one thing I would like to say, if it pleases my Lord." I nodded as I knew she would say it regardless of my approval.

"Nightmares can be seen as bad omens. Never take them lightly. A nightmare is only as powerful as the fear that drives it. You must finish the dream, Lord Marcus, and conquer it. When you do, the nightmare will haunt you no longer."

I knew there was truth to Liza's advice. I have always forced a premature awakening from the night terrors; never have I challenged it. *Next time I will finish it and defeat my fears,* I reassure myself. This is the last thing I remember before the horrific event that had transpired in my parents' bedroom.

Liza's panting becomes heavier as she gasps for air. "We must reach the guards and alarm them of the situation," she proclaims with strained breaths. The guards will not be of any help since they will be absent from the keep. Every year, my father would permit all of his guards to have a day to their families. Many of them are pre-occupied visiting the brothels outside of town, while others travel to see their children and wives. Liza knows this, but given everything that just transpired, it must have left her dumbfounded.

"Marcus, please answer me. Tell me you know that this is not a dream? I need you to focus and be attentive to the situation. If we do not escape, we will suffer the same fate," Liza whimpers. The tears earlier have dried up and have chaffed my skin and my eyes are sore and swollen. The images of my parents' bed chamber vividly stay with me. Finally coming to terms with it all, I break down and admit that I am never to wake from this. This is no nightmare. *This is real. My parents have been murdered.* I fall to my knees from the thought of never seeing my parents ever again and the brutal death that has befallen my family.

Liza realizes that I have come to my senses and releases my arm for a moment. Without hesitation or thought I clench my fists and bring my bare knuckles to the hard concrete ground repeatedly in a fit of anger and fury. Water and blood swirl and mix together on the ground as I continued to beat against the hard, grey stone. Tremendous force surges through each punch, causing my hands to bruise but I do not stop. I pretend the stone I am pounding is Payne. I raise my head and peer at Liza with swollen and bloodshot eyes.

My parents are dead. My light is extinguished. Everything that I swore to become - a noble, dutiful and prodigal son, a knight, a husband, a father - has all been taken from me by Payne. Liza sets her hands around my shoulder and spins me around so that I am looking at her. Her black eyes gaze into my soul with pity and sympathy. I am still fuming as my heavy breathing causes my chest to move in and out and my shoulders up and down. She places her arms around my back and hugs me gently.

"We will survive, Lord Marcus, for the sake of your parents and your noble name. We will return and reclaim all that is yours."

I do not care for my home or my name. *I want Payne's bloody head on a stick!* My thoughts are filled with that of pure rage and hatred. Liza and I look at one another as we continue to run.

The yard is disturbingly empty and the two guards who are normally posted at the front gates are absent. We shuffle towards the stables connected to my parents' keep where we know horses are always readily available. The stable boy is also missing. He never requires a special event to have an excuse to drink himself to a stupor. Three horses remain in the stables and luckily two are the royal mares. The spotted horse is the one I am accustomed to riding. It is a white horse, with brown marks, and a bushy tail. He was given to me on my seventh year and I named him *Hope*.

The other horse we take is a dark black stallion dressed in a leather saddle and muzzle. He is the oldest, but fastest and most obedient. He towers over the rest of the horses and was once my father's most prized possession. Its mane is always combed and shined, and he sets an example to the younger horses in becoming submissive and dutiful. My father named him *Edwin*, the name of the first Sunborn. Edwin was also a large, powerful man who surpassed most men in both physical build and noble stature.

"Where are we going Liza?" I ask. She is clutching her stomach and looking down at the wet ground, lost in thought.

"Somewhere far away, Lord Marcus. Thalia has many small towns and provinces that can shelter us from Payne. You understand that from this moment forth our lifestyle will change completely? We will fend for one another and keep our identities a secret as to not raise suspicion," she instructs.

"What about my father's banner men? Surely, he has friends that will lend us aid. My birth right alone should be enough to rally my father's allies to stop Payne. I am a Sunborn and that should mean something," I remark. Liza did not seem keen on the idea. *She knows something about the situation that I do not.* "What is it, Liza?" I ask, persistently "Why do you hesitate to agree?"

She waits, and then speaks slowly, "Marcus… Payne has planned this for some time. He plans to frame your mother as the murderer. Word will spread that your father committed adultery with Gwyneth and he will soon lose his land and his gold to his heir. As the last surviving Sunborn, you must exist to receive it."

How does she know that he has planned this? Did she know about this plan all along? I wonder.

She continues on, "Payne is a dangerous man, Marcus. Far more dangerous than any man I have known. For the time being, we must lay low and not interfere. There are many nobles in Thalia that are jealous of the Sunborn's riches and prestige and will support the destruction of your family name," Liza explains.

"How could you know all of this, Liza? How did you know Payne planned this all along? Father and Mother took you in from the streets and gave you a life that many with your stature could only ever dream of. Do you not care for me and my family?!"

"Marcus, I promise on the life of my unborn child that I have no connection to the dastardly events which occurred. I am as terrified as you are. Payne has fooled me into believing that he and the rest of my former friends were content with living here. You must believe me," she begs.

I cannot help but believe her. Nothing in me could hate Liza. She has been my friend, parent, and guardian for the last few years. Pyke, Gwyneth, Timber all contributed a part in the ploy but not Liza. They are as guilty as Payne. *I will kill them all.*

I look away from Liza and drive my heels into the sides of Hope. The horse snorts and wails as it lifts itself and begins to gallop. Liza follows my lead as we both escape the keep. I stare back one last time at my home. Memories skitter through my mind; my childhood, my mother's light green eyes, her light golden hair, my father's boisterous laugh, his imposing yet gentle glare, and both of their smiles when they held me. My heart sinks inside my chest and my stomach turns with sorrow and loneliness. *Never again will I see them or hear them,* I cry.

The keep begins to shrink smaller and smaller as we ride into the distance. The two towers and the front gate transform into something hideous. It reminds me of the mocking and twisted smile that donned on Payne's face as he took my life away from me. The same demonic smile he had on his pale and slender face while he carved holes into my family. I promise myself that I will take everything from Payne as he had taken everything from me. My life will be dedicated to his destruction. I close my eyes and take in the darkness as it surrounds my body and soul. *I am no longer a noble and no longer a Sunborn. My life is dedicated to avenging my family. Marcus Sunborn is now an avenger.*

CHAPTER TWELVE
LIZA SKYLAR

My heart races as the horses gallop at blinding speed. The horrors that Marcus and I just witnessed today will haunt me forever and I can only imagine what it has done to poor Marcus. I *failed him,* I think devastatingly. *God, I failed the boy.* Marcus is a child who was forced to grow too quickly and now has lost even more than his childhood. Lord Edward and Lady Jaina were the world to him and now his parents have been taken away along with his youth and innocence. I promised to protect him from the darkness but I failed due to my naïve perception of Payne. *I will never forgive you Payne. How could you betray me again!*

Ten years we lived with the Sunborns and in that time they have provided food, shelter, a purpose and most importantly a family. They sacrificed their lives and put their trust in us. My mind travels back to Lord Edward's bed chamber as Payne rips out Edward's heart; the dagger methodically cutting through his chest while Payne lavished every second of it. Blood ran over the golden yellow bed sheets and covered the majestic topaz carpets. At the end there was nothing left but death. The images and smell still linger in my mind. I pull on the horses reins and the horse reacts swiftly to my command. I could not hold it back any longer. Since the gruesome events, there is a sickening knot in my bowels which has withheld my nausea but I can sense it unraveling. Quickly jumping off Edwin, I drop to the cold, wet, and dirty ground and release every meal I harboured in my stomach from today. An acidic, vile, stench arises from my mouth and continues as the nightmarish events unfold in my head in slow motion. My feelings are ejecting out of me in a physical, yellow, and putrid form.

The faces of Lord Edward, Lady Jaina and Gwyneth keep flashing before me. I hold on to a tree and a biting cold rushes through my veins due to the wet bark being moist from the night breeze. My noises startle even the horses. Edwin neighs and snorts but stops as soon as Marcus calls out his name. I attempt to breathe through my nose but the cold air attacks my nostrils. I resort to gasping for air through my mouth and pant heavily. My throat is raw and sore and my eyes sting from the tears. Marcus hops off Hope and stands next to me, careful not to glance in my direction. After all of my grotesque vomiting, I realize that I must save him before he is lost to this torment. I knew how easily one can put revenge and hatred above everything else and Marcus deserves better than that. Payne will pay for this but not by soiling Marcus' hands. Justice will be served and it will come from the state. This way Marcus will earn the right to his father's legacy.

The black stallion grows impatient again and starts to pound the ground with its mighty hooves as to indicate that we need to continue moving forward. Marcus seems to be in a trance as he just stares ahead into the forest. *Where do we go from here? I ask myself. Pesoleen Harbour is the closest town and is a few days ride west of Apollon.* The harbour hosts some of the fastest ships in all of Thalia. *Perhaps a boat could provide us safe passage past the sea and somewhere safe until Payne gives up his search for us.* It is costly but we still possess the two gifts which were meant for Marcus' parents. *If we sell them, it may provide us enough gold to board a ship and travel across the sea... but then what?* I question myself.

Marcus' travels have only been within Apollon and never beyond its borders. I have only ever occupied the homes of others and even then I have no recollection of the towns or provinces except for Nasgrath, Pesoleen Harbour and

Sallandar. The path east leads to Sallandar, the merchant town, however, that would be unwise. Too many of populous can recognize Marcus by his appearance. Sallandar is the merchant capital of Thalia and has had many tidings with the Sunborn clan. Even the gifts we purchased for Lord Edward and Lady Jaina were purchased from there as well. Too much risk came from revisiting areas that could potentially identify Marcus. Nobody knows or cares for Liza Skylar but the Sunborn name is renown throughout Thalia. When word is out that the last heir of *Edward the Light* is still alive, there will be many seeking us for a hefty reward. Payne will see to it that we do not live a day of comfort until we are dead. *Perhaps the safest route is Nasgrath.*

There are two types of people that inhabit the town of Nasgrath; the nobles and the poor folk who occupy the slums referred by the wealthy as, "lowborne". The nobility of Nasgrath keep their distance from the slums almost religiously. They treat the district as if it is infested with the plague and rightfully so. The slums are in fact littered with cutthroats, pickpockets, thieves, orphans and turn cloaks. *The perfect crowd for a runaway noble and his naïve guardian,* I dreadfully sigh. Again, *Edwin* flares his nostrils and snorts in my direction. Finally, Marcus broke his silence. "Edwin wants us to move along. These woods are ancient, even older than my parents' lineage. I do not know what creatures live in these trees at night," he says with bitterness and mistrust in his tone. "Have you decided on our destination?"

"Nasgrath, Lord Marcus," I reply as reassuringly as possible. "We shall make our way to Nasgrath. It is a three days ride southwest from our current destination. I cannot continue calling you Lord Marcus either. We will attract unwanted attention." Again I receive no reaction from Marcus.

What do you expect you foolish woman, I think. *The boy witnessed things that would make war veterans cringe.* I climb back onto Edwin's saddle and take hold of the leather strap. The wind grows colder as did Marcus' demeanour.

As our horses stride along the narrow forest road, various noises and creatures lurk from every corner. Crickets are chirping in the leaves, the bushes rustle with small creatures, owls sitting in high trees and hooting, wolves howl from a far off distance and the winds roar in our ears as both horses ride alongside one another. They seem fairly anxious to continue but press on. The world seems dark and bleak. Edwin and Jaina's death seems to have sucked the very life away from Apollon. The forest path twists and turns in various directions. The trees look alive with some portraying sad faces while others look malicious and evil. I have never witnessed this side of Apollon. Few stars are covering the sky and only a pale full moon lit our path.

We keep a steady pace for a few hours until finally passing the forest and coming upon a stream heading south. The horses head to the river and eagerly drink the water. Marcus remains silent while the horses continue to gulp.

It is unbearable to see him like this. "Marcus, we must continue until we find proper lodging. There must be an inn somewhere nearby for us to rest."

An inn did appear a few hours downstream and seemed deserted and shady but we have little choice, since this seems to be the only inn, before Nasgrath. We decide to investigate. As we approach the lodge, a sign swings from the roof top. I stop to examine it and it reads *Knights Rest. I could do rest without the knights.*

There is an abandoned and miniscule stable on the side of the inn that will suffice. All Marcus and I require is a little food in our stomachs and few hours of sleep. The stallions willingly enter the hay ridden shelter, showing sign of exhaust from travelling through the night. "Marcus, please stay here while I examine the inn," I request. He listens and I proceed to walk through the wooden door cautiously. The door creaks and I have trouble opening it since the wood has warped from the murky weather and the river water is seeping into the ground. Entering the inn, dust gathers under each footstep I take and the wooden floor is uneven. The room definitely looks to be deserted. Cobwebs and empty bottles cover various corners of the room. In the back of the room there is a chipped wooden table which appears to have many pieces of parchment and ink. I walk towards the table and look around. "Hello. Is anyone here?" I call. No response provokes me to project my voice this time, "Hello! Is anyone here?!"

The noise of a cane stomping the floor makes its way steadily towards me with a flicker of a dim light following closely behind. Each thump of the cane is followed by a grunt and the mixtures of these noises become almost rhythmic. An old wrinkly man suddenly appears from the room behind the table, holding onto his wooden cane for support and sliding his feet on the stone floor. He is bald with snow white eyebrows and his skin resembles worn leather. The clothes on his body is unfittingly small and tight as though he is wearing a young boy's attire. The bottoms of his brown and tattered pants only reach his knees while his shirt barely covers his belly. Stench of cabbage and musk fills my nostrils the closer he approaches but I welcome any smell resembling food. *Anything to help me forget what Marcus and I witnessed moments ago in The Guiding Light,* I tell myself. My only concern for this man is that he possesses a gentle demeanour and a warm bed.

"Oh I thought this old man's ears were fooling him. Age brings many blessings and unfortunately even more curses. Being hard of hearing is one of those curses, my dear. Pardon me, here I am prattling away. How may I be of service m'Lady," he says with a stammer.

"Good eve, sir," I reply with as much calmness I can muster in our situation. "My son and I seek shelter for a few hours and some food. We have journeyed far and are weary. Is it possible to ask you of this small inconvenience?"

"Ah m'Lady, you have come to the most honourable of lands. Apollon is ruled by a just and noble family and they shelter the lost and hopeless and give them a path. They lead by example and as fellow Apollonians, we try to follow this same ideal," he says proudly. I shudder at the idea of what Apollon will transform into once Payne has his clutches around it. The innkeeper heeds me no mind and continues advising me.

"Please, bring in your boy before the nights chill takes him. I will warm the pot for some soup to fill your bellies. Unfortunately, this old man only has beets, carrots and barley but I trust it will make due," he says with a cheerful smile.

"We thank you for your hospitality good sir. The boy and I lack any form of payment though. Is there any deed I may perform or some duties you may require of me?" I ask desperately.

"Ohhh… m'Lady. This old man is far from ready to be charmed by the likes of a beautiful lady such as you," he laughs and coughs consequently.

Taken aback, I say, "Good sir, I did not mean...", but the innkeeper interrupts with a smile and waves his hand before leaving to prepare the soup. Listening to his sound advice I exit the inn and search for Marcus. I find Marcus sitting with his arms crossed around his knees and places his head tucked inside them. *Console him you fool,* I tell myself. Walking over, I soothingly place my hand on his shoulder. He does not stir from his position. Instead, I hear Marcus whimper in his arms. I sit next to him and wrap my arms around his body and his sobbing increases. Tears pool in my eyes as well but I did not make a noise. This is much more his lose than mine. *I must be strong for him.*

Once we cease our crying, I rise to my feet and extend my hand to Marcus. At first, he did not react to my gesture but I maintain my composure and keep my hand steady. After a few moments, Marcus raises his head to look and places his hand into mine as I assist him to his feet. Silently, we both walk towards the inn, our hands clasping together.

The scent of mixed vegetables filled the air as we enter the inn replacing the original smell of dust. The old man had already prepared the soup and placed it on a table closest to the fireplace. There is no flame in the fire place to keep us warm but a lantern sits beside the fresh soup and it is more than either Marcus and I could ask for. I thank the innkeeper again for his kindness and he nods with a gentle smile.

Marcus and I sit on opposite sides of the table. Splintered oak benches reside on either side. Sitting on the old benches made my legs and bottom feel raw after the long horse ride. I peer over at Marcus to see if the vision of food rouses any emotion but the sudden sound of wooden stairs creaking draws my attention. An elderly woman waltzes down the stairs. I did not see or hear her when I first entered and the innkeeper never mentioned another occupant. Before I have an opportunity to question the innkeeper about the woman, he interrupts me.

"Oh my dear Margaret... this is Lady... I am sorry my dear. I do not believe I had the pleasure of hearing your name," he realizes absentmindedly and turns his attention back to me.

"My name is Katherine and this is my son Arthur. We thank you again for your kindness my Lady and Sir. We only ask to stay as long as you can keep us." I chose the names of my former Masters in Nasgrath as they were the first two names that came to mind.

The stranger is an overweight woman with an enormous bosom. Her skin was rosy pink and her eyes much more youthful than her age. A bonnet covered her hair, but strands of fiery red still manage to escape through. The Inn was dark but I could tell she was not all too pleased with our arrival unlike her cheerful husband. Margaret grumbles noises of discomfort as she wobbles her way down the stairs. "The beds are made you old fool," she utters displeased as she eyes down her husband. "You best be paying us and be on your way as soon as the sun rises."

"Margaret, mind your manners. We rarely have visitors these days," the innkeeper pleads. "Please excuse my wife, she has forgotten her manners in our bedroom. The lack of company tarnishes ones social skills."

"No offence taken my Lady," I reply in a friendly tone. "We will be on our way as soon as the sun lights our path." Margaret ignores me and continues into the backroom behind the table. I turn to Marcus and notice his eyes are focusing on the red beet soup. "Arthur, is everything alright dear?" I ask, knowing full well what he is thinking. *Please play along Marcus.*

He gazes up emotionless and responds with a courteous, "yes mother," and proceeds to drink his soup. Thankful, I heave a sigh of relief. The soup is steaming and gives off an alluring aroma. My stomach grumbles and urges me to eat. I pick up my spoon from the table and swirl the red soup around in circles. The carrots and barley are coated in the red liquid which leaked off the beets. *Red… more red.* The soup gives off the appearance of blood and the beets floating in my soup bear a resemblance to hearts. I drop my spoon and escape outside to hurl again. This time there was nothing but yellow bile that exited my body. Marcus rushes out to check on me this time. He waits for me to finish and holds my arm for support. "Come mother, we must rest and leave as soon as the sun permits."

When we re-enter the inn, I notice Margaret standing by the desk with the innkeeper at her side. She has her arms crossed and is tapping her wooden shoes impatiently on the worn out wooden floor. "We will not have you damaging the bed sheets," she claims bitterly. "If you cannot hold in your meal then you will be asked to withdraw from our premises and leave this night. Do we have an understanding?"

"Yes my Lady," I reply. "I will be fine once sleep takes a hold of me. Please, may you show my son and I to our rooms?"

"I will do no such thing," she says angrily. "Those stairs will be the death of me if I continue climbing them. I have prepared a room with two beds. It will be the first room to the right. Now off with you."

Marcus and I take our leave and head up the stairs. Margaret and her husband begin to argue as we climb one step at a time. It is a one sided bashing as Margaret yells and belittles her poor husband to no end.

The door to our room is already open when

we approach it. Two lanterns hang above our beds. Marcus shows himself in and claims the bed furthest from the door. I enter second and sit on my side. The beds are made of straw and definitely something that neither of us is accustom to. Silently, we both make prepare our sheets without even glancing at one another. Normally, this role would fall on me as I was responsible with the preparation for his sleep but with everything that has transpired today, I do not know if I can handle Marcus rejecting my help. We remain quiet for a few minutes until frustration took control of me and I can no longer take it. "Marcus. We will avenge your parents, I promise. Payne will pay for what he has done," I claim. Marcus turns to me and finally breaks his silence.

"Mark my words Liza, he will pay. I will do such inhumane things to him and everyone involved that I will be seen as the monster, not him. I will avenge my family through death. Payne wanted me to learn hatred. Well now I have learned and it will be his destruction. That is my purpose and my reason for living. You are either with me or against me Liza," he growls. Marcus turns away and lies on his bed, folding himself up to keep warm.

I realize at that moment that the sweet,

cheerful, caring and innocent Marcus died along with his parents back in Apollon. What lay across from me is someone else; still the same boy age of ten but now spiteful and full of hatred. Evil festers in the soul of Marcus Sunborn and I have to do what I could to light his path as he and his family has done for me the last ten years. If he turns to murder, he will become no different than Payne. I bring myself to my knees beside my bed and clasp my hands together to pray. *Please God. Watch over Marcus. Protect him from the impurities of this world and guide him back to the path of righteousness,* I plead. Every bone in my body aches as I rise up to my feet. I blow the room's lantern out and rest my head on the bed. As soon as my body hit the bed, fatigue takes its toll and I doze off.

The morning sunlight makes its way through the window cracks of our room. The light shines directly in my eyes almost blinding me. I want nothing more than to remain asleep but I know time is scarce and we need to rise and make our way to Nasgrath. My eyes remain closed as I remove the bed sheets. "Good morning Arthur," I mumble after a great big yawn. Silence. One eye opens to see if he is still fast asleep in his bed. There seems to be a lump curled under the blanket. "Arthur?" I ask and again no answer. Rubbing my eyes, I force them open and notice that Marcus is gone. Jumping out of bed, I rush to the bed sheets and franticly swing them off the bed only to find a stack of hay. Panic and terror took control of me. I start calling out his name. "Arthur, where are you. Arthur!" but there is no response. I run down the stairs and out the door. *God save me if they found us.* Running to the stables to check on the horses, I spot Marcus stroking Hope gently.

"Shhhh. You will wake Margaret if you continue yelling," he snarls. "The old man asked us to ready our horses and leave before she awakens. He did not ask for payment. I have a satchel with bread, cheese and carrots for us to eat when we make camp again. Now make haste mother."

Relief washes over me. I sigh and walk towards him and planted a kiss on his temple. *How could I be so foolish as to let the boy be the adult?* I ask myself. Lord Edward was right. He did provide Marcus the tools he needs to survive and now I need to guide him. I must sway him from the path that Payne has forced him to follow. He must fulfill his parents' wishes of becoming the true heir of the Sunborn. How though? How will we ever stop Payne?

Marcus is already saddled and ready to journey forth to Nasgrath. "Lead the way mother," he says. "Once we are there I will begin to plan. Nothing will stop me from fulfilling my destiny. Payne will die by my hands." I hop on Edwin in silence, cup my belly and heave forward towards our new life.

CHAPTER THIRTEEN
PAYNE BLADESTORM

Anarchy, chaos, confusion, doubt, misery, despair, disbelief, and opportunity are but a few words I could use to describe the atmosphere surrounding the deaths of the Sunborns.

A few days have passed since the guards decided to get off their lazy good for nothing arses and take notice that their Masters have not left their tower. *That will change once I am Master of this domain.* Pyke, Timber and I made sure to remove any trace of our involvement and snuck through the tunnels back into our daily routines. When the guards returned from their whoring and drinking the night after the celebrations, everything ran as it normally would. Even the ones charged with keeping Jaina and Edward safe in their chambers did not bother to investigate the absence of their Masters. Only after two days passed, did the massacre of Jaina, Edward and Gwyneth reach our ears.

Everyone seems to believe that Jaina killed Gwyneth and Edward. According to the rumours,

Jaina cut both their hearts out once she realized of their affair and then slit her own throat because she could not bear the pain of what she has done. Marcus has gone missing and there have been parties deployed in every direction searching for him. *They will not find him if Liza is with him.* Within a matter of time Pyke shall read the last Will of *Edward the Light* which will promptly grant me rights to all of his treasures, rights, property and land. Then the fun begins.

Darkness and light came and went for three nights as I patiently awaited Pyke's audience. Time stood still as my patience grew thin. Most of my idle time is spent making potions and elixirs. Ingredients grow scarce and I do not have the time or willpower to gather any until this ordeal is over. On the fifth night, I notice torches lighting the path to my domain and the sound of horses riding towards my tower. Leaving my alchemy behind, I head down to the entrance to greet the strangers. Two riders on horseback and a fat man on a mule approach my training fields. The two guards are stocky men with burly moustaches and pink faces. The one on the left has an enormous two-handed axe strapped to his back and wears thick white chainmail armour. The man's shoulders are twice the size of my own. A plain steel helmet sits on his head and plate leggings cover his lower half. *I have never seen this one before.*

The horse is dressed in silky white linen from the saddle and drapes down to the horse's lower calves. The horse's head and muzzle are decorated with dark leather. A pole with a different sigil than the one belonging to the Sunborn home is held in the goliath's hand. The flag is pure white with black linings on each side of the borders. In the middle of the flag sit two silver axes parallel to one another.

Although the first man is unknown to me, the second one seems familiar. After a few moments of examination it dons on me. "Hail, former Master of Blades," I call out mockingly. He is wearing the same armour as the time I almost sliced his throat wide open. Everything about him is the same with the exception of the emblem. It is no longer of the Sunborn. Not only did he lose the match that day but he also lost his title and the one thing that made him different than the mediocre, poor excuse for louts that Edward called his guards. "How fares the arm my lord?" I ask with a smirk. His eyes look over to his right with frustration before his gaze returns to me.

"Why not come here and find out you mangy dog," he respond with enmity.

"I see your mouth has not been affected by the defeat," I answer unamused. Ignoring the brute, my attention now turns to the fat man behind them. The two giants overshadow him but he stands, seemingly due to his inability to ride a horse. He struggles mounting his mule while I examine the other two. He finally gives up and looks in my direction with disappointment.

"Hello Lord Payne," the man calls out and waves. The voice is definitely Pyke's but I am reluctant to believe it is him as his outfit actually fits his overweight body. A flashy purple doublet conceals his lard. Normally, his outfits are either too revealing or too short for this stature. He believes his body is God's gift to women so he enjoys flaunting his flabby belly to the public. He wore a top hat uncomfortably on his head. His pants are the same colour as his doublet. The purple makes him look like an overgrown grape.

"Pyke? They finally found attire that could fit your "curvaceous" body? What brings you to my humble abode at this late hour?" I ask this knowing full well the reason.

Ahem, he clears his throat. "This is regarding Lord Edward's will. These two noble gentlemen are here to accompany you and me to the keep. There seems to be-," before he could finish, the crippled behemoth interrupts.

"Something is amiss and we intend to find out what it is. You will follow us Payne. Your audience is required."

Something is definitely wrong. It seems as though I have no choice, I tell myself.

Kill them all…show no mercy, the satanic voice whispers in my head.

"Not now," I say aloud.

"Excuse us m'Lord?" questions the giant on the left. "Did you refuse our request?"

"I will be only a moment. I need to gather my belongings," I reply as I walk back to my keep. When I enter my tiny room, I compare it to Edward and Jaina's bedchamber and smile knowing it will soon belong to me. I begin to collect all of my essential belongings for this affair. My traditional black attire is neatly folded on my bed. I undress from my current training garb and wear my black battle apparel. The *Silent Sisters* hang from the wall with the fire from the torches glimmering and intensifying their golden hilts. I stride over, taking a moment to marvel at my tools of destruction. As I reach to grab them, Dark Heart's voice enters my head and demands, *kill them all!* One of the *Sisters* drop from my hand, the sharp tip noisily impaling the wooden floor. Shaking my head, I bend down and pick up the dagger, immediately placing it in the sheath of my garb. Leaving the room, I take one final gander and mutter, "good riddance." I spit on the floor for good measure and head downstairs to meet my guests.

A destrier is waiting for me alongside Pyke. I saddle up to the horse with ease and we take our leave back to the *Guiding Light.* No words are spoken during the voyage back to the keep. Leaves rustle in the wind as the horses trot along. Pyke and I ride in front while the two men follow in the rear. I look over at Pyke and notice sweat dripping underneath his top hat. One of his hands is busy trying to keep his hat from falling while the other holds on to the saddle straps. It is always amusing watching Pyke struggle with anything but counting gold.

Never leaving my tower, except to travel through the secret tunnels, I had not realized how twisted and gloomy the trees in my vicinity are. Beauty and wonder are ever present within Apollon but this forest seems dead and deprived of life. *Just like Jaina and Edward,* I remind myself pleasingly. We near the *Guiding Light* and are greeted by a crowd waiting impatiently for our arrival. Hundreds of torches are lit and even more low mutters are heard. When the two gate guards notice our arrival, they stomp their lances on the ground and open the large steel gates.

Everyone gazes upon us as we gallop towards the main hall of the keep. Some of the crowd stares with discontent, some with disbelief, while others smile and cheer. Timber is standing with his enormous arms crossed at the far end of the main hall. *My monster,* I smile to myself. The two titans riding to my side pale in size when compared to Timber. As we finally reach the entrance of the main hall, we disembark from the horses and hand them to the drunken stable boy. I can hear Pyke groan and grunt trying to lift his leg over the saddle. One of the guards decides to be heroic and assist Pyke. Once he realizes he could not lift his leg without assistance, he calls over a few more men in an attempt to free the poor horse from the cow sitting on it. It takes three guards to lift Pyke off the horse. Each man holds on to the next from behind and pulls. Pyke finally lifts his leg high enough and with the three men pulling, he quickly topples off the horse. Unfortunately, the first guard could not bear the weight and let go of his grip causing Pyke to fall backwards on top of the fool. The other two men lift Pyke to his feet and dust him off but the man underneath him can barely breathe. "I think my ribs are broken," he wheezes in pain. Two others swoop down and drag the poor bloke away. After the fiasco, Timber, Pyke and I stand together while the two gargantuan men that accompanied us are stationed on each side. Pyke removes the parchment from his sweaty doublet and prepares to read it to the masses.

"We summoned this meeting to settle an important matter. Here in my hand lies the final will of the late great Lord Edward," he yells at the top of his lungs as the parchment is held high in his fat hands. "The last will of Edward Sunborn shall be read aloud for everyone to bear witness. The two men standing to our sides shall attest to these words and deliver the news to their Masters as we appoint a new Duke of Apollon."

Pyke points to the left as he starts his introductions. "Lord Stanley Dreadford, the champion of Castle Grey Axe, General of Lord Daniel Grey Axe's armies," he summons. Lord Stanley bows his head to the zealous crowd. Pyke continues. "No stranger to Apollon, on my right stands the former Master of Blades and now newly titled General of Star Strike keep, Bartholomew Royce." Bartholomew threw a menacing look towards Pyke regarding his announcement of his former title but then looks back at the crowd and raises his fist in the air as a salute. Some cheer his name while others are silent either not knowing who he is or not caring. Pyke allows the crowd to tire of their chanting. As the voices subside, he completed his remarks. "We thank thee both for blessing us with your presence m'Lords."

Smoke encases the sky as the torches lite the garden. Clouds form around Apollon, as if an omen of some unnatural disaster is about to occur. Everyone stands awaiting the final words of *Edward the Light*. Pyke plays the crowd much like a prostitute charms her clients. Taking his sweet time, he unravels the parchment deliberately with caution and turtle like speed. His eyes move rapidly, reviewing the writing as he admires his own workmanship. A smile appears on his fat, white face, portraying the yellow and gold from his teeth. Angry shouts arise from the mob. He clears his throat again, wipes his nose followed by spittle of drool that is coming down his mouth before he continues to read.

"I, Edward Sunborn, Son of Maximillian Sunborn, Duke of Apollon and Lord of the *Guiding Light* decree that when I pass, my son, Marcus Sunborn is granted all the treasures, property, lands and title "Duke of Apollon". For any reason that my heir is incapable or God forbids passes before his time, all the treasures, property, lands and title of "Duke of Apollon" will be granted to the most capable protector of my home - The Master of Blades and Potions." *There it is.*

Uproar and upheaval take the air as the guards express their displeasure with the announcement. Lord Dreadford stands straight, chivalrous, and unfazed by the sudden outburst yet Lord Bartholomew joins the crowd. His one good arm lifts up and down as he roars along. *I wonder how large the target is on my chest.* Many did not recognize me or even know who I was in person. They have only heard of me by name and by title. Winning over peoples' admiration or approval has never been my intention. Unfortunately, it is time to become the shepherd to the flock of sheep which currently want nothing more than to trample over my carcass. *Kill them all,* the voice returns. "Shut up fool," I respond.

Once the chanting subsides, someone yells from the back of the crowd. "Where is Lord Marcus? We demand an explanation as to where the young Lord has disappeared to." Others nod and raise their voices again in defiance. Pyke assures them that everything is being done to locate him and the "traitor" Liza if they are still alive. Knowing Liza, I feel as though these chances are slim but it must be done. *She will be half way across the world,* I assure myself. I wait silently against the gate doors, my eyes directly gleaming towards the crowd. The scar on my face stings due to the heat from the fires. The mixture of the crowd and the sensation in my face only feed my irritation. Another man comes forward. "What kind of Master of Blades can claim to be a protector when he cannot even protect a child?" He points at me challengingly. "You, sir, are an outsider to us. No one knows of your so-called fabled fighting ability. I say you prove yourself to us!" he shouts as he turns his head left and right seeking approval. Pyke attempts to retort to the comments but I extend my hand and cover his mouth to stop him from speaking. Everyone else turns silent as well almost as if I had hundreds of arms, forcefully shutting their mouths.

"You wish to challenge me Sire?" I ask in a low threatening tone. He did not answer. "How many of you know Lord Bartholomew? If you doubt my abilities ask him or Lord Samuel on how deadly I can be." Staring down the crowd, I await for someone to challenge me. *Kill them all,* the voice calls out. *I just might do it,* I reply to it with frustration and malice.

"Well? If you have the courage step forth and take my title. If no one has the manhood to take it from me then I shall take my rightful title as Duke of Apollon," I say with confidence. I walk left and right of the crowd reviewing the faces of my new army. *Soft! All of them,* Dark Heart exclaims. Suddenly the crowd parts as a man clad in a short sword and shield steps forward.

He is young and possesses eyes of a trainee, yet is decorated and adorned as a knight. A heater shield rests on his left arm with the Sunborn symbol embedded on it. The chest plate he wears is decorated and enlaced with rubies and reinforced iron. Steel spikes are jutting from the elbow sockets and his leg plates are simple but heavily plated with iron. His knees to his feet are also equipped with the same precious metal as the plate armour, again with spikes protruding from his heels and knee sockets. He has long blond hair which hangs from his head to his lower back. Physically, he is not bulky or muscular but he does possess height. He stands above six feet and with his long sword extended, he would easily reach ten feet. His face structure and demeanour reminds me of someone but before I have the chance to remember who, Lord Bartholomew shouts, "No son! Do not do this. You cannot fight this... this monster." *Ah the son of Lord Bartholomew. I will finish with him what I couldn't with his father.*

"Father, please stand back. I will avenge you and our family name. Once I defeat this heathen, you can return and rule as "Duke of Apollon". There is no one more deserving than you!" he turns and barks in my direction. "I, Radford Royce, eldest son of the great Bartholomew Royce, former Master of Blades and current General of Star Strike Castle, challenge you to a duel for title of Master of Blades and Potions as well the Duke of Apollon."

Cheers explode from the crowd as they recite together, "Royce! Royce! Royce!"

Timber yawns and moves towards the crowd, pushing away guards left and right as if they are mere babies. After a few minutes, a large gap between the two sides is created by Timber, giving us ample room for a duel. The arrogant Royce boy smiles and flicks his golden hair back as he unsheathes his sword. He waves it in circles, taunting me to remove my blades. "You are not worthy to face me with weapons, boy," I tell him. *Toy with him first. Show these fools why they should follow us,* the voice demands. *Then kill them all!*

I lift my right hand and curl it into a fist, laying it dormant near my chest. Twisting my body to the side, my left hand extends half way, open and ready to parry his attacks. As an assassin, there have been many instances where I had to kill men with my bare hands, especially those I deemed unworthy of feeling the touch of my *Silent Sisters*. My hands were built for destruction and are more than enough to handle my challengers.

"What is this foolishness?" he laughs. "Can you believe this imbecile?" he asks the crowd. A burst of laughter fills the air. "So be it. Let it be known that Payne Bladestorm perished at the hands of the Radford Royce in one mighty swoop!" He swings the sword rapidly at my head and I immediately duck. Radford definitely has speed and form but I am faster and stronger. Again, he extends the sword to pierce through my skull. I simply sidestep, staring straight into the eyes of the boy. His eyes open in disbelief, as he barely sees me move. I am staring at him with determination. The sword came at my face again but this time with a side slash. Ducking the swipe, my open palm finds his perfectly shaped nose. When my palm connected with his nose, a loud *crunch* noise resonates from it and the crowd yells out in unison. Radford stumbles backwards, drops his sword and holds his nose as blood gushes over his face, armour and blond hair. "It seems as though your armour is no longer silver *my Lord*," I say in a mocking tone. "Your sword is also on the ground, please pick it up."

He roars in anger, veins bulging from his neck and temple while he picks up his sword, Less cocky than before and a bit disoriented, his blows become less calculated and precise but now he is wise enough to distance himself from my strikes. He attacks as a fencer would and his heater shield is up at all times. Unlike his father, this young boy would not be as easy to tire. Iron is extremely difficult to penetrate and this particular armour has no openings. If anything, it is much deadlier than the sword which he wields with all of the spikes sticking out from different areas of the armour. Radford's only weakness is his head which he did well to cover with the shield. He places all of his might into swinging his sword hoping to penetrate my swift defences. The setback of his attack pattern is that it leaves him open to counter strikes. An experienced knight understands how to distribute his strength equally between sword and shield but Radford has become infuriated and lowers his shield with every downward swing. *Use the shield against him,* I tell myself. His next swing is aimed at my chest but steel cut air as I flip backwards. *Now!* I punch the heater shield sending it back into his face.

Metal connects with flesh as the shield he was using earlier for protection becomes a tool for his own demise. Unfortunately for him, the shield strikes his already broken and twisted nose. This time I did not allow him to recover. Radford almost fell backwards from the force of my blow but I was there to stop him from tumbling. Before he is able to comprehend his dire situation, my palm is against his back, holding him up. Startled, he drops the shield and attempts to use the spike on his elbow and swings his arm backwards. Expecting such an attack, I dodge and by the time he recovers from spinning in my direction I am already up and ready to attack. With two fingers extended, I quickly jab the inside of Radford's neck, connecting with his cricoid cartilage below the adam's apple. Both his hands cover his neck and his breathing is caught. He lowers his head down to gasp for air but it is quickly met with a furious knee strike to his nose again. Tears fill his eyes and he could no longer see through them. His head snaps backwards and I grab his long hair in my hands and pull down, dropping him to the hard cement ground. I lift the head of Radford Royce and look at his father with a smile. I place one hand on his temple and the other on his chin and quickly spin my hands in opposite directions of each other, snapping the neck of his only son. The neck bones crack grotesquely as his father disembarks from his horse and runs over to see his dead body.

Bartholomew kneels, sobbing like an infant who has just been scorned by his parents. "I will kill you!" He screeches with strands of spit plastering his mouth. *Kill them all,* the voice urges again. Without hesitation, I reach for my daggers hidden in my garb. With blinding speed, the *Silent Sisters* find Bartholomew's neck, cutting deeply from one ear to the next, almost beheading him. Instantly, father and son are re-united in the afterlife and lie dead on the floor under my feet. It is a beautiful creation; a painted mosaic which only I could create from violence and carnage. *Much better,* the voice whispers with a satisfied tone.

Lord Stanley Dreadford has not flinched nor made a move. Pyke is smiling and Timber continues to shows no sign of emotion. The same could not be said about the rest of the spectators. Their faces speak volumes. There is complete silence with the exception of the crackle of the sparks coming from the torches. *No one shall dare defy me.*

"From this day forth, we shall no longer be known as the *Guiding Light*," I yell with bloodlust still lurking in my veins, awaiting any opposition so I could strike again. Not one individual argued or dared to speak. I calm my nerves and walk back over to Pyke's direction. "Was that proof enough of my capabilities to protect these lands Lord Stanley?" I ask wiping the blood from my blades on my black sleeves.

"There is more to ruling than brute force and killing aptitude but as far as those traits are concerned… If you did not look human, I would think you were a demon."

"Politics will be handled by our Master of Coin. Tell your Master and the other nobles that I will not succumb to the soft hearted ways of the Sunborn. This is a new era of rule, an iron fist. Apollon will no longer be the salvation of the weak and the saviour of the decrepit," I proclaim.

"As you say m'Lord," he replies. "I will let my Master know what has transpired and will pass my condolences to Lord Star Strike about his General's defeat. If you will excuse me now, I have seen enough bloodshed for one night. I will be going to my quarters."

I nod but never took my stare away from my daggers. My army stands ahead of me cautiously awaiting my guidance. "Hear me," I shout to the fearsome crowd. "If you wish to serve and are capable to do so, I will make this home the strongest and most feared in all of Thalia. No more will we cater to peasants and lifting those who cannot walk on their own. If you obey, then you have a place in these walls. If you defy, you will suffer the same fate as the *noble* Royce family. The dungeons will no longer be occupied by spiders and rats. Your new executioner and jail keeper shall be Timber. Mark my words; he is not one to trifle with." Timber nods in approval.

"Lord Pyke shall handle all of the affairs when it comes to audiences, gold, treasure and politics. I am not to be disturbed unless by him. Training will fall upon me. If you cannot maintain the level of discipline and skill in training then you shall be cast out of your position and made a steward. Expectations will be set high. Champions will be chosen for combat training and recruiters are needed to scour the lands for capable bodies. No longer are we to light the path for the meek and helpless. From this day forth we uphold justice through battle. From this day forth we cover the light that was once the Sunborn and relish in the darkness that is Payne Bladestorm. Let all fear and cower before Castle *Eclipse*."

Mixed roars, cheers and mutters emerge from the crowd as some chant my name which only increases over time. "Payne! Payne! Payne!" A few moments ago the mere sight of me made them laugh and doubt my worthiness but now they cheer for me as if I am their Messiah. *They are sheep and you the shepherd,* I remind myself. I close my eyes and the noise slowly disappears in my mind even though the crowd seems to be getting louder. In my mind, I am standing on top of the dead bodies of hundreds of victims I have murdered. The bodies of Bartholomew and Radford are now part of the collection. There are still faceless bodies underneath me, but soon those identities will be revealed. Across the carcasses stands another figure cloaked in black with red eyes and a twisted white smile. *We will find them,* the figure says re-assuring me. *Then it shall be their faces you see.* An army of darkness stood obediently and ready to conquer behind me yet the figure across the way still stands alone, confident and maniacal. *Soon, it will be my time,* it whispers before it disappears.

CHAPTER FOURTEEN
OLD MAN VENOM BOLT

These old knees have been planted; bent on the cold, dark, stone ground for ten days. In my youth this type of ordeal would have barely been a burden, but at the age of sixty my limbs and bones are not what they used to be. I despise being called "old man" by the younger apprentices but there is an undeniable truth to it. To make matters worse, as I age, my past memories begin to return to me.

Lately, all I have thought about is my foggy past existence. Any who join this secret covenant are trained not to remember their life prior to being servants of darkness but the last few days I cannot help myself. Memories invade my mind and force me to recall a life before my calling and before my old age - a time when I was a strapping lad born into wealth and power. This was before the Second Great Holy War. When my purpose in life was to wine with nobles, feast with warriors and sleep with whores. My parents never approved of my whoring or my drinking though it mattered not. Woman could not resist my charms nor my looks.

My hair was once black and straight, slick in a knot compared to the dry and white hair currently occupying my scalp. My eyes are an arresting shade of sky blue and I once had perfect cheek structure and a smile guaranteed to seduce women to drop their garments. When my charms and good looks did not convince the ladies to bed me, the coin in my purse was persuasion enough. Every brothel in Thalia knew of my name. The amount of coin our family possessed was obscene. Even the emblem of my house was represented by a coin purse, spilling with loot, while the golden banner colours shone brilliantly. Brothel owners would line up their inventory of whores by the dozen to sway me to fund their business. Some promised two screws for the price of one if I returned for business, while others offered discounts with every visit. Yet there was only one that I offered repeated visitation. *The prostitute that changed my life*, I reminisced.

All of these memories returned to me in pieces. In the last few days, all of my dreams have been bits and pieces of my shameful actions when I was a youth. I had a hard time distinguishing whether these dreams were memories or just fictitious events my mind was conjuring but I could not shake them. Each passing moment, these memories occupy my thoughts but there are many things I cannot remember. My father or mother's faces are a blur and my friends a distant memory. Allies, companions, lovers, and whores alike are hazy. I cannot even remember my own real name, though there is someone I do remember.

Snake Charmer they called her. No other woman captured my attention and lust as much as her. I first laid eyes on her at Pesoleen Harbour if my memory serves me. The brothel was lavish and the mistresses were bountiful. A few companions and I had a night of drinking and brawling. We smashed a few louts before the hired mercenaries escorted us out of the tavern. Having not been satisfied with how my night ended, I convinced the boys to continue our fun elsewhere. A brothel stood erect only a few minutes away from the tavern. *Sinful Seduction* was the name of the whorehouse. The hour was late but intoxication eliminated any sense of time. We wanted women and that is what we would have.

Four grown men, aroused from the sensation of battle, all stumbled towards the whorehouse. When we arrived we all knocked wildly on the steel door, which stood in our way. Constant knocking was met on deaf ears and soon we started shouting profanities and throwing anything we found on the ground to attract the attention of the brothel mistress. Finally, the door creaked open as chubby fingers pulled on the edge of the door. A fat woman stood staring. Reluctantly, she welcomed us in and we all tried fitting through the door at once, laughing and pushing as we acted like drunken idiots. Once inside, we stared at the mistress of the home. She was dressed in purple silk with her brassiere struggling to hold her giant bosom in place. The dark portions of her nipples were visible through the top. Her underwear, suffocated inside her crack and a mask covered the lower half of her face. Men would find her completely hideous if it were not for her eyes. It was known that mistresses who worked as the head of a brothel practiced seducing men with only their gaze. The outside of her eye was purple and the inside a shade of light green. The perfect description for her eyes would be *sultry*.

Some of the men were raving that they would give her a night that she would never forget but only soft laughter came from her mask. She moved and we followed like sheep and she the shepherd. Her hand lifted suddenly and we all stopped beside a set of long winding, velvet stairs. A light clap from the mistress' hand caused different women to appear from above from various directions.

Every one of the women had qualities that made them differ from one another. There were ones with large breasts and thin waists. Others had small breasts and thick hips. Many were white while some were dark skinned from across the sea to the east. Those ones were the whores that garnered the most attention from curiosity. As the men picked their women, another came down after the pack.

She struck me like an unforeseen arrow. Her lips were full, eyes slanted on the side and half open as if she just awoke from her beauty rest. Her skin was tanned perfectly, not too dark or too white with supple round breasts and perfect sized nipples. Jewels and pearls covered her ears, neck and belly. There were no blemishes or scars to be seen. Her legs were long and her torso shaped like an hour glass. *A goddess finally worthy of my heart,* I recall thinking. A snake lay on her slender shoulders almost as long as her. She moved slowly and elegantly causing every man and woman to stop and stare. The fat woman introduced her as Snake Charmer hailing from the Eastern part of the world. People across the sea were known for two skills; loving making and combat. Women were said to pleasure multiple men at once as one man could never fully satisfy them. Being in a drunken stupor, I could barely stand but that had no effect on my erection. *It* stood ready for the challenge. The fat one recognized my arousal but more so the emblem on my chest. Recognizing the famous sigil, her thoughts turned to money.

"I see you fancy our prized possession, m'Lord," the Master of the brothel said gleefully. "She is not cheap and I cannot guarantee that you will find her methods to your liking. If you are a man who must conquer and satisfy a woman, then I caution you with that one. She bites."

"Mistress," I called out to get her attention not even recognizing that she already introduced the lustful woman to me. "How much gold for her," I asked. No amount of gold would stop me from having her. Never had I seen something so beautiful. The green and yellow scaled snake around her neck hissed as her hand stroked its head. She paid me no mind which made me want her even more. *Soon you will be stroking my head,* I thought cleverly.

"We ask for one hundred gold a night with that one, m'Lord."

"One hundred gold?!" I gasped. "I could open three brothels with that much coin. No woman is worth that amount let alone for one night." As the words escaped my mouth so did the

Snake Charmer from my sight. She started to escalate up the steps, taking her time purposely so I could notice how foolish I would be if I did not pay. It definitely worked. When she was out of sight, my mind would not allow me to let her go. *Coin is something that you have plenty of but a woman like that comes once in a lifetime,* I told myself. "So be it… one hundred gold. Take me to her chamber," I told the fat mistress.

"This way, m'Lord," she replied as she bent low, emphasizing the rolls on her stomach. I followed her up the velvet covered stairs. Both anxiety and excitement struck me simultaneously. I had prided myself on pleasing women. My manhood was my weapon. That confidence withered as soon as the door to her chamber opened. She lay on a throne of silk green pillows which covered the top of her bed. The room was full of wonderful aromas and candles from the Eastern part of the world. A snake was draped on her waist, slithering its way to her as she had her legs crossed. Using one finger, she stroked the side of her curvy buttocks up to her skinny waist in a repeated fashion. Her head rested on her other hand. Her silky black hair ran down the side of her body and was draped to the bottom of the floor like the bed sheets.

"She is all yours, m'Lord, but remember she

is not your typical whore. There are things she will do to you that not even your imagination could comprehend. I leave you with these words," the mistress said as she bowed again and took her leave. I thanked her and my attention immediately turned back to my treasure.

"What makes you think you are worthy of bedding me?" She asked as she continued to pay me no heed. Her accent was flawless and barely different than my own. "Men in this part of the world are pathetic at the art of love making. All you know how to do is shove your member forward and thrust. Love is not sword play. No one in the east has been able to satisfy me and they are twice the men you are."

"You have never met someone like me before, m'Lady," I answered with a confident smirk. "Is that snake going to be joining us as well?" I asked.

"If I play with your snake then you must play with mine," she replied slyly.

The Eastern woman lived up to her reputation. Never had my seed been so eager to release from my cock. First, pleasure escaped my body and then pain entered as she kept hold of my *snake* and jerked it up and down. It took everything in me to fight the pain and release her grip. Out of mercy, she loosened her hand and shoved me away. My erection maintained but the self-confidence I once had dissipated. "You see? Pathetic. This creature gives me more pleasure than you ever could. Now, let me be. I must finish what you could not," she said as she waved me away. Lifting my pants and taking my leave, I vowed to conquer her.

I continued to visit the brothel every day and paid a ludicrous amount of gold in the process. Every night, I entered her chamber envisioning myself making her moan and beg for me but instead I was the one begging for more. My coin purse became lighter and I required more gold to pursue my new found obsession. Father's vault of treasure began growing smaller and unfortunately this did not go unnoticed. Two of my father's guards followed me to the brothel and reported back to him regarding my whereabouts and the location of his missing gold. Once I returned to our massive dwelling, my father and mother requested my presence. My father forbade me to ever visit any brothel again. If I betrayed his orders, he promised to wipe the establishment from his lands forever. I have heard stories of my father's bravado, yet even then I could not stay away from her. My visitations only increased as I borrowed gold from other noble friends, promising repayment in a short period of time but that did not last very long. My father's guards stormed the brothel, killing ever man and woman whether they were noble or peasant, making their way to her bedchamber but the Snake Charmer refused to run. "Fleeing is for the weak. Let them come. I will teach them how Eastern women deal with cowards," she exclaimed.

Five men entered with swords, shields and leather armour. My father followed behind. He glared at me at first then turned his attention to the Snake Charmer. His hand raised and he pointed at her as the men walked towards us. There was fear in my heart but she did not flinch. One of the guards grabbed her by the arm and said, "You are a beauty. How about you pleasure me before I kill you?"

"You are not worth my time or touch. Leave here with your dignity and your lives." The men bellowed in laughter but she did not find it amusing. *I cannot let them hurt her,* I told myself. The guard reached around and grabbed her breast. She did not squirm or fight back. His hands moved up to her neck and started to choke her. *Do something before they kill her,* I thought. Suddenly, my body reacted on its own. The guard was too distracted to notice but I had removed his sword from his belt buckle. A swift downward slash came unexpectedly and severed his limb. Gushing velvet blood squirted from his open wound profusely as he released the Snake Charmer to cover the remainder of his arm. Either the alcohol had taken its toll or my wits had left me. Every man serving my noble house looked stunned and confused. My father, normally a man of no emotion, showed such fury and anger that his usual pale, chiselled face turned red as the blood dripping from the sword which I held.

"How dare you!? You treacherous little bastard! No one raises arms against me, especially not my own blood!" He turned to his men as each of them stood in panic and dismay. "What are you waiting for fools?! Kill her and leave my good for nothing son alive so I can punish him for betraying me," he barked. The men took up their swords and let out a battle cry.

Two men came running at me with full force. The first was a fat oaf, whose steps rumbled the floor each time his feet hit the ground. His girth made him an easy target but if he were to land on me, it would be my demise. What he had in size, he lost in speed. My father was not planning to kill me but that is easier said than done. My opponents knew I was not holding back and looking forward to taking their lives if they pressed their attack. The ogre pressed towards my direction, roaring with his sword raised high. I waited patiently to strike, and inches away my sword found his stomach. Battle cry turned to an alarming grunt of pain. The blade found his sternum and plunged through. One second I was standing with the blade inside his stomach, the next I was on one knee, ripping him in half. The second guard stopped in his tracks as he stared at his fellow soldier dropping to the hard floor. Without wasting another moment, I lunged in his direction and caught his jugular, splitting through every muscle and tendon.

I remained standing sweating, bloody and drunk. There were two bodies lying between my father and I. The Snake Charmer was being encircled by the other two dolts who treated her like a mere woman. They laughed and snickered and surrounded her like vultures to a dead carcass. Her hands moved up to her hair, looking marvellous and beautiful with her tall and slim body. Both guards came at her with vicious speed. Before I could blink, her hands untangled her hair and both men dropped like heavy boulders. She tied her hair with poisonous venom hair pin. They were as long as my hands and deadlier than my sword. Her eyes turned towards me full of lust and passion. *This is what makes this woman feel alive.*

"You leave me no choice. I will have both your heads on pikes," my father screamed.

"Leave us old man before the same fate befalls you," the Snake Charmer scoffed. "Your son does not need to lose his father this night. Go back to your home and forget that has happened."

"Stupid cunt. I will enjoy ripping your tongue out as that useless twit of a son watches. Then I will keep you alive long enough just so you can watch me punish him."

Father charged at her but stopped as soon as I jumped in front to deny his attack, yet he made no attempt to halt. I was ready to die for her but I did not have to. I recall my body turning cold with the anticipation of cold steel ramming through my chest but it never happened. A hand reached behind me and lifted my chin up.

"Open your eyes," she whispered in my ear. Both eyes opened at once and could not believe what I was witnessing. Three enormous snakes wrapped my father in their coils. The first snake was emerald and black. It hissed at father as it wrapped tightly around his legs. The second was the largest of the three and it was the one that she kept with her at all times. Yellow and green scales shimmered as it bound my father's waist and arms. Its mouth remained open, ready to attack if any sudden moves were made. The third was brown and small but it was still enough to choke the life out of its victim as it rotated around his neck. There was nowhere to turn or anything else my father could do to release himself of his captivity. At her behest, each snake could kill him in ways that I could only imagine. *What should I do? He is my father,* I wondered. All thought of family left my mind once I heard the Snake Charmer's heavy breathing behind me. Her hand moved down my sweaty chest and stomach and into my trousers. She jerked roughly and I responded with sighs of pleasure. "Take me now. Show your father the man that you truly are," She moaned with excitement.

I turned to face her and ripped what little garments she had on. We were fully exposed but this only fuelled our passion. Her eyes were wide open and she had a smile on her face. "This is how a man should be! Harder you worthless excuse for a man," she yelled in ecstasy. I thrust deeper and deeper, feeling our bodies against one another. My free hand found itself groping her breasts and moving to her buttocks. "Yes! That is how you pleasure a goddess. Keep fucking me while that useless old man watches how I take his very life away." I hear my father fighting for air and his life behind me but I could not stop. *This is what I longed for,* I reminded myself. My body moved like a battering ram, putting its full force inside of her. My hand which was around her neck relocated itself close to her mouth. Fingers full of blood, dirt and sweat entered her sweet opening and she let them in willingly. Her tongue swirled around my fingers and made me want to explode inside her but not this time. This time I will satisfy her.

Once my hand exited out of her mouth, she spat the blood and dirt in my face. I let loose with a slap to her cheek which made her want me more. There was nothing I could do any longer as my seed raced out of me. "Keep going! I am almost there," she roared. I finally accomplished what no man could ever do. She arched her back and screamed in pleasure as her nails dug onto my thighs. Between her legs felt like a waterfall. Never had I felt manlier until that moment. My father's voice was no more as he struggled no longer. The snakes bit his entire face until he was barely recognizable.

From that day forward, I was branded a murderer and hunted by my family guards and fellow banner men and worst of all the royal guard. *All of this for a woman,* I recall telling myself constantly. *All for a woman whose name which I cannot remember.* Yet, we both ran, night and day, trying to live a meaningless life. We no longer had a physical connection either. The one thing that bound us and ruined my life was now gone. She no longer wanted to touch me, while I was too caught up with the consummation of guilt for murdering my flesh and blood. We never stayed in one town for more than a week. My appearance constantly changed to keep the guards suspicions low and allow us time to breathe. Sometimes I shaved my head, and other times I grew different variations of facial hair. Food was as scarce as our lust for one another.

One day, my guilt consumed me to the point of insanity. I decided the only way to rid myself of these feelings was to destroy the cause of all my misfortunes. I decided that night to find refuge in the wilderness rather than an inn. I gathered wood, grass and fallen leaves for our beds and sparked a flame for the night to keep us warm. She was growing thin and dirty but her confidence and ego was still intact. Disgusted by the idea of sleeping outside, she did not speak to me all night and just lay in bed staring at the sky. Eventually, she grew tired of doing so and her eyes slowly began to close. I pretended to do the same so I would not arouse her suspicion. Once I was sure she was asleep, I awoke with a dagger in hand and sought out to end her life and my ever-haunting guilt. Unfortunately, it was not going to be easy. I had to overcome three dangerously poisonous obstacles which, unlike her and I, could stay up all night.

She slept naked with her serpent guardians planted strategically to protect her during her slumber. The smaller brown snake slithered at her side, moving up and down the leaf bed while the emerald serpent slept above her, hanging from a small oak tree. The largest of the three lay below the bed, stretched as long as two men. They have acknowledged me as one of their own and trust me outmost, just as my late father had once. I was about to betray them as I did him.

I moved quietly, dagger hidden behind my back. Venom from the largest of the snakes was the most potent. It hissed as I approached perhaps feeling something was amiss, subsiding once my sharp blade chopped its head off cleanly. The other two did not react to my attack as I was fortunate enough not to face their wrath. I learned much about poisons from the Snake Charmer. Using that same knowledge, I coated my dagger with some of the serpent's blood. Standing above the bed, I admired everything about her. The luscious curves, puckered lips, her soft skin; everything about her was beautiful and graceful but she is the reason for my misery. To end my misery I had to be rid of the cause. My hand moved swiftly and proceeded to make a miniscule cut on her elbow where the roughest skin grew. She moved uncomfortably but barely woke. The poison seeped slowly into her system and took its toll overnight. I left knowing that the venomous nature of the snake would kill her before she woke. *I was truly alone*, I cried.

Within that year I went from a loathing, drunk, noble and rich womanizer to a cowardly and homeless murderer. To eat, I hunted and started mercenary work. The crossbow became my only companion and there was no truer shot in the Realm of Thalia. Even alcohol could not blur my vision and accuracy. I could hit any target I hunted and because of this, my popularity and name grew as did my clientele. People spoke of me in fear and whispers of my name reached the ears of my current Masters. Their identity has been shrouded in mystery for millennia. Only a handful of people knew of the secret organization and even less served them.

I was travelling to a tavern for drink, food and hopefully word of work when I noticed a man dressed all in black walking in my direction. Due to a blackened hood, his face was not visible. Both hands were inside his sleeves as they draped low. *A priest perhaps,* I thought. But priests wear white, not black, I reminded myself. I kept my pace but was ready to attack if the shadowy figure tried anything. As we crossed paths, he moved one hand out of his sleeve and dropped a note on the ground and continued on his way. I stopped and grabbed the small paper from the ground. *'Habitamus in tenebris... Meet at the church after midnight... your sins will be abolished'* was all that was written. *Who was that and does he know of my past,* I wondered as fear crept into my thoughts. The sin of killing my own father, and then the she-devil which turned me into a killer, bothered me relentlessly. Only hunting and drinking calmed my guilt, but only temporarily. Their faces came to me in my sleep and at times in my work as a mercenary. Desperation took hold of me and I decided at that time I would do anything to liberate my mind of the sins.

My reminiscing of the past halts suddenly as I hear my Masters approach in the dark. *Thank goodness. I was almost trapped in that forsaken past of mine and my knees are hurting,* I think bitterly. Each has a distinct sound to their steps. The only thing I know of my Masters is that there are two women and two men. All four Masters take their seats in the pitch black hall.

"Rise *Venom Bolt*," the eldest male demands. He is the leader of the group and the one who asserts himself most often. All orders are approved and given through his will and voice. I rise to my feet sluggishly as my knees *creak* like rusty cogs. "What word do you have on the traitor?" he asks.

"Yes, old man. Please do tell us of how you plan to amend this failure?" asks the obnoxiously screechy young female. She sounds the age of ten or maybe younger but barks orders and insults like an army general. Her voice bounces off the closed walls in the tight room and rings in my ears. On cue, the sound that usually follows hers is one of an equally young male. *Siblings for certain,* I deduce.

"Shut up. You are so bloody loud. Next time just whisper your pointless insults rather than screaming them," he retorts with a hiss of disgust.

"Behave yourselves," exclaims the soft spoken and sultry voice from the calmest of the four. "Let Venom Bolt speak of what he has learned these past few years."

"Thank you, Masters. I am still working on Dark Heart's whereabouts and his activities. I will be moving to Nasgrath shortly and investigating a situation which caused him to betray us. There is also activity in Apollon which requires our attention. Edward Sunborn has lost his life as has his family. Another stepped forward to take the title of Duke and he goes by the name of Payne Bladestorm. He served for many years as his Master of Blades and Potions but seldom left his keep. We should be wary of this unknown figure and I plan to examine him and his intention further once I locate Dark heart's whereabouts.

"So be it," the eldest responds. "Ensure that Dark Heart remains your first priority. This new Duke possesses no threat to us and we are aware of his new position. If he ever is to become a threat, you cannot destroy what you cannot see. We have controlled Thalia for millenniums and no one has ever stood against our might. This *boy* will fall like the rest; and you, Venom Bolt, will be the one to do it. Now be gone and do not return without Dark Heart's head on an arrow."

I bow and await the four to take their leave. As they disappear in the dark, I make my departure. My past has come back to haunt me and now I understand how it feels to be betrayed by the one companion whom I considered a son. His treacherous actions have scarred me for years. I now understood what my father must have felt when I turned my back on him. *I will punish you for your deceit Dark Heart. Darkness will consume you and I will bring you back to justice.*

CHAPTER FIFTEEN
ARTHUR LOWBORNE

Only a few months have gone by since our arrival in Nasgrath but it feels like an eternity. I could not believe that a place like this could exist so close to my former home. Overwhelming sickness, decay and death litter the slums of Nasgrath. Men and women fornicate in public without shame or concern of scrutiny. The children observe and mimic without understanding the heinous acts they are committing. Half of the infants are orphans having lost their parents either to famine or disease. The adults do not watch over them, as food is already scarce thus caring for others only shorten your chance of survival. Despite this, the population continues to reproduce like roaches. Everyone lives on the street since there are no homes in the slums. The closest structures to resemble houses are huts made of wood and hay. Scouring the nearby woods, the decrepit and young alike, gather large branches as foundation support and grass as roofs and beds for their shelters. These lodgings rarely last longer than a few weeks before they are destroyed by weather or thieves looking to prosper from selling the wood. Coin is absent in these parts, however wood fetches a decent price in the market place.

Our plan is simply to keep our identities hidden from the world until the birth of Liza's child. While we wait, I monitor the actions and events occurring within Apollon. Hopefully a rebellion will occur against Payne and his minions as soon as the other nobles learn of my parents' murder and the culprit behind it. It is only a matter of time before my father's banner men take action to reclaim *The Guiding Light* and place Payne in the dungeons. Liza and I will then resurface with our true identities and convince the Royal family to trial Payne for his actions and bring him to justice. Once the child is born, we will seek assistance from the other nobles in Nasgrath and offer a large reward for any who will provide us shelter and assist us in keeping our identities secret until my title as rightful heir to Apollon is restored. Until then, we are forced to live as Arthur and Katherine lowborne, mother and son enduring the hardships of Nasgrath's slums until the appropriate time to strike.

Although I have been struggling, "mother" is no stranger to this lifestyle. When entering Nasgrath, I was told the first lesson to living a new life was letting go of the old, an exercise that I still practice every day. The second lesson is to always protect oneself. Nothing in the slums comes easy and everyone only looks out for themselves. Simple objects found littered on these dirty streets can become a tool for survival and could be the difference between life and death. People are simple-minded but dangerous in their own ways. Unpredictability is as dangerous as any weapon and mother has witnessed many murders in the slums. I have seen children and adults alike walk around without garb yet they all seem to possess a handcrafted tool for protection. Some of these items were simple hand-made weapons, such as a rock tied to a stick to imply an axe; others use remaining branches or pieces of wood sharpened to use it as a spear. They will never match the might of a true steel sword or lance, but the weapon is as dangerous as the man wielding it. These "savages" have no remorse when it comes to killing.

Lastly, the most important lesson is to avoid the Noble District at all costs. Any "lowborne" found in the Noble District will be tied up in the middle of the market and stoned to death by the nobles; even if anyone were to slip away unseen, guards are stationed in each district near every home to watch for intruders. The market place is the furthest I am allowed to venture. I try visiting the wondrous market as often as possible but I tread lightly when I do. I make numerous trips daily to find food to feed our bellies and my trusty pocket knife lies at my side, ready to keep the thieves at bay. I obediently never step foot past the market district. Yet part of me knows that in my previous life I outrank all of the supposed nobles in Nasgrath. That is when I remember the first words of advice. *I am no longer Marcus,* I remind myself. *Arthur... I am Arthur lowborne, son of Katherine lowborne.*

My appearance has changed as well. My hair is no longer golden and straight but instead is tangled in knots and unwashed. Dirt covers the blonde giving me streaks of brown in various locations. Without any methods to groom myself, my hair has grown beyond my shoulders, almost rivalling my mother's in length. I am taller as well, stretched further by at least two feet. Strange how much change can occur within a year and how different I look at the age of eleven. My legs sprouted, arms thickened, and shoulders broadened. The constant travel to the forest and back paired with the consistent need to construct new wooden homes weekly has advanced my muscle build. If anyone from my past were to lay eyes on me they would have a hard time believing I am Marcus Sunborn. The only remnant of my past lies in my green eyes. When I exact my revenge, I want Payne to peer into these eyes which are identical to my father and mother's. *The last thing he will remember are these eyes when I kill him,* I tell myself.

Exhaustion is starting to take over my body as I return home with wood and grass to construct a new home for mother and myself. The last hovel withered due to a week straight of harsh rain and wind. My legs ache from bending and lifting. My skin, which was once soft, is covered in cuts, scrapes and dirt. Filth and holes adorn the baggy cotton top and bottoms I wear. The leather on my shoes is eroding and beginning to rip from the front, exposing my toes.

As I approach the alley I see mother resting her back against a broken half wall, rubbing her belly. Lately, her stomach is growing immensely. She complains of pain and often throws up, decorating the already disgusting streets. According to her, my unborn sibling is trying to get out and join our family. *This is not a world for any child,* I thought.

Katherine rises to her feet when she sees me approaching. A lazy smile forms on her face. "Arthur, welcome back," she said. She extends her arms out to assist me and I gladly hand over the grass.

"How are you feeling mother?" I ask. Calling Liza by the name Katherine has been difficult to remember, but referring to her as mother is not. She is the closest thing to a parent I have, even before my parents were. However the extra weight from her belly caused her much pain and difficulties, thus lately I have been the one taking on responsibilities and taking care of her.

"Better today, Arthur," she replies warily. "The baby has been less fussy and it kicks less frequently. Is this enough grass and wood to complete our haven?"

"Aye, it should suffice. I have been collecting wood and grass for three days. This should last us for a few weeks and give us shelter from the storms. Have you eaten today?"

Katherine looks down at her stomach and presses it as it lets out a thundering grumble. "There is no food left for us. I am sorry, son, but our rations are depleting because of the third member of our family."

We both venture forward to the alley where our broken home barely stands. My feet are heavy and my skin raw from the long walks gathering material. Katherine wobbles left and right as she struggles carrying the grass in her arms. Every now and then, she needs rest and places the grass on the muddy ground, leaving behind grass whenever we continue. My stomach begins to grumble now as we come within reach of our destination. Food has been hard to retains and in short supply lately due to Katherine's insatiable hunger. "Rest, mother," I tell her as I drop the wood on the ground. "We will visit the marketplace tomorrow and gather food and water." I arrange the grass into a cushioned bed for her to rest on. I stack the wood into a triangle and dig them into the muddy ground so it will hold during the night. The remainder of the grass is set aside for later use. Removing my dagger and resting it beside me, I close my eyes and fall asleep as fatigue takes its toll.

Katherine and I decide to explore the market district the next afternoon. The marketplace is quiet at nights, but robust and populated during the day. Merchant competition is fierce so many shops make an effort to differ from one another. Some create signs with ludicrous names, such as *God's Gift*, which sold basic fruits and vegetables. Because of this name, religious nobles and travellers flock to the owner, who will recall divine stories of how he came about his products. The opposing fruit vendor is aptly named *Sweet and Sour*. The seller had been losing business lately after his competitor deemed his product as "Satan's

Forbidden Fruit". To display truth in his accusation, he hired a con man to buy fruit from the vendor and pretend to be possessed by an evil demonic force upon consuming it.

Katherine and I were walking back to our alley when this farce took place. The man's mouth gargled, and he dropped face first. As the crowd came closer to inspect him, he started to tremble violently on the ground, like a fish hooked on land. Once the shaking subsided, he rose and his eyes were a pearl white. The owner of God's Gift came running out of his shop and began pointing and shouting, "See! The Devil has a hold of him! Do not eat this man's fruit!" Some religious fanatics were convinced of the act instantly and started to accuse the shop owner of being a Devil Worshipper. To solidify his product as being divine, the shameless owner of God's Gift hurried back to his shop and returned with a blood orange, which he proclaimed was given to him by a prophet to battle demonic possessions. Red juices ran from the traders hand as he ripped the orange into several pieces. Shoving the orange down the open and twisted mouth of the man possessed caused him to instantly "regain" his humanity.

"What happened?" he asked dumbfounded, "Last I remember was buying fruit from that man."

He pointed towards the old man sitting behind the counter of the Sweet and Sour shop.

"You, good sir, have been tricked by the devil worshipper and have tasted the forbidden fruit!" He spun theatrically, finger pointed at the audience and then back to the owner. "You see, good people of Nasgrath, my fruit will save you. Shop at God's Gift and you will be blessed." Katherine and I later saw the shop owner pay the acting victim gold for his convincing performance.

Ever since that day, the owner of Sweet and Sour has barely made enough money to replenish his stock. His fruits have begun to rot which made the shop stink of mold and decaying fruit. The owner of Sweet and Sour has a family of three young grandchildren left in his care after their parents were killed for trespassing on the Noble District. He has owned the shop for forty years and is the longest trader in the merchant district of Nasgrath, yet he has no way of defending himself. The old man himself is decaying like the fruits in his shop. He lacks teeth, his gums are swollen, eyes barely open, and his skin is dark brown like tanned leather. He clung to slivers of white hair strands on the back of his head. I decided to avenge the old man myself. Marcus may have pitied the man, but would never act upon his feelings due to his noble standing. As Arthur I am different. Mischief and exploits are my calling. Never will I allow my doubts cloud my judgement. Marcus stood by idly while his nightmares came into fruition with the travesty befell his parents; Arthur will not make the same mistake.

On a clear and starry night, when all the shops would normally close, I came to bargain with the old man. Sweet and Sour has been the only store to consecutively remain open from dusk till dawn. The owner was hoping that some weary and hungry buyer would magically appear, seeking for fruit as a source of food. The stench of rotting fruit wafted through the clear sky. This would normally have made me gag, but the smell of rotting fruits was welcome in comparison to the scents within the slums. When the old man noticed me appear, he jumped to his feet and began reciting his best song and dance in order to promote his product. "Come in, come in, young Master," he said merrily. "If you are looking for fruit, there is none finer than Sweet and Sour. One taste of these delicious delicacies and you will be begging for more."

Unimpressed and unfazed, I persist forward with purpose. Everything he stood for was taken from him; honesty, hard work, sincerity and dignity, all gone because of a low life, greedy bastard. Whenever I witness people who prey on the weak, it reminds me of Payne and I crave revenge. Anger and hate overwhelm me and my thoughts return to the room where he murdered my parents.

"I am not here for your delicacies old man. I am here to help you regain your reputation and destroy the one who has taken your business and slandered your name," I replied.

"Boy… you look no older than my youngest grandson," the old man whistled through his teeth. "Do not involve thy self in the world of grown men. There is only pain and suffering at the end."

"I know a thing or two about pain and suffering, especially to those who are undeserving of it. Are you not tired of being away from your family? Have they food in their bellies? How much longer can they feed on fruit not fit to feed the homeless?" I questioned.

"What would you have me do? The man has marked me as a devil worshipper and furthermore displayed his 'miraculous' fruit power in front of all of Nasgrath. Nobody dares approach my stand any longer," cried the shop owner.

"Nothing, do nothing," I repeated in a

threatening tone. "But if you hire me, I can guarantee you gold in your pocket and out of his grubby hands."

"Hire you? Boy, I barely have enough coin to keep my store open let alone feed my family. How am I to pay you if I have no gold? Even if I did have the gold, how am I to know I can trust you or that your end of the bargain will be upheld?"

"Let us make a wager then. In three days, I will deliver you the same earnings you would have made before these accusations against you. If I pull through, I want you to provide me with fruits… fresh fruits which I can take home with me every day," I answered.

The old man looked at the sky as he rubbed one hand on his scruffy and unshaven chin, pondering my words. After a few moments, he looked back down in my direction and said, "If you get caught then I have no ties to your crime. If you succeed, see me before sunrise and I will provide you with enough fruit to last you the day. We will continue to support one another as long as it remains safe to do so. Do we have an understanding?" He asked.

I smiled and nodded. "Three days old

man…that is what I ask for. I will bring you gold before sunrise in exchange for the fruit." A lowborne with gold is less suspicious than one with fruit. Gold is easy to hide in my tunic and I can carry it from the slums to the market place without worry. The plan I devised requires me to stealthily cut the coin purse that was glued to the side of the devious owner of God's Gift. In order for my plan to work, I needed an accomplice and I had the perfect partner – Liza. *Katherine,* I reminded myself, would be the perfect decoy.

Upon my arrival to the sorry sight of the structure we called a home I noticed Katherine was waiting with a worried look in her eyes. This has become as customary as the kiss on my forehead Liza gave when I went to training in my past life. "You are becoming reckless, Arthur," she complained. "If you wish to live long enough to see your family avenged then you must tread carefully. People go missing in Nasgrath every day and no one questions it, especially ones who reside in the slums." Knowing full well I would not listen, she stayed up every night, fearing that one day I would not show.

"You should rest, mother. Remember that you are living for two." I touched her belly and felt the baby kick.

"Correction, Arthur, I am living for three," she scorned. "You must return sooner. I cannot take the late nights any longer and neither can she."

"She? What makes you think that it will be a girl?" I asked, curiously.

"It has always been my dream to have a son and daughter. God has heard my prayers and sent me a sign. I had the most vivid dream of a young girl as I slept last night. She reminded me of a version of myself only younger, happier and innocent."

"What if you had a dream about your childhood?" I questioned her.

She shook her head, "I have never been happy or innocent. Enough talk of me. Why were you out so late again?"

We sat together under our hut as I explained my agreement to help the owner of Sweet and Sour. I asked for her participation in my scheme to take the gold from that charlatan who ruined the life of an innocent. "I just need your involvement once. In good faith, I promised the old man I would delivery his money to him in three days and we will never go hungry again," I tried to explain convincingly. She stared at me with her dark, round eyes. After a few seconds of silence, she said, "Promise me this isn't about revenge."

"What do you mean?" I retorted. "This is for our survival. Besides, I have no quarrel against the heathen who ruined another man's life. I just want justice to be served."

Silence filled the air again but Katherine's gaze spoke in volume. She knows me too well, I realize. The truth is that I did take the situation personally. Payne had torn down my very existence by tricking my father into trusting him. He used my family and our land, devouring our resources for his own gain. I knew there was something dastardly about him, as did my mother, but I did not react or try and convince my father further. After nothing was said for a few minutes, I rose angrily and blurted out, "Fine! If you will not help me, then I will do it myself."

Katherine grabbed me by the arm and pulled me back down. "My fear is for us and my child, Arthur. I know how you feel. There was once a time that revenge was my very purpose for living. It consumed my soul. Please know that I am only helping you because I do not want you to go through life living this way. You must not lose yourself to the evil darkness. Remember the light,

Arthur. Think of your parents, your home, and your noble bloodline. Think of me," she said.

Her words hit me like a flailing mace to the skull. I was so caught up in my hatred for Payne that I was becoming him. Scheming and not caring for anything but revenge. I could have killed the God's Gift vendor if need be in order to achieve my goal. Not because he deserved it, which he did, but because the situation reminded me of Payne. Promising that no harm would come to anyone, I told Katherine of her role. She would buy some fruit from the shop and then faint in front of the store. Trying to not ruin his reputation, the vendor will panic and come out of his shop to tend to Katherine. This will give me the time I needed to enter his shop and take the gold that he kept hidden underneath the counter. The plan would be best executed during the busiest time of the day which is a few hours before the sun set. During these hours, the streets are covered with buyers and it would be the ideal time to plunder his loot as his daily earnings would be the most profitable.

Once the third day arrives, I attend to my daily routine of gathering materials in the forest. Today, I am wearing special attire to help conceal my identity. The top is a light green cotton doublet with a hood resting on its back. My bottom consists of short slacks which matches the colour of my top and hangs low to my pale ankles. These gifts were bestowed upon me by the old man. His eldest grandchild grew too quickly and had some clothing which fit me perfectly. I gladly accepted the new garb as mine were becoming unbearable to wear. Completing my task, I return home and review plans with Katherine. Once we both understand our roles, we part ways and head towards the shopping district.

The market place is lined up with vendors in a straight line vertically up and down the street. Behind each shop are multiple lavish homes with enormous balconies, belonging to wealthy families without noble bloodline. They mostly consist of merchants, warlords or mercenaries. I perch on a stone balcony of an abandoned home looking below more than ten feet high, monitoring the activities of the busy street. People rush along to each seller trying to bargain and save coin on purchases while merchants push their products on oncoming pedestrians. Many entitle their items as the greatest, tastiest or mightiest in all of Thalia, still most are ignored. Most of these claims fall on deaf ears except for one merchant. The owner of God's Gift is busy spewing his stories to the masses as they quickly flock to buy his "magical" fruit. I look across at the old man withering in his humble shop. The only flock surrounding his store are flies and maggots. I hope he saved some fresh fruit for us. My attention turns to locating Katherine. I easily spot her as she looks marvellous, wearing her finest dress my birth mother had gifted to her. Clear blue, strapless and snug, her figure compliments every feature. Katherine took the time to wash her hair today in the forest river as I was harvesting our material. She could pass for a noble with her beautiful face and full figure. Even with her belly showing, Katherine is lovelier than most in Nasgrath.

Vendors took notice as well. Shop owners approach her trying to persuade her to take notice in their product. Jewels, clothing, and crafts are thrown in her direction as they gush over her beauty and bless her unborn child. Shooing away the sellers, she maintains her focus on the task at hand. God's Gift is bombarded with buyers and much of his stock is being depleted quickly. Katherine stands in line patiently as others quickly leave the store with their purchase. She keeps a lovely smile on her face and acts as if the heat and uncomfortable attire is something she is accustomed to. When Katherine finally reaches the head of the line, the owner takes immediate notice of her beauty and her belly. He rushes around his counter and stands facing Katherine. A devious smile wraps around his face. "If I knew you were in line alone, my Lady, I would have come to you instead," he compliments slyly.

"You seem to be doing well, good sir," she replies while reviewing the shops merchandise. "The wait is worth it from what I have heard. Is it true that your fruit are gifted to you from God?"

"You flatter me, my Lady. Aye, you have heard correctly. My fruit are picked by the hands of the almighty himself. He has gifted me again by bringing you to my humble shop. Please grant me the opportunity to offer you a free sample." He grabs a ripe red apple from the counter. *Once she bites into it, our little plan with take form,* I remind myself. Katherine bows courteously and holds the apple in hand. As the apple enters her mouth and she bites down, I jump off the balcony and cover my head with my cowl. Looking ahead, I notice Katherine playing her part. She cups her belly and screams in pain. Her acting is more than convincing. Katherine loses balance and falls to the ground, attracting the crowd and the owner of the shop. *This is it,* I tell myself. My feet move rapidly down the street, passing various stores as I aim for God's Gift. The closer I approach my target, the louder Katherine screams. I eye the coin purse behind the counter and push through the distracted crowd and snatch it quickly and continue moving. Once I am out of sight, I turn back to see Katherine. She is crying and screaming. Her eyes are tightly shut and her breathing is heavy. Sweat pours down her face and the crowd yells, "She is in labour! Someone help her!" A part of me wants me to stop running and go back to help her but another reminds me of the mission. *The weak cannot avenge. You must keep going,* I convince myself. I did not turn back. Instead, I keep moving towards the slum hoping that Katherine will forgive me one day for leaving her in her time of need.

CHAPTER SIXTEEN
KATHERINE LOWBORNE

Something is amiss. Pain is coursing through my body although no apparent harm had befallen me while speaking to the shop owner. *Could it truly have been the fruit?* This became an afterthought as my abdomen seizes and muscles contract. I stiffen as it becomes difficult to breathe. All I want to see is my "light". *Marcus. Where is Marcus?* I wonder helplessly. In a finer state, it would dawn on me that the Marcus I want no longer exists because of me. The boy who once considered me as precious as his mother changed the night his parents were killed. Now there is only Arthur, a revengeful and destructive shell of his former self. My body reminds me to take precedence over worry for Marcus through surging pain. I try to calm myself but all I can do is hold my belly as feet seize and voices murmur around me. Someone yells aloud and I try to make out the words, but I cannot focus on anything but the agonizing discomfort. I scream in order to relieve some tension. The crowd around me gasps and the discomforting begins to creep its way into my thighs and lower back. *Is this God's way of punishing me? I consider. I did just have fruit from a vendor who claims his products are a gift from God.*

The cramps are now becoming long and fierce. They become so unbearable that I squeeze my eyes shut and let out a long and deafening shrill. Tears run down my eyes and I take a few moments to adjust to the light before opening my eyes. I realize I am on the dirty ground of the market place with the storeowner hovering over my body; behind him stood a crowd of Nasgrath's populous. There are nobles as well as lowbornes, priests, mercenaries, royal guards and vendors. Mothers are holding their children to their breasts and covering their ears, and men argue amongst each other, trying to figure out what is transpiring. It seems all of Nasgrath is present to witness my suffering - all except the one who matters most. Arthur is nowhere to be seen. Momentarily, the sun disappears as the overgrown owner of God's Gift bends over and says, "My dear madam, what type of pain do you feel?"

Words cannot escape my mouth as dry flakes of white skin fall in my throat. I choke a bit and cough up saliva. From a distance, someone shouts out with a frail voice, "She is with child and is likely delivering right now you oaf." Everyone turns their heads to see who is speaking. The crowd parts as an elderly woman with a wooden crutch drags herself to the front. Feeble and delicate, the old woman has grey hair tucked into a bun. Her back is hunched forward and supports what barely remains of her green dress. She is not wearing any shoes and her bare feet expose her talon-like nails. Leaning on a wooden cane for support, she is standing above me, staring at my face. For an instant, I become lost in her stunning eyes. They are the most unique hint of grey circling a light purple. That distraction is instantly overtaken by contractions and my hand clutches my stomach as the pain comes through faster and more intense.

"Old woman, how do you know she is with child and this is not a sign from God for her to be punished?" asks the merchant.

"My *name* is Magda, scoundrel. You still try and promote that ridiculous notion of yours, even as a helpless lady struggles near your shop?" she replies scornfully. The owner is taken aback by her stern response and harsh but accurate accusation. "I know she is with child because I have been a midwife my entire life. These are signs of a woman about to give birth. Make yourself useful and fetch warm water, clean cloth, a piece of wood and anything to support her head."

With all the background noise from the crowd I barely hear what she says to the owner. I ask with a groan in my voice and sweat on my brow, "what is happening to me?"

Before Magda could respond, the obese vendor jumps out and looks at the crowd and shouts, "It is a miracle! People of Nasgrath, witness the power! Witness the power of God's power! His almighty has bestowed upon my fruit the gift of life!"

Before he can continue any further, Magda grabs her cane and crashes it against his foot without remorse. He yelps and tumbles to the ground with a loud *thud*, holding his now bruised foot. Dust drifts through the air as he rolls back and forth. A guard pushes to the front of the crowd with the materials requested by the midwife.

"Here is what you requested, Magda," he offers in a deep and gruff voice. "Leave Balthasar in my care. The fat dope will not be shamelessly promoting himself any longer. The last thing this city needs is an investigation of a dead woman and baby on the streets. These markets drive Nasgrath. Be done with this before word spreads to the royal guard."

The old crone tilts her chin up and utters something under her breath before turning her attention back to me.

"As for the answer to your question, my dear, you are with child and about to give birth in the presence of all Nasgrath."

No… not like this. I never wanted it to be like this. I attempt to force myself up to my feet, but the overwhelming pain will not allow me to move. My pelvis feels as if it is going to burst and I let out another scream. Magda grips my hand tightly and brushes my hair with her wrinkly, dirt stained hands. She reeks of garlic cloves and spices but it is comforting having someone here with me.

"Child, listen to me very carefully. Even within the confines of one's home, there is a risk for infection for both you and the child. The possibility of death for either of you is even higher in our current circumstances, but if you listen to my every instruction we may yet see you both well and healthy," she murmurs with a smile, exposing her missing teeth. Clasping my fingers into hers, I hold on tightly and struggle a nod of approval before the pain again becomes intolerable. She removes the hand which was brushing my hair and signals the guards to come closer. "You, skinny one," she points at the guard in the back. "You look like you could barely hold your sword let alone pin down a woman who is about to give birth. How about this stick though? Is this light enough for you?" He does not answer but as instructed, takes the stick from her hand. "Fantastic," Magda says with a guffaw. "I want you to place that in her mouth and do not let go." Her droopy face turns to me again. "You, my dear, will need to bite this as hard as you can. I will not be here to comfort you while I deliver your child. Pretend it is the bastard who left you here on your lonesome to bear this burden."

I close my eyes as the thin, armoured man kneels behind me and places a wool blanket underneath my neck to hold my head up. The wooden stick is placed in my mouth and the bitter taste of bark and dirt invade my taste buds. I want to hurl, but the stockier guard holds me down so I have no chance to fight back. Panic ensues as the memories of my rapist returns, and my hands and feet react on their own trying to free myself from the strong grip of the giant man hovering on my side to no avail. It does not take long for me to give in to the pain and I moan in response. Magda quickly signals to the last guard to assist in holding my limbs down. Magda moves closer and speaks softly, "Think of what makes you happiest and keep yourself there. I will need you to push with all of your strength. If you want this child to live, then you must fight for it."

God, please help me through this, I plead to the almighty. Closing my eyes and trying to pry my thoughts from the pain, I attempt to think about the things that made life joyous. Instantly, the image of a Lord Marcus when he was first conceived came to mind. I see the smiles of Lord Edward and Lady Jaina and remember the joy it brought them to see the birth of their healthy baby. I held him in my arms even before his mother. At that moment, I realized the beauty and pain of giving birth. Lady Jaina cried tears of agony for hours but it all vanished as soon as she heard the wailing of her newborn son. Soon I will be holding a child of my own, but I must first survive this ordeal. Keeping focus on what little memory of happiness I could muster, I notice that the pain subsides slightly. The rapid contractions continue to shudder through my body but hurt less with the distraction of Marcus and the Sunborn family. Magda notices the comparable calming in my demeanour and says, "Good, dear, we are almost there," as she continues to stroke my hair with her dry and wrinkled hands. Memories of Marcus are instilled in my mind and his smile warms my heart. The way I used to kiss his forehead before each training lesson makes me realize how much I wish he was by my side. Perhaps having a sibling will bring that innocence back. This child must survive not only for me, but for Marcus as well.

The diversion only lasts briefly as reality sneaks back in. Panic arises from the crowd and the old hag screeches to one of the guards. "Quick, bring a bucket of water and some towels!"

I feel thick liquid running down my legs. My eyes open so I can fully understand the reason behind the commotion. The guard who was holding the stick in my mouth is cringing and his face is turned to the away. He is no longer holding the stick to my mouth so I take the opportunity to see what the commotion is about. A stream of blood is flowing between my legs and onto the brown sand. The sight of it makes my stomach writhe in pain and a dizzy spell takes over so that my head slams back against the hard, sandy ground. There is much chatter within the crowd and frantic movement around me. I find Magda's hand on my forehead as she continues her attempt to comfort me. She utters something like encouragement to keep pushing. My body is steps ahead of her and is doing exactly what it is built to do. However, with the level of pain, I have to fight to stay awake.

The sun which gleamed above me begins to fade as a figure, fully cloaked in black, appears above me. Everything around him turns pitch black and abruptly everything around me fades. Magda, the guards, and the crowd disappear until it was just the unknown figure and I.

"Who are you?" I manage to ask. No response, though I could hear soft breathing from his hooded face. "Answer me!" I demand. He bends to one knee and places a hand on the ground next to my face and reaches into his garb with the other hand. A sharp noise resonates from his pitch black attire. His lean frame is over me and his hidden face is parallel to my own. All the warmth and sweat which I felt earlier from the sun is replaced by a chilling and ice-cold shiver which slithers into every pore of my body.

"You thought you could escape me, didn't you?" he asks with a familiar voice.

"Who are you?!" I demand again.

"You carry my child, Liza, and I will not allow it to be born into this world."

As soon as I realize who the dark figure is, I am frozen out of sheer terror. "No. You are not real, you cannot be. Somebody, anybody, please stop this man," I wail.

"No one can hear you, Liza. I will not make the same mistake as before. This time I will take the life of both the bastard child and the whore who does not seem to learn from past mistakes." I try to push him off me, but I am weak and he weighs more than a horse. My breathing ceases as he lies atop of me. A sinister smile forms across his face as he holds a golden black dagger in the air, ready to strike.

"Goodbye, Liza. May you and our baby find peace in the after-life."

Aiming his weapon in between my legs, he brings it down with blinding speed. I let loose with a deafening scream, as I push as hard as my body allows. Exhaustion finally defeats me and my eyes shut instantly. I am not sure what has transpired with Payne and my child but my body and mind demanded rest whether it be in death or in life. Everything turns cold and dark, but all of the pain subsides and I am finally able to sleep.

CHAPTER SEVENTEEN
PAYNE BLADESTORM

The stench of nobility still lingers in these towers. They were once occupied by the Sunborn, former Masters of the *Guiding Light,* and traces of their existence still exist even after their demise. I had the newly appointed maids replace the colourful and golden drapes with darker, stiff cotton. The large beds, once covered in lavish sheets, are now empty and barren. The carpet with the enormous insignia of the Sunborn remains smeared with the blood of Jaina and Edward. Pyke requests the removal of the carpet, but I have instructed that it stay in the room as a reminder of my conquest. The sun, which encompassed the once golden emblem, is now a dark and dull umber. At times, I glare at this sun and I experience an out of body sensation which brings me back to the night when Edward's tongue was hammered like a bloody and limp piece of meat. The night my dagger struck Gwyneth's beating heart, ripping into her chest as the blood trickled onto the luminescent carpet. The sun itself bleeds for the noble Sunborn clan.

Since their murder, the clouds have sealed the sun from Apollon, drastically shortening the days. I prefer the new atmosphere, but others are less than pleased with the sudden change in scenery. *No matter. It suits the new Lord who rules these lands;* the sinister voice would stir within me. I nod my approval. Farmers, fisherman, hunters and gardeners have all filed complaints to the guards, but it falls on deaf ears. There is vast belief that God is punishing Apollon for the scandalous events leading to the murder of the Sunborn clan by their own family.

Pyke continues to plea for me to have the object removed, since it reminds him of the dastardly deeds we committed. He feels as though it will also upset any former Sunborn support and increase the difficulty of recruiting a new regime. Those sanctimonious bastards can keep their loyalties and allegiance to whomever they like. Only the strong and unquestionably corrupt will serve my kingdom. One thing I have learned from serving my former Masters is that the most powerful pawns are the ones who are wicked, evil and without morals yet unquestioning and brainwashed to their ideologies and goals.

Alas, after days of jabbering in my ear I came to a compromise with Pyke before I succumbed to the urge of killing the fat lard. Since the blood is a symbol of a triumphant moment for me, I would not remove the rug. Instead, I had Timber furnish a large oak table to cover a large portion of the stain. It is a magnificent sight to behold, with jewels streamed along the four sides of the table, a sequential pattern of rubies, and onyx flowing from one end to the next. Two black runners hang on each side with the new insignia of this castle stitched in the centre of the fabric. Covering the center of the table is a large replica image of the *Silent Sisters*. The daggers look exquisite and remarkably identical to the two which hang from my sides. From the detailed dragon heads and ruby casings, to the golden hilts and onyx blades, this is one of the talented blacksmiths finest creations. But as beautiful and fitting as this table for my new abode, it is also the cause for long, mundane days of placing ink to paper. Being a Duke has too many political duties and penmanship responsibilities for my liking.

Once a day, the Master of Coin climbs my tower, heaving and puffing. He staggers over to my desk, winded, and carefully piles a stack of documents, which are either decrees of allegiances from other provinces and nations or simple parchments from the local townsfolk. The latter mostly consist of pleas from farmers or small market owners, asking for my blessing and for exemption from the tax increase recently changed by Pyke. Pyke would read the letters while I barely listen and each time the topic of the tax hike is mentioned, I would notice a foolish smirk appear on his face.

A simple signature with a stroke of ink is required for me to place judgement on Apollon, though I prefer the use of my daggers. I care not about the snivelling beggars and their petty lives. My goal is simple: kill those who took everything from me. Soon I will have an army large enough to compete with *them*. There is one place where I can sate my pleasure for destruction, and that is in the dungeons with Timber as he tortures treacherous nobles who oppose me or have declared to wage wars upon my rule. The goal is not just to punish these prisoners, but more importantly to gather information on the Assassin's Guild. So far all those who have been tortured do not have the slightest clue of their existence, but I am convinced there has to be a connection to the nobles of Thalia and the Assassin's Guild. I have given Timber the freedom to do what he must in order to break their will until they speak the truth. Despite this, pleading and bribery seem to be all his victims offer before Timber disembowels their organs and melts their bones in the pits of his flame-filled cauldron. The mute is instructed to disrupt me only if one of his victims speaks of the Assassin's Guild though I can clearly hear their agony and screams from the basement to the fifth floor of my chamber. The noises are a melody to my ears and sometimes they re-awaken the evil inside.

Standing near my window, I watch as the clouds continue to darken the sky and I hear the ever annoying wheezing of my Master of Coin approach the chamber doors. He raises his hand to knock on my door ever so lightly. "Come in, Pyke," I respond reluctantly. The buffoon pushes the door open with one meaty hand as the other rests on his knee to support his beefy body.

"What news do you bring me today?" I ask.

Pyke raises his free hand and waves it left and right, indicating that he needs time to catch his breath. Annoyed, I say, "One day, your weight will be your undoing. Take your time, I will have a seat and whenever you feel that my time is more important than yours, then you may speak." I walk over to the oak table and have a seat.

Why do you deal with this stupidity each and every day? The voice asks.

Pyke may be a grotesque sight to the eyes but he

is trustworthy and has his uses, I answer.

"Perhaps we should put you on the training fields with the other soldiers until you are fit to climb a measly five floors," I tease.

That notion brings his torso to a vertical position. He takes a deep breath in and exhales loudly as drool exits the side of his mouth. This annoys me most about the man. He has a never-ending supply of saliva. "I pray that was a joke, Lord Payne," he says in a raspy, dry voice. "May I please have a glass of water? I fear that I may be of no use without a voice."

You are barely a use now, the voice snickers in my head.

I sigh and pour him a cup of cool water and sit back down. He slowly waddles towards it and with one large loud gulp, inhales the liquid.

"Ahhhh, refreshing," he says while wiping the drool from his mouth. He spilled half the water on his outfit. "Thank you, my Lord." I remain in my chair staring at him with disgust and impatience. Realizing my glare, he yelps an apology and begins his task.

"We have letters from Destonia, our

neighbours in the northwest, as well letters from your scouts deployed for recruitment and those seeking the whereabouts of Marcus and Liza. Which shall we begin with?" He asks knowing full well my answer.

"Begin with the scouts seeking Marcus and Liza."

"Very well," he mutters. "According to our scouts, there were horse tracks heading southwest. The stable boy confirmed that two horses went missing the night that Marcus and Liza escaped. Amidst all the rain and mud, the scouts followed the faint trail to an inn which once *used* to be owned by an old man and his fat wife," he read. Pausing for a second, he looks up with an obscene grin, hoping I caught onto the key word in his parchment.

"They denied seeing anybody until the very end. Even as your scouts cut the bacon off of the pig, she would not squeal. Her husband attempted to grow a backbone so he lost his head. The last thing she cried was, 'Long live the Sunborn' before her bloody flesh was burnt in front of her inn," Pyke laughs as he read the report, as if he finished a very humorous anecdote.

They will never accept you as their ruler, the

voice taunts. *Kill them all and be done with this world.*

As frustrating and infuriating as the entity inside me can be, it does pose a valid point. Outrage spills across Thalia as word spreads of my ascension to Duke. Many nobles think it a travesty that someone with lowborne blood is ruling a house as acclaimed and respected as *The Guiding Light*. Furthermore, many believe it sacrilegious that I renamed this castle to *Castle Eclipse*. The bloody Sunborn clan are revered as Gods in Apollon. All the bards in Thalia sing songs of the sun itself giving birth to an avatar, one which we humans call Edwin Sunborn. The fabled tale claims the Sun watched humans turn to greed and violence as the world was in turmoil. The Sun wanted to intervene, but its power was too vast and destructive. If the Sun attempted to purge greed and violence from the world, then it would also take with it the innocent and good that were caught in the middle of the power struggle. Therefore it gave birth to Edwin Sunborn, said to be a titan of a man, who built Apollon with his bare hands. He was a simple blacksmith and carpenter but those who knew him treated and basked at him as a God. When the rebellion came, it was Edwin who led the revolt against the criminals and brought justice and peace back to Apollon. Now the nobles watch as I desecrate the very existence of everything the Sunborns once were.

You do it for the sake of vengeance, the voice reminds me eerily. "For justice", I reply aloud, forgetting that Pyke is in the room.

"Justice?" asks Pyke suspiciously. "I agree that killing the two innkeepers is justice in your world, my Lord".

He mistakes my comment with his former remark but it works in my favour. I nod and ask, "What takes them southwest of Apollon?"

"Memories," he answers as he lifts his head up to give me a look of satisfaction.

"Memories… what are you talking about, you fool? Stop speaking in riddles and answer me. What lies southwest of Apollon?" I ask again impatiently.

"Where it all began," he says with a whisper as drool ran down the side of his face.

I hate the fat fuck. Gut him and let us find another plaything who knows how to obey, the voice demands.

Ignoring the noise in my mind, it suddenly

came together. I cannot help but laugh, which startles Pyke.

"I give the woman more credit than she deserves," I proclaim mockingly. "She has been residing in Nasgrath with Marcus and likely has taken sanctuary with a noble banner man who owes allegiance to the Edward Sunborn. Send all our scouts there immediately and stop any rumours of his existence. The last thing we need is word of Marcus Sunborn being alive and well. When they are located, make sure we kill the nobles who have assisted them and Marcus, but leave Liza alive. I will do the punishing myself. Is that understood?"

"Understood," Pyke answer. "Shall I give you the news of Destonia?"

"Go on, but be quick. I grow weary of listening to what these bastard nobles have to say about my rule."

"You may be happily surprised with the results this time," Pyke confidently remarks. "This letter does not come from the Lord Gaston Fate, but from his Chancellor. He seems to have grown tired of serving Lord Fate and wishes to move up in the ranks."

I sigh with disbelief. "What does the treacherous worm request?"

"Lord Fate grows old and frail, and has no children to his name. His wife was unable to bear him any children, and thus he has no heir. Yet Lord Fate wants to give the rule to his soon-to-be of age nephew."

"So the worthless scum would like us to kill the nephew, I presume?" I ask rhetorically. "How will this benefit me?"

Pyke continues. "When he gains control of Castle Fate, he will fully pledge his armies and banner under Castle Eclipse. The army has two thousand strong and are trained by the finest in the north."

"The finest in the north only tells me that they will need to be retrained," I chuckle. "Yet, an additional two thousand men sounds appealing. What makes him think that they would follow his lead so easily?"

"Castle Fate is very superstitious, as are all the members within its ranks," Pyke explains. "Their belief is simple and archaic. Everyone in Destonia believes that life is predetermined from birth and that God paves their path and destiny.

No one fights their rank, their prestige and their roles. The concept of Fate controls their lives and actions. Soldiers serving the head of the house also deem the Lord as their God, destined to lead and command them to their dying breath, hence the name of their land, Destonia." Pyke rolls the parchment up and places it back into his doublet. "Shall I command some of your less than 'virtuous' guards to handle the situation?"

"No, leave this to me. This requires precision and expertise that none of my sell swords and cut throats possess. Besides, I need to leave this hovel before my mind leaves me."

Is it my turn to come out and play? The voice asks.

I can do this on my own, I tell it. *You are too rash and bloodthirsty; your actions would only raise suspicion.*

My blood thirst is what allowed you to survive this long.

I ignore the voice as I wave my hand in a dismissal manner.

One day, I will be the one in control and there will no longer be a need for this farce. Everything will die, even you, Payne, the voice rings in my head for a few seconds until it finally fades.

CHAPTER EIGHTEEN
OLD MAN VENOM BOLT

I cannot recall the last time I disembarked on duty, leaving behind the Holy City of Saint Aran. I believe two decades have passed, though at my age time becomes irrelevant. Now I set sail across the ocean on my final and perhaps most important mission: to bring justice to my former student, Dark Heart. Nasgrath seems to be the first viable location to investigate, as that is where his persona changed. The day he lay with that wench is the same day something changed within him. He no longer wanted to serve our cause or be a tool of justice for our Masters. Everything I trained him to become had almost instantly disintegrated. He did not even reply to his name, and I questioned him about the arguments he was constantly having with himself. Perhaps he was facing his past as I have recently been doing.

He was my finest pupil but the Masters warned me about Dark Heart; they professed feeling an evil within him that was unnatural. But not since my time had someone been so deadly in the dark arts. I heeded my Masters' advice and kept a close eye on him, but as I spent more time with him I began to forget their warnings and grew fond of the boy as a son. I admired him not only for his abilities, but for his determination to rid this world of evil and his undying loyalty to our Masters. The Dark Heart I knew should have been able to defeat me during our confrontation the night I left him with a scar, yet here I stand. Something was different about him. He did not seem to possess that same intensity or confidence. His aura did not feel as menacing. *Has he forgotten who he was?* I ask myself.

My hand covers my face as I shake my head. *Impossible. No one ever has ever come back from the identity wipe.* Yet as of late, I have been reminiscing of a time too long forgotten. I have even started to remember the faces of those who once were a part of my previous life. *You are Venom Bolt. Do not forget it,* a voice hisses in my mind. *Yes,* I reply. *That is who I am, who I have been, and who I always will be.*

Metallic creaks resonate in the dark room of my cabin as the ship enters shaky waters. The ship rock violently as the water crashes against the stern and pours on deck. It reeks of fish, spices and vegetables. A supply ship by trade, it delivers goods to Nasgrath regularly and seems to be the fastest ship to do so. Travel from Saint Aran to Nasgrath is five fortnights sail east. The ship is large enough to hold twenty passengers, the crew, as well as a fair amount of cargo.

The Captain of the ship is a grizzly man by the name of Nomad Highsea. He wears a blue bandana to conceal what remains of his balding head, a grey jacket, white undershirt, brown belt, blue slacks and long leather boots. A bottle of wine always rests in his slimy and wet hands. Drinking is as much a part of his life as sailing. His most prominent feature is his long black beard, which is braided in various knots and colours. He has been growing it since the day his chin sprouted its first hairs. Each knot and colour represents the various regions of Thalia that he has sailed to. The top braid is white, representing the Holy City of Saint Aran. Next to it is a purple braid signifying the colour of Castle Mane, known for their Lord who loves breeding horses. The shades are endless, as is the length and width of his beard reaching his knees. When he was chattering about what each colour represented, he pointed at the brown strand and told me it is what he chose to represent Nasgrath. Brown is the perfect colour, as it represented the shit and filth populating Nasgrath.

The Captain demanded a hefty fee to have

me as a passenger. Ten gold pieces is enough to travel thrice to Nasgrath from Saint Aran but he ensured me that he has the fastest and safest boat in all of Thalia. Pirates are notorious in these waters, as Saint Aran and Castle Mane are the only two provinces on the small islands; anyone caught by pirates would find no assistance from other fleets. Between each of these islands, there is nothing more than vast amounts of blue water spanning as far as the eye can see. The Captain assures me that no pirate has ever dared to board his ship.

"The crew and its Captain are known throughout the lands as the most fearsome and deadly trading cargo ship," the Captain brags. "All of my crewmates are trained ex-mercenaries, har har har," he laughs as he attempts to justify charging such a ludicrous amount of gold. Ultimately, I paid the fee only because it was the first ship leaving to my intended destination. Money has never been an obstacle though time is a whole different matter. Time is the one thing I can never recover. *I must complete this mission before time takes from me what no other can: my life.* I feel death's grip tightening around my neck each day, waiting for time to take its toll before it comes for me.

Three days pass since we set sail and there

has been no sign of life, save for the seagulls flocking over our heads. Staying within the quarters that the Captain provided, I take the time to meditate, thinking back to my experiences in Nasgrath and the locations best suited for Dark Heart to find sanctuary. He is not one to be careless, but perhaps the woman has changed him. Maybe he lives a normal life and has even become a father. Perhaps I can turn a blind eye if I see he has turned to a life of fatherhood and houses a family.

No, he will be killed by your hands, hisses the voice in my head. *You failed to do it last time and failed our Masters. Venom Bolt does not fail,* it reminds me. I agree with my persona and recite the words of our order. *Habitamus in tenebris, we live in darkness.* No one can know of our existence and he has lived without a trace for over 10 years. *I must find him before we are exposed and end the grief this has caused the Masters.*

My thoughts are interrupted by the sound of Nomad Highsea's leather boots stomping towards my cabin. Although my appearance has deteriorated over the years, my hearing has never failed me. I cover my head with the black hood attached to my tunic, hoping that he would leave me. But knowing the Captain, this would be asking too much.

Nomad's drinking becomes most excessive after the sunset. A complete metamorphosis occurs, turning the stable and ever-confident Captain to the blundering oaf that he becomes once mead takes over. His crew sends him on his way once when they realize he no longer can navigate the ship and his deck hand commanders the ship and navigation until the Captain is himself again. Lately, I have the "pleasure" of his company.

The cabin door begins to *creak* as it opens slowly and a bearded figure peeks through the door. I do not turn my head to face him, but I use my peripherals and realize that the Captain has a ridiculous smile on his face exposing his missing teeth and bruised gums. Even outfitted in a fully black cloak and hood with brown leather pants in a barely lit room, he seems to find me. His eyes open with excitement and slams the door open as it smashes against the wooden wall and bounces back into him. The fool is knocked back and I relish the seconds of peace I have until he tries again. This time, he opens the door cautiously and yells, "Old man! Have you been here the whole time?! Why do you refuse to join our merry company on deck and instead stay here by your lonesome? There is so much to see out in the ocean." I ignore him but he continues forward. "So be it, I will be your company again tonight!" He sits next to me, his shadow towering over my body and his beard resting on the damp wooden floor. The smell of wine fills the air as the aroma of grapes, pears, spices and honey surround us. Nomad places the cup in front of me, offering some of his drink. "I appreciate the hospitality but I have not drank for years and I shall continue that tradition, if I may," I say as I continue staring ahead.

"Perhaps that is why your beard and hair are white as snow, old man, har har har," he claims as his bellowing laughter booms throughout the room. The smell of wine on his breath and the cabin bring back blurred memories of my youth, when I was a foolish noble with nothing to lose and everything to gain. My nose has not caught the scent of alcohol for ages. It has almost become non-existent to me, as the Guild of Assassin's does not permit sinful activity such as drinking.

"Fine", he sighs. "If you shall not have drink with me, then tell me about yourself, old man. Someone your age should have some stories to tell," the drunken Captain remarks.

"I did not pay to keep you company or to tell you about myself," I reply bitterly. "Our agreement is to get me to Nasgrath safely and that is what I expect from our arrangement."

"Bah! No gold can buy friendship and company such as mine, old man," the Captain smacks his chest with pride. After a few seconds of blissful silence, he says, "So be it, I will then tell you about myself and my adventures. I am sure they will amaze and surprise you. Perhaps THEN you will share something about yourself."

Ignoring the Captain's voice as it ricochets off the cabin walls, my thoughts drift to how my final task would unfold. Every scenario plays out in my mind. Focusing on the failures first, I think about all the ways that this mission would be the end of me and learn from the possible mistakes, finding ways to eliminate error. The success of every duty comes from understanding the strengths of your enemy. Dark Heart has been an enigma for all these years. Even my Masters, with their vast knowledge and reach in Thalia, have not seen or heard of his whereabouts. This is where my mission differs from the rest. In every case, we would have the element of surprise and knowledge of the situation and the target - from their whereabouts, to their family, weaknesses and strengths, and their routines. But this target is different; he knows more of us then we know of him. This is the reason why I have been chosen to stop the biggest threat ever to face my Masters. One thing is certain: his biggest weakness will be Liza and his child, if one even exists. She will be his downfall. My venom will drown them both.

The Captain carries on with his stories until he is interrupted by frantic footsteps in our direction. The wooden door swings open as one of the crew members pushes the door open. His face is drenched in water and he is panting heavily as if he just swam across the ocean and back. Nomad turns and stares puzzled at the man standing at the door. Raising his cup high, sounding annoyed, he asks, "What is the matter?"

"Captain, pirates! There are pirates approaching our deck! They demand to see you right now!" he exclaims.

"Huh?" The Captain says stupefied. "Pirates? What are pirates doing out here? More importantly, do they know whose ship this is?"

"Yes, Captain. I have professed your name and all they did was spit on our vessel and laugh."

"You promised no problems and safe passage, Captain," I remind the Captain as I give him a cold stare. "If you delay or do not rid these pirates from your ship, then I will be asking for a third of my gold back."

"It will be handled. Do not worry, old man. Just stay in the cabin and out of harm's way, and let the mighty Nomad Highsea handle everything," he proclaims in a drunken yet proud voice.

The Captain leaves the cabin to confront the pirates and I do as I am asked. *You only have one goal. Do not interfere with this nonsense,* the voice in my mind demands.

The door remains open and I turn my head to peer through the opening. Twelve of the Captain's men are standing in a horizontal line with their hands gripping the sheathed swords on their belts. The pirate Captain is standing on his ship, leg on the mast and a wide grin showing years of corrosion within his mouth. His teeth are corroded and jagged with pieces missing in various places and his gums are a dark purple. He is decorated in a green coloured tricorne on his head, a blue jacket, tanned belt which holds his fencing sword, blue pants which only reach his ankles, exposing chaffed and bruised ankles and dark shoes cover his feet.

"Captain Nomad Highsea," the pirate calls out. "I am Blunder Deepblue, Captain of the Kraken Elite and dread of the three oceans. You have the unfortunate mishap of sailing in our waters. We only request your gold, your goods, and your ship. We leave you with your lives but you will have to swim to safety and from the looks of it, you will not make it very far with this rag tag crew, bahahahaha," he laughs with the rest the pirates following his lead. "Please, be quick and quiet about it. Or else we do prefer the violent way."

"We have nothing of interest on our ship," Nomad Highsea claims. "Our goods are gathered in Nasgrath and delivered to the Holy City of Saint Aran. You and your crew are threatening an empty ship. I will provide you with what gold we have, but first you must promise us safe passage."

The pirate strokes his cheek and removes his sword from its holder. "Do not lie to me, Nomad Highsea," he taunts. "My men are hungry and we know that you possess food onboard. The wonderful smell of fish fills the air and our noses can smell it coming from your ship. So how about we give you death and take your gold and fish," the Captain threatens as he smiles an evil smirk.

The men behind him roar in approval. I examine the men on our ship and can tell from their reaction that Nomad was exaggerating about his ship crew. Most are shaking at the idea of a battle and the ones who are steady look too seasoned to do battle with the pirates. These men are as much mercenaries, as feeder fish are sharks. The pirates will kill each and everyone one of Nomad's crew.

Do not interfere old man, I am reminded again.

If I do not, then it will delay our mission, I reply to the voice. *If I remove their Captain, the rest of the pirates will fear this ship and most likely leave.*

What if they do not? Do you plan to fight all of those men?

I nod and swing the door open as all eyes turn to me. My hood covers my face; I do not wish to reveal myself. I take slow and frail steps so as to not alarm anyone. Captain Nomad turns to me and says, "Old man, I cannot protect you if are on deck. Return back to the cabin until we have finished dealing with these lowly pirates." Brushing off the advice given by the Captain, I continue casually lingering to the center of the deck.

"I suggest you listen to your Captain, old man," Blunder Deepblue agrees. "This is no place for the meek and frail. Your time will come without having your throat slit by my men. Your mortality seems to be at its end by the looks of it, bahahahaha," he laughs insultingly.

Make it quick. These fools do not deserve death by one such as us, the voice tells me.

"Leave this ship immediately," I warn the pirates. The opposing ships laughter is even louder now and the pirates begin spitting and pointing their swords at us in amusement.

Finish this now, the voice commands in a sinister tone.

I reach behind my cloak and in an instant remove my crossbow which is attached to my back. It is already loaded with three arrows all aiming right at Blunder Deepblue's direction. While they are all busy mockingly laughing, I release all 3 arrows. In an instant, all laughter ceases and the only noise coming from the pirate ship is the sound of choking and gasps. All three arrows impale different locations. The first penetrated through Captain Deepblue's jugular, the second through his mouth and the last in his only good eye. His body instantly falls backwards onto his ship; the rest of his crew can now witness their fate if they wished to challenge me. There is a moment of disbelief.

"I will not repeat myself. Leave us be before the rest of your crew meets the same untimely fate as your Captain," I threaten.

Disgruntled and confused, they quickly gather themselves and raise their bridge off our ship before sailing away. Our ship is in equal shock and awe from what has transpired minutes ago. The silence quickly transforms to cheer, as the men comprehend their safety. Nomad stumbles over and lays his sweaty hand on my shoulder and shakes me. He has a smile that spans from ear to ear.

"The payment that you made for the travel will be returned in full, old man. You are a hero to this ship and will always be welcome," claims the Captain. I nod with appreciation and head back to the cabin to continue my meditation. *Soon enough, that will be the fate that Dark Heart will face,* the voice convincingly says.

I grunt and sit back down on the floor to begin my meditation for the remainder of the voyage. The Captain should not interfere any longer unless I request clean water to quench my thirst and food to satisfy my hunger.

Two days pass and I finally break meditation. I have dismissed all human emotions and am ready to complete what I have journeyed to do. The Captain approaches my cabin and informs me that the ship is now being anchored to the port and places the gold back in front of me. I open the sack and toss half the gold to the Captain. He catches the gold in the air and thanks me. Lifting myself to my feet, I feel my back is stiff and my joints hurt. I may be able to forgo all of my human emotions but my body does not cease to remind me of my aging. I step outside the cabin and the sunrays burn my eyes. I have been secluded in darkness for two days straight, but I sense I have finally arrived. The mixture of shit and dirt hovers in the air and invades my nose. *Nasgrath. The stench of death will soon cover this town,* I think as I disembark from the ship.

304

PART III

CHAPTER NINETEEN
ARTHUR LOWBORNE

My feet keep moving but my mind is stranded in one place. The agonizing scream that emanated from within the crowded circle surrounding Katherine continues to haunt me as I rapidly move down the murky slum alley. It sounded as if the fruit she ate was devouring her flesh from the inside out. The small distraction of the heat from the dirt ground was my only saving grace. I would rather have the soles of my feet burned and the jagged rocks, wood and glass stick to my heels than to think of the shame of leaving behind my only family. Inevitably, my focus turns to the pain shooting through my legs. My breathing is heavy but I keep up my pace for the fear of being caught. The stolen coin purse begins to weigh on my mind and body the more I think about Katherine and how I abandoned her. When I first snatched the coin purse, I barely felt the burden as the excitement and thrill of success surged through me but now that the feeling has subsided, I feel like a boulder is weighing me down. I look back to make sure no one is following me. The emptiness of these alleyways are common before sundown and I want to ensure that I make it back to our hovel before the sunsets as thieves and bandits lie waiting in the darkness. The sun's presence is starting to dissipate as the sky turns a bright orange. Soon, the darkness will devour the bright blue sky and that is when I would be safe. As the market disappears from my sight, it took with it the smell of fruits, vegetables, baked bread and all of the delicacies and replaced those pleasantries with shit, dust and body odour. But a sense of reassurance fills my heart and for the first time I am happy to see the slums. My hand reaches in my pocket to ensure that my dagger still resides hidden within my pants. I feel the dull blade against my skin and feel an overwhelming feeling of security. Amongst the decay and debris, the slums are full of unpredictable degenerates who will kill any unwary, unfortunate soul having anything worth stealing.

Paranoid and unnerved as the sun sets, I begin to sense eyes peering from various corners and crevices of the woods as if cave bats were waking from their slumber. These bats however, have hands and feet with an insatiable hunger for money and food. The thrill and security which comforted me earlier has turned to a sense of fear and caution. My hand instinctively pulls the pocket knife out of my pants and I continue to run with it by my side. Suddenly, I notice my heartbeat increase and my breathing becomes heavy and audible. My eyes squint as dust flings in the air and blurs my vision and the suffocating heat amplifies the already unbearable stink. Our wooden shack and grass stands at the far end of the slums close to the forest. *A little further*, I tell myself. I am so caught up with the idea of getting back safely that I do not realize the sudden appearance of thick wooden log being swung in my direction. Again, I naturally react as I drop to my knees and slide on the rough surface, scraping and bloodying them along the way. Cat like; I jump to my feet and turn to face the culprit who tried to bash my head in with the piece of lumber. The swing sent the assailant forward and stumbling.

"You missed, idiot", a voice calls out behind me.

A butch, pimple covered boy waddles over from the dark alley to the side of the stumbling attacker. He is also holding a blunt piece of wood with a few rusty nails attached to them. He points ahead of me and waves his chubby hands over. Two slim built boys, who were no older than the age of seven, slither out from behind a grass home. They did not possess weapons and are likely here to intimidate by outnumbering their opponent. The boy who originally swung, finally regains his footing and stands beside the two boys with slumped shoulders and a frown.

"What is the meaning of this?" I demand. I shift my body and slide the coin purse from my rope belt into my pocket, trying to be inconspicuous. Unfortunately, one of the younger boys watched my action and points his finger towards my pocket.

"Gus... Gu...Gust...Gustav," he stutters while his hand shook violently. My attention turns to the stuttering boy and glare at him with anger. He is covered in black soot from head to toe. His ribs concave through his half-ripped long sleeve shirt. Skinny cheeks rub against his mouth and I can see the outline of his jaw as he moves his mouth. His teeth are sharp and spaced awkwardly and his eye lids barely remain open. If it was not for his movement and speech, I would have thought him to be asleep. He resembles more a skeletal figure than a human. "He just put something in his pocket, Gustav. I think he is hi.. hiiii... hiiidddening something of worth."

"Is that so Flynn?" Gustav grins as his greedy eyes lurk towards the sack of gold occupying my pocket. "What is the hurry? Is your mother going to beat you if you don't make it home on time?" he taunts with a laugh which mimics that swine snorting.

"Yeah, is your mother going to beat you?" The one holding the weapon repeats.

"I hate it when you repeat what I say, Argo!" yells Gustav. Argo quickly turns his smile into a frown again. Gustav returns his attention back my way.

This one is definitely their leader, I tell myself. Pimples and warts cover the boy's face and scale down to his arms and feet. Some of the pimples are bloody and pus is oozing from his cheeks. Deep scars are mapped all over his face. He scratches at his saggy chest with one arm and holds his log with the other. His once white shirt is now brown and red from dirt and dry blood. "I said… What is your hurry?" he repeats his question.

Without hesitation I reply, "Get out of my way and all of your lives will be spared." Both Gustav and Argo burst out laughing, one sounding like a pig and the other like a weasel.

"Did you hear that boys? He will spare OUR lives if we move!" Gustav exclaims in a cocky and belittling tone.

"Yeah, spare our lives!" Argo echoes in a similar tone. Gustav grabs a deformed rock from the ground and tosses it past me trying to hit Argo. Instead of hitting its intended target, the rock unexpectedly flings towards Flynn and pounds him on the forehead, nearly toppling him over. The young boy who appeared with Flynn snatches him by the wrist and holds him steady while Flynn attempts to recuperate. The trickles of blood gush from the gash above his raggedy hair. Flynn's hand begins to shake uncontrollably and his eyes are full of tears. Argo tries to aid him as well but subsides as soon as Gustav yells, "Don't even think about moving Argo! Let the baby cry and bleed. There is no room for the weak in our group." Argo's face turns pale as he keeps turning his head towards Gustav and Flynn, thinking of what he should do. Ultimately, he stays planted and did as he was commanded to do, like a dog obeying his master. It is despicable.

"Do you not care for your friends?" I ask. "He needs aid, some stitches or medication. If that gash were to become infected, there would be no way of finding him a priest or doctor to heal it."

"Stitches? Medication?" Questions Gustav, as he snickers with a repulsive snort. "Where are you from? We can barely afford bread and clean water and you want me to find him stitches and medication? Let him die, one less bastard to contend with. These are MY dogs and pawns. If they cannot obey or do simple tasks such as taking down a little shit like you, then they deserve to die," he proclaims in a sinister tone.

At that moment, something came over me. My eyes widen and my heart feels as though it is beating like a hundred drums and everything turns black. It is, as if something…no… someone took hold of my body and soul and all I could do is watch helplessly from a distance. My mind is still intact and I want to reason with my body but it is too late. I lunge at Gustav, both hands around his wide throat. He is completely unprepared for my attack and stumbles backwards, falling on the dirt with a loud *thud* as his head meets with the unforgiving ground. The weapon which he held is now to his side and his hands are busy trying to pry me off his neck. I squeeze with all my might as Gustav turns a bright pink. His cheeks swell and he squeals while fighting for air but to no avail. More than ever, he resembled a pig. Something inside tells me to stop but I cannot. This felt right but wrong at the same time but the urge to punish took over my sense of right and wrong. I want nothing more than to kill this boy. He reminds me of Payne with his lack of regard for others, only using them as pawns in his schemes to better himself. *This was how it has to be. It starts with this poor excuse for a human being,* I convince myself. Marcus was calm, collected, and noble using what skill he had in battle only for defensive measures. That was what his noble father had thought him.   Arthur is different. He is a survivor, merciless and cunning and right now, I want to be him. Gustav's eyes start to roll back until only white is visible. His struggling has also subsided and his hands loosen from their grip on my forearms. An unintentional smile forms on my lips. I am enjoying this. My fingers tighten as hard as they humanly can. *A few more seconds and it will be over,* I think triumphantly. I am so caught up with the task at hand that I did not realize two pairs of boney hands have wrapped themselves around my chest instantly. Argo and Flynn are pulling with what strength they could muster and suddenly I find my grip loosening. "Why?!" I scream as I attempt to grasp onto Gustav. "Why would you help this shit, when he would just watch you die if you were in his place?!" They did not bother answering and instead they heaved even harder than before. My hands could no longer handle the pressure. In a blind rage, I quickly let go of Gustav and fling my elbows left and right, knocking both Argo and Flynn off my back. My urge to kill every one of them intensifies and that is exactly what I am going to do.

The dagger lies still on the ground covered in debris and mud. I walk over and lift it off the ground and take hold of it and callously start lurking towards Argo. It was only fitting that I dispose of him first as he tried to do the same to me. Argo holds his mouth as blood rushes from it. He spits out a few teeth that I managed to elbow and fearfully crawls backwards, pleading for his life. His pleas only enrage me. *Stop! This is not how to handle this situation! You have proven that you are a better fighter than these fools. Stop this now!* A voice deep within my mind begs. I stand still for a few seconds, staring at my hands. One is holding a dagger so tightly that it feels as if it is an extension of my arm. The other is full of blood and spit from Gustav. *What am I becoming?* I ask myself. Before I could think any further, Flynn had the opportunity to pick up the log and swing at the back of my head, knocking me to the ground. I lost my sanity and went berserk. Without hesitation, I rise in anger and thrust my knife into his stomach with full force. We both hit the ground but I am the only one who got up. Argo came at me next and only found the sharp end of my dagger slicing his throat instantly. He drops gasping for air as bloods spills from his open wound. Gustav is still unconscious but not dead. I wanted to change that. The voice of reason which once enter my thoughts is now all but gone. My head pounds with pain and rage and I feel the veins of my temple pulsate. As I approach his helpless body, I could not help but picture him as Payne. The anger inside me boils as both hands gripped my dagger and bring it down with blinding speed into his heart. Gustav squeals one last time before the light vanishes from his eyes. Only one remains.

He stood staring at everything transpiring without flinching or running. He did not speak, shiver, nor move. All he did was gaze at me without any emotion. I pluck my dagger out of Gustav's body and watch as a fountain of red liquid pours from the puncture I made in his overweight body. Once I had my fill, I turn my attention towards the boy. There is no fear in his eyes and that must change. I extend my dagger in his direction, point and begin to move for the kill like a predator finding his prey. He continues to stare in my direction, this time his mouth opens yet he makes no sound. I pick up my speed and am an inch from driving my blade into his eyes but a familiar voice yells out, "ARTHUR! STOP!"

This voice did not come from my head this time but in the distance. My knife finds itself a fingers length away from the boy's eye. I hold my knife close to his face and the hand not holding the dagger holds my attack hand back. I shake uncontrollably and am holding my breath. I feel as if my body has been possessed by a demonic entity. Regaining my senses, I drop my dagger and pull my hand back as I continue to shake. My conscience returns and I finally realize what I have committed. Falling to my knees, I put my hands on my hair and pull, screaming in denial. I cannot believe I am transforming into the man I despise more than anything. It is as Payne said the final time we trained, "maybe I should be calling you *Young Dark Heart.*" I finally understand the darkness he referred to.

CHAPTER TWENTY
KATHERINE LOWBORNE

Never have so many emotions run through me in a mere few hours. I suffered unfathomable pain from an unexpected public child birth, lost more blood and endured more pain than I could possibly imagine, witnessed the father of my child take my life only to have it be a hallucination, and then when I was freed from that nightmare I was given the one thing I desired more than anything, a new born daughter. *A perfect addition to our small family,* I think as I hold my child in awe. She is so frail and small. Her eyes remain closed but her other features are a mix of myself and her father's. She has her father's slender nose and traces of dark string like hair. Her skin is darker than most natives in Thalia, so she has inherited that from me. Her little chubby fingers moved without rhythm or purpose. I recall when Marcus was born and how he cried excessively and moved his little baby parts uncontrollably. She is different though. For someone who was brought into the world in the harshest of environments, she is oddly at peace. *Perhaps she inherited her mother's will,* I pray. I am handed a raggedy blanket to cover her body and protect her from the sun. Unaware that the crowd is still surrounding me and whispering to one another, I remain perched against a massive guard which stood protectively watching over me. I was leaning against his legs and he did not flinch. He just stared into the crowd with a stalwart demeanor. His duty came first and right now it was to protect my baby and I from harm.

I sit a while longer, absorbing the newfound idea of being a mother but at the same time I realize something was missing. Marcus is nowhere to be seen. I pray that nothing happened to him during this ordeal. There were many people present to witness my childbirth and it would have been just as easy for him to be caught as it was for him to escape. I need to return to the slums to make sure that he is safe. Once I am able to move, I pat the soldier on the leg and he looks down at me and nods. The large guard bends over and grabs me by the waist and lifts me to my feet with utter ease. The other guards finally manage to disperse the crowd once everyone had their share of gossip. A story I am sure which they will tell everyone in town. When the streets finally empty, the guard turns to me and says, "it is my sworn duty to get you home safely my Lady. Can you manage the trek?" I nod but did not take my stare off my child.

He looks at the other guards and yells, "You are all dismissed. If the Captain Commander requests a briefing, let him know I will provide one upon my return." The other guards salute with a pound to their chest and return to their post. The guard did not ask or question where I live but if he knew it is the slums perhaps he would not bother escorting me home. With that doubt in mind, I decide to keep that information to myself and gladly take his offer. He extends his hand to mine and lifts me to my feet with ease. I realize that Magda has been watching over me the entire time. I smile in her direction and she returns the gesture. "This old lady will be accompanying you as well," She says. "You are in no shape to be making this journey home and this is no place for a child either."

By the time we leave the marketplace, the sun was already setting beneath the mountains of Thalia. Any mother would normally rest after giving birth in order to allow the scars and rips to heal naturally but in my case I could not afford the time or gold for that service. Magda did her best to heal me for the journey but I fear it was not enough. The longer we walk the more I can feel my stitches unravel. Moments into our march towards the slums, blood begins sliding down the inside of my thigh and makes its way to my ankle. I gather all of my strength and continue moving forward with an uncomfortable limp. I hold onto my daughter as securely as I can and whisper in her tiny ears, "I will never let you go," and kiss her forehead. "Soon, you will meet your brother and we will name you together, as a family."

As we approach the slums, a rancid smell invades our nostrils as the marketplace vanishes and the wasteland comes into view. Even my newborn becomes irritated and begins to show signs of discomfort but that quickly subsides as I place kisses on her cheeks and sing softly in her ear. The last thing I want to do is rouse suspicion in the slums. People have no sympathy for newborns, children or women. I am thankful that the massive guard decided to escort us home although his emotionless expression has changed to that of disgust. He did not expect someone dressed the way I am today to be living in this sty. I peek at Magda and see her struggling to land her wooden cane on the uneven and mucky ground. Her support has now turned into a handicap in the slums but she did not show any sign of discomfort. *What a strong woman,* I praise her in my mind.

The stitches continue to rip steadily and the idea of string ripping my skin causes me to feel ill but I have to fight it. Magda recognizes the look of pain on my face and requests the guard to go ahead and scout the area. She slowly makes her way to my direction. "The stitches are not holding together are they?" she asks disappointed.

"They are fine," I reassure her. "It is not too far from here, a little longer and I will be able to rest." She peers at me with her purple and grey eyes, knowing full well that I am lying.

"Dear, you forget I was a midwife long before you were born," she states as she smiles with her missing teeth exposed. "You have lost a lot of blood and you cannot afford to lose more. I will tell the guard to hold the child and we could try to re-apply some of the stitches."

I look at my daughter and could not imagine parting with her even for a second. Magda senses that I am not going to relinquish her to anyone and instead of pursuing the matter she just turns away and walks ahead.

The guard, who is steps ahead, suddenly stops and signals us to hide and be quiet. Two tall grass homes standing side by side assisted in concealing us. We peer behind the two hovels at massive guard. He did not hide and even if he tried, there is no home tall enough to cover him. We overhear noises coming from not too far ahead of the homes and it sounds like there is a confrontation.

"What do we do?" I ask in a fearful tone. The last thing I want is to have to defend myself and my baby, especially in my current state. Travelling with Payne and my former companions did instill some battle prowess in me but it was minimal training and only when Payne wanted to get close. Those sessions usually lead to a more "intimate" turn of events.

"Quiet, woman," the guard demands, pursing lips and placing his finger on them. Crouching, he sneaks over to one of the taller grass homes and glances from the side. We sit in silence while he surveys the environment. He remains slightly crouched and stares in silence until a scream startles all of us. The screech is not that of pain but of anger. "Please God, protect us," I pray aloud. Our guard jumps back and upright, removing his sword from its leather holster. Magda stands with both her skinny hands atop of her cane and sighs.

"Put that sword away, you buffoon," she orders. "We are here to escort this young lady and her child to safety, not pick a fight with the locals." He reluctantly nods in agreement and inserts his sword back into the leather casing. Deciding that staying put would put us into more danger, the three of us move quietly down the street in hopes of avoiding the situation. The bodies become slightly visible as we pass by them unnoticed. There is what appears to be five children having a physical confrontation. A young boy who has dirt blond hair similar to Marcus lay on top of another larger boy, choking him. The scene sends shivers down my spine. *That could have been my child,* I think to myself as I witness the aggressive act. Two others are latched on the blond one, trying to get him off but he violently swings his arms and knocks them both down. He rises from his victim's body and faces the other boys and at that moment I recognize his face. *My God… Marcus!* I try to yell to him but my voice catches in my throat.

For whatever reason, he seems to have regained control of himself. Standing still, he looks down at his hands intensely. A jolt of fear strikes my body and turns my blood cold seeing Marcus like this. He remains motionless and it scares me but it is better than him hurting these frightened boys. Even outnumbering him, they will have no chance against Marcus. With his training, Marcus is a formidable foe for seasoned fighters. I sigh in relief and look at Magda. The wizened old woman recognizes that I have a connection to Marcus just by looking at my facial expressions. Magda taps her cane to gain the attention of the guard. She makes a motion to him with her head to break up the fight and he acknowledges the request.

He appears behind the hut to make his move but before he could even take step forward his movement is halted when one of the boys strikes Marcus on the back with a wooden log. I gasp and almost drop my baby. It is all happening so fast that I barely have time to react. Marcus loses all control of his emotion. It is like watching Payne with his swift and powerful movements. Toppling the boy down with his might, Marcus drives his dagger deep into the helpless youth's stomach. *No Marcus, please stop!* I beg but the bloodshed persists. Another boy attempts to stop Marcus but only found the sharp end of his dagger cutting through his throat as if it was warm butter. *I am failing him,* I cry as goose bumps appear on my arms and legs and my face turns pale.

Marcus begins walking back towards his original victim with spiteful and callous intent. I shut my eyes and try speaking out again but all I could picture is Payne driving his dagger into Edward's heart. *This cannot be happening. Why is this happening? God, please give me the strength to speak, to stop Marcus from becoming HIM.* I take a deep breath and open my eyes. In that split second, Marcus is rapidly moving to his last target. Finally, my voice returns and I manage to project so loud that the entirety of Nasgrath may have heard me.

"ARTHUR, STOP!" I screamed with little energy remains. He suddenly stops in his tracks. *It worked. Thank God, it worked!* Marcus drops on both knees and places his hands on his hair, shouting and sobbing. Magda approaches me and extends her arms to hold my baby. I am reluctant at first but I am responsible for Marcus… no Arthur and he is family. He needs me and I want to be there for him. Loosening my grip on my new born, I gently place her in the arms of Magda and thank her with a weak smile. The guard is already taking action by assisting the only survivor in the vicious attack. He asks the boy where he lives and whether he needs to be taken home but he just stared past him, deeply focusing his gaze at Marcus. It was menacing and even more terrifying that he did not say a word or show any sign of human emotion. *He is obviously shocked and distraught over the death of his friends,* I tell myself. Marcus' sobbing becomes overwhelming and I rush to him forgetting that I still had stitches. Every step I take, I feel them rip but every step also brings me closer to Marcus. It is a sacrifice I have to make.

Blood continues to run down my leg while Arthur has blood running down his hair. We both have witnessed too much bloodshed for one life time. His once golden hair is now red. I did not know how to approach him so I carefully extend my arm out and whisper, "Arthur," but no reply came. I try again. "Arthur… son, it is me," I say louder as my hand moves closer to his shoulder. The moment my hand touches his shoulder; he shrugs viciously to remove it. His crying ceases but his hands did not loosen their grip from his hair. I put my hands out to touch his, softly brushing them along with his hair. After a few minutes, Marcus drops his guard and lifts his head up. Smiling at him, I bend low and kiss his hands and forehead. He wraps his hands around mine and profusely apologizes.

"I'm sorry," he cries. "I'm so sorry! I never meant to hurt anybody." Our arms tightened around each other and I let him continue crying on my shoulder but I could not do this much longer as the damage between my thighs has become profoundly more painful. I squirm in discomfort and Marcus notices the red river flowing down my leg.

Marcus looks at me in a concerned manner

"I will be fine, Arthur," I reply. "I have some wonderful news to share with you!" Before I could finish my sentence, my mind freezes, my sight vanishes and everything turns black. The only thing I hear is, "Mother! Mother! Wake up! Help, please!"

"Mar….c….u….s," I whimper and that was the last thing I remember before I lose consciousness.

CHAPTER TWENTY ONE
PAYNE BLADESTORM

Destonia is aptly named as the *impenetrable castle* with impossibly high stone walls and steel gates tall enough to tower over some smaller mountains. The residents of Destonia have all submissively given in or become accustomed to the idea that God himself took pieces of the largest mountains and sculptured them into the most monstrous palace in all of Thalia. It is said to be so tall that if anyone were to ever reach the top and look beyond, they would be able to see all of Thalia from every direction. A Bard's tale sings of one hero who succeeded in scaling the walls and was gifted with the esteemed title and blessing from God as "King of Earth's Heavens." This was the first Duke of Destonia and the beginning of Castle Fate. Before I embarked on this hellish journey, Pyke had warned me about the humidity and sun in the regions connected to the desert but I did not heed his advice. I have traversed through many locations within Apollon to seek ingredients for my alchemy, yet the only place I can recall being this scalding would be the Sallandar Deserts. However, unlike Sallandar, there is beauty and peace to be had in Destonia.

As I stroll through the different towns on my horse, I recognize the simple life the residents seem to enjoy. The lack of monetary needs is refreshing in a world where gold and power rule. Farmers' harvest only enough grains to feed family and friends and do not use their trade to profit. Fishermen did not have an overabundance of catches and seem to only reel what is necessary for the day, knowing that water is scarce in a dry land such as theirs. Even the animals look healthier, since Destonian citizens take special care to value all of God's creations. Hunting is prohibited unless it is as self-defence or else essential in response to an epidemic or famine. Most of their nutrition comes from gathering of fruits, vegetables, nuts and fish. With such simple lives, one would imagine Destonia to be a poor province although it is the contrary. The most rare and valuable gems originate from the gem mines, which stretched every few miles. The demand for these gems is so great that it alone is the source of income which keeps Destonia wealthy, therefore allowing for the creation and purchase of some of the rarest and formidable military armour and weapons in all of Thalia. *Soon, these resources and army will belong to me.*

Each town seemed more cheerful than the next. Children litter the streets with laughter; the elderly commune together and exchange stories about their youthful days, women gossip about their neighbours while the men go about their daily work. Not a single individual paid me any mind. *I could have walked in with an army and these God loving religious fanatics would pay me no heed.* Striding along, I cannot help but admire the beauty and complexity of the architecture. The population live with little means but no expense is spared in the creation of the churches. Exquisite and elegant monasteries exist in every town for worship. Etched in each door is a depiction of an enormous angel descending from the heavens and blessing the miniscule people beneath which represent the citizens of Destonia. A majestic halo rests above the angel's head and is composed entirely of topaz, while the grass which the mere worships are kneeling on is made of emerald pieces, shining in the light and illuminating the luscious green. Jewels and minerals run along every door and wall and every window are depicted with scenes of angels and God. Even the windows and portraits within the church are laden with rubies, amethyst, sapphires and other luxurious gems. Within each church, I can hear the prayers and ramblings of a minister manipulating the masses. From soft-spoken priests to the loud and obnoxious, the sound of sermon is resonates from every citadel and the believers follow the words like gospel. *Like sheep herded by their shepherd.* It sickens me to know that people succumb to the words of a mere human just because they say it is given to them by God. *Delusional fools.*

Before my departure, I commanded Pyke to draft a parchment to specify the purpose of my arrival. The letter indicates that Castle Eclipse intends to join forces with Castle Fate under one regime and in doing so making us one of the most powerful military alliances in all of Thalia. Of course it will all belong to me, but the parchment claims all rights to Lord Gaston of Castle Fate and his young nephew and future heir, Henry. Unfortunately for both of them, it will never come to pass and the one true ruler will be me. Lord Gaston Fate is frail and feeble. His body is diminishing rapidly from an undiscovered, unknown debilitating disease. He should be easy to dispose of but the nephew proves to be the real challenge. Pyke did mention Henry sharing similarities to Marcus: determination, loyalty, hard work, and honesty. On the other hand, he likely possesses the same characteristics I hated about the little bastard as well. With that information in mind, I took the time to brew a poison that will be untraceable in the blood stream and has no physical effects on the body and mind - an extremely rare mixture of dragon lilies and spider venom which are found in Dragon's Wake, an island situated across the seas to the east. The poison will enter his blood stream and in minutes inflame each major organ causing them to slowly rot within. If timed correctly, he should perish in his sleep, making it appear as if it were God's will. The mixture lay in a pouch within my black robe. Once I have disposed of them both, the Chancellor will gain his rule and hand over the armies of Castle Fate to my command.

Why bother letting him live? He will betray you just like everyone else, the sinister voice whispers in my head.

This is an opportunity to expand our armies and I do not fear the Chancellor, I reply. Do not interfere. We do not need blood on our hands this time. It would be a shame to ruin this rich garb which the maids worked so hard cleaning. I still see a bit of blood in the fabric from the last noble's dead body after Timber finished torturing him.

The heat emanating from the sun is becoming unbearable and I begin to perspire heavily. My traditional black cotton hooded robe is riding in my satchel attached to my horse but the silk pants and long sleeve silk shirt I am wearing begin to blotch with sweat stains. Luckily, due to my constant creation of potions, my natural smell has been replaced over the years with herbs and spice and the sweet scents of rare plants; seeping their way into my glands. I look down at the clothing and shudder at the thought of Timber melting the bones of one of the nobles he was torturing in his smith shop before saving the getup for me to don. The clothing fit fairly well despite being a fair bit constricting for assassin work, but the disguise is a necessity according to Pyke. My preferred attire is not *appropriate* for such an occasion. My sigil of sun and moon forming an eclipse was also sewn on the blue silk doublet. The wrist sleeves are white and fluffed with gemmed cufflinks sewn as buttons. The pants drape down to my ankles where leather black shoes occupy my feet. My black hair is tied in three knots and hangs down my lower back. I am certainly dressed the part, though I want nothing more than to burn the clothes on my body. They represent everything I loathe in this world. Nobles do nothing more than leech off the land and look down upon the poor and weak; they manipulate and use others until they are no longer of worth, and are killed or discarded like garbage. My former Masters built their guild and power based on the same premise - using the poor and helpless for their own gains. Once I have armies, I will come down upon them like a tidal wave and destroy the guild and its leaders once and for all.

Castle Fate is still a few miles away but is quickly becoming visible. What I had originally thought were clouds are in actuality the enormous white stone gates of the castle. Songs and tales do no justice to what my eyes witness. Even for a God, these walls seem impossible to comprehend. I stare into the sky and see no end to the stone. The leisurely gallop of my stallion becomes an echo in my ear and the world around me becomes small. I cannot peel my gaze from the unfathomably tall stone castle walls. Clouds look to be closer to earth than the top of those gates.

This is exactly why you need me, Payne. You lose focus too easily, the voice mocks me. With that remark, my head comes back down to earth and the sounds and sights of Destonia return with it. Not to be outdone I mentally reply, *I need you as much as I need this rash developing on my arse.* I smirk, satisfied with my remark.

After what seems to be an eternity, I finally arrive at the front gates where an immense bridge covers an even larger portcullis. My horse stops and I feel its legs jerking and shaking. I disembark and gently pat its back. It neighs and with what minimal energy it has, it trots over to the closest rock and nearly collapses on its side. Closing its eyes, the horse begins to inhale heavily as its dark nostrils flare with each exhale. The sun is setting behind the castle and the sky is turning is pigmenting into a blood orange. *A perfect night to collect our trophies, do you not agree Payne?* The voice asks.

"Do not interfere with my plans. We only get one opportunity for this," I command. Angrily, the voice responds loudly in my head, *Soon, I will be the one commanding you! You are nothing without me, Payne, nothing...* the voice fades, inferring temporary closure to our dispute.

I close my eyes and squeeze my temples with my fingers, attempting to ease the raucous pain. Gradually the voice disappears but I know it is not the last I will hear from *it.* I squint up at the two balconies erect on both sides of the bridge and notice that a torch is lit only on the left side of the bridge. Upon closer assessment, I see left right side is absent of sentry. No more than a few moments pass until I hear a thundering *creak* coming from inside the gate as the bridge lowers ever so slowly. The sound of chain and metal cling and turn as the guards attempt to hold the structure together for its descend. The earth shakes as the bridge moves from the heavens to the ground. I stand my ground but realize I am being elevated slightly from the tremors.

I cross my arms and wait impatiently; I have never been one for patience. When the bridge finally collapses to the ground, debris is tossed in the air and dust clouds form, covering my vision. I lift my tunic to cover my nose and close my eyes and wave my unoccupied hand back and forth to clear the sand. When the earth finally settles and the lifted portcullis is raised, four men on horseback ride towards me. Each man bares the banner of Lord Gaston Fate, a silver flag with a blinding white border and a golden maiden in the middle wearing a halo. One of the men shouts, "Lord Payne Bladestorm?" I lift my right hand up and signal once, annoyed. *Who else would it be, you moron.* Once they confirm my identity, they move forward with even less haste. When they finally are within a few feet, the two men at the front of the pack dismount and hand their banners to the two soldiers in the back.

"My Lord, where are your guards and escorts?" The skinny guard to the left asks in a confused manner. I point to the horse that is still resting near the rock.

"That is my companion and it did a magnificent job guarding and escorting me to your noble castle," I reply. Removing the parchment from my belt, I hand it to the feeble guard and explain, "The details of my visit are inked within this scroll. Please, show me to my quarters and inform Lord Fate and the Chancellor of my arrival. Also, tell the Chancellor to pay me a visit before this night is over. I will speak with him in private about how our nations uniting will benefit Lord Fate and all of Thalia."

I walk over to the horse on the left and saddle. Startled, the horse neighs and raises its feet but I hold on tightly. It struggles violently despite the soldiers attempt to calm it, though after a few minutes it finally settles. I pet the horse and look back at the two soldiers holding the banner and closest to the gate. They understand my demands and part silently. My horse turns towards the castle and trots forward. I point at the horse resting near the rock and yell to the soldier on the left, "Make sure you keep that one alive. That will now be your horse."

Castle Fate is much less the spectacle inside when compared to the enormous stone gates towering over the skies on the outside. The stone used to build the castle seems to be ancient and archaic. The castle is light brown with shades of white with only one window on each side of the castle and upper floor. Three towers protrude upwards and hang loosely to each side from the base. Whoever built the castle was either blind or drunk, or perhaps the rumbling from lowering the bridge is the reason for the disproportional structure. Large banners with Lord Fate's sigils are draped from each tower. Large, dry roots and vines have entangled themselves throughout the castle walls and cover the majority of the east side. A stable pen is attached to the west, and it is perhaps the most impressive sight within these walls. The Destonians pride themselves on waging "Holy Wars" when God commands, and favour a military built primarily of cavalry. Multiple young and brawny stable boys tend to the horses. *If the stable boys look this strong, I wonder how the army looks.*

I pull on my horse's reins making it stop in its tracks. Observing the middle tower, I realize that a pale and hunched, bony man is staring at me intently. His eyes are dull and grey, almost lifeless. He would not be standing on his own two feet if it were not for the companion to his right holding his underarm for support. *That must be Lord Gaston Fate, and the other could be none other than his Chancellor.* The Chancellor seems more weasel than human. His eyes are abnormally parted, and the edge of either eye is painted in red mascara resembling the eyes of the cultures in the Eastern continents. His nose is straight and thin like an arrow, and his mouth wide and thin lipped. There seems to be no pigment to his skin. Next to him I would look as dark as Liza. His hair, pulled back sleek, is long, straight and fair. If the Destonians were not so naïve and trusting, they would notice how untrustworthy the man is by his physical appearance alone. I raise a hand to acknowledge their presence and the Chancellor waves back. *Time for the fun to begin,* I smile.

CHAPTER TWENTY TWO
OLD MAN VENOM BOLT

Nasgrath brings back many painful memories; memories of a time that I thought were long gone and forgot in the annals of my mind. Recently everything that has transpired before my transformation into Venom Bolt has begun returning in fragments. The voice that once kept me focused and guided my hand in completing my Masters' orders can no longer suppress the past. *What is happening to me?* I wonder. *Habitamus in tenebris... we live in darkness,* I remind myself. *Habitamus in tenebris* is something all assassins are taught as a mantra. Not only does it remind us to conceal our identities but also remind us that our pasts no longer exist. The method was meant to be absolute, forever binding; yet my past continues to break through the barrier. Memories began resurfacing after my last battle with Dark Heart, my first *true* loss in battle. *I must find him and bring him to justice before he reveals our location, or worse, decides to let the monarchy know of our existence.*

As an assassin, I am an elite soldier - an

avatar of death and darkness to the unjust and cruel. Our guild has structure and purpose with virtues such as justice, peace and stability. We selflessly keep this ungrateful world from collapsing, performing our duties without thanks or recognition. We are not branded heroes or given rewards, yet we tip the scales in every war, politics, and significant events that have shaped Thalia's past, present and future. The Masters, all knowing and all powerful, determine victories before the wars even begin. To this day, their identities remain a secret, shrouded in eternal blackness. Only the coveted *Shadow Walkers* have the privilege to be in their presence and hear their powerful voices, though even their eyes cannot see through the darkness that shadows their true identities. If we consider the Masters as Gods, then Shadow Walkers would be their Generals. Shadow Walkers are the highest class of assassin and there is only one per generation permitted into the order. For another to be chosen, the previous Shadow Walker must lose in combat to death causing them to forfeit their title. Only once has there ever existed two Shadow Walkers in the guild at one time.

It was my proudest moment when *he* was chosen to be my equal. I replayed the event over and over in my mind for years, reminding myself of the reason why I have always seen something special in that boy. It is the only time I can recall feeling a kinship with anyone; the closest I felt to being a father. I watched him grow, training him to be deadly and focused. When it was time to pass the torch to him, my finest and most prized pupil bested me in battle and yet refused to kill me.

He was a young lad during those days. It was a time when my already snow-white hair began transforming into a dull shade of grey. Time, the ultimate assassin, was finally creeping up on me from the shadows, and I felt it was time to allow someone else to have the honour of being the right hand to our Masters. There was certainly no one the Masters would deem more appropriate than my disciple. Dark Heart was demanded by our Masters to challenge me for the role of Shadow Walker. His training was not complete, yet he was undoubtedly the most skilled assassin in the Guild. Dark Heart simply needed more time and time was something I could not offer him if I lived.

I did not have the heart to kill him. No one had bested me in decades and I cared little for my pupils past their training. *He* was different. Never before had I considered a student to be like a son. I let Dark Heart win the battle, knowing that he would fulfill the duty of Shadow Walker with honour, pride, courage and justice. But instead of obeying the laws and killing the former Shadow Walker, he put his daggers down and offered to help me to my feet. I urged him to finish the deed or we would both be executed, but he just stared through the pitch-black room refusing my advice. Our Masters were hidden in darkness during the battle and if it were not for our heightened senses we would think it abandoned. Our Masters sat in silence for quite some time.

Sweat was dripping from both of our brows. I remained on the ground, embarrassed at the notion of purposely losing only to have my successor disobey rules that have been sacred for generations. I remember observing Dark Heart and noticing something different about him at that precise moment. He was not the malicious killer I trained him to be. Whether he felt affection or a bond towards me, he neglected to end my life. After a few minutes, the *Black Queen* rose and proclaimed for the first time in history that two Shadow Walkers would exist at the same time. It was an unprecedented turn of events. From that day forward, we were equals. No longer student and master but fellow Shadow Walkers, hand in hand, we would purge all the evil in Thalia. That was how I wanted to die, knowing that I raised someone as a son and left behind a legacy to be proud of. Instead, I am now hunting the very man I once considered my own flesh and blood. *He must be brought to justice,* I remind myself. *Emotions will not get in the way this time.*

I wait patiently for the sun to set before I set out and hunt my first interrogation. Dark Heart knows that our Masters have noble spies and henchmen working for them, thus I begin in the Noble District. Dark Heart's first goal would be to identify the Masters' true identities. Besides the Shadow Walkers, there is another class in our guild who are referred to as *Wraiths* - those who have a connection to the Masters indirectly. These Wraiths are the eyes and ears of the Masters and are bound by servitude. In return for loyalty, their nobility, wealth and stature are protected. Orders are transmitted from priests who work tirelessly in the citadels of every city and country in order to spread the commandments of our leaders to their subordinates. These priests are known as *Wanderers,* and their purpose is to whisper the word of our Masters in secrecy to their subjects. Wraiths would never have the knowledge of our Masters' location or names, but Dark Heart is resourceful. He could turn a simple piece of knowledge and investigate every angle until the pieces come together, and he discovers their identities.

Every past and present assassin is trained

and groomed to be a killing machine on the island of Saint Aran. Seldom do our Masters ever grace us with their presence, either for a battle for a new Shadow Walker or to give instruction on critical orders. They exist elsewhere, however the location is a mystery even to me. Dark Heart would not take the chance to travel to Saint Aran, where he would be surrounded and outnumbered by his former brethren. His priority would be to seek out information on their true location. I must stop him before he learns too much.

I sit atop a large tree, peering down at the immaculately decorated homes and yards. Looking west, I witness the marketplace vendors all leaving, save an old man selling fruit and a young boy of twelve or thirteen handing him something. My gaze focuses even further west and I notice the despicable slums. *How could one place as the Noble District exist in the same city as the slums,* I shake my head in disgust. The existence of the slums irritates me, yet I cannot understand why. Nasgrath only serves as a location to find my target so why does my mind and soul feel disturbed by the idea of such poverty? Suddenly a glimpse of my past remerges. I close my eyes and witness a younger version of myself standing idle while my father sits in an elaborately decorated chair while writing ledgers. He moves his mouth and my mind zooms into his moving lips so I could make out what he was saying. The only words I could read are, "Peasants are filth. It is your duty to look down upon them". He utters a name but before I can puzzle together the word, I return to the present day. *Not again. Why does this keep happening?* My visions are clearly my father continuing to haunt me. *Maybe your relationship to your father reminds you of the way you were with Dark Heart,* whispers Venom Bolt in a mocking hiss.

Perhaps, I agree. *Let us not lose focus on our task.* There was no physical way of identifying a Wraith. Their identity was only ever exposed to those who knew of *Habitamus in tenebris.*

There are two hundred homes in the Noble District. There exists, at the very most, ten Wraiths in each province. I will have to infiltrate every home until I find all of them. My hand instinctively reaches for my lower back and squeezes. *I am getting too old for this,* I sigh as I prepare for several days of work.

I begin to descend the tree, jumping nimbly from one giant branch to the next. The tree stands mightily, over seventy feet tall, and is perhaps older than the town itself. Each branch shakes steadily as my feet lands swiftly to the next. Upon reaching the gate that separates the Noble District and the market, I sit crouched while I observe the patrolling patterns of the multiple guards within the Noble District. It is tradition during every mission to wear a black hooded cloak in order to cover our faces and blend into the night. Underneath my cloak I have both venom coated daggers, *Basilisk and Hydra,* as well as my trusty crossbow, *Medusa.* This is to be a covert mission, mostly involving stealth; but I always prepare for an unexpected skirmish. In my years, there is one rule I have come to learn and that is to always be prepared for a fight. I memorize the guards' patterns after a few patrols. *The guards walk in a straight line from bottom to top, stopping at each home for a few minutes,* Venom Bolt hisses in my mind. I nod in agreement. I wait until the guard at the far left patrols past the first five homes then leap off the gate on to the first rooftop.

I land carefully and creep to each corner of the homes. There are four windows on the top floor of each home and four windows below. Nobles love natural sunlight, thus their windows are oversized and easy to enter, increasing the need for guards. I nimbly place my feet on the brick wall of the house and grab on the roof, sliding my body off the top and to the side of the home as I sidestep towards the window frame. Due to the heat and dry weather in Nasgrath, it is common for many of the windows to remain open during the night. The ocean breeze blows cool air into the home and enters my cloak and down my back. A combination of perspiration and air cause me to shiver. Wooden window frames swing lightly from side to side, delaying me from entering the home quicker than I would like. I adjust my fingers on the roof shingles and patiently wait until the wind ceases for a fraction of a second and the frames movement subsides and jump inside the top floor chamber.

My eyes automatically adjust to the room and my senses heighten as I am surrounded by darkness. A husband and wife are asleep side-by-side. The husband is snoring while the wife is twisting and turning in her sleep. Neither of them have a blanket or clothes covering their bodies. Fumes of alcohol and the stench of fornication clouded the room. I can smell the sweat coming off of the man in his bed, reeking of wine and his natural body odour. Again, visions of my younger self appear in a brothel. I am in bed with a whore, and I am pouring a cup of red wine unto her breast and laughing while sticking my other fingers in her mouth. I can almost whiff my own bodily sweat as I continuously enter the woman. I gain a glimpse of a reflection of my younger self while he laughs, and I realize his teeth are fangs and his eyes are empty. A multicoloured snake slithers in and out of them, hissing and flicking its tongue at me. I need a few seconds to understand the meaning of the vision, but before I can decipher anything the reptile strikes and my eyes open. My hands are trembling slightly and I can feel my legs weaken. I close my eyes for a moment to collect myself.

What is the matter, my love? An unfamiliar voice enters my head.

Who are you? I ask reluctantly. *Where is Venom Bolt?* No answer came from within. Suddenly, I am in a trance once more. The image of a giant serpent with human features appears with the same colours as the snake circling inside my previous vision. This being's lower body is that of a snake, scaled and long. It stands on its tail with bare exposure from the waist to its neck with full firm breasts and a distressing green liquid oozing from its nipples. Her skin is beautiful and exotic, her eyes are slanted and her hair lengthy and black. She stares at me with her sultry eyes and hisses at me with her long split tongue. She exposes her fangs and points at me with one finger, beckoning me to come closer. Her nails resemble sharp, white spikes. I cannot resist her instructions, mesmerised by the creature that stands in front of me. Every step I take forward her belly grows in size, and the green slime from her nipples no longer drips but instead pours out rapidly. As soon as we are at arm's length I stop.

"Who are you?" I inquire. She smiles at me with sharp fangs white as ivory. Her hands find her belly and she cups it. She jerks her head back and screams, "You killed us!" I want to open my eyes to understand who and what she is, but I cannot. Something is forcing me to endure this mental anguish and I could not stop it from progressing.

"I am sorry… I was a foolish young man with no appreciation for life," I reply pathetically.

"Nothing has changed. Now you are an old man who has no appreciation for life!" she hisses. "You continue to kill and destroy all that is around you. Do you even remember my name? Do you remember yours?"

"Names do not matter, only the mission," I answer as I am trained to do. Again, I try to open my eyes but it seems as though my mind continues to want me to endure this agony. *Where the hell are you, Venom Bolt?* I wonder.

"So be it," she says. "If you refuse to remember then I will remind you. Your name is…"

Before she can finish, my eyes re-open and

my foot is in unbearable pain. Somehow I reacted in time and punctured an arrow into my own foot. I grip my teeth and allow the initial pain to subside. Luckily, these bolt tips are not covered in poison or I would be completely paralyzed for hours. As quietly as one could in this circumstance, I pull on the arrow carefully and bear the pain. I hear the sound of flesh, bone and muscle rip from my foot, leaving behind a puncture in my foot and wooden splinters.

Old man, so nice of you to finally join us, a familiar voice hisses.

"Venom Bolt?" I ask cautiously.

Who else were you expecting? I believe you almost fell asleep on me.

Embarrassed to tell him the truth, I jump back on the window and climb on the roof. Ripping the bottom part of my cloak, I tie the fabric around my bleeding foot and take a deep breath. *Alright, let us start our mission.* Recovering as quickly as my body would allow at my age, I lift back up to my feet with a grunt and return back inside the home. *Habitamus in tenebris... time to locate the Wraiths.*

CHAPTER TWENTY THREE
KATHERINE LOWBORNE

Every part of my body is stiff. My skin feels tender, my muscles pulled, and my joints ache immensely. I run my tongue along my mouth and feel coarse skin all along my lips. I bite down on a piece of dry, flaky skin attached to my lip and tear at it to allow the pain to assure me that I am still alive. A trickle of blood runs down my mouth and I let out an involuntary sigh of relief. A tickle irritates my throat almost, as if a feather strokes it playfully. I instinctively attempt to bring my right hand up to my neck and rub out the soreness and itch, but my arms will not respond. Looking down, I realize both my hands are tied behind my back along a wooden post. I try to free myself from the knots but they are tied securely. Whoever took the time to bind my arms has done the same with my feet and along my torso. There is no escaping this confinement, even disregarding the amount of blood I have lost and emptiness in my belly. *Blood... belly,* and it suddenly dawns on me. I open my eyes wide and scream, "My baby! Where is my baby!?" No one answers my plea. "Marcus... Marcus, where are you?"

"Arthur, not Marcus, mother. It was your plan to give us different identities and names, remember?" a faint voice answers from a distance. I could hear his footsteps approaching me from behind. I shudder at the very idea of his presence. I fear him after what I witnessed in the alleyway, *I fear him… my god, I FEAR Marcus.* I dig deep within myself to push that fear aside and find courage once more.

"Why are my feet bound?" I question him hesitantly. The rope twists at the smallest adjustment, causing rashes to develop on my ankles and peeling the skin off my legs.

"It was Magda's idea," Arthur claims. "Do you not recall what occurred two days ago?"

I have been unconscious for two whole days? Why do I not remember anything? Feelings of panic and anxiety begin to inch their way into me.

Arthur ignores my puzzled expression and continues, "Magda had instructed the guard who accompanied you that night to bind your feet. It was to prevent you from making any sudden movements. The last thing we need is for your wound to re-open. Magda has been here every day looking over you and your daughter," he corrects himself, "My sister. I am to summon Magda as soon as you wake."

I want to ask where my daughter is but before I could, Arthur pulls out a rusted pocket knife and looks me dead in the eyes. His beautiful light green eyes once full of joy, innocence, pride and love are now tired, defeated and without soul. To avoid him from noting my awkwardness, I look down at my ropes and plead, "Marcus, can you please free me from these binds. I promise to be cautious with my wounds." He looks behind the post and places his knife carefully on the thick rope and with one slice, cuts them off. I wrap my hands around my wrist and rub gently so as to not rip at the already tattered skin. Both my wrists have traces of dry blood and bruises. Even with my already dark skin, they stand out in a deep purple. "You moved too much in your sleep, mother. Under normal conditions, these ropes leave only slight bruising but you subconsciously fought against them," Arthur explains.

I do not remember being tied up, let alone my dreams. I only want to see my daughter. Though before I can respond to Arthur, he moves to bring my child to me and place her in my arms. I instantly swell with mixed emotions of joy and disappointment. I am disappointed in myself for leaving both of them for so long. Bringing her fragile body closer to my bosom, I notice my daughter seems thinner than when I first held her and her skin darker due to exposure to the sun. She is cradled in a fleece and is sound asleep. Tears run down my cheeks and land on her blanket causing a moist spot to appear. Seeing my daughter peacefully sleeping removes all of the pain from the hardships endured. Perhaps while I was unconscious, I fought to free myself knowing that my child and Arthur were waiting for me. When she was born, I promised to never forget the way she looked when I first held her. I remembered her brown skin, her little chubby cheeks, and her tiny hands and feet, as soft and smooth as if she was washed in milk. Yet, at this moment she does not look like the same child.

"I will never let you go again," I whisper soothingly in her ear so not to wake her. Her head tilts to the side and she smacks her lips together and yawns but does not open her eyes. I cannot help but smile. Unabashed, Arthur studies the two of us, but I dare not catch his eyes. Something about him has changed and it continues to scare me.

"I will fetch Magda, mother. She wanted me to inform you that a child needs her mother's milk," he said shyly, quickly reverting to the young boy I love. "I have left bread and fresh fruit inside our home." He loosens the remaining knots around my feet and waist. The skin on my ankles burn as the warm sunlight scalds my raw, reddened skin. I wince silently, attempting to endure the sensation.

"I will be away late into the night, fetching our food from the fruit vendor. Magda will be here shortly. Take care mother and please remember not to move too often. You are still recovering," he instructs in a worried tone.

I nod without breaking my gaze on my daughter. No more than few moments pass before I realize Arthur has already left for the market. I want to confront him when he returns and let him know how disappointed I am with his actions. The way he murdered those boys in the alleyway was inexcusable, but this is neither the time nor the place. My daughter's health takes precedence over everything. I scan the area to see if anyone else is near and once I confirm that I am alone, I lower one of my sleeves and bare my breast. I hold my child close and she instinctively takes to me like a leech. Nothing could have prepared me for the soreness that comes from breastfeeding. My baby suckles hungrily with all of her might, trying to absorb what milk I have to offer. I want to re-adjust her positioning for comfort. I remember Lady Jaina placing two fingers into Marcus` mouth in order to loosen the pressure on her nipple but that thought quickly escapes me once I see the amount of dirt that cover my hands.

When Lady Jaina fed, she barely showed any signs of discomfort. She cradled Marcus closely and regarded him with pride and love. It is memories like that which remind me how much I miss Lady Jaina and Lord Edward`s company. If only she were here to guide me through this new experience. Her voice and affection would be enough to comfort me. *I hope you burn in Hell for eternity, Payne.* I clench my teeth. Anger seeps through my soul. The very thought of Payne makes my blood boil. He has done nothing more than deceive, manipulate and destroy everything I love and care for. The baby fastens on tighter and I wince. *I suppose there is one gift he has given me.*

My stomach grumbles loudly reminding me that I need to eat. I warily pull on my child to have a moment to feed myself but as soon as she is removed from my breast, she instantly cries. A high pitch wail echoes through the slums in rhythmic fashion. Rising to my feet, I hold onto my baby and quickly skitter over to our hut, singing what little children melodies I learned from Lady Jaina when she sang to Marcus. I am hoping to cheer her up but we both need to eat in order to survive these conditions. A wooden pail is in the corner of the straw hut filled with ripe fruits. Red and green apples, yellow pears, oranges, bananas and pomegranate all stacked on top of one another. The very sight of food makes my mouth salivate. I walk over to the bucket and snatch an apple. I crave the orange, my favourite of the fruits and the juiciest, but I cannot stand the thought of releasing my daughter to peel it. I place the apple in my mouth and clench down, taking a massive bite. The sound of the crunch after my bite is loud and gratifying. It even startles my baby long enough for her to stop crying. This apple is the most delicious thing I have ever tasted, although I have enough sense to realize that even eating a crunchy beetle in my state of hunger would be as delightful. I ceaselessly consume the fruit without taking breaths in between. Before I know it, my cheeks are filled and I choke slightly.

"Slow down, my dear," a familiar voice says behind me. "You don't want an apple to be the reason why your daughter grows up without a mother." I turn around embarrassed and realize that Magda has been behind me the entire time, watching as I stuff my face.

Magda is standing in her usual way, hunched over, depending on her wooden cane to remain upright. She has a delicate smile on her face. It seems as though she is happy to see me moving again. I smile back and ask, "Would you like any?"

"No thank you, dear," she graciously replies. "I have already filled my stomach with food. The boy had fetched me to tell me you have joined the world of the living. We feared that you were not going to wake."

"I am sorry to worry you, Magda," I apologize. "Never would I have wished a burden such as this on you or my son. Thank you for everything and if there is anything I can do to repay you, please name it."

She rubs her wrinkly chin at the thought of my offer. Her eyes gaze at me intently and her demeanour changes from a friendly smile to an expression of curiosity. *There is something troubling her.*

"What is the matter, Magda?" I ask eager to find out. For a split second, I place my attention elsewhere but my baby quickly reminds me with a loud, mouth opening cry. This prompts me to lower my sleeve again and curl my daughter into my arms as she returns to suckling. I am becoming familiar with the sensation though she seems to test me by sucking harder each time. Magda laughs at my discomfort, coughing and wheezing in between each chuckle.

"It will get better as time goes. Your body will adapt," she promises, playfully. "Katherine, I do have a few questions for you but I am unsure about how to ask them."

"You have never been one to shy away from expressing yourself. After everything you have done for my family, the least I could do is answer your questions," I reassure her.

"If you insist," she nods in approval. "How are you and Arthur lowborne truly related or perhaps the real question is who exactly are you two…your true identities?"

The question catches me completely off guard and I feel my stomach plummet. I drop my apple as I lose control of my breathing. When I permitted Magda to ask me anything, I never expected it to be *this*. Hoping to save my lost demeanour, I swiftly respond with an uncomfortable laugh and ask a question of my own, "What do you mean our true identities?" Her kind expression changes to one of sternness. Her brow furrows as she sighs.

"Katherine - if that is your real name - by now you should know I am no fool, and can be quite insightful even at my old age. I have lived in Nasgrath since I was a youngling like the one you hold in your very arms and I have never seen a child who looks like Arthur and woman of your *colour* were only slaves. Yet here you are without a Master and with a so-called son who resembles those from a different region of Thalia. You said that you would do anything for me and all I ask for is the truth."

I promised to protect this family. Nobody can be trusted anymore but despite my caution; part of me wants to trust Magda. She has done so much for us, though so did previous so-called companions who had gained my full trust only to destroy everything I cared for.

"I am sorry, Magda. I still do not quite know how to answer your question. I am Katherine lowborne and Arthur is my son," I repeat unwavering, hoping that she would not pry any further.

"Still playing the ignorant damsel I see," she mumbles annoyed at my response. "I will be taking my leave then and you will no longer see me as I do not wish to involve myself further with people who keep secrets from friends." Magda raises her cane and juts the bottom of it into the ground to propel herself to her feet. She glances at me with disapproval and disappointment, then turns around to take her leave.

My conscience is troubled. I look down at my baby and my heart melts. If not for the old crone who is about to leave forever, I would be here alone in the dark as Arthur commits himself to his duties. My sanity and my child have been saved thanks to Magda and her wisdom and friendship.

"Wait, wait, Magda. I do not understand the reasoning behind your question but... I will tell you what I can only if you promise to take it to the grave with you," I whisper reluctantly. Her hand pauses as it lifts the tent drapes, before she drops them to face me. She has a wide smile from one ear to the next.

"I knew you would come to your senses, my dear. I only want to be here for you and your family," she claims almost too gleefully.

I re-live every event as I tell our tale from

beginning to end. With each passing minute, the heavy burden on me seems to wither away and I feel liberated. I describe life growing up as a slave in Nasgrath, my relationship with Payne, my colleagues and the demise of the Sunborn with the exception of Marcus. Magda stares at me in disbelief but does not interrupt me once as I complete my story.

"Magda, please say something. Your silence is killing me," I beg for her to speak. She does not move and continues to contemplate everything quietly while rubbing her chin.

"Unbelievable…It is a miracle that you made it this far with that poor boy. Everything you have told me seems unreal and I have seen much in my life," Magda says in awe. "So Arthur is the last heir of the late Edward Sunborn? He does possess his father's features and does resemble a native of of Apollon. It was a wise chose to bring him to the slums… Wise indeed. Nobody would expect a noble to ever step foot in this filth."

I nod in agreement, relieved that Magda approves of my decision. She is wise, kind and a welcome blessing from God. Her guidance has been my support through all of these recent life-changing tribulations. Magda continues to examine me with her uniquely coloured eyes but does not utter a word. Instead, she waves over to me and I walk over and help her up from her seated position back to her feet. She thanks me with a polite tap on my shoulder and proceeds to leave the tent.

"Magda," I call out before she exits the hovel. She stops and moves her head slightly but does not face my direction. "Thank you for everything you have done for us… and most of all keeping my secret." She returns to her original position and continues on.

CHAPTER TWENTY FOUR
PAYNE BLADESTORM

Hundreds of soldiers stand in parallel lines, unwavering, at attention and ready to follow commands given by their Master. Not one eye glances in my direction as I enter the main halls of Castle Fate. Each man is outfitted in glamourous silver armour with a halo attached to the top of his helm. Round, golden armlets glitter as each warrior holds a shield in one hand and a sword in the other. *Their discipline is impressive.* In the distance, I observe a skeletal figure dragging his feet ever so slowly down the elongated halls. At his side is a weasel of a man. *The Duke and his pet,* the voice in my mind whispers. *Or is it the other way around?* It almost appears as if the Duke is a puppet and the Chancellor is his puppeteer with the way they stood together. The Chancellor is walking at the same sluggish pace as his Master and I can tell by the expression on his face that he wants nothing more than to rid himself of the dead weight he is forced to carry around, yet he plays the part of a loyal subject well. Without an heir, the Chancellor would take title of Duke of Destonia, a title worth everything that he has to bear. The only obstacle is the Gaston Fate's nephew who is next in the line to receive the title of Duke.

I focus my attention on Lord Gaston Fate. His attire is fashioned to rival that of royalty. Made from the finest silks and linen, it is light in fabric in order to keep it from putting pressure on his frail body. With a white tunic made of silk and golden pantaloons to match, his clothing is well-expressed for someone who is to represent the will of God. As the monasteries within Destonia, his tunic is interlaced with topaz in various areas. Unfortunately, the weaver who sewed this outfit together from the most delicate material did not imagine that a jewel crafter would place so many gems onto the garb. The Duke's shoulders and wrists are weighed down by the lavish jewellery. Duke Gaston's head wobbles uncontrollably as he approaches me. As they come to a halt, the Chancellor bows while trying to keep the Duke in an upright position to greet me. "Thank you for making this long trip, Lord Payne Bladestorm, Duke of Apollon and Master of Castle... Eclipse now is it? I am Chancellor Triten and this is Lord Gaston Fate, Duke of Destonia."

I bow slightly at the Duke and smirk at the Chancellor's introduction. I take a few moments to assess the Duke's physical state. At this point, there may be no need for me to even lift a finger to end his life. Gaston Fate unexpectedly raises his head and looks deep into my eyes. His gaze is fierce, almost seeing through our true intentions. His mouth trembles as if he wishes to speak but does not possess the strength to speak it.

I was informed by Pyke that before his "attacks", Duke Gaston Fate spoke in old tongue and made references to an imaginary son which he never had. Every so often, he did evoke the native language of Thalia, calling out for his wife while sitting in the main hall, eating his soft food and drinking his soup. Now he can barely even open his mouth without passing out. Lady Nemaria, his wife, was a devout priestess chosen to wed Gaston on the day she became a woman. This was customary for every ruler of Destonia yet the only thing they consummated was miscarriage after miscarriage, eventually leading to a depressed Lady Nemaria taking her own life.

Fate... it is the one word that these fools hold above all else. It was God's will and Lord Gaston's Fate to be childless.

Hypocritical mongrels, I think in disgust.

I smile in Lord Fate's direction mockingly,

knowing full well that he has means of coherent speech. My eyes then return to the Chancellor. "Where is the Duke's noble nephew?" I inquire. "I would meet the future Duke of Destonia with proper introduction."

"My Lord, Henry Fate is currently training on horseback and will not be joining us until well into the night. He is dedicated to his rigorous training so that one day he can defend the lands of Destonia. The boy is the closest thing to a son that Lord Gaston has and has just turned the ripe age to rule," Triten proclaims. "Yet he is ever hesitant of the role... No Duke of Destonia has ever been crowned with the title any earlier than the age of twenty. Poor Henry is only thirteen." An evil grin appears on the face of Chancellor Triten, as if to say that he is expecting this to be child's play.

Triten has every characteristic of a classic villain. His overly exaggerated expressions, sharp tongue, greed driven eyes and plain appearance alone should have signalled some cause of alarm. Yet everyone besides the Duke seems oblivious.

"There will be time for pleasantries with Henry. I would like to retire to my quarters and please prepare a proper bath for me as I have been on the road for days. I will change and sup with yourself, the Duke Gaston, and Henry, if he has concluded his training."

The Chancellor waves over to one of the statuesque soldiers. The lifeless body comes to life and moves stiffly in our direction. Each step he takes causes the ground to ring with the sound of metal clashing on ceramic.

"Take Lord Payne to his chambers. Have the maids prepare a warm bath, and lastly inform the kitchen to have a proper meal cooked for our guest. "The sentinel silently nods, obliging to every command made by the Triten.

"If you will, Lord Payne," the Chancellor bows and sways his hand toward the right side of the room. I take my leave, following the guard and examining my surroundings while he escorts me to my quarters.

While the outer layer of Castle Fate is dull and aging, the inside is brimming with decor and marvel. Each wall tells the tale of a previous Duke who ruled and their contribution to Destonia. The very first carving depicts enormous hands with a glow around them descending from the clouds, holding a man draped in a golden cloth, wearing a crown. Below the godly hands are images of men, women and children, kneeling down and bowing to their new ruler. The next wall portrays another

Duke on a horse with sword in hand, pointing to the sky with an army of angels behind him. Above the army again is another portrayal of what seems to be the hands of God but with another child. *The child of the current reigning Duke and soon to be new ruler of Destonia,* I tell myself. Each wall is glittered in gold and white marble and each Duke that ruled in the various eras all possess one common trait - a silver sword which points to the sky. *So many precious minerals wasted on such useless tales.*

"Soldier," I say trying to get the live statue's attention. He pays me no mind and proceeds to march forward. I ignore the rude behaviour even though I am tempted to plunge my dagger through his back. "The silver, white marble and precious stone used in the engravings... how fare the miners in locating these precious minerals?" I query.

"The miners fare quite well, m'Lord," answers the soldier in a deep and low voice. "Marble comes in daily, as does the iron, onyx, topaz and jewels. Our mines are filled with guards for protection in order to prevent thievery especially of the *silver* you mentioned," he explains in a mocking tone that did not sit well with me.

One more time and I might have to follow my urges to end his life. My breathing quickens.

Being a Duke has its benefits, but I do miss the thrill of the hunt and the ability to kill at will without any obligations or remorse hence, why I decided to embark on this mission on my own rather then send an emissary. Not only due to the delicacy of the situation but also because I long for the excitement of spilling blood. Lost in my own thoughts, I did not realize the soldier was still speaking. His last few words caught my attention. *Did he say mithril?*

"Repeat that last sentence," I demand.

"We do not possess silver in our lands but something far more valuable. The very rare metal, mithril is what you see on the walls. The mines, which possess these metals, are amongst the most guarded. Only the richest of Dukes and nobles can request the purchase of mithril. I believe the former Duke of Apollon had made purchase recently."

The thought of Edward buying mithril put a smile on my face. The mithril he purchased helped create the very weapons that took his life and provided me with a means to exact my revenge. God must be punishing him in the afterlife by leading me to the *Holy Grail* of the most valuable metal in Thalia. *If there is a God, he or she is definitely more sinister than I could have ever imagined.*

We ascend a massive flight of stairs leading to the second floor of the castle. The next floor is very similar to the first except without a great hall leading to a throne room and entertainment hall. Instead, it is a maze of narrow hallways with rooms on each side. The walls are still engraved with images of past Dukes just like the first floor. This floor only illustrates the life of three Dukes with the last image representing the most recent Duke. There is a notable difference between these carvings compared to the previous twelve. The image of God holding a child is absent, an accurate portrayal of Gaston Fate, the childless Duke, the first of his kind.

We near a room at the end of the narrow hallway to the left and the guard unlocks the door and steps in. I follow him in the room and dismiss him with a wave of my hand. The door behind me shuts and I am finally alone to plan the day. This is a time sensitive task as the poisonous elixir I created will only be potent for a few days and the travel itself to Destonia has taken away much of my valuable time. I have only two nights remaining before the poison renders useless.

The room is quite small compared to my chambers in Castle Eclipse but it will do. Steam enters my bedroom from the bath situated in the next room and I welcome the sight. I unbuckle my leather belt and untuck my tunic from my trousers and take them off, placing them on the floor next to the tub. I unbraid my hair and with one leg at a time, I step into the smoldering hot bath and drown my body into the water. I lay my head down and let the water drench my black hair. Closing my eyes, I turn to meditation and envision how the next two nights will unfold.

The first night will be all observation. In a few hours, I will learn my victim's habits and routines at dinner. The frail Duke is simple enough. He is attached to the Chancellor's hip and does not venture too far from his own bedroom during the night. Henry, the Duke's nephew, seems to be training himself for his future role as ruler of Destonia. The potion I concocted is specifically made to end his life. The poison is most effective when the target is fatigued or physically spent. It will flow through his blood stream and seep into as many vital organs as it can, and due to his exhaustion from training his body will not be able to fight the effects if administered in the evening during his time of rest. The report from my scouts is that Henry trains vigorously day and night, only stopping for food and water to replenish his body. During the day the boy is relentless but during the night his vitality is drained.

The second night, I will need to make my presence scarce and not be seen in the castle until the events have transpired. Once Henry and Gaston are dealt with, only then do I wish to be found in my own chambers, oblivious to the situation. Along with the initial letter of introduction, I had Pyke draft a second parchment to indicate my interest in observing the monasteries and traditions of Destonia so that I can bring my findings back to Apollon in order to educate our people about the *advanced* cultures of Destonia. With this official document, there is no reason for anyone to suspect me in the castle during the day or night. Pyke also provided me with details on Henry's morning rituals. A priest is said to visit Henry's room every morning to pray. They pray to give him strength for his training and to ask God to cure his uncle's degrading disease. *Tomorrow will be their last prayer together;* I smile while I enjoy the scolding water against my skin.

While no one suspects my presence, I will be scouting the ancient castle, locating hidden doors and entrances to the Duke's bedchambers. *This is a mission of stealth and precision,* I remind the dastardly voice which would instruct me to leave a bloodbath behind. Yet there is no response this time.

"Perhaps it has finally given in," I mutter triumphantly.

Before his bed hour approaches, the Chancellor's personal maid will serve young Henry a beverage containing the potion. While Henry is dying by the hands of my creation, I will find a way into the Duke's chambers while he sleeps and suffocate the old man. His death should not arouse suspicion, as he is barely alive to begin with. The priests will assume it an act of God for his time to pass this world and live in the next.

I replay the outcome of both deaths over and over again and each time my confidence and excitement grows. I am one step closer to having my revenge. I did not wish to keep our guests waiting too long, so I rise from my now mild bath and wipe myself with a fine lamb skin towel, watching as the water is absorbed from my body. Fresh clothes await hanging on a string rope near the window. A silk and black sleeveless shirt and grey wool pants are provided for my audience with the Duke and his nephew. The outfit is simple with no special ornamentation but the quality is outstanding. I dress myself and head for the hallway. Before leaving down the stairs, I examine each room in case I need to *relieve* someone of their duties on the day of reckoning. Luckily, there are no servants or guards to be seen. This entire hall must be dedicated to guests. After I complete my examination it is clear that I will have complete privacy and no disruption besides the odd visitation from the Chancellor or his personal maids. I descend down the stairs and sigh with annoyance, *time to play the role of a noble Duke.*

As I approach the bottom of the stairs the sickening voice that has been silent for most the day creeps its way back into my psyche. *Don't be weak; kill them all,* it buzzes eerily.

"One day, I will kill you," I reply, not realizing that I have just blurted those remarks out loud in the presence of the Chancellor, Duke and a young boy who fits the description of Henry. Triten and Henry look up at me with a startling expression. The voice in my head laughs and disappears once again. I walk to the table and say, "Apologies for startling everyone. Please ignore the outburst."

"Quite alright, Duke Bladestorm," the young man answers politely as he stands and bows. The Chancellor rises from his seat still confused over my vocal eruption and extends his palm, directing it towards the boy.

"Lord Payne Bladestorm, I have the honour

and privilege of introducing you to the Duke's nephew and soon to be heir of Destonia, Lord Henry Fate." The boy's resemblance to Marcus is uncanny. It is almost as if I am being introduced to his future twin. He has identical golden coloured hair, soft white skin and green eyes, though he is taller in height and more muscular. Even his demeanour is similar in the way he bows, all noble and proper. I want nothing more than to slit his throat, but not tonight. This one dies a different way.

Putting aside my will to kill this boy, I respond with a proper noble gesture. "The honour and privilege is my own, young Henry," I smile casually.

When the pleasantries are complete, we all take our seats with the exception of Duke Gaston who is already sitting. During our initial meeting, the senile fool gazed upon me with suspicion and it seems as though he has not stopped. He endures his watch with his suspecting eyes. I gesture at him with a smile and turn my attention to Henry. "How is your training, Henry?" I ask trying to keep the focus on Henry and not the Duke's intense staring.

"Thank you for asking, my Lord. I have concluded my jousting and sword play training, and prior to that horseback riding and archery lessons," he answers wearily. "I will have to excuse myself earlier then I would like but the training drains what little energy I have left."

"Of course," I say in a reassuring tone. "Being a Master of Blades and Potions, I can appreciate the fatigue that comes along with training. Let us enjoy our meal and discuss your training in more detail and perhaps, if time and energy permits, your goals in successfully ruling Destonia."

As we took sips of our soup, Henry tries to explain his daily regimen of training. Henry's training reminds me of Marcus'. Mornings consisted of literary studies while the afternoons were in the fine arts. While Marcus focused on blacksmithing and jewel craft, Henry prefers the arts. His passions are playing the harp and the flute. He sits for hours, fine tuning each instrument to ensure the perfect melody. Henry claims that music helps calm his mind and is his favourite part amongst his daily routine and just like Marcus; it is the evenings that he dreads most. Every evening, he equips the same armour as the soldiers, saddles up on his steed and jousts for hours. Jousting is a tiring affair for grown soldiers and knights so I can only imagine the toll it has on Henry. It did not end with jousting. His training would then consist of archery. Whenever he grips his fork and spoon I examine his hands and witness the effects of his training. Each finger is damaged and his hand has scratches, cuts, callouses, and inflamed veins. He claims to shoot over three hundred arrows a night and from the looks of his fingers, that number is not an exaggeration. His night concludes with swordplay. Three trained soldiers with wooden training swords surround him and come at him one at a time, slashing, jutting and poking Henry until he fends off each attack successfully. Then they would switch to attacking in twos and eventually threes.

"I know this is not the appropriate supper conversation, but how fares your body to the soldiers' attacks? Is it a similar situation to that of your hands?" I pry.

Henry curls his hands into a fist, embarrassed at the sight of his damaged skin.

"It is alright, Henry," I smirk and point at my eye where my scar sits. "These are reminders of our failures but also can be our motivation to become stronger. Never hide your battle scars as they are what make you a man."

"Well said, Lord Bladestorm!" the Chancellor interrupts with an impressive tone.

I turn and give him a sharp stare, making the weasel sink back into his meal.

"Now, please Lord Henry, let us see those manly battle scars," I insist.

Henry still shows signs of discomfort but as every good little noble he knows his station and it is below mine. Henry careful lifts his tunic. His pale skin is red and purple from bruises and scars, some fresh and some old. Almost every inch of his torso is covered in some form of physical deformity.

"It pains me to see such a young boy with so many scars but I am honoured that you show such determination and dedication to your duties. Destonia is in good hands," I praise him with a twisted smile. *With all of those cuts, the poison might be easier to seep through his body when he is bathing.* Turning my attention to Gaston Fate, I notice his stare has not faltered. *Soon, old man, those eyes will never open again.*

CHAPTER TWENTY FIVE
ARTHUR LOWBORNE

I rest atop a balcony staring into the distance, past the market place and towards the docks. *If only I was free to leave this cursed life and start anew.* I know this could never be possible while Payne was alive and on the hunt for us, though it does not stop me from imagining a life where I control my own fate. The five-storey high terrace permits a perfect view of Nasgrath.

Lately, all I want is to be left alone. The burden of being an eleven-year-old boy forced to play a grown man has changed me. And now there is a child in our lives to complicate things even further. Everything about Nasgrath is devouring my energy and youth and I cannot escape my responsibility to protect Katherine and her newborn. I sigh deeply as the idea of fleeing on a boat across the ocean escapes my mind. By now the sun is setting and Magda should be with Katherine.

Magda, who has been a blessing to Katherine, is perhaps her first friend since my real mother. Her knowledge as a midwife is invaluable and her friendship has been vital to mother's survival. I recognize that without Magda, both Katherine and her new born would be as good as dead; yet something about her concerns me, almost as if she is hiding something but this could also be a product of my environment. I have become a increasingly paranoid and untrusting.

At the very least, I have come to trust one person in Nasgrath. The Sweet and Sour fruit vendor has prospered ever since Balthazar's mockery during Katherine's incident. The customers and other vendors were so repulsed by his self-promoting while a woman was in agonizing pain that they no longer even speak with him. Thanks to Magda and the royal guards, he has also been exiled to a different location in the market and prompted to change his product name to *Balthazar's Standard Fruits*. If it were my decision, I would have taken away his right to ever sell again; nonetheless, there is some justice still left in this world.

I watch as the old man closes his shop for the day and completes his last transaction with a satisfied customer. Our usual hour to meet is almost here and I have quite the appetite. My stomach grumbles as a reminder. I place a hand on it as to tell it that soon it will be fed. As the fruit seller is about to finish his task, my attention treks elsewhere for a few moments and I forget my hunger. Gruesome images of me murdering troubled youths as well as the murder of my parents still haunt me to the point of disturbed sleep the last few days. Each time I relive those dreams, I see the boys in my parents' room rather than the alley. I have no remorse when I use my rusty knife and pierce it into the bodies of those boys. Each time I stab and cut, I can see Payne's evil smile on their faces and a sudden outburst of uncontrollable rage enters my soul. Everything around me becomes a crimson bloodbath. It is almost as if I am possessed by an uncontrollable blood thirst. Once I kill those boys, I see the dead bodies of my parents next to them. *You still blame yourself, don't you?* A voice asks behind the closed doors of the bedchamber. An innocent boy peers through the door watching me perform the murders. At first, I just see a glimmer of an eye, but as I walk closer to it I can eventually see clearly the person hiding behind the door. His face is identical to my own but younger, innocent and brimming with life. It is the Marcus before the murder of his parents. My heart swells with joy to see myself so healthy and clean but my admiration of my previous identity is brief as an arm abruptly wraps around my shoulder. I look up the lanky form only to notice it belongs to Payne. He is looking around nodding in approval of the carnage I have committed. He then turns to the innocent boy behind the door and extends his arm out, plunging his dagger into his heart. I always wake in a cold sweat.

Am I becoming like him? If it were not for Katherine stopping me in the alley, who knows what would have become of me? I could not stop the murder of my parents and now I have the blood of three boys on my hands.

My head spins from the recollection of my nightmare and I lose my footing on the balcony causing my body to trip forward. I quickly react and catch myself before I fall five stories down to my death. Shaking my head clear, I remember my eventual goal. Nothing will stop me from taking revenge on Payne. No matter how I reassure myself, I cannot stop my tears.

You miss them so much. You cannot rid yourself of the person you once were. You must remember the past, your family, their demise. Let it fuel your vengeance but do not become the very man you want to kill, I lecture myself. Grabbing the ledge with both hands, I propel myself back on the balcony ledge. The market place is pitch black and clear of buyers. Only the old man and I remain. I hop down each story as swiftly and agilely as possible so I do not wake the owners of the homes. The balconies are slippery and brimming with dust and small pebbles but I have learned to control my speed and accuracy, landing on the edge of each balcony until I reach the bottom floor. I do this in my bare feet because of how rough and scaly my skin has become due to the harsh environment in Nasgrath. After a few seconds of scaling the building, I land on solid ground and I start walking towards the old man who is already packing fruits in a sack.

"Ahhh... Young Arthur, always on time," the old man whispers. "How are your mother and sister doing? Have my fruits kept your bellies full?"

"They are well, thank you kindly for asking. The fruits are a blessing. Both my mother and sister are eating well. How are your grandchildren?" I ask politely.

"Everyone is doing fine dear boy. They are happy and healthy once more thanks to our *fruitful* arrangement," the old man snickers quietly to himself. He hands over the sack of fruits to me and I tie a knot on the front end to avoid anything from spilling out. I thank him and am about to take my leave until he stops me.

"Arthur," he says in a worried tone. I twist

my head slightly to let him know I am listening. "There were strange men from Apollon under the orders of Duke Payne Bladestorm seeking out two fugitives by the names of Marcus Sunborn and Liza Skylar. Apparently, these two criminals are involved in the deaths of the late Edward and Jaina Sunborn. These mercenaries came to my shop with descriptions of the two and I denied ever seeing the fugitives... but I have a feeling I know them both," his voice lowers so no one else can hear us.

My hand reaches for my dagger hidden in my tunic. *Please be careful with your next words, old man,* I plead.

"Be forewarned, but rest assured that your secret is safe with me, Arthur. Everything you did for me and my family will forever remain in our hearts and souls. As far as I am concerned, Marcus and Liza never stepped foot in Nasgrath."

"I appreciate your loyalty," I express my gratitude and removed my shaky hand from my tunic. "Do you recall their appearance and their numbers? I would like to know what I am facing."

"Five men led by a bald, medium sized man. His most prominent feature was a brand on his forehead of a half moon. He seemed the most dangerous of the five. The others just seemed ordinary trained mercenaries, deadly still, yet the one I described stood out amongst the rest. They were garbed in black leather shirts, brown tanned gloves and pants, dark leather boots and each carried cutlass swords."

"Did you happen to hear where their next destination may be?" I probe.

This is bad... very bad, I tell myself. I cannot protect myself, Katherine, and her child from trained, armed men. Running will also make us stand out. What do I do now?

"Their next location seemed to be the Noble District. I overheard them speaking of Lord Edward having had many friends in Nasgrath that would blindly assist the two fugitives. The slums seem to be a safe location for the time being. There are over two hundred homes to investigate in the Noble District before their attention turns elsewhere. I would say you have two nights before they start searching all lowbornes," the old fruit vendor advises.

Two days is not enough time, but it will have to do, I cringe at the thought of telling Katherine. She finally found peace with the birth of her daughter and now the very man who took our old home is haunting us in our new one.

"I have provided you with extra food due to these unforeseen circumstances," the old man interrupts my thoughts. I wave my hand in acknowledgement and hastily take my leave back to the slums. I scurry along the main road west heading towards the putrid smells of the slums. Even a blind man would be able to find his way to this filth. The hard, sandy ground slowly transforms into mush, dirt and mud the further I go west. I race as fast as my feet will take me across the narrow streets. Sharp pieces of wood sticking from the ground poke and scab at my feet, festering new wounds on the existing ones but I run through the pain. The urgency of the news given to me by the old man takes priority over everything. *I need to make it home to give Katherine the news.* Never before have I been this excited to be in the slums.

My pace slows down as I enter the alleyway where the incident happened not too long ago. *This time I will not be caught by surprise.* I watch for signs closely with every silent step. No one hides in the darkness this time but that does not stop me from being cautious. I retain a steady pace but I do not wish to linger here for too long. Gossip and rumours of my ruthless attack on the boys has made the people of the slums fear me. Though most of the residents in the slums can now identify me and stay far away when I am nearby, the family members of those boys want nothing more than to exact revenge. My fair hair and green eyes only aids in making me stand out amongst the typical citizens of Nasgrath, and the news of my actions has launched my reputation even further.

Once I pass the narrow alleyway, my heartbeat regains its normal rhythm and my heavy breathing subsides. I stop to catch my breath and clear my thoughts I suddenly sense a presence behind me. My body starts to seize with fear, but my instincts drive me to turn and face it. Without even thinking, I reach for my dagger from the rope belt around my waist and spin to encounter my foe.

It is the sole survivor from the group of bullies staring at me and baring his teeth. My posture returns to an upright position. We stare blankly for a few minutes. I know the anger and resentment he feels towards me; I can almost feel his emotions coming off him, but he and I both know that he would be no match for me.

Show mercy and let the boy live. Remember who I truly am and what I am avoiding to become. Portray the kindness that made you your father's son.

"I know you cannot speak but you can listen. I am sorry about what happened to your friends. I did what needed to be done out of defence and it was you who attacked me first."

His expression did not falter. Perhaps a show of good faith and kindness will help ease the situation. The sack in my left hand drops to the ground and I put my dagger away. I can tell the expression on the mute boy's face is that of mistrust and his eyes still flare with rage. I reach into the bag and pull out a ripe green apple, two oranges and a few yellow pears and offer it to him, hoping the boy understands that this will never replace his friends but it is an attempt to offer amends. Food is scarce in the slums and lowbornes usually kill one another in cold blood for a crumb of bread. At first, he hesitates but eventually he cannot resist. He wipes the drool off his mouth and bites his lip while thinking. His belly grumbles furiously and he places his hands on his flat, skeletal stomach. Instead of waiting for the boy to approach me, I walk a few steps towards him, which startles him, and he shuffles backwards.

Be patient, he will come, I tell myself.

The fruit is becoming heavy and my arms tired of holding them, so I sigh and retract my offer. Before I place the fruit back into my sack, the mute makes a leap towards me and snatches the fruit from my hand and jumps back. Smiling as to show him that I am pleased with his decision, I close the bag and place it on my shoulder. The boy crunches into the apple as he runs back into the alley. I am glad to have had this last encounter with the mute. It provides me with a small sense of closure that I need before I leave this life behind and return to my former self. I turn my attention back towards my hovel and sprint forward, trying to make up for the time.

CHAPTER TWENTY SIX
OLD MAN VENOM BOLT

Over one hundred homes have been searched and not one Wraith is within them. Last I remember, Nasgrath should have close to ten in the Noble District and I have not been able to locate even one in the last day. *I wonder if this change is a result of that rape incident with Liza,* I ponder, *the one event that changed how the Guild utilized Wraiths.* In the past, my Masters chose the richest and most powerful figures in each land and manipulated them to work for our cause. This worked well until some of the wealthy forgot their place and their newfound riches and position swelled their egos, not unlike the rapist in Nasgrath who abused his privilege. When you are deemed a Wraith, the guild provides protection and wealth beyond imagination; but as with everything in life, there are limitations. The fat bastard, who gambled all of his richest away and lost his soul to alcohol and publicly raped a woman on the streets, was disposed. My Masters had tasked me to discard him and his family but I did not make it there on time. Instead, he was made into a spectacle for all of Nasgrath to see.

What transpired that day changed Dark Heart forever. He had learned of the man's identity and took it upon himself to instil his own type of justice before I could get to him. At the time, he possessed the prestigious title of Shadow Walker, but after his change our Masters never fully trusted him. That night he inadvertently learned of what and who Wraiths were, something which the Masters were not ready to disclose to Dark Heart.

He tortured the rapist until he confessed of our Masters' involvement which only imploded the already volatile situation. He also repeated our sacred vows to Dark Heart in order to prove that he was under their orders and that only gave more reason for Dark Heart to distrust us. The bastard divulged the truth about Wraiths as well and ever since that day, our Masters have been careful with whom they appoint.

It is time, old man, demands Venom Bolt. My knees crack and my wrists hurt as I assist my body to get up from a kneeling position. I place my hand on my lower back, trying to rub the pain away. *Let us locate this Wraith and move on,* Venom Bolt hisses impatiently. Nodding in agreement, I swoop down and begin my search through the second half of the Noble District.

My foot has swollen drastically since last night's incident. *Next time step with your foot, you old fool, not put an arrow through it,* I mutter angry to myself. Every landing, I stumble slightly and want nothing more than to scream. It isn't only physical pain I am dealing with. Sleep has also been difficult; every time I close my eyes to rest, the Snake Charmer invades my thoughts. She continues to relentlessly reveal a past that I no longer wish to recall. I am no longer that person and as far as I am concerned the past can stay buried with her and those vile snakes.

In my most recent dream, the Snake Charmer and I lay in bed together fully in love and what seemed like a finished fulfilling sexual act. She placed her head on her hand and looked to me. Her lips moved but no noises came out. I tried to read her mouth but could not. When she tried to repeat herself, I awoke with a throbbing pain in my foot. All I managed to understand was the first word: *Cecil.* I know the name but something did not allow me to recall its significance. Was *it my part of my past or hers, or was it the name we wanted to give our child?* I wonder. Venom Bolt quickly intervenes with an angry pitch when he notices that I am thinking of a time long past. *Old man, remember who you are. There is no past, just the present and the mission. Habitamus in tenebris.* I refocus and await sunset. Still, in the back of my mind, I fear that I am losing control of my emotions and I do not understand how or why this is happening.

A few hours pass and only a dozen homes left to investigate. Something is certainly wrong. Twelve homes remain and all of them are too close in proximity with one another. To have more than one Wraith so close to one another would be foolish. Still, I push forward and inspect each home. Some homes are vacant with no signs of furniture or décor, while others are occupied but have no response to my presence or our secret code. Wraiths are trained to react without hesitation to *Habitamus in tenebris* even during their sleep. These fools slept uninterrupted with drool running down their cheeks. Once I complete infiltrating the last home and find no trace of a Wraith, I return to the rooftop and want nothing more than to shoot an arrow through someone's eye to alleviate some of my frustration.

No Wraiths in the Noble District... what is going on? I sit for hours and meditate. A clear head will be needed to figure out my next move. Nasgrath is too vast for me to search every inch for clues of Dark Heart. As I sit concentrating, a frail voice whispered from a distance, "Shadow Walker."

At first I ignore the voice, thinking my mind is playing tricks on me. How could anyone possibly know of my existence? The voice eventually stops calling out and there is silence once more. Seconds later I hear the sound of an object project towards my skull. I open one eye and catch the pebble in my hand seconds before it hits my forehead. Curious, I stand and peer over the rooftop with *Medusa* in hand. Below me is an old woman with a cane and a grin on her face.

"Who are you?" I ask reluctantly with a whisper. Her grin grows wider.

"I assume you have been looking for me and it seems as though I found you instead. *Habitamus in tenebris,*" she recites.

I am in utter disbelief. *Her? She looked as much a noble as a donkey looks a horse.*

"Wraith, what is the meaning of this? Why do you not reside in the Noble District?"

"Why don't we talk in a more secluded area," she suggests. "You can put that deadly weapon away as well. It has been some time since I last had any contact with the Masters and now I get their deadliest weapon looking for me. Let us meet at the marketplace where it is deserted. I am slow and it will take me but if you have waited long enough to find me what is a few more hours?"

Fantastic, a Wraith with personality, I sigh. I jump off the rooftop to the ground and wince at the pain that shoots up my foot and body. The Wraith is no longer in sight. I put *Medusa* back in its holster behind my cape and discreetly move towards the market district.

Desolate, barren and without any sign of life, the marketplace is completely empty. Even so, I hide in the shadows in case of any guard or vendor revisiting the area. I have waited over an hour for the Wraith and despite her warning, I am growing restless. Something I have not been for ages. This folly has taken its toll on me and my patience. My tuned hearing recognizes the sound of a wooden cane stomping on the ground and slow paced footsteps approaching me. In the distance, I see a hunched figure. She is unaware of my location so I creep out of hiding to meet her.

"Explain to me why you are the only Wraith left in Nasgrath, and why the Masters chose one so... old?" I demand looking for answers. The old woman lets out a laugh.

"Old, you say? If you think I am old, son, what does that make you?" she replies with a toothless open smirk.

She makes a valid point, old man, agrees Venom Bolt.

Shut up, I retort bitterly.

"It has been some time before the Masters tried to reach out to us. After the incident with the rapist, many of us never received messages or orders again. Money ceased from coming in and someone was hunting down most of us. What was his name again? Dark Heart, I believe. That one was ruthless," She grumbles.

Why has this information never been relayed to me? I wonder.

"I was sent by the Masters to kill that very man. What information can you give me about his whereabouts? Has there been sighting of him in these areas, or news of him in Thalia?" I ask.

"Not Dark Heart. That name has never existed beyond the Assassin's Guild, but there has been lots of movement in Apollon."

She tells me of the Duke of Apollon's murder by his wife for infidelity and their only heir perishing in a training accident. A maid who seems to be an accomplice in the murder has escaped and is being hunted by the new Duke, a man named Payne Bladestorm, the former Master of Blades and Potions. *Two things that Dark Heart excelled at was combat and alchemy,* Venom Bolt reminds me, as if I needed to be reminded.

"How do you know all of this? Was there any description of the new Duke, perhaps a scar or physical characteristic?

"I have never seen the new Duke or have had the privilege to be in his presence. I do know he bested a famed knight and his son in battle, and changed the name of the former *Castle Guiding Light* to Castle Eclipse. He has been known to be very adamant on training his soldiers in combat and is seeking to grow his numbers."

That sounds like something he would be planning if he wanted to attack the Assassin's Guild head on.

"There is something else though," the Wraith says. "The heir of the Sunborn clan has not perished as the reports say. As a matter of fact, he lives among us but uses a different name. His mother's maid is also with him under a different alias."

"Have you seen them?" I inquire. She nods.

"It would do me well if you could remember my generosity when reporting back to the Masters. My name is Magda... but Magda the midwife should be sufficient," she says, a look of greed in her eye.

"Tell me everything you know."

As the Wraith tells me her story my eyes widen with disbelief. *She IS here,* I think triumphantly. "They both live at the end of the slums near the forest," she points west. "Do what you will but when you return to the Masters, remind them of my loyalty and hard work."

"I will but what name should I give them for the reward?" I ask curiously.

I thank her for all the information and with a burst of speed; I make my way towards the slums to find Marcus and Liza.

CHAPTER TWENTY SEVEN
PAYNE BLADESTORM

The second day is here and I am putting the final pieces in order to execute my plan. What might have originally been a chore should now be an easy task thanks to the open cuts and scars on Henry's body. The poison should spread quicker than originally anticipated. The potion along with the instructions has been provided to the Chancellor and he ensures me that his personal maids will distribute the mixture in Henry's bath tonight. The only other task remaining is to kill Gaston Fate without a trace of breaking and entering or foul play; a death disguised as a natural event. *This will be child's play,* I think confidently. There is no need to shed blood this eve.

Waking from my bed, I open my eyes in a dark room and peer at the window in my tower. I get out of my bed and stroll to the wooden window, pushing the curtains and allowing the blinding light to pour in. Rays of sunlight cover my body and face and I completely despise it. Raising my arm to shield my eyes, I peer down and look to the courtyard below. My room is stationed above the stables and I can hear the buckets of water and dry grass being moved by the stocky figured stable boys. Looking further ahead, I see a guard yawning at his station on his watchtower above the portcullis. Nobles scurry along with their daily routines like ants without a single worry in the world; fools ignorant to the real world. They live in a fantasy world created by money and shelter, knowing nothing of famine, poverty or the cruelty of the world. When I was abandoned by my parents and forced to survive on the streets, not one noble lifted a hand to assist me. Even when I was recruited, trained and raised by the Assassin's Guild, they used me to accomplish their own goals. When I finally found someone - something - worth living for, they did not take into account my service. Rather than thanking me for my efforts, they tried to kill me. The truth about this world is you either let the system choose your life and be a puppet, or you fight and choose your own fate.

How do you expect to have revenge/justice when you are too cowardly to accept me as a part of your existence Payne, asks the deep and malevolent voice inside me. *If not for me, you would not even be standing here. I make all the difficult decisions and keep us alive. It is I who will take everything from them and anyone who stands in our way, not you!*

I jam my fingers into my temples and squeeze the sides, rubbing fiercely in hopes that the voice would just leave and never return. Admittedly, its words ring true. There have been times when I stood victorious and unsure of what transpired knowing full well that my body was being moved by something else which resided in me.

When I trained as an assassin, my alter ego took control of my body often and I naturally allowed it. At first, the entity did not have a name; I mistook it simply for something that lives deep within everyone. All humans possess a dark part of themselves which lies dormant until they are pushed to the brink of insanity. Dark Heart is the name given to this entity inside of me - a voice that taunts me every waking day. A very small percent of trainees actually accomplish awakening their *calling* and most will perish from deadly training. Once you feel you have found your *true self*, you are put to the test and are forced to fight another fellow recruit until only one is left standing.

Combining our training and new persona, assassins follow a new path of servitude and obedience. Our pasts mattered not and in my case, the past was something I never wanted to remember but something was wrong in my relationship with my alter ego. Instead of supressing my past, I am constantly reminded of my whore-loving father and useless good for nothing mother and their mistreatment of me. I wanted to forget more than anything but it would not allow it. Dark Heart was cruel and bloodthirsty, and our co-existence only mattered when my daggers were in my hands ready to take a target's life. Besides these moments, we were always in disagreement.

My mentor and his alternate personality worked in tandem and never resisted one another. It was the one aspect of my training that I never mastered. I kept it secret from my teacher and past Masters, hoping they would not notice that Dark Heart was undisciplined and uncontrollable. It seemed as though Dark Heart wanted to keep the secret as much as I did. He only presented himself during situations in which victims were involved or battles were fought.

Because of Dark Heart's lack of discipline, I have never rid myself of my past. It is meant to be my support and guide, help me walk a new path in life. Instead, all Dark Heart did was murder and collect hearts, never assisting me in forgetting the past. Lately, it is lingering in my dreams as well. The dream begins with my victims underneath my feet, bloodied, hearts missing and the army I amass standing at attention behind me. I stand in the centre wearing my assassin cloak, holding both the *Silent Sisters.* But lately my glorious dream has started becoming a horrific nightmare. Instead of hovering over the dead as I normally am, my body is added to the pile with my heart missing. Looking down upon my still cold carcass is my reflection but more sinister, remorseless, and bloodthirsty. The face that bears a resemblance to mine stares down with pitch black holes in place of eyes and smiles, revealing its dark sharp teeth. "*Kill them all,*" it whispers and the words echo in my mind, growing louder by the second and consuming my thoughts. The words linger for hours, eventually becoming unbearably booming and I wake up in bed sweating and shaking, unable to sleep. He is trying to take control. *I will never let you have my soul,* I say in my mind, hoping it hears me. I shut the wooden blinds, dress in my plain, yet expensive fabrics and prepare to break my fast.

Bread, pork, eggs, and various other delicacies are arranged at the table. The Chancellor and Duke sit together at the head of the table, waiting for my arrival. To spite the dying noble, I walk ever so slowly down the final few steps leading to the grand hall. With spoon in hand, Triten feeds Lord Gaston with a look of disgust. Every time Duke Gaston slurps his soup, the

Chancellor's eyes would roll. It was quite comedic as the Chancellor would like nothing more than to shove the spoon down the Duke's throat and end his misery but the Duke is no fool. He purposely slurps louder each time the spoon touches his lips, knowing full well it irks his servant to no end.

Finally reaching the bottom step, I decide to introduce myself to the unaware Chancellor. "That is dedication if I have ever witnessed it, good Chancellor," I sarcastically mock him. "Would it not be more fitting to have slaves or maids perform such a task that is well below your stature?"

"Lord Payne!" he jumps excitedly, almost sounding like a child preparing to receive a gift. "Thank you for joining us this morning. I know you have a busy day today outside these walls. The Duke's well-being is my responsibility. I trust no one but these able hands to keep him sustained. There are many in this home that I mistrust especially with the Duke's current state. Besides, I believe you and I need to exchange some words before you depart?"

Nodding, I take a seat and snatch a loaf of bread on the table and start to rip it apart piece by piece. A maid stumbles over to the table and almost spills a glass of milk on me. I move in time and the milk splatters on the wooden bench. I give her a nasty stare and she quickly apologizes and refills the glass and places it gently on the table before skittering away. I sit back down and drink the glass of milk before inquiring, "Has Henry begun his training this morning?"

"Yes and he should not be returning until later into the evening," he answers as he wipes the Duke's mouth. Looking down at the bowl, the Chancellor sighs and beckons over to the maids. "The Duke has finished his soup. Take him back to his chambers and call the priest from the church. Let him know that the Duke would like his weekly recital to be performed sooner than usual." Two young females respond with a respectful bow, wrap Duke Gaston's arms around their shoulders and attempt to lift him. As they lift him to his feet, he turns his head in my direction and his mouth frowns, almost pleading to me not to follow through with my plans. *I am sorry old man, you are a step to a greater justice,* I think. Once the Duke exits the room, Triten slides closer, like a snake slithering in the grass.

"Is everything prepared for today?" He probes anxiously. I reach into my cloak and hand him the transparent bottle, which contains the poison I crafted. His eyes grow in bewilderment and amazement as he claps excitedly. "Instructions again if you may my Lord," he requests.

"Have one of your trusted maids pour this into Henry's bath a few hours before he has completed his training. When Henry steps into the bath, the poison will seep into his cuts and wounds, attacking every organ in his body, burning through him at a snail's pace. It will increase in speed and progression once the boy is asleep and his body is fatigued. Three or four hours into his sleep, every organ in his body will have been melted at the same time. He will die peaceful and quickly. There will be no screaming, no pain, and most importantly, no sign of murder or misconduct."

The Chancellor could not believe his ears. He brings the bottle to his face and examines the contents within the clear flask. "You are quite the man, Lord Payne," he exclaims. "Remind me to never cross you."

"I am sure it will not require a reminder," I remind him in a threatening voice.

"Of course not, my Lord," the Chancellor quickly replies. "As for the Duke, I have requested one of my most trusted guards to open the cellar door which leads to his bedchamber. At the back of Gaston's tower, there is a wooden door we leave locked from the inside and can only be unlocked in the same fashion. One of my servants has already unlocked the door for your entrance. This is an escape route in case of attacks from enemy forces or unsuspecting fires. A wooden ladder will lead you to the top of the tower and into his bedchamber. The trap door is placed right in front of the main door chambers. Two guards are always placed outside the Duke's door to protect him from intruders. Please be stealthy and cautious, as any sudden noises within the eerily quiet bedroom could alarm them of a presence other than the Duke's."

"Excellent," I offer my approval. "I will make short work of the Duke, leaving no traces of my presence. His death will look that of a natural cause and with those two out of the way, you will become the new Duke of Destonia and I will have disposal of the two thousand plus soldiers who will secretly serve me."

"Destonia will be at your command, my Lord," Triten claims with a villainous smile. "Oh, and one last bit of pertinent information... I assume you will not be climbing those eternally high walls on your secret return so the only back in unnoticed is *behind* the castle. There is a stone door that is hidden quite well. Seven torches are lit on the back of the castle walls. The fourth torch is the key to the hidden door. Put your hand into the flame and you will feel a lever; that is your way back in. Now, if you will excuse me, I need to perform my final duties for the morning. Until next we meet, my Lord."

I signal my hand in dismissal and finish eating the remaining food left on the table. The room empties shortly after the Chancellor leaves. With some silence, my thoughts travel to the other side of the continent, pondering how the search for Liza and Marcus is progressing. I could care less what happens to Marcus but Liza is still salvageable. She has been the only person in my life to ever give me hope for something more than this. The day I met her was the first time I resisted Dark Heart. The longer she stays by my side, the easier it becomes to control myself, to reach past Dark Heart's demands and killer intentions. She is also the first person to ever accept me, to love me. I want nothing more than to have her by my side when I am triumphant. I want to give her the family she has always wanted, in a safe Thalia.

You think the bitch will ever forgive you for what you have done to her and Marcus' family? snickers Dark Heart. *You took the life of your first unborn child, and that made me so proud. Then you proceed to live a lie for ten years, planning and succeeding in destroying the family that you vowed to protect. It was magnificent the way we dismantled Gwyneth, Jaina and Edward. I usually do the dirty work but this time you were with me every step of the way. Sometimes you surprise me and I wonder if you really are trying to do what is right for Thalia or if you are just finding excuses to justify your lust for murder.*

My hand trembles at the memories of killing my child and the Sunborns before I remember my resolve and that every action leads to the greater good of Thalia. Everything I have done after leaving the guild, I did to gain power to overthrow the mysterious hand of Thalia's true rulers - the Masters of the Assassin's Guild.

"You will never take away my determination. I do what I must for the good of the land, for the sake of my future family," I say, trying to convince myself in the process.

You have no future or family. You have only me, and the sooner you accept that truth, the sooner you will gain the power you seek, Dark Heart promises. I rise from the table, furious and flustered. I will not sit and trade words with Dark Heart today. This is not the time or place. Grabbing the last piece of bread from the table, I depart the empty great hall and make my way to the decorated double doors leading outside the castle walls. Using both hands,

I push the doors wide open and keep my head low, covering it in my hood. The two guards at the front gates need to recognize my departure but those were the only eyes that I want as witnesses so as to any additional avoid unwanted attention. The enormous portcullis has already been raised and the drawbridge lowered and I suspect it is due to Henry's departure for his training. I pick up my feet and speedily walk towards the stone gates when I realize that not a single eye is veered in my direction. The populous seems devoid of any care or worry. *I forgot how carelessly inattentive Destonians are.* My pace slows down and I naturally return to my regular speed. I even lower my hood as I come within reach of the guards. They both continue to stare into the horizon while I pass them, neither of them glancing in my direction. I turn to face them, hoping they would have the wits about them to realize who I was. Both guards move their heads slightly to one another and then back to their original position. They bow simultaneously in acknowledgement of my presence and return to their duties, looking like stone figures. As long as they see me leaving the premises of the Castle gates, then I have completed the first phase of my plan. "Now to wait for nightfall," I mutter impatiently.

I watch the sun settle into the mountains

from atop a hill behind the castle as the Chancellor suggested. A short, middle-aged man appears with a torch in hand and makes his usual rounds of lighting fires. He yawns and scratches himself as he ignites the multiple wooden torches attached to the castle. As soon as he completes his task, he returns whence he came. The moon shines down on all of ancient walls of Castle Fate exposing every crack and deformation that has occurred over the years. Just as Triten mentioned, there is seven torches lit outside the large stone structure, the wall spanning for what seems to be hundreds of yards. Finally reaching my destination of the fourth flame, I look down at the fire and wonder how literal the Chancellor was when he mentioned the switch being "inside" the flame. I look underneath the wooden torch and there seems to be no contraption. Touching the sides, I only feel a warm sensation of heat emanating from the fire.

I guess the switch must be inside.

I unbuckle my leather belt and remove it from my waist and tie it around my hand to avoid scarring. I cautiously place my hand around the flame at first for a few seconds, trying to get a feel for the pain. Once my body and mind comprehended the sensation, I quickly thrust my hand into the fire, rapidly trying to locate the lever. It did not take long for the flame to burn through the leather belt around my hand and pierce through my flesh. The stench of leather and skin fumes with the smoke and enters my nostrils. I cover my mouth with the other hand and scream into it as my skin burns. I frantically search for the lever and finally locate it at the bottom of the torch and pull up. The scolding hot lever rises and drops and I pull my hand out and shake it uncontrollably, trying to shake off the pain. My cuffs and leather are fully burnt; luckily I only find traces of minor burns and small boils on my skin. The pain is sharp and uncomfortable but I instruct my mind to accept the pain and endure.

Remembering that my presence is needed elsewhere, I look away from my hand and back to the castle walls, realizing that a trap door beside the fourth torch is now exposed. I slide through the door and enter the castle grounds once more. There should be a wooden cellar behind the castle. After briefly searching for it, I notice a door which has a dim light coming from inside. I place my hand underneath the door and pull softly and it opens with a tiny *creak*. Entering the room, I see a steel handle on the inside of the door with a lock. I grab the cold steel handle and the boils and burns on my hand send a sharp pain through my body as the mixture of hot and cold elements mix and wage war on my palms. Instinctively, I want nothing more than to release my hand from the door handle but I have to endure. If I cannot cup a door handle, there would no way I would be able to grasp my dagger. The door screeches and dust drops from the top of the frame as I close the door behind me. *I guess this cellar is used as often as the Duke's member.* The ladder described by the Chancellor stands tall in my view and the bedchamber above. I climb one rung at a time with a smirk on my face. I could not help but think about Gaston's nephew in his bath. Each step up the ladder makes me wonder if my poison is seething through Henry's organs, imploding and melting within his body. By the time I reach the top of the ladder, Henry should be lying in bed and very much dead. *Time to finish the old man,* I ready myself.

Reaching the top rung, I lift the trap door lightly and grab it before it crashes to the ground. Letting it down gently so it does not make a noise, I enter the room. Quite the sight for a dead man, the room is lavish beyond that of the Sunborn. Everything is covered in golden silks and jewels. Various gems and minerals such as mithril, topaz, diamonds, rubies and gold cover the crown moulding of the walls. Even the walls are painted in gold. Two large windows are to the side of the bed, each with a lavish wooden frame and an engraving of an angel carved into each one. The

Duke's bedframe is made of copper and could fit at least four people. If I were a thief, this room would exist as a fantasy come true; though the most precious prize to me is lying in an enormous bed, frail and dying. His bed sheets are comprised of material resembling golden silk and he is drowning in several blankets. Beside him, the holy book sits open on a nightstand. *I hope he recited his last prayers before I finish this.*

I slowly creep to the bed and loom over the figure of the old man who is barely breathing. I place a finger below his nostril and a warm breath of air touches my finger. *I suppose I will have to continue with the plan.* His bed is masked with various pillows that I can use, ranging from soft colours to dark shades. I reach for the darkest one I can find since the last thing I need is for any trace of blood on a light pillow. I raise the pillow above his head and slowly begin to lower it. Gaston suddenly opens his eyes as if he has felt my presence in the room all along. I cease the pillow's descent and drop it to my side and stare right back.

Gaston opens his mouth and releases a *hack,* perhaps a cry for help. It is pitiful witnessing how helpless and weak this man has become. Even the late Edward Sunborn stood as a mighty giant against this corpse. I smile down at him and raise my finger on my lips, pressing him to be quiet.

"This will be painless, my noble Duke. Your nephew has already passed away by now and there will be no evidence of foul play. Your life is barely worth living. I took it upon myself, from one Duke to the next, to be so kind as to help you end it," I say mimicking the most compassionate I can take. The Duke's lips purse together and he closes his eyes, almost as if he is ready to embrace his destiny. I bring the pillow back to a raised position and before I drop it, he opens his mouth and with all of his might spits a ball of yellow, chunky phlegm out and towards my face.

I have dodged arrows, outmanoeuvred knives, parried swords, and other viciously rapid objects but this...*this* unexpected and vile projectile smothers my cheek as a blob of yellow spit rolls down my face. The scent of saliva and decay is disgusting. I clench my teeth and instinctively clutch my daggers and remove them from their holsters. The sound of metal rubbing against leather fills the air as I swiftly raise them and almost plunge them into the Duke. Hands shaking and anger rising, I have to use all of my willpower just to stop myself from gutting him. I pull back my dagger slowly and sigh. The Duke never flinched. He continues to stare at me with an unwavering, fearless and taunting look. The spit slides down my face leaving a trail of mucus from cheek to my chin and lands on to Gaston's forehead.

Do it! Demands Dark Heart. *Snuff the light from this old man's eyes. Look at the way he scoffs you. A dying man mocks you and doesn't flinch at the sight of the Silent Sisters. He can sense your cowardice and so can I. If it were I, this old man would have died from my murderous presence alone.*

"Shut up! This is not the time for you to intervene! It has to be a clean death," I yell aloud, forgetting that there are two guards situated outside of the Duke's door.

I lower my voice again and try to regain composure. "Do you not fear me, Gaston?" I interrogate him with a sadistic tone. Gaston does not waiver nor blink. If anything, his resolve is stronger than ever. He begins moving his right arm underneath his blanket and removes the covers, exposing a skeletal hand. The Duke raises his hand wearily as he struggles to find the strength to reach his destination. I cannot help but curiously watch what he has planned in this situation. The hand reaches mine as he places his palm on my knuckles and attempts to push the dagger down to his abdomen. He wants me to kill him. He wants everyone to know that his death was a murder rather than that of natural causes.

"A murder is the last thing we need," I whisper as I halt the dagger from going down any further. Yet, my hand does not completely wish to stop. Something is convincing me to move it from Gaston's stomach over to his chest. *What is happening?* I worry as I lose control of my body. Sudden images of my father crash into my mind and I shake my head trying to remove them but it is too late. His voice, his stench, his appearance are all I can see now.

"Watch as I fuck this whore, you useless mutt. You were an accident, a pitiful accident!" he shouts as he shoves himself inside the stranger. "Come over here and watch this whore enjoy the way your father fucks." When I do not abide to his command, he removes his member from the prostitute, stumbles over with an overgrown belly, smelling of alcohol and sex, and commences into punching me repeatedly in the face until I am bloody and unconscious. I try to fight the memories but my father is on top of me, naked and angry. He is wailing away with his hairy, giant closed fists and I feel each blow as if it were happening to me right now. The last thing I recall is closing my eyes and Dark Heart laughing. Falling unconscious, I can sense him taking over. I am afraid of what is about to happen next. *This is going to get bloody.*

CHAPTER TWENTY EIGHT
DARK HEART

Thump, Thump, Thump.

A few seconds later, the old man's heart quickens and becomes less rhythmic and more unpredictable. So much colour in this room and it bothers me. I just want nothing more than to smear it with Gaston's blood. Payne is weak, has always been weak. When he discovered me deep in his soul during his deadly training, I did not awaken to save his hide but to save my own. Every human has the ability to be ruthless and soulless but only the Assassin's Guild understands how to rouse us and channel our abilities and persona into our hosts. We are a means of guidance and logic, a guide for them when they have doubt or uncertainty. Assassins work together with us and as a unit we are near invincible. But I refuse to be used the same way Payne was by his "Masters". This flesh believes he has been using me but all along I have been taking advantage of his self-doubt, insecurities and false sense of justice to satisfy my own lust for death. We used to get along when all he cared for was killing but our co-existence ended as soon as he met that little succubus who infected his heart and mind full of thoughts above a different life. Then he started making grand plans to be the saviour of Thalia. I only participate because the plan includes opportunities to murder others and collect hearts.

Speaking of murder and collecting hearts. I look down at the Duke. Both my hands stop shaking and I smile as I bring my free hand down on the Duke's chest. His heart beat increases and I oh-so badly want to rip it out. Without hesitation or doubt I pierce the left side of the Duke's chest, aiming for his heart. As the *Silent Sister* impales Gaston, he takes his last breath in and arches his back in pain. This act makes me feel complete. I *must* collect. My trophies remind me of my power, my dominance over *my* prey.

I lower my face close to the Duke's and place my eyes right above his and watch his every expression as the dagger resides in his chest. Red liquid spews from Gaston's mouth and onto the silk sheets. I rest my head on his chest and listen to the heartbeat once more. I can feel the warmth of fresh blood dispensing from his flesh and onto my chin and mouth. I lick the blood and rejoice in the metallic taste. His heart is pumping uncontrollably and red body exits his body form the whole I am enlarging. His lavish bedding is no longer and array of colour, but instead is drowning in a dark red pigment. Tears and sweat appear on the Dukes tormented face. Sated by the man's agony, I grip the hilt with both hands and carry on, harvesting the dying man's heart.

I resist the urge to finish this quickly; like an orgasm, it never lasts long enough. This act is what excites me the most. This is my form of foreplay and I perform like a man looking to tease his partner until they beg for it to be over. I do not require the touch of another human, unlike Payne, yet this is different. Nothing is more exhilarating than having power over life.

By now, Lord Gaston has fainted from the pain I made him endure. I place my ear close to his mouth and no sound comes from the opening. *This one didn't last long,* I think, hoping Payne can still hear my thoughts. As usual there is no response; he is still unconscious, dealing with his abusive father. I unleash my daggers from his body as the three sharp prongs rip at his flesh and bone, and the sharp blade slices through the remaining intact veins and arteries. Blood drips on the copper bedframe and the once golden hilts of my daggers now have speckles of crimson colour as my black blades turn a dark red. I do not even bother wiping the mithril before sheathing them back into their leather holsters attached to my belt. I watch intently as Gaston's heart pulsates with an irregular beat. Gaston's mouth is open and an unpleasant smell comes from within insides. Blood covers both sides of his cheeks and trickles into his white beard. I cup my hands together and dig them deep into the dead man's chest, scooping his heart out. The remaining few tendons and muscles rip as my hands grip at the small, frail organ. The pulsating has ceased. A sinister smile forms on my pointed face. The task is complete. Gaston's life vanquished and Henry should be disposed of as well. The only thing left is to bring Payne back to consciousness and let him clean up the mess he so wanted to avoid.

Before I free Payne from his torture, a knock comes from the bedroom doors.

"My Lord," whispers a timid and youthful voice. "It is your nephew, Henry. I wish to see you this night, Uncle, as I have not been feeling well and I was hoping that spending time with you would give me strength to continue training tomorrow."

What in the bloody hell is he doing moving

around, I wonder frustrated. *He should be a dead corpse in bed by now. The Chancellor had better played his part or else we will have two bodies to dispose of.*

The idea appeals to me all of a sudden but this is *too* careless. I cover the Duke's body with clean blankets and cover the hole in his chest with a dry pillow and quickly sprint behind the door as it opens carefully. Henry pokes his head through the door and says, "Uncle?"

When the Duke does not respond, the rest of Henry's body enters the room. He is walking awkwardly while holding his throat. I can tell that he is on his last legs. Most men would be lying in a pile of their own drool but this boy is strong. His training has given him a physique capable of enduring pain, and his will to live is impressive. There is no doubt that Henry would have made an honourable and noble Duke, just as Marcus Sunborn would. Unfortunately, just like Marcus, he is an obstacle in Payne's plans and needs to be disposed in order for my continue killing spree to continue.

About halfway to Gaston's bed, Henry falls to one knee and struggles to raise himself back up.

"Uncle, can you hear me? I think it is the will of God to punish me as I feel that my body is withering from the inside. I-I-I am sorry Uncle..." Henry's voice echoes and trails off as he falls on his stomach and then collapses on the ground with a light *thud*.

This has turned out better than I could have imagined. Now we have an alibi for the murder.

I search the room for a sword and find a collection of mithril blades hanging above a stone dresser in the right side of the room. They are identical replicas of the swords in the pictures that Payne examined when he traversed through the castle to his guest room. Nine different mithril swords hang neatly in their appropriate leather holsters. I reach for the seventh sword and remove it from the holder. It is the smallest and easiest to use, and I need a blade that can match the marks of my dagger; the edge of this sword is not precisely identical, but it will do. It would require a weapons expert to thoroughly examine them in order to identify that it was the wrong blade. Placing it in Henry's still hand, I lift his body from the ground and drop him on top of the bed near his uncle. I dip the steel sword into the fresh bloody corpse of the Duke and smear some of it on Henry`s hands and face.

"You are a weak, ungrateful bastard... just as the Chancellor claimed. A boy your age could not handle the pressure that was bestowed upon you so you took the life of the one man who treated you as a son," I whisper in Henry's ear.

The details behind how and why the heart is removed will be overlooked and the more prevalent matter will hold precedence. For the first time in Destonia history, a trueborn Fate will not be ruling. I take a deep breath and soak in the beauty of my work and admire the bloody mess I created. *Now is the time to awaken Payne.* I close my eyes and wait for Payne to regain consciousness. *Enjoy the work I perfected, you dismal excuse for an assassin.*

CHAPTER TWENTY NINE
KATHERINE LOWBORNE

Arthur has not returned from his nightly meeting with the fruit vendor. The hour is late and there is an eerie night breeze today. I pray he did not encounter adversaries today on his trip back. Every sunrise is a reminder of the life Arthur and I must endure just to survive. He had everything before this and all because of my misguided trust in Payne did he lose not just a family but a home. I promise to do what I can to help him reclaim what is rightfully his.

A few hours after Magda left my side, I fell into a slumber hoping to awaken to Arthur and my daughter together as a family. I wake up to an empty home but at least savour the sweet smell of my tiny daughter. It is refreshing to have a different scent than the usual morning "delights" provided by the slums. Her presence gives this horrific life some desperately needed beauty, hope and goodness. I gaze at my child with amazement and awe. Her fingers wiggle gently and she constantly places her upper lip on the lower one trying to moisten them. I move my hand gently on her head and stroke her tiny hairs as she coos. I look around to see if there is any food available for me to eat. The bucket of fruit has leftovers from the night before, but some of the fruits are drying up while others are bruised and rotting. Last night, the apples were red and yellow and now they are brown and soft from heat. I hope Arthur returns shortly.

I return to caring for my child. Removing the sheet covering her loins, I want to ensure she does not need changing. Magda placed a few clean cloths aside for me to use, one for wiping and a few as a cover. It takes some adjustment to cleaning her bottom but the act brings me closer to my child. I grab both her feet together and lift lightly and wipe. The cloth comes back clean and I smile at her and plant a kiss on her cheek. I pin her cloth back together and hug her once more. We lay together side by side in the corner of our home and I feel as though all of my past sins and sorrows wash away when she is in my arms. I look down at her and begin to think of names that would suit her.

Arthur promised he would assist in naming my daughter but I cannot help but think of a few on my own. The first name that comes to mind is Jaina - in honour of Jaina Sunborn, mother of

Marcus - but I fear that would only bring Arthur painful memories of the past. Magda is another name I consider because of the invaluable friendship and support she has shown me during my trials and tribulations. I quickly decided that there is only one Magda and the name does not suit my daughter. I raise my head to the sky and begin to contemplate. The dark night is a magnificent creature. A full moon hangs in the starry sky, casting down a light on the slums. *God's kingdom was a sight to behold,* I marvel at the view.

The day my time comes, I hope he will forgive my sins and permit me into Heaven.

This small child is the closest thing to Heaven on Earth. Heaven... the idea of it gives me peace. Perhaps I shall name her Nevaeh, wondering if Arthur will approve. The thought of finally associating a name with daughter excites me. *Where are you Arthur?* I decide once again to close my eyes and take a small nap with my child.

The sound of footsteps surrounding my hovel wakes me from my sleep. "Arthur?" I whisper aloud. When no response came, I ask again but louder. "Arthur, son, is that you?"

One set of footprints multiply to two and then three and four until five men hover around my home. A chill runs up and down my body and I clutch my baby close. I can feel an evil shadow surrounding my home. Something sinister waits outside. "Who are you?" I ask, with a tremble in my voice.

"Liza Skylar, we are here under the orders of Duke Bladestorm to escort you back to Castle Eclipse, preferably in one piece," mutters a harsh and deep voice.

This is not happening, I panic. *How did they find us?*

"I think you have mistaken my identity for another, my name is Katherine lowborne, a citizen of the slums and I have a daughter and son," I say hoping that I sound convincing.

"There have been no reports of her with child, let alone two," yells a voice from the other side of the tent.

"Katherine was it? Let us assume that you are not Liza Skylar and that you are indeed a citizen of this filth. Tell me of your children in every detail; their appearance, age, fathers name and birthplace."

They must be searching for Marcus.

I remind myself of the promise I made the night we escaped the gruesome murder of Edward and Jaina Sunborn. Marcus is and will always be under my protection as long as I live. When I refuse to answer, one of the men waves the grass skirt door aside and enters the hovel. He glares at me with a sadistic and murderous look. A scar of a half moon is branded on his forehead.

"You match the physical description provided to us but there is no mention of a child. Who does that child belong to?" demanding an answer. Once again, I decline to answer.

"*Tsk,* you are as stubborn as he described you to be. He only asked me to bring you back but nothing about a child."

His hand reaches behind his cloak and he draws a straight short sword. "Now, I will not repeat myself. Come with us and tell me where Marcus Sunborn is. If you cooperate I will let you and the child live. One life for two seems like a fair trade."

I grip my daughter tightly and back away into a large body at the back of my tent. Large hands push me back and I stumble forward.

"Marcus died while we were escaping," I

say with tears running down my cheeks. "I buried him in the forest of Nasgrath a few months ago. You are wasting your time. If you want to take me back to Payne, then so be it, but leave my child in my arms, alive and breathing."

Please do not come home tonight Arthur, I plead.

The stone-faced man has yet to blink once. He continues to stare and takes a step forward. "If that is the case, then you will not mind if I sit here until the sunrise. It will be easier to travel in the light. Until then, I will have my men stationed outside and I will remain in here."

His attire is similar to Payne's original garb. A black hooded cloak, black pants, brown gloves and tanned belt. The brand of a half-moon seems as though it is intentional. He catches me looking at it far too long.

"Brand of Castle Eclipse and given to those who survive one-on-one session with the Duke himself," he chuckles as he points a thumb to it. "Notice how I said the word "survive"? He took my fingers in exchange for my life." He removes his left glove and displays a hand with missing fingers. I almost want to vomit at the sight of his disfigured hand. He glances at it and laughs then puts his glove back on.

"*Fingerless John*... that is my new name and for Fingerless John, failing is not an option. I do not want to be renamed *Headless John*."

With eyes shut, I rock back and forth hoping my baby stays asleep but unfortunately she is already awake and begins to fuss. I try to calm her but am distracted as soon as one of the other men outside my tent alarm Fingerless John of another presence nearby.

"Sir, someone has just arrived and by the looks of it, he matches the description of our other target."

Fingerless John turns his attention back to me and shakes his head, disappointed in my lie. "If this turns out to be Marcus Sunborn, then it will be his life and this child for yours. You had your chance."

I try to reach for him but he steps outside before I can snatch his cape.

"Marcus!" I scream. "Run! Do not come any closer! It is a trap!"

It is too late. I hear four of the men moving while one stays behind. *Why, God? What more do I need to do for you to forgive me?*

CHAPTER THIRTY
MARCUS SUNBORN

Katherine's screams and pleas for me to escape fall on deaf ears. Nothing will stop me from saving her and the baby. I will never let another person I love be hurt by criminals and murders. I stand with my dagger out and sack of fruit on the ground. Sweat pours down my face as four men, all very large, approach me. Each one guffaws at the sight of my battle stance and weapon but I do not waiver or feign. This is not the time to be cowardly; It is the time to stand up and be courageous and do something that I was not able to do in the past and protect my family. All four of the men draw their swords and circle around me like vultures.

They are not here to take me alive and I will show them no mercy. These mercenaries seem untrained and undisciplined, I can tell by their demeanours and attitudes. I feel like my old self, like Marcus, a composed, and courageous young man. Arthur is mischievous and daring, but I have been as unfocused and callous as my alias. The first man underestimates me by approaching with his sword down and an amused laugh. As soon as he is within arm's length, his laughter stops as I jerk forward and stab my dagger into his sternum and rip open his belly. He looks down with disbelief and tries to thrust his sword into my body but I anticipate the attack and step aside. I bring my right elbow down and knee up into the middle of his arm, compressing it and loosening the grip on the sword. There is a brief moment that allows me to snatch it from him with my left hand. He gasps for air as blood runs down his mouth. With sword in hand, I swing upwards at his abdomen, hitting dagger and flesh. The dagger rises further up his stomach, exposing entrails, while the sword split him apart from chest to throat. The first man falls down, his blood and guts lying on the ground mixing in with the stench and dirt of the slums.

The remaining three men turn and look at one another. They signal the man in the middle to step forward. He steps forward with much more caution than my previous opponent. Learning from the mistake of his fallen comrade, he circles around with sword in hand and a defensive pose. The stance has so many openings I can exploit; there is no possibility that these men were trained in armed combat by Payne.

The first battle is always the most difficult

and with each battle won, my confidence and fighting ability grows. My first opponent was fortunately a dolt and underestimated me from my age and size. My new opponent is no better but takes the situation seriously. His movement is awkward as he staggers to the left and then to the right, dragging his feet and scraping dust from the ground. He looks as if he could be drunk and trying to either confuse me or entertain. He swipes his sword in various directions while dancing towards me. The closer he gets the more openings I find; with the sword swinging in my direction, he leaves either of his sides open to an attack. Both his feet shuffle on the ground every few seconds as he moves in. That is where I attack first.

Before the mercenary can move any further, I charge towards him and perform a sliding leg sweep. I topple the man onto the ground and the back of his head snaps back into a sharp rock. His eyes fold and blood pools from his skull. The other two men sigh with disbelief and step back simultaneously. Neither of them is sure of what to do next until a voice calls out from a distance.

"Let him pass."

The two men step aside, gritting their teeth and growling at me like hungry dogs fighting over meat. I cautiously move towards the voice coming from the direction of our home. A single man is standing firm with a bastard sword in his hand. *This one is different from the rest. He* is composed and relaxed even after watching me kill two of his men without effort.

"Katherine?" I call out. The man turns his ear to my direction acting as if he did not hear my call. "Where is Katherine?" I question firmly.

"Are you referring to Liza? There is no need to pretend any longer, Marcus," the bald man says as he parts the grass skirt covering the home, exposing Liza and the baby shaking in the corner. As soon as she lays her eyes on me, she stretches her arm reaching out for me but the man closes the skirt.

"Now be a good girl and stay put. I will deal with you later," he threatens Liza. "As for you, boy, don't think I did not notice how you killed my men. I did not expect it to be *that* easy but their death was assumed a certainty. These worthless cowards are with me because Lord Payne instructed I bring them along as disposable convoy."

Liza's life is in my hands and I have to save her. I grip my sword tighter with intent to maim. Both hands on the hilt to ensure full power in my thrust, I gain momentum and close our distance with blinding speed. The man reacts with precision, piercing his sword with force into the dirt ground and steps behind it. His right hand is out and feet gripping the ground, heavily digging into it. The tip of my sword clashes with the front of his blade and sends me stumbling back as steel strikes steel. He looks up at me with a smirk and lifts the front of his sword out of the hollow ground.

"Hmmm. Do I look like the four fools behind you, boy?" He asks mockingly. "If you are going to attack with full steam, you best know your opponent first. You are not the only one who has trained with the former Master of Blades and Potions," he points back to the home in declaration, "Their lives depend on your victory."

I remain calm even after the taunts and threats. *A clear mind and steady hand is necessary when facing a worthy opponent.* These are the words of my late and noble father. Closing my eyes, I take a deep breath and bring the hilt of my sword to my abdomen and let it rest gently in my hands. The man notices my sudden change in behaviour so he removes his sword from the ground and clutches his bastard sword, lowering it pointed forward and close to the ground. One leg moves forward and one back in a defensive stance. I make the first move and swing at his neck, hoping to sever his head from his shoulders, but he counters with a quick upper sword thrust causing my hands to vibrate from the clash and I slightly lose my footing from the force. His sword comes crashing down on my shoulder but I adjust in time and cover my flesh with my own blade. The weight from his sword pushes down on mine causing my sword to cut into my shoulders and pierce the skin. His strength far surpasses mine and is becoming more apparent as he brings me down to one knee. I do not have much time to think about how to escape this dire situation; defending myself in this position any longer will result in me losing right arm. I adjust my body to the left and drop my sword as I roll my body away from his attack. His blade plummets to the ground unexpectedly and his body jerks forward. I scoop a handful of dirt and toss it in his eyes. The man coughs and rubs vigorously, shouting and cursing furiously under his breath. An opportunity arises to retrieve my sword, and I slide to my original position to snatch the blade from the ground. Without hesitation I swipe, connecting with the man's left hand, causing him to scream in pain.

Getting back onto my feet I ready my next strike but halt as the man grips his left hand and twists and turns his body in pain, screaming and cussing. Feeling a surge of confidence with the results of my attack; I am sure this battle will not last long with the man's hand being severed. His body stands suddenly still and the once painful expression on his face is replaced by laughter. He blinks uncontrollably and rubs his eyes to remove the excess dirt while laughing. He picks up what remains of the left glove off the ground and sighs with disappointment. Turning his attention to me, he waves the glove in my direction with a looks of annoyance. "These fingers have already been claimed by Lord Payne. Fingerless John does not intend to lose any more fingers today. I need to be careful with you boy."

While Fingerless John tries to recover from the dirt clouding his sight, I take advantage and press my attack. Our swords clash as I push my offense and John counters with parries and blocks. I force him back with my thrusts and jabs, but none of my moves can penetrate his defence despite with his eyes blinking uncontrollably. Frustrated and fuming, I put my full power into an impaling forward lunge, hoping to end the battle with one move. Fingerless John reacts instinctively and I find myself losing my footing again and rush past him through the grass door and into the hovel. I startle Liza but she is relieved to see me alive. I glance quickly and see her eyes are puffy and red from crying. She is unaware of what is transpiring outside and is glad to see me alive but I do not have much time to recover. Both my hands are occupied from my fall as I tried to keep myself from landing face first. As I rise to my feet, I notice Liza's smile turns to an expression of shock as her mouth opens and eyes widen. A cold steel tip pricks the back of neck, causing me to shiver. *I failed to save them.*

"Drop the sword and step outside… both of you. Leave the child here," Fingerless John demands with a sinister low tone. Dropping my sword, both Liza and I stand and gaze at each other, perhaps for the last time. Turning around, we are both led outside by Fingerless John to face what he has in store for us.

Liza keeps looking back at her baby in the hovel and cries as we both stand stiffly side-by-side. "It will be alright Liza, I promise. Nothing will happen to the baby or you."

Liza looks at me and says, "Nevaeh. Her name is Nevaeh. Is it agreeable with you?"

"Nevaeh," I smile. "It is a beautiful name Liza. I am in full agreement." She laughs with happiness and fear in her voice. We both turn our attention back to Fingerless John, who is not swayed by our conversation to show mercy.

"Borro? Mathis?" He calls out. "Where are you fools?" No answer comes from the darkness behind him. He spits, "No matter, they are expendable. Now, to end your miserable life, Marcus, and leave this godforsaken filth of a shit hole you call home."

As he is about to drive his cold silver steel into my chest, an arrow zooms in his direction with such speed that we do not see it until it strikes the back of his shoulder, making him scream out in pain. I gaze up, startled, to see Fingerless John fighting against the pain. He relentlessly pushes on and before I can react his sword is an arm's length from my heart. Trying to brace myself I shut my eyes and lower my head, anticipating the cold blade piercing my body. Few breaths escape before I hear the whizzing of arrows and the loud squelch of penetrating flesh. I seem to still be conscious and breathing, so I open my eyes and see the tip of the blade, dripping with blood, and inside another body.

Her hands are stretched out and her head is down, long black hair running down her back and a hole inside her stomach. Liza stands determined and resilient, like a wall of flesh, protecting her cub. *Red... Blood... Again... this can't be happening again,* I shake as I realize what just transpired. Arrows cover Fingerless John`s back, head and spine. His body is draped on the cold ground, all the while his hand hangs onto the hilt of his sword.

She looks down at me with blood running from her mouth and she coughs, trying to say something to me.

Get up, Marcus! You need to help her. There is no use trying to convince myself as I am paralyzed by images of my family's slaughter. My only remaining family has just been killed protecting me. Liza grabs the sword with both hands and pulls with what strength she has left. The sword exits her sternum and she drops to her knees, trying desperately to breathe. She places one hand on her belly and another on the ground to bring herself to her feet and turns to face me. Her arms struggle to wrap around my shoulders and she slowly places a final kiss on my head.

"Marcus," she whispers weakly in my ear. "Take care of your sister and yourself. Remember your family and I will always be watching over you both... Please... keep Nevaeh... safe and... Marcus... I will always love you."

Her chin rests on my shoulders and her soft breathing ceases. My arms squeeze around her and my hands tightly clutch the fabric of her top. I start recalling our times together; from my lectures, to morning breakfasts, all of our talks during my baths, our trip to get my parents gift and just listening to her soft voice and beautiful laugh. My heart sinks into my feet.

"Liza. Liza, please wake up," I cry. She does not stir or move. "I cannot… I do not know what I will do without you. You promised we would be a family together and we would reclaim what is rightfully ours. I cannot live without you."

A hooded figure draws near from the darkness where the two mercenaries once were. My hands still shake as they tighten themselves around Liza one last time. Tears and blood cover my face. My nose is running as I cry out loud.

"Argh!" I yell in the cold dark night. My throat is raw and dry but I force my anger out. The hooded figure is standing in clear view, an old man with white hair, two green and gold daggers and an oversize crossbow. He bends over and examines Fingerless John before removing the arrows from his dead body.

"I was hoping this man was Dark Heart, alas, I was mistaken. I was too late to save you, Liza. Damn my old age," he says mutters to himself.

He clutches his hand on Liza's shoulder, trying to pry her off my body but I do not allow it. I hang on tighter and he detects that I am not ready to let go.

"So, you are still alive, boy," the old man sighs. Nevaeh is crying from inside, which prompts the hooded man to turn his attention toward the tent. He releases his hand from Liza's shoulder and pointedly walks over to the home and enters.

"I am sorry Liza. I am sorry. I am sorry," is all I can repeat.

Moments later, he comes out holding Nevaeh wrapped in his cloak. "Marcus Sunborn, son of Edward Sunborn, the last heir to Apollon, and travelling with Liza Skylar. That can only mean that Dark Heart now calls himself Payne Bladestorm and has seized the title Duke of Apollon," the old man talks to himself, seemingly trying to piece together the puzzling events. He looks to me next and says, "Marcus, I need you to focus. Liza is dead, but it is not for naught. She has given you the opportunity to live and to avenge her and this child. I would imagine you want nothing more than to make Payne suffer?" he asks rhetorically. "I will give you that chance if you listen carefully and follow my every instruction. I take some blame for what has transpired here as I am Dark Heart's, *Payne's*, mentor."

Before he says another word I react without thinking. With a growl, I let go of Liza and lunge at the old man. Seconds later, my face is to the ground, my mouth is covered in dirt and his hand is placed firmly atop of my head.

"I said to *listen* and *follow*. As I was saying, you could obtain the same level of skill as he or I, perhaps even surpass us. You and I are seeking the exact same goal, the death of Dark Heart." He ceases resistant from the back of my head, allowing my face to rise out of the dirt.

"Now, I have gold in my purse, enough to lead you to a ship and travel to a holy land called Saint Aran. There, I need you to travel northeast of the pier past an abandoned village, following a river and into a cliff. Within this cliff there will be a church with a few followers and priests. You will see a one winged angel once you enter the church to confirm you are in the proper location. Are you following so far?" he questions. I do not answer him, but he takes my silence as confirmation.

"I need you to sit there from dusk till dawn. You must visit every morning and stay every night until the moon is at its fullest. When the time is right and you have completed the first step of initiation, a priest with a *third eye* will approach you and whisper these words, *Habitamus in tenebris.* You MUST repeat the words back. I want you to practice these words on your travels. *Habitamus in tenebris,* we live in darkness. From that point on your training will begin and if you succeed in completing the ordeal, I promise you will be ready to face anything and everyone in Thalia."

He finally stands and allows me to breathe exasperatedly. Grabbing my hand, he helps me back to my feet and places the gold purse into my hand, closing my fist around it. This entire time he has held onto Nevaeh. His balance is inhuman.

"I will raise, train and protect her until your training is absolute and you return to this world reborn. By then I hope to have killed Dark Heart myself, but in the event that my age gets the best of me, you are our only chance," he claims.

"Now, go. Your sack of food is safe. Take any of the swords left behind by these men and head to the pier. Look for Captain Highsea and tell him Old man Venom Bolt sent you. He will take you to Saint Aran safely."

I stare at the old man defiantly. "I will not

leave until I say my proper goodbye to Liza. She deserves better than this. Her body must have the proper burial and passage to the next life. I must bury *someone* in my family. I did not even have the chance to say goodbye to my brutally murdered parents. Please, give me this last request," I now plead with tearful eyes. The old man agrees and hands Nevaeh to me. His arm wraps around Liza's stiff body and lifts her onto his shoulders. He grunts and put his hand on his lower back.

"Where would you like to bury her, boy?" He inquires impatiently. I point to the forest.

"She always walked towards the river in the mornings and spent most her time there. I want to bury here in the forest near the river."

We pace for what seems an eternity. I weep at the sight of Liza's motionless body on his shoulders. The only other person I love as a mother has been taken from me. I will never see her laugh, her smile; feel her kiss on my forehead, or her stern looks. I will never hear her voice or her wise words of advice.

I will train and return with power. Marcus is weak and Arthur is reckless. I will become something more.

Once we arrive by the river, we use our hands and dig a grave deep enough to fit her body comfortably. Both of us are exhausted by the time we finish but it is a necessity; I have to do something right for once. We both lift her body and place her into the ground gently. Placing a kiss on her head, I whisper, "I love you, Liza. I am sorry I could not protect you but I will avenge us all; you, my parents, Nevaeh and all of Apollon. I will make you proud." I grab a handful of dirt and begin to cover her body.

After an hour, Liza is buried deep in the ground and both Venom Bolt and I are washing our hands in the river while Nevaeh rests wrapped on a smooth boulder.

"Do you remember everything I told you, Marcus?" tests Venom Bolt. I nod in silence. "Good. You will leave immediately and wait at the pier for the Captain. He should be returning tomorrow after noon. He only travels to Nasgrath once a day, so it is imperative that you wait at the pier early and not move until he arrives. Repeat the words I taught you," he demands.

"*Habitamus in tenebris,* we live in darkness," I repeat and before he can react, I turn and take my leave. I head southeast towards the piers and the only thought that crosses my mind is Payne. I do not trust the man but my vengeance outweighs my logic. If there is anywhere in the world that can provide me with the tools and training to kill that menace, then I will endure everything until the deed is done.

I will make you suffer beyond imagination. I will return a force to be reckoned with and will save Thalia from your wicked grip.

CHAPTER THIRTY ONE
OLD MAN VENOM BOLT

As I hold Liza's daughter in my cloak, I am overcome by an unexpected rush of emotions. For the first time in decades, my humanity returns and it causes me confusion and pain worse than anything I have ever felt. My lips tremble underneath my burly, white mustache and my eyes water. The images of the Snake Charmer, no, *Alexia*, appears in my mind in full human form. She was beautiful, strong, and sensual. She possessed everything I was seeking for in a partner. Alexia bore my child and was ready to raise a family and live her life growing old by my side. At the time, I did not share the same resolve as her. I let the death of my father cloud my mind and riddle me with guilt, feeling as she was to blame for my lack of family and nobility. My old habits were hard to extinguish. Alcohol and prostitution made me weak. I drowned my sorrows in bottles of strong liquor yet I could still recall sneaking out at night to bed random whores. Alexia was an intelligent woman and knew all my doings, yet she stood by my side despite my heinous actions and obvious flaws.

The Royal Guards were in every major city searching for the two of us, but I was tired of the running and hiding. I craved a new identity and life with Alexia by my side, though I knew I could have never escaped my past. So, I took her life to save my own. The child in my arms now reminds me of a time when I could have been a father. I could have lived a simpler life, happy with a family and wife who adored me. Instead, I killed her and my unborn child out of cowardice.

I am sorry old man, whispers Venom Bolt with a low hiss. *I cannot subdue these feeling any longer. I have tried to battle your psyche and repress these thoughts for years. Slowly and surely your past pushed has relentlessly to the forefront. As much as you believe you are fighting your past, I believe a stronger part of you wants to remember.*

A part of me acknowledges I want to remember what it feels like to be human again. An assassin's life has provided me with a fresh start, restored my reason to live and allowed me the training to forget a life that only brought me pain and misery. I do not understand when and how my past has re-opened but, like my mortality, it is inevitable. I look at the child and cannot help but wonder how it would feel to be a grandfather.

I vow to protect this child and raise her as my own. "For you, Alexia, this will be my redemption," I say to myself hoping for forgiveness.

Marcus should be close to the pier now and I had scouted the area before I arrived to ensure there was no one else who looked suspicious. I wonder if sending him down the same path as Dark Heart and myself is wise. When I looked into his eyes and delved into his soul, I saw nothing but vengeance. He could become another monster.

Then again, he could also become our saviour, Venom Bolt counters.

The information given to me by Magda the midwife was disturbing. Marcus witnessed a gruesome display of savagery when his parents were murdered. A young child of his age should be playing with friends and thinking about girls, not be running from assassins and fighting for his survival. That same tragedy could fuel him to become the weapon our guild is seeking for the next generation. I once believed Dark Heart would become such but his upbringing differed too much from Marcus'. While Marcus was loved and cared for by those who surrounded him, Dark Heart was tortured, abused mentally and physically by his peers and family. Marcus knew the value of humanity, humility and love because he was witness to it for most his childhood. Dark Heart only understood suffering and the anguish that humans can cause one another.

Have confidence, old man, Venom Bolt hisses. Marcus will become what Dark Heart failed to be. He will turn into an honourable and just-seeking member of the Guild. You and I both saw something in the boy. He has lost everything and you have given him purpose again. Let him walk his own path under the guidance of our Masters.

I look down at the child and whisper, "I hope you're right, old friend."

Putting the child down carefully, I lean over to scoop water from the river and wash my hands of the dirt.

Venom Bolt, do you believe I failed Dark Heart as a mentor?

I am not one to harbour feelings for others, old man, he hisses in reply. Perhaps Cecil will be a better choice for that task? I only understand the art of killing. My instincts are predatory.

Cecil… a name long forgotten. Could I overcome the coward I once was and give this child a parent it desperately needs? I ponder.

An image of Alexia appears in my mind. Her belly is full and she softly smiles and I can only imagine her words, "Cherish this child as if she was our child, Cecil. Give to her what you would your own child. Love her and protect her. You are never too old to learn something new."

The thought fills my heart with joy - an emotion that I am no longer accustomed to in my old age. This has been an evening of realization and redemption. My shoulders feel light as a feather.

You were right. I am not too old to learn something new.

I bring the child closer to my chest and remember Marcus calling her Nevaeh. I am still required to complete my mission, but now my attention is required in two places and as two different. I wrap Nevaeh tighter in my cloak and look past the forest towards Apollon and my final task.

CHAPTER THIRTY TWO
MARCUS SUNBORN

My fingers dig into my chest where my heart beats as if I am afraid it is going to fall out of my body. Each beat causes me excruciating pain, both emotional and physical. I feel a weight pressing down on my lungs, blocking my ability to breathe. As I stumble through the forest, I cannot help but think of Liza. Her warm smile, brown skin and soothing voice is no longer in this world and it is entirely my fault. I grit my teeth and clench my other fist, looking for something to hit so I can release some of my anger. Knowing it would not bring back the dead, I decide to hold my anger in and let it be my drive.

I could have warned my parents of my nightmares, but I held my fears in and let them become reality. Their deaths were as much my doing as Payne's. I could have talked to them and explained my fears and my dreams. The omens were a warning I neglected. Because of it, I lost a mother and a father.

When Liza and I escaped Apollon, I gave her my word that I would avenge my parents and protect her from Payne but I accomplished neither, and now I have lost a dear friend and the last person in this world who I cared for.

After an hour of walking, I finally returned to the slums. I return to our grass home where the incident occurred. A powerful force compels me to walk to it. I stand in front of the hovel, once a sanctuary, where Liza and I spent our nights sleeping, eating, laughing and praying. With a rush of rage, I run over to the home and begin tearing it apart. I dig my fingers into the grass fiercely and rip apart the sides and collapse the roof. The branches and twigs cut my hands and puncture my nails until my skin shreds and nails chip, but this does not stop me. The wooden sticks that hold my home in place are now in my bloody hands. I grasp them tightly and start slamming them against the ground, bending and chipping them until they break. Each time I smash and crack a piece of wood, I picture a piece of Payne's body breaking. This is what I have become, a boy consumed with hatred. I harbour the images of my parents and Liza; not the loving times but the ones where they bled and suffered, and where I failed to protect them. I let the images stir in the depths of my soul and permit them to empower me. This is all I have left in my life - vengeance. I then toss them as far as I can and with every throw, I let out a savage scream to the point where my throat aches and my voice disappears.

In my current state, I have no way of protecting Nevaeh or stopping Payne but with the opportunity given to me by old man Venom Bolt I can become someone with the power to do so. I attempted being honourable and loving, but I know now those emotions are for the weak. I tried being rash and sneaky but those traits are for rats and lowbornes. The strong are ruthless and hateful. These are the traits I must acquire to be skilled enough to stop Payne, and he has already provided me with a lifetime of fuel for both. The only thing left for me is to board Captain Highsea's ship and travel to my new destiny. Once I complete dismantling the wooden dump piece by piece, I set my sights back to the pier.

The moonlight still shines bright on Nasgrath as I approach the market place. I was only a few minutes away from my destination, but before I departed I wanted to let the old fruit vendor know that my presence was no longer going to be in Nasgrath.

When I arrive at the market, everything has been neatly packed away and the shop has already been covered with a cotton cloth. I raise fabric and expose wood on the side of his shop. I carefully carve in my message on the inside: *never utter my name to anyone. I am no longer here and you never knew of my existence.* My hand aches from pushing the blade into the board. The dry blood and chipped nails embedded in my hand and fingers make the whole experience uncomfortable but I need to ensure he keeps quiet about my existence. Once I complete the inscription, I cover the store with the cotton cloth once again and make my way to the ship harbour.

I do not sleep this night. I sit cross-legged at the docks awaiting the ships to arrive, as ordered. During my wait, I let the disturbing deaths of Liza and my parents fester in my mind. The continuous and revolving memories made me realize the truth about the world. Evil controls it and they take advantage of the innocent and good. Each moment I witness Payne's daggers enter my father I grow stronger. Every time Payne slices my mother's throat I become more vengeful. The numerous times I open my eyes and see the bloody blade of Fingerless John inside Liza, I grow more hateful. *I will use these feelings to grow powerful and protect Thalia,* I say confidently.

As the sun sets and rises again, numerous boats enter the pier and others leave. Captain

Highsea's ship finally arrives early in the morning. The Captain steps out and stretches his arms. I can smell the alcohol and sea from his clothes. He scratches his beard and lets out a jolly laugh that echoes through the pier. I march over and startle him, as he was not prepared for a visitor this early in the morning. I only mutter two things to him, "Saint Aran. Old man Venom Bolt," and place the sack of gold in his hand, entering the ship.

The Captain does not answer, hesitate, or resist. As Venom Bolt mentioned, the Captain would know what to do when I mentioned his name. The crew unload the remaining cargo and restock what needs to be shipped back to Saint Aran. Once they complete their duties, one of the members of the ship rings a bell and yells back to the men to embark the ship for departure. I did not go inside the quarters. Instead, I stare into the sea as the ship steadily sails away. I have always wanted to see the rest of the world but out of choice and with a clear conscious. The ship rocks and shakes the deeper we sail into the vast waters. The waters become violent and powerful but I do not falter. I continue to watch as it vividly smashes against the wooden boat with power and beauty. As I admire and revere the ocean and the endless water that inhabits it, the memories of my parents and Liza begin to wash away. The further I get from Nasgrath, the more I want nothing more than to start anew. The water is determined to erase my old existence and take me to my new life in Saint Aran. I reluctantly give in and adhere to the idea of my resurrection.

EPILOGUE

Landing on familiar ground I travel back in time, four years, and recall the beauty and wonders that once inhabited these lands. The sun beaming its rays on the vegetation, flowers growing in gardens, the green grass and large fields of wheat, farmers and fishermen harvesting and fishing, children playing knights and mercenaries with one another. I used to walk these paths as a child and admire every stretch of land I passed.

That was a different time and place. I was an innocent boy, naïve, and kind hearted, always wanting to please everyone. That boy died in the lands of Nasgrath, and any trace of his existence was buried with the last person he loved. There is no love left in my beating heart.

Most of my past is a blur though not completely forgotten as my Masters would have wanted. Four images have been implanted in my mind since I was ten, and no matter what my training is meant to provide, I would never forget those moments and faces. I also still know my previous name was Marcus Sunborn and I have not forgotten what that boy had to endure to become *this*. Although only a few years older, I no longer feel like a young boy, and now go by the name *Morningstar*. The entity came to me during a dire moment of my training and we discovered one another. Training and age has also made me unrecognizable in appearance – I tower in comparison to my former self in height, muscles now toned and built, and long blond hair draped to my shoulder. The only thing that has remained from my past is the green eyes which my mother possessed. These eyes have seen so much in such a young life and there are many more things to see – in particular the death of the man who caused so much misery to this world. After completing all my training and missions, I finally proved that I am ready for the task of killing Dark Heart. My Masters agreed to allow me the opportunity to exact my revenge.

I step foot on Apollonian soil for the first time since the day I escaped over four years ago. Smoke rises from villages and traces of fire scars, which replaced the once beautiful lush and green grounds. The towns were once populated and filled with life, now only to be littered with the bones of the deceased. Most of the homes are abandoned; for many they served as a grave. The ash fills the air, polluting the sky and changing its once blue colour to grey. Even the sun cannot penetrate through the thick layer of smoke. It is a travesty seeing my birth home devastated this way. I have no time to mourn as my one goal is to infiltrate Castle Eclipse, rescue the old man if he is there, and do the one thing that the guild has been attempting to accomplish for years. *Habitamus in tenebris,* I remind myself. I live in darkness, and in darkness I will destroy the man who took everything from me. My destination is only a day away on foot. The battle I have been waiting for will finally come to pass and I will bring justice to Thalia.

ABOUT THE AUTHOR

P. Mail was born in 1983 and moved to Canada in 1989. Raised in Ottawa, he is a graduate of Carleton University and more recently resides in the Greater Toronto Area. Although his first literary work, Dark Heart is just the beginning – he's currently working on completing book two of the Dark Heart Trilogy.